TEMPLE SECRETS SERIES

ALSO BY SUSAN GABRIEL

FICTION

The Wildflower Trilogy:
The Secret Sense of Wildflower
(a Best Book of 2012 – Kirkus Reviews)
Lily's Song
Daisy's Fortune

Trueluck Summer

Temple Secrets Series:
Temple Secrets
Gullah Secrets

Grace, Grits and Ghosts: Southern Short Stories
Seeking Sara Summers
Circle of the Ancestors
Quentin & the Cave Boy

NONFICTION

Fearless Writing for Women:
Extreme Encouragement & Writing Inspiration

Available at all booksellers
in print, ebook and audio formats.

TEMPLE SECRETS SERIES

TEMPLE SECRETS & GULLAH SECRETS

SUSAN GABRIEL

WILD LILY ARTS

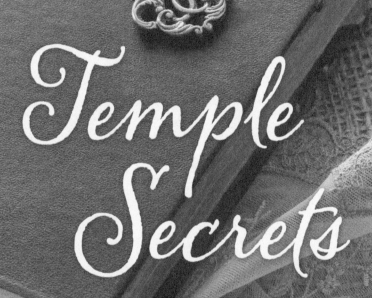

Temple Secrets

Susan Gabriel

CHAPTER ONE

Queenie

I ris Temple has been threatening to die for three decades, and most of the people in Savannah who know her want her to get on with it. Queenie looks up from the crime novel she's hidden within the pages of *Southern Living* magazine and takes in the figure of her half-sister, Iris Temple, across the sunroom. Everything about Iris speaks of privilege: the posture, the clothes, the understated jewels. Not to mention a level of entitlement that makes Queenie's head ache. An exasperated moan slips from her mouth before she can catch it.

Iris's gaze shifts to Queenie. Her eyes narrow, the adjoining crow's feet forming a close-knit flock. The look delivers the message that even though Queenie is solidly middle-aged, she is to be *seen and not heard* like a child.

As Iris Temple's companion for the last thirty-five years, Queenie lives the lifestyle of a Temple instead of a Temple servant like her black mother, grandmother, and great grandmother. With the precision of a Swiss clock, Queenie is reminded daily that she is not a *true* Temple—though they share the same father—any more than Sunny Delight orange drink is considered *real* orange juice. She is simply a watered-down Temple—albeit several shades darker.

As she does every morning, Iris studies the local newspaper from headlines to classifieds in the lavish sunroom facing the prominent Savannah square. Wicker furniture with rich fabrics mingles with antiques and tropical plants, as gold elephants the size of laundry baskets offer their polished backs to hold Iris's porcelain teacup.

Focused on the society section, Iris licks her lips as though relishing the fact that the Temple family is one of the elite families of Savannah. Their photographs appear in the newspaper with a regularity that Iris's constitution rarely achieves. As if on cue, Iris's stomach rumbles, and she fidgets in her chair. If treated more kindly, Queenie might feel sorry for Iris's discomfort and offer to make her life easier in some way.

For years, Iris Temple's unpredictable illnesses, usually of a gastrointestinal nature, have manipulated everyone around her. Just last week, a stomachache canceled a Daughters of the Confederacy charity event, and gas pains dismantled a family reunion planned for over a decade. Other social events Iris deemed unworthy of her time were aborted by attacks of acid reflux. To what does Iris Temple attribute these ailments? Gullah voodoo.

Within seconds, Iris's stomach rumbles again. Yet her attention has not left the newspaper.

"Oh my word, listen to this," Iris says.

Queenie exhales as Iris begins to read.

"Miss Iris Temple, of the Savannah Temples, will be hosting the 20th annual charity bazaar for the Junior League this coming Saturday. The grand matriarch, also known as Savannah's grandmother—" Iris balks

and looks as though she's swallowed something bitter. "Savannah's grandmother? Is that supposed to be a compliment?"

"Oh, I'm sure it is, Iris," Queenie answers, all the while thinking, *Savannah's grandmother, indeed. Never mind that you're eighty years old and have one grandchild who you've never even met. Or that you don't have a nurturing bone in your body.*

Queenie anticipates what will follow: Iris's angry letter to the newspaper on embossed Temple stationery that will insist that the reporter be dismissed and Queenie called upon to hand deliver the bad news.

Voodoo or not, most people—including Queenie—consider Iris Temple to be a first-class fake. What she blames on folk magic is merely an excuse to bring the fancy families and institutions of Savannah under her control.

And if that doesn't work, there's always that damn ledger, kept in a safe at the bank, documenting secrets about rich and powerful Savannah families. Secrets, Queenie has been told, that their great-grandfather began collecting before the Civil War and that every Temple has contributed to since.

Well, not every Temple. Iris has never asked my thoughts on anything, never mind what I'd like to put in that "secret" book.

It's true. Iris has noted every affair of prominent men, their illegitimate children, mental illnesses of wives, and any dishonest money dealings she's ever become privy to. According to Iris, two entire pages are devoted to Queenie. Given the Temple family's inclination to lie if it benefits them, Queenie questions how many of those so-called "secrets" are true. But she does have one that could do some serious harm if it got out.

"Did you call the restaurant about tomorrow night?" Iris asks.

Queenie looks up from her crime novel and gives the expected response. "Yes, Iris, it's all been arranged." And then thinks: *Only you, Iris, would counteract a voodoo curse by following a strict diet that consists of no sauces, no spices, and no intermingling of foods. You might as well be eating the Temple Book of Secrets!*

Part of Queenie's job as Iris's assistant is to make certain that chefs in downtown establishments follow these strict dietary restrictions. Chefs hate being told what to do. But if any fail to meet her requirements, Iris will make sure that they never work in Savannah again.

"And did you tell them about my special condition?" Iris asks, turning to the classifieds. "You know how delicate I am," she adds. "Fragrances make me nauseous."

"Yes, Iris. I made them aware," she says, thinking that Iris is about as *delicate* as a piranha.

Fragrances include perfumes and scented body powders, soaps, shampoos, and detergents. Every maître d' in town has been alerted not to sit Iris next to anyone who might fall under the scrutiny of her superior olfactory system.

"What about the Catholic charities meeting tomorrow?" Iris asks. She takes a sip of tea, the sunlight bouncing off the gold inlay of the cup.

"I'll see to it, Iris." Queenie resists rolling her eyes. *It would be more of a charity for Savannah if Iris didn't show up.*

For the privilege of living in the big house and being Iris Temple's companion, Queenie pays a steep price. Among other things, she is required to arrive thirty minutes early to every meeting of the Junior League, the Daughters of the Confederacy, and any other event that Iris Temple is scheduled to attend to ensure that they are fragrance-free. It's on these days that Queenie feels like little more than a trained bloodhound, sniffing at the heels of Savannah's elite. More than once, she has had to approach a prominent Savannah resident and request she go to the restroom and scrub off expensive fragrances dabbed behind her ears and on her wrists. This seldom goes over well, leaving Queenie to feel blacker than she already is.

Queenie knows how the rich women of Savannah feel about her. She has overheard their whispers, their cutting remarks about her color, her place. No matter what she does, they—like Iris—will never see her as legitimate. They never see her for the woman she is and never think of the burden Queenie carries because of Iris's insistence that she play Prissy to her Scarlett O'Hara to have a decent life.

Yet deep down, Queenie knows that she's more real than any of them and is as entitled to her life as Iris is. She is well aware of what their daddy left behind when he passed over. Not that she's seen a penny of it. Yet Iris has promised to leave her the house when she finally passes to the Great Beyond. And for that, Queenie will tolerate just about anything.

"I smelled one of those horrible dryer sheets, yesterday," Iris begins again, her nose upturned.

Queenie sighs, thinking of her periodic sleuth for scents while strolling the beautiful Savannah square where the Temple house stands. During this surveillance, Queenie must ascertain whether any housekeepers in the area are using scented dryer sheets. If so, said housekeepers risk losing their jobs, and their employers risk having their secrets revealed. Secrets Iris has told them are stored in the bank vault.

As a result, most of Savannah—regardless of race, class, gender, or age—is waiting on Iris Temple to die. If for no other reason, so that life can return to scented bliss. Fantasies of Iris's demise have indeed graced Queenie's thoughts many times. It is time for Iris to step aside so Queenie can head the Temple clan. She looks around the room, thinking of how she might redecorate, adding more color.

"I know it doesn't bother you to smell the dryer sheets," Iris concedes. "But if you were a *true* Temple, you'd understand. You just don't have our level of sophistication."

There it is, Queenie thinks, *as predictable as Old Faithful, and just as full of toxic vapors.*

To distract herself from doing Iris harm, Queenie thinks back to when she came to live with her thirty-five years ago in 1965. She was twenty-two years old when she made this fateful choice.

Iris was forty-five. It was Mister Oscar's idea—Iris Temple's husband—that Queenie join the staff because of a particular fondness he had for her. A fondness which extended to the bedroom.

Queenie lifts an eyebrow and studies Iris. *Did she really never know what Oscar was up to right under her nose?*

The Temples are one of the richest families in Savannah, Georgia. Iris's father—also Queenie's father—made a fortune in the invention and production of prosthetics. A generation after his father, a surgeon in the Civil War, removed thousands of limbs that his son seemed destined to replace.

Though Queenie has seen none of the Temple money except for a meager monthly allowance, she and Iris live in a large Victorian house listed on the national registry of historic homes. A house used at the end of the Civil War by Union officers reveling in their victory during General Sherman's March to the Sea. As the story goes, these Union soldiers were told to burn the mansion to the ground, but they refused to do any damage to it, given its rare beauty. The extinguished torch is now encased in the Temple foyer, where it was left all those many years ago. It is also the house where the present-day Junior League conducts annual house tours to raise money for orphans in a country many of them cannot pronounce, and none would ever dream of visiting.

An oil portrait of Edward Temple, Iris and Oscar's only son, glares at Queenie from across the room. Their daughter Rose's portrait was taken down and stored in the attic twenty-five years before, replaced now by an original Audubon. Queenie keeps in touch with Iris's estranged daughter, Rose, who lives on a horse and cattle ranch outside Cheyenne, Wyoming. Rose has one child, Katie, who graduated from college and now works in Chicago and is Iris's only grandchild, whom she has never met. Queenie pulls a photograph from her pocket that arrived in the morning mail of Rose and Katie in Chicago. She smiles.

"What are you looking at?" Iris asks.

"Nothing, Iris," Queenie says. She slides the picture back into her pocket. Of all the Temples, Queenie likes Rose best. Yet Iris has forbidden Queenie to ever speak of her. Rose's existence has been totally erased. No photographs. No memories. Nothing.

Rose was ten years old when Queenie came to live here, and Edward was seventeen and away at boarding school. Queenie's mother—fondly called Old Sally by everyone who knows her—was still working for the Temples then but would be replaced by Violet in 1980. Violet, Old Sally's granddaughter, spent a lot of time at the Temple house when she was growing up and was Rose Temple's best friend.

Queenie glances at her watch and then at Iris's empty teacup. She always calls her mother after Iris finishes her tea and retires to her bedroom for her morning constitutional—a ritual that easily lasts until noon. Queenie would never call her mother in front of Iris unless she wanted to aggravate her half-sister for the rest of the day. The two women are like fried okra and a dainty watercress sandwich and do not mix.

At one hundred years of age, Queenie's mother, Old Sally, lives on the coast of southernmost South Carolina in a house she has lived in her entire life. She was born in the year 1900 and has seen a century's worth of change. Yet Old Sally still practices the family trade of root doctoring and folk magic in the way her Gullah ancestors did. Just yesterday, she got a call from someone in New York City who is flying to Savannah to have her work her spells and cure their environmental illness. This kind of thing happens all the time. Queenie has never practiced the family trade. Perhaps it is the Temple blood in her that refuses to participate. But her mother is quite versed in it.

Seconds later, Iris screams, and Queenie bolts upright, her book and magazine flying, as Iris's teacup crashes to pieces on the marbled floor. Queenie has never heard Iris screech and has to admit it is an interesting change from the silent roar of her half-sister's delicate constitution.

"What is it Iris, what's wrong?"

Iris's mouth gapes as though she is reading her own obituary. She points a boney, bejeweled finger at a section in the classifieds, her hand shaking.

Queenie comes to Iris's side and leans in to read:

FOUND. One Book of Temple Secrets.
First Secret to be revealed tomorrow.

"Sweet Jesus," Queenie mutters under her breath. "The shit has just hit the fan."

Iris's stomach gurgles in ready agreement.

CHAPTER TWO

Violet

As the grandfather clock in the hallway strikes seven, Violet serves dinner in the grand dining room. Miss Temple sits at the head of the elongated table while her Aunt Queenie takes her place at the far end of the mahogany monster Violet has polished so often she now has tennis elbow without ever lifting a racket. Violet and her aunt have always been close. Like sisters almost, though Queenie is seventeen years older.

The evening meal always looks like a BBC mini-series Violet would never watch. Sepia tones surround an efficient servant (that would be her) serving a grand dame and her half-breed sister elaborate meals while standing nearby to meet their every need. The room is lit by a cumbersome chandelier—one she can only reach with a tall ladder when she dusts—that was an original feature of the house before it was converted to electricity a hundred years earlier. Violet can't imagine what it was like to work here then, yet her ancestors would know. Her grandmother, who people call Old Sally, has told her stories about washing all the clothes and dishes by hand. Violet shudders with the thought.

After she serves Miss Temple her usual bowl of clear broth soup to begin, the meal can easily last a solid hour while her employer grinds every morsel of food to a lifeless pulp to aid her uncooperative digestive system. In contrast, Aunt Queenie finishes her meal while it is still hot—a lovely piece of flounder, with rice and mixed vegetables—which Violet makes separately.

While Violet stands stationed at the door, she remembers her youngest daughter Tia's question to her this morning:

"Mama, when will I have to start working for the Temples?"

Tia is fourteen, and the question shocked Violet. As she told Tia, she will never, *ever*, let either of her daughters work as servants. Never. Violet gives her foot a strong tap now to seal the promise. She will be the last of a long line. Her children will never know what her life has been like, and she is glad. *Never,* she tells herself again, standing straighter. If she can save enough to open her own business, she won't be at this job much longer anyway.

Life is too short to spend it waiting on rich white people, she thinks. At the same time, she is grateful for the job.

When Iris isn't looking, Violet winks a hello to her Aunt Queenie. In return, Queenie gives a brief nod and hides a smile behind her napkin. Queenie makes the entire situation of waiting on Miss Temple bearable. They are like two soldiers in a foxhole together, their fates linked by a common foe.

Shadows grasp the corners of the room, winning out in a tug-of-war with the light. The dark wood of the doors and moldings adds a veil of heaviness to the room. Period furniture, heralding the time the house was constructed, gleam with over a century's worth of lemon oil rubbed into the grain by her ancestors, and now by Violet. History, in this house, is as heavy as the curtains that cover the floor to ceiling windows. Every day, Violet yearns to throw open the curtains and let some fresh air into the rooms. She is convinced air from the last century is still trapped in the corners.

As far as she knows, Miss Temple is the only member of Savannah's upper class who still insists that they dress for dinner. Violet is also the only housekeeper and cook still required, even in the year 2000, to wear a blue uniform with a starched white apron on top and white shoes. A look meant to remind Violet of her place and perhaps the 1940s. As Violet has observed, things are slow to change in the Temple household.

However, on this particular evening, Miss Temple has not changed from the clothes she wore that morning when Violet cleaned up the spilled tea in the sunroom. Something from the newspaper had Miss Temple practically in tears. Not that Violet has ever seen her employer cry. Violet isn't that fond of crying, either, but at least she knows she can do it when a situation warrants. Yet Miss Temple's lack of dinner etiquette strikes her as odd.

Violet lifts an eyebrow to ask Queenie *what's up?*

Queenie shrugs and widens her eyes with the message to stay alert.

No one speaks during meals—another of Miss Temple's dinner rules—so Violet is left to listen to the old grandfather clock ticking away the seconds of her life and the click, click, clicks of silver on china, along with Miss Temple's persistent chewing, accompanied by her guttural rumblings.

Violet pulls a small tincture bottle of vanilla, cinnamon, and ginger root from the pocket of her apron to dab underneath her nose. A scent, oddly enough, Miss Temple never notices. The tincture is the only thing Violet has been able to find to counteract the smell of the potent exotic meats and Miss Temple's occasional reaction to them.

Tonight's reactions are more forceful than usual. Perhaps because of what was in the newspaper this morning. After the first course is finished, Miss Temple lets out a belch found more often at a Georgia Bulldogs game than at the table of one of Savannah's most prominent families.

It remains a mystery what causes Miss Temple's ailments. No matter how many specialists she sees or what radical changes she makes to her diet, her condition does not improve, making Violet believe that it is entirely possible that her grandmother deserves more credit.

"Are you reading during dinner?" Miss Temples barks at Queenie as if she's caught her buying sweatpants at Wal-Mart.

Violet snaps to attention.

"Answer me," she insists. If Violet had the nerve, she would tell Miss Temple to quit being such a bully. But, for now, she can't risk losing her job. Besides, Queenie knows how to take care of herself.

"If you must know, Iris, I was praying," Queenie says.

Miss Temple pauses as if aware that even she can't trump God.

"No need to worry, Iris, I'll put in a good word for you." Queenie glances heavenward, whispers a few words, and then winks at Violet.

In response, Miss Temple's stomach roars like a thunderclap. Anticipating what's next, Violet dabs another application of her tincture to her upper lip. Over the years, Violet has become as adept at reading Miss Temple's dark moods as the experts on the weather channel are at predicting hurricanes. In the current fore-cast, her employer's stormy disposition has changed from a watch to a warning.

Miss Temple coaxes into her mouth a piece of rattlesnake that Violet sautéed in butter and onions. In the last decade, she has learned to cook things she would have never dreamed would end up in her kitchen. Miss Temple chews with so much vigor it makes Violet's jaws hurt. Her Gullah ancestors would much sooner run from a snake than to eat one. When Violet was a girl, her grandmother told her stories about whip snakes, which were said to bite their tails and roll like a wheel to overcome their victims. At that moment, she pines for her grandmother's stories, as well as her red rice, okra soup, and shrimp and grits. She has come a long way from her Gullah roots, though she's not so sure this is a good thing.

No one expected Miss Temple to live this long. Her physical woes have plagued her since before Violet started working here and have intensified over the years. Meanwhile, Miss Temple's face takes on the color of a confederate gray uniform worn by one of her ancestors in the portrait gallery. Violet is smart enough to fear what is coming, but luckily it doesn't seem to be about the food.

"I was at my attorney's office today trying to sue the newspaper when I received some alarming news of a different nature," Miss Temple says.

Violet and her aunt exchange a quick look.

"Sometimes those closest to us betray us," Miss Temple says, sounding like a Hallmark greeting card gone wrong.

Her eyes narrow and change from tired blue to a steel gray. A pause follows, the distance between lightning and a thunderclap.

Violet fears for Queenie more than herself. Miss Temple can be spiteful when she wants to be, especially to Queenie.

"It seems my attorney has found a most distressing letter," Miss Temple says.

"A letter?" Queenie asks, appearing calm. "From whom?" Both Violet and Queenie know it is safer not to react.

Miss Temple tightens her lips and then wipes her mouth on a silk napkin graced with a prominent monogrammed "T" in gold thread that Violet has laundered and ironed hundreds of times.

"Did everyone know except me?" Miss Temple asks Queenie and then turns the question toward Violet, who takes a step back. It is not like Miss Temple to notice her.

"I've fought my entire life for the recognition I deserve," Miss Temple begins again. "My father would have much preferred his only child to be a son. It doesn't matter that I've solidified the Temple dynasty during my tenure."

Violet has never heard the Temple matriarch talk like this. Does it have anything to do with the threat in the newspaper this morning? Something to do with the secrets?

"Are you okay, Iris?" Queenie asks, as if she, too, has noticed the change.

"I've been thinking about the past more than usual, that's all," she answers. "Nothing good can come of it, of course. It's probably because of those damn secrets."

"Do you want to talk about it?" Queenie asks.

Miss Temple's eyes widen like confiding in Queenie is about as appealing as desegregation. "Must you be so common," she says to Queenie, her words coming out in a huff. "Of course I don't want to talk about it, especially not with someone who isn't a *true* Temple. How could you possibly understand?" She sighs, as though putting Queenie in her place isn't as satisfying as she hoped.

Violet hates it when Miss Temple takes out her frustration on her aunt, and she opens her mouth to tell her so, but Queenie shakes her head to stop her.

"My father was a brilliant man except for sleeping with the servants," Miss Temple begins again. "But I have to put up with you as a constant reminder of his indiscretions. Have you ever thought about what it's like for me to deal with my father's bastard child for over half a century?"

Violet steps closer to defend Queenie, but Queenie shakes her head again. In most cases, it's best to just let Miss Temple's rants play out, like a tea kettle releasing its steam. It doesn't help that someone is threatening to leak secrets to the newspaper. However, this latest news seems to have distracted her from even that.

"Of course it was Oscar's idea," Miss Temple continues. "He could be quite persuasive when he wanted to be." She rubs her temples as though smoothing a splitting headache. "Did I ever tell you that I married him just to make my mother angry? He was from a family of tailors." Iris gives a short laugh. "*Beneath us*, my mother said."

Violet always wondered how Mister Oscar ended up with Miss Temple. He seemed way too nice for her.

According to Queenie, Miss Temple refused to take his name when they married, so she could remain a Temple. She also insisted that Edward and Rose keep the Temple name. Queenie told Violet that Miss Temple treated Mister Oscar's parents horribly, as well. They were never invited to the Temple mansion, and she didn't even attend their funerals.

To Violet, family is sacred. Having never known her parents, she doesn't take family for granted.

"I shouldn't have changed it," Miss Temple says, talking to herself.

"You shouldn't have changed what?" Queenie asks.

Within moments Miss Temple's mood shifts, like the wind has changed direction and the storm downgraded. However, Violet and Queenie know better than to relax just yet.

Miss Temple turns to Violet again. "You are lovely," she says.

Violet stands straighter. Her employer never pays compliments. She gives a quick, "Thank you," wondering what this has to do with a found letter.

As Queenie can attest, to capture Miss Temple's attention is rarely a good thing. She has observed more than one casualty from her employer's venom. Violet thinks of Rose, Miss Temple's daughter, who hasn't returned to Savannah in decades. Venom goes a long way when used to poison a relationship, and Violet never wants to pass on anything like that to her girls.

"Are you married, my dear?" Miss Temple asks her.

Violet looks at her aunt and then back at Miss Temple. Should she refuse to answer?

"Iris, leave her alone," Queenie says, but Miss Temple waves her comment away.

"I'm married to a man named Jack," Violet says, hoping her response will end the tension.

"What does this Jack do?" Miss Temple asks.

"He teaches English at the community college." Violet lowers her eyes.

"Do you have children?" she asks.

Violet hesitates. Then she thinks about how hard it will be to find another job without a reference from Miss Temple.

"Two daughters," Violet says. "Sixteen and fourteen."

Miss Temple looks thoughtful.

Violet's face feels hot, and her heartbeat races. She steps toward Queenie's end of the table, wanting to flee. Under the table, Queenie makes a slight motion with her hand, as if guiding jets onto a tiny aircraft carrier at her feet. In their foxhole, Queenie and Violet have developed a type of Morse code, using a series of eye and subtle hand gestures to relay Miss Temple's moods. If not for the seriousness of the situation, Violet would feel foolish making these gestures.

Meanwhile, Miss Temple scrutinizes Violet, as if overcome with great curiosity. After the main entrée is finished, Violet gathers the empty plates and goes back into the kitchen. She returns with crystal dessert goblets, each filled with a scoop of blackberry sherbet. Violet waits near the kitchen door. Beyond this door is her territory, her safe place. The heightened tension in the room causes goosebumps to rise on her arms. Queenie must feel it, too.

In their agreed-upon mayday signal, Queenie winks twice and jerks her head left, like the return on an old typewriter. Through gestures, Queenie tells Violet to save herself. Violet, however, refuses to abandon Queenie no matter how many times she winks and returns her carriage.

Not only are Violet and Queenie bonded as niece and aunt, but they are close like people who survive natural disasters are close. When Miss Temple has nothing for her to do, Queenie often helps

Violet in the kitchen and knows intimate details about her and her husband, Jack, and their two daughters, Tia and Leisha. Sometimes Tia and Leisha come over for the day if they don't have school, and Queenie and the girls have Parcheesi tournaments in the kitchen, just like Violet, Rose, and Queenie did decades before.

After taking her last bite of sherbet, Miss Temple nods, a signal to Violet that she is finished.

As Violet clears the table, Miss Temple pats Violet's hand and thanks her.

Violet swallows a gasp and shoots an alarmed look in Queenie's direction. Miss Temple never touches anyone, especially not a servant. Nor does she thank anyone for anything. If saved from a raging river, Miss Iris Temple of the Savannah Temples would expect her rescuers to thank her for the privilege of keeping her alive. Hubris she may have inherited from her father, a man who supposedly never liked children and made a daily practice of ignoring her. It is this fact alone that helps Violet tolerate her.

Queenie signals for Violet to save herself, but Violet refuses to leave. Miss Temple is up to something big. Something that feels dangerous. After having observed her employer for over twenty years, Violet knows one thing for certain: a predator is still a predator, even with claws retracted.

Miss Temple stands and stares at Violet like she is seeing her for the first time.

"Iris, are you sure you're all right?" Queenie asks. "You've had a big day with the threat of the *Book of Secrets* getting released."

"Of course I'm all right," she says, her tone dismissive. But she doesn't look *all right* at all. This crisis seems to have cracked her hard exterior, at least for now.

Violet and Queenie follow Miss Temple into the foyer, where she announces she's going to bed early because she has a big day tomorrow.

At the base of the grand staircase, Miss Temple gives Violet a quick, tight embrace in a rare act of affection that feels more like a frontal version of the Heimlich maneuver that Violet learned in a Red Cross class. In response, Violet gasps, waiting for her ribs to crack, and then lowers her eyes, wondering if she should be terrified or relieved.

Miss Temple lets out another belch to rival her other emissions for the day and says, "Damn voodoo curse," glancing back like she holds Queenie responsible.

Ascending the spiral staircase, Miss Temple releases a long, slow sigh that sounds like a lonely train whistle fading in the distance.

CHAPTER THREE

Queenie

The next morning Queenie chews a fingernail as she wonders who is behind releasing the coming secrets. Iris picks up the morning paper, skips the society section entirely and goes straight to the classifieds. Queenie lost sleep the night before, worrying that her secret might be the first one revealed. She imagines there are many people in Savannah with this very same fear.

As Iris runs a finger down the column, Queenie covers her ears awaiting the scream but hears a shriek instead. Iris's lips disappear into her scowl.

"Who is doing this?" Iris points at Queenie as if she should know.

Queenie has no idea who is behind it. If she did, she would offer them every penny in her savings account to keep her biggest secret out of the newspaper. Meanwhile, in all the years she's known Iris, she has never seen her this unnerved. In a way, she finds it as refreshing as those scented dryer sheets Iris hates so much.

Iris throws the newspaper at Queenie and pieces cascade to the floor. Despite a personal visit to the head of the paper and another trip to her attorney, the first secret has appeared anyway.

"Get the car," Iris orders. She walks out of the sunroom and climbs the stairs, heavy-footed like a child having her second tantrum in as many days.

Queenie quickly gathers the newspapers and reads the first secret in the classifieds:

Several Savannah patriarchs have mixed-raced children.
Contact Iris Temple for more information: 912-944-0455.

Queenie lets out a guffaw to go along with the relief she feels that the secret released is not one of her own. Even though she is of mixed-race, that scandal is old news. Almost immediately, the phone rings in the hallway, and Queenie answers it.

"Keep your damn mouth shut," a male caller says before a loud click severs the call.

"Uh, oh," Queenie says. She'd better warn Violet not to answer the telephone today.

AN HOUR LATER, Queenie sits in the waiting room of Bo Rivers, Iris's attorney, someone who probably has his own share of secrets in Iris's book. Queenie wonders if he's someone who actually might have access. It would be just like Iris to store a copy with her legal representative in case the banks failed. Iris could be a little paranoid sometimes.

Behind a heavy door, Queenie can hear Iris's raised voice and the low mumblings of Bo Rivers as he tries to calm her. Seconds later, Iris appears from behind the door and slams it and then strides past Queenie, who scurries to follow. For an old lady, Iris has some pep. It reminds Queenie of when power walks were in fashion. Not that she ever did one. *Wouldn't want to ruin my girlish figure,* she says to herself and slaps her large hip. She has never understood why white women have to be skinny to be happy. Even Oprah falls for it from time to time.

LATER THAT AFTERNOON, Queenie waits in the grand foyer, where the telephone has not only been unplugged but removed entirely. It is Queenie's job to accompany Iris to the Piggly Wiggly grocery store across town. All household errands are relegated to Queenie, except for one, which Iris insists on doing herself. This errand is to order exotic meats from Spud Grainger, the butcher at the Piggly Wiggly, with whom Iris had a storied affair in the 1970s. An affair—Iris told Queenie after having too much sherry on All Souls Day in 1983—that she blames on an article she read in *Vogue Magazine* concerning the free love movement.

Free love or not, what that man ever saw in her, I will never know, Queenie thinks.

"How do I look?" Iris asks, her scowl softened. She joins Queenie with purse and keys in hand and dabs at her hair as though it might actually move.

"You look, uh, stately," Queenie says. *And pissed,* she thinks, but she's not about to say that to Iris.

"I've decided to put the morning behind me and go to the market as planned," Iris says. Her face twitches, the closest she comes to a smile.

Queenie doesn't voice her skepticism. She's never known the Temples to keep the past behind them, and they have a house full of ghosts to prove it.

Though she can afford a multitude of chauffeurs, Iris insists on driving herself. Queenie follows Iris out the front door and around the side to the carriage house. Although cutting through the kitchen would make much more sense, Iris refuses to use any door that might be considered a servant's entrance.

Once inside the car, Queenie buckles up and says a silent prayer that they reach their destination unharmed. Then she kisses the sweetgrass bracelet her mother gave Queenie for protection. Between the good lord and her mama's Gullah magic, she figures she has her bases covered.

Despite the snail-paced speed, a drive with Iris always proves harrowing. As far as Queenie can tell, Iris has never once used the rear-view or side mirrors on her black Lincoln Town Car. Instead, she uses the sidewalks in town as a kind of bumper car railing, to keep track of the edge of the road. All because Iris is so vain that she refuses to wear her eyeglasses in public. What Iris lacks in accuracy, she makes up for in spite. Anyone she endangers with her recklessness, she deems somehow deserving. Some days it is all Queenie can do to not hang out the window and scream, "Get out of the way!" to unsuspecting pedestrians on sidewalks up ahead.

In the fire lane near the entrance of the Piggly Wiggly, Iris brings the Town Car to an abrupt stop and ejects herself from the car while leaving the engine running. The persistent alarm from inside the Lincoln does nothing to remind Iris that she may want to turn off the car and take the keys out of the ignition. Queenie completes the task and reminds herself that someday she will have to take the car keys away from Iris on a permanent basis, an action she looks forward to about as much as back-to-back root canals. Iris is not the type to give up control of anything, especially large, life-threatening motor vehicles.

With the sophistication of Savannah royalty, Iris enters the Piggly Wiggly. Queenie follows not far behind as store employees exchange their usual looks, as well as a few new ones. Queenie guesses that word has spread about the *Temple Book of Secrets*. Although Savannah is not a small town, it has some similarities. Gossip is savored, chewed, swallowed, and then digested until it comes out the other end as compost, which is then used to create more secrets.

Iris walks down aisle three toward the meat department in the rear of the store. Despite being eighty years of age, her posture is impeccable, as if a flag pole extends from crown to coccyx. And though she is of average height, perhaps five feet, seven inches, she seems much taller than everyone else. Even her wrinkles appear to align themselves properly, and her solid white hair is coiffed to perfection like she and the Queen of England share hairdressers.

Queenie serves no particular function on this outing except to fulfill her half-sisterly duty as a companion and keep her mouth shut. Afterward, she will get her hair washed and relaxed at the Gladys Knight and the Tints Beauty Parlor located in the shopping center adjacent to the Piggly Wiggly, a reward she looks forward to all week.

Iris arrives at the meat counter and gingerly clears her throat to get Spud Grainger's attention. When this doesn't work, Iris crescendos her query from *pianissimo* to *forte*. He turns around, causing Queenie to think: *If there was ever an example of love's blindness, it is Spud Grainger's affection for Iris Temple.*

Their affair began two years after Iris's husband, Oscar, died unexpectedly of a massive heart attack while in a compromising position in his office with Queenie. Spud Grainger was a bag boy at the Piggly Wiggly at the time and a part-time jazz musician. The affair ended after six months, at Iris Temple's insistence. Heartbroken, it is rumored that Spud Grainger never played the saxophone again.

"My dear Iris Temple," Spud says, his southern accent smooth and lilting. "You get more beautiful every day."

"Oh, Mr. Grainger. How very kind of you." Iris radiates a smile that has received minimal exercise over the years, and her bottom lip quivers with the effort. Once weekly, Queenie marvels at her half-sister's transformation into a somewhat pleasant human being while in Spud Grainger's presence. Not to mention, it is extra impressive that Iris can do this amidst the hullaballoo around the *Book of Secrets*.

Spud Grainger is not a day over sixty and has aged well. A solid white mustache hides his slightly crooked front teeth. He also has an affinity for bow ties. Today's tie is lime green, with thin red stripes that match the beef tips on special, displayed in the glass case in front of him.

At least he doesn't mind a little color, Queenie thinks.

The elegant butcher wipes his hands on his perfectly clean white apron and steps into the aisle to kiss Iris's extended hand. A girlish giggle escapes her octogenarian lips.

When Queenie is unsuccessful in hiding her smile, Iris shoots her a look that could stop a wildebeest in a dead run. No matter how many times she gets these looks from Iris, they always shock her. Iris returns her attention to Spud and her face colors slightly from Spud's consideration. She tilts her head upward as if this noble gesture might command the color to recede. They speak affectionately about the weather.

Damn, y'all, how many different ways can you describe hot? Queenie wonders, for Savannah is as hot as a furnace in Hades for six months out of the year.

Iris hands Queenie her leather handbag, heavy enough to contain the wildebeest from earlier. As instructed, she reaches inside the bag for a linen envelope containing an order written neatly on Temple stationery. She hands it to Spud Grainger, who thanks her kindly.

Exotic meats, Iris Temple will tell anyone who has the misfortune to ask, are the only thing her delicate, voodoo cursed constitution can tolerate. Whether the strong medicine of these exotic animals is meant to counteract the spell she is at the mercy of, remains a mystery.

Antelope, alligator, buffalo, elk, kangaroo, and ostrich are flown in from all over the world at great expense. Not to mention iguana, llama, rattlesnake, and yak. Exotic animals associated with nursery rhymes or the stars of animated Disney movies Queenie watched with Violet's daughters. Animals that would have fought harder if they knew their capture would result in ending up in Iris Temple's gullet.

Spud Grainger studies the list. He smiles and pets his mustache, as if Iris's exotic orders, as well as her exotic nature, have captivated him.

"The caribou may take a while," he says thoughtfully. "But I'll give Violet a call as soon as it comes in."

A line of Savannah housewives forms behind Iris. Queenie overhears at least one mention of secrets and that Iris should be ashamed of herself. Luckily, Iris doesn't hear them, but that doesn't stop her from eyeing their khaki shorts and New Balance sneakers before inclining her chin heavenward like she's on the trail of an unacceptable scent. She wrinkles her nose and furrows her brow. Though the 4th of July is three months away, Queenie anticipates the upcoming fireworks.

"Chanel," Iris says to Queenie in a whisper that can be heard from the front of the store. The look on Iris's face reveals her complete and utter disgust.

Chanel no. 5, as Queenie has been told countless times, is the fragrance of the terminally middle class. Iris abhors the wannabe rich or any other kind of rich that doesn't involve money that has been around since the Confederacy.

Spud Grainger gives Iris an apologetic look and motions to the line forming behind her. Iris stops mid-sniff and thanks Spud, another kindness reserved only for him. Before leaving, she turns to the gaggle of Savannah housewives and gives them a parting hiss, like the rattlesnake she had for dinner the night before. Queenie offers the women a quick apology, but the final word comes from Iris as she departs. Meanwhile, two children holding a box of Lucky Charms cover their noses and run in search of their mother.

Back at the car, Queenie gives Iris the keys to the Lincoln and Iris drives—at the speed of a handicapped snail—the 500 yards to drop Queenie off at the hairdresser.

"I'll be back in two hours," Iris says. "You'd better be finished."

Queenie nods as the grand matriarch drives off to conduct another errand, running over the curb and missing by inches a stop sign at the end of the parking lot. Queenie never questions the nature of Iris's other errands, but just last week when returning to the car to retrieve her crime novel, she found a bucket of Kentucky Fried Chicken bones crammed under the back seat, the bones picked clean, like an exotic jungle animal had feasted on them while lying on the plush leather seats.

So much for voodoo and special diets, Queenie thought at the time, as she held the bucket of bones and smiled back at Colonel Sanders' emblazoned image. If Iris keeps this up, hardening of the arteries may take her out, but Queenie's not so sure she has the fortitude to wait for natural causes. Although violence isn't really in her nature.

HER HAIR RELAXED AND STYLED, and all the latest gossip discussed —most of which has to do with the *Temple Book of Secrets*— Queenie puts the charge on Iris's bill and waits outside, fanning herself with a real estate flyer pulled from the box in front of the beauty shop. Queenie has only seen the *Temple Book of Secrets* twice, both times while in Oscar's office, before the ledger was moved to the safety deposit box. No matter how much Queenie begged, Oscar refused to let her look at it, saying Iris would kill him, which she probably would have. The book was kept in the bottom desk drawer that locked with a key Oscar kept on his key chain. It was moved to the bank vault a few years after his death.

Within minutes, the shiny black Lincoln rounds the corner, rolls over the sidewalk, and hits a green trash can that bounces off a silver Toyota wagon before coming to rest at the north end of the parking lot.

"Good lord, this woman is an accident waiting to happen," Queenie mutters.

Queenie is an excellent driver herself. Oscar, Iris's husband, taught her when she was sixteen in an equally big Lincoln Continental. In exchange for the driving lessons, she agreed to climb into the back seat with him and show him her breasts. At the time, this gesture seemed a small price to pay to use the Temple cars. *Of course, this is a secret I doubt ever made it into Iris's precious book.* But others might have. She wishes now she had caught a glimpse of that secret book, but Iris keeps the key to the deposit box locked up, too.

If Queenie's own secrets are revealed in the classifieds, she might be looking for a new place to live. She gulps with the thought. While some southerners follow the motto: *What would Jesus do?*—seen on car bumper stickers as *W.W.J.D.*—Queenie is more prone to ask *W.W.O.D.? What would Oprah do?* Having watched nearly every episode of Oprah since the early 90s, Queenie's best guess is that her hero would put a team of lawyers to work on it. Unfortunately, Queenie doesn't have that kind of money.

The Town Car rounds the final corner and veers in Queenie's direction as if Iris is playing a game of geriatric "chicken." Queenie debates whether to jump aside but decides to hold her ground.

"Just try it, old lady," Queenie says, her teeth gritted in determination. She locks her ample knees in place, grateful she has some substance to her. "If it's my fate to go to the Great Beyond at the hand of that smelly witch, then so be it," she adds. "But I refuse to be the first one to flinch."

The Lincoln lurches twice before screeching to a halt and then stops only inches away from Queenie. So close that heat drifts from the engine and further relaxes her hair. Queenie gets inside and slams the door while Iris's wrinkled lips glisten in the sunlight from her latest rendezvous with the Colonel. The grease relaxes her face like a kind of Botox injection while the smell of his secret recipe of eleven herbs and spices permeates the closed car.

After several attempts, Iris coerces the Town Car into drive and hits the curb three times before reaching the main road, causing a family of four to frantically scatter into the good hands of an Allstate Insurance office.

"God in heaven," Queenie shrieks. "Watch where you're going!"

"Keep your commandments to yourself," Iris says with a sneer.

ON THE SLOW RIDE HOME, instead of worrying what secrets of hers might end up in the newspaper—a legitimate concern—Queenie entertains herself by daydreaming of Iris Temple's accidental death while choking on one of the Colonel's chicken bones.

CHAPTER FOUR

Violet

Violet rubs her left shoulder that has ached all morning. The day before her daughter Tia broke her leg in 4th grade, this same shoulder predicted it. It happened before Mister Oscar—Miss Temple's husband—died, too. Since she was a girl, Violet has known her arm is hooked into a higher level of consciousness. As a result, the minute it begins to ache, she automatically breaks into a sweat.

A sense of urgency accompanies her drive to the Temple house as she wipes a thin layer of perspiration from her upper lip. She has taken this route through Savannah hundreds of times, yet something about this morning feels different. Nearing the house, a blast of pain radiates up her arm. She rubs it and sighs her anguish.

"What are you trying to tell me?" she asks.

Anyone who heard her talking to a body part would assume

she was crazy. *But I guess I'm only crazy if I hear it talk back.* Violet smiles despite the pain, as the throbbing continues. Meanwhile, she catches every traffic light and is still five minutes away from the Temple mansion.

When Violet pulls her car into the carriage house, the throbbing intensifies, and her blouse is soaked straight through. Her deodorant works overtime as she turns off the car and gets out. Even though she grew up in Savannah and has never lived anywhere else, to go from air-conditioning to the sweltering Georgia heat is shocking at first, like stepping into a pre-heated oven.

After she walks into the kitchen, she stands still and listens, purse still in hand. The house seems quieter than usual. Violet has the family *sensitivity*, as her grandmother calls it, a sense of invisible things, like the different entities in the Temple house. Now that the *Temple Book of Secrets* has been in the news, the ghostly presences have seemed especially strong. Violet can usually tell where the spirits are that live in the house, by the energy they give off. It's like tuning into a distant radio station. Violet turns her head to intuit her next move while the entire house appears to be holding its breath.

"What's going on?" she asks any spirits listening. She's never known them to answer back. *But there's a first time for everything,* she tells herself.

Having read once that so-called *sensitives* often come from tragic backgrounds, Violet wonders if her psychic ability has anything to do with her being an orphan. She has no memory of her mother, who died in an automobile accident when Violet was a baby, and she never met her father, who left town when he found out her mother was pregnant with Violet. For whatever reason, her grandmother never speaks of either of her parents. And even though her grandmother and her Aunt Queenie raised her, at times, Violet feels all alone in the world.

Now that she thinks about it, her Aunt Queenie seems worked

up about that secret book, too. While Violet used to always retrieve the newspaper from the front porch, it is now Queenie who gets it before she even arrives.

Mysteries are everywhere, she thinks. But this is nothing new.

Out of habit, she checks the kitchen counter for the note Miss Temple always leaves. In the two decades Violet has worked there, her employer has critiqued every meal, leaving detailed feedback on Temple stationery for Violet every morning. In all that time, she's never been told she did a good job. If something is prepared well, it simply isn't mentioned. To Violet's credit, Miss Temple's communications have become shorter over the years, but she doesn't know what to think about there not being a note at all. She looks around the floor to see if it might have dropped. Sometimes if the Temple ghosts get rowdy in the middle of the night, things get moved. But nothing is there.

After retrieving two aspirin from the cabinet, she fills a glass with water, takes the pain reliever, and then glances at the clock. Queenie is usually already downstairs by the time Violet gets here, but not this morning. Her shoulder tells her again that something isn't right.

Violet leaves the kitchen and walks into the dining room. With every step, her shoulder tells her she is getting closer to whatever she needs to find, like in a childhood game of hot and cold. She steps into the grand foyer, which could use a touch up with the dust mop.

"Queenie?" she calls. "Miss Temple?" She waits and listens again. The only sound is her old friend, the large grandfather clock ticking in the entryway that smells of the lemon oil she rubbed into the wood yesterday.

Upstairs, Queenie's bedroom door opens and then slams. "Is that you, Queenie?" Violet calls.

Queenie steps to the railing wiping her eyes.

"My heavens, that's the deepest I've slept in years," Queenie says. "You would have thought I took one of mama's elixirs."

Violet exhales her relief. "With all these nuts worked up about those secrets, I was worried," she says.

"There's still plenty to worry about," Queenie says. "For one thing, Iris is going to give me hell for sleeping so late. Is she in the sunroom yet?"

"I haven't heard a peep out of her," Violet says.

They turn to look in the direction of Miss Temple's room at the end of the hallway.

"Maybe she's overslept, too," Violet says.

"That wouldn't be like her," Queenie says. "She's usually up at dawn doing her calisthenics on the balcony." Queenie approaches Miss Temple's room and knocks on the door. "Iris?" Queenie says.

Violet winces as her shoulder sends her an urgent message that perhaps she relaxed too soon. "Be careful," she calls after Queenie. She waits downstairs in the middle of the foyer as Queenie knocks again and then slowly opens the door.

"God in heaven!" Queenie shouts, disappearing into Iris's room.

Holding her shoulder, Violet runs up the stairs to find Queenie shaking Miss Temple, who lies lifeless on the bed.

"She's not waking up, Vi." Queenie's voice sounds an octave higher than usual. "All this mess about the *Temple Book of Secrets* has gone and pushed her over the edge."

Violet has never heard Queenie sound this frantic, and it scares her. She seems to be the one over the edge. Moving closer, Violet notes Miss Temple isn't breathing. The left side of her face droops like it has somehow melted from the heat. Violet dials 911 from the telephone by the bed. She gives the address to the operator, who assures her that someone is on their way. Meanwhile, Queenie is giving Miss Temple mouth-to-mouth resuscitation, evoking Jesus and Oprah as she pumps her chest.

"Don't you dare die on me, you old witch," Queenie says.

Given how Miss Temple has treated Queenie over the years, Violet considers her care heroic.

"Help is on the way," Violet says to Queenie, who repeats the message to Miss Temple.

"She's been so stressed about those silly secrets," Queenie says. "Plus, all that reminiscing and speaking in riddles last night at dinner. And asking you all those questions? What was that about?"

"I don't know, but look," Violet says.

A note rests on the nightstand that is written in Miss Temple's handwriting. In all capital letters, it reads: MAKE APPT TO SEE BO RIVERS ASAP. CHANGE THE WILL!

"Do you know anything about this?" Queenie asks.

"Nothing," Violet says. "But it looks like that's one appointment Miss Temple won't be keeping, at least not today."

Sirens approach in the distance and stop in front of the house. Violet runs downstairs and opens the door for paramedics. As abruptly as it started, the pain in her shoulder stops. In the next instant, she feels the whole house breathe, the Temple spirits offering a collective sigh of relief.

CHAPTER FIVE

Rose

You finally got your way, Mother, I've come home.

Rose Temple pulls the rental car in front of the Temple house and takes in its stoic presence. Despite the car air conditioning running on high, she begins to sweat. Courage is called for, but it is also mid-April in Savannah, and temperatures are already approaching ninety degrees. When she left her house in Wyoming that morning, there were eighteen inches of snow on the ground.

It has been twenty-five years since Rose returned home to Georgia. In its grandeur, the house she grew up in always seems unapproachable to her, an architectural replica of her mother. It belongs to an earlier time, when gentlemen strolled the squares with ladies wearing bonnets and carrying parasols, mirroring the aristocracy of Europe. The house rests among mature palm trees, magnolias and live oaks. Spanish moss clings to the oaks and waves in the warm breeze. The pink camellias, having already dropped their blooms, make way for abundant pink, white, and red azaleas that hold onto their last blossoms of the season as if to prove their resilience. She could use some of this resilience herself right now.

Rose gets out of the car, and it feels good to move. After spending the entire day sitting in cars, airports, and planes, her back has been complaining.

A small group of tourists stand on the sidewalk and look up at the house.

"Hey, do you live here?" a lady asks. Short, perky, and middle-aged, she wears a T-shirt that reads: *I Heart Savannah.*

"I used to live here," Rose says. "A long time ago."

"I can't even imagine," the lady says. She nudges her friend with an elbow as if Rose is some kind of celebrity.

Just because you grew up in a mansion doesn't mean you had a happy childhood, Rose wants to tell the woman. Yet, there were moments of her childhood that were incredibly happy. They just didn't involve her family.

Five days ago, Rose received a frantic phone call from Queenie at six in the morning. Rose's mother was unconscious, having suffered a massive stroke. Queenie had gone into a long explanation over the phone about how the *Temple Book of Secrets* had caused her mother's collapse. In a weird way, it made sense that her mother might fall on the same sword she'd been wielding all these years.

Rose considered not coming to her mother's death bed. After all, she lives far enough away that she almost has a legitimate excuse. But for some reason, she feels the need to see her mother one last time. For closure, if nothing else.

The Temple mansion looms above her. In the shadow of the live oaks, Rose feels herself become more protective. Twenty-five years ago, she broke off contact with her mother for reasons of self-preservation. Given the amount of inheritance she chose to forgo, most people would not understand her choice. Luckily, her husband, Max, had spent enough time with her mother to understand and be supportive.

After walking through the black wrought-iron gate to the east side of the house, Rose follows the groomed pathway through the garden. She pauses outside the kitchen door, looking back over the mature landscaping and dense shade sprinkled with handfuls of sunlight.

"God, I've missed shade," she says aloud. She could have saved a fortune on sunscreen and moisturizer if she'd never moved to Wyoming.

The magnolias emit an aroma reminiscent of her childhood. The garden, lush with growth, resonates with vibrancy. This is the part of the house that Rose was always drawn to. As a girl, she imagined it her secret garden after she read the book by the same name. The garden is hidden from the street and has a high brick wall around it.

A stone fountain graces the east wall, an impish looking gargoyle spouting water from its center. Moss covers the stones at its base and climbs upward, a green beard stretching to connect with the face. Koi fish live in the broad base of the fountain and flash like golden gemstones through the murky green water. Sounds of the trickling water almost lull Rose into the belief that nothing bad could happen here.

The salty smell of the sea travels on the breeze. Compared to the dry air of Cheyenne, Savannah drips with moisture. It clings to Rose and pulls her clothes close. She closes her eyes and takes in the faint smell of salt water, the ocean only a few miles away. Whenever she smells the sea, she thinks of Old Sally. She wants to see her again.

Rose fans her overheated face and chides herself for forgetting about the heat. It is too hot for blue jeans, a cotton shirt, and her cowboy boots. At least she left her Stetson at home. Her clothes help her remember who she is now. She isn't the lost young artist who left here twenty-five years ago. She is the woman who co-owns a thousand-acre ranch and sells her art in a prominent gallery in Santa Fe. Yet as soon as Rose exited the plane in Savannah, she felt herself weaken. It is as if her past has been waiting in the baggage area to be claimed, and she is now saddled with it again.

Memories greet her everywhere. She looks up at her mother's bedroom window, half expecting to see her standing there. In the heat, a chill crawls her spine. Walking the garden path, she takes in the regal live oak she played under as a child that stands in the center of the garden. Branches of the oak are as thick as entire cottonwood trees at home. The oak's massive limbs touch the ground in places. The roots rise up to greet the limbs, and it is hard to tell which are which. Moss carpets cover the ground underneath. As a girl, Rose and her best friend, Violet, created a doll hospital under this tree. They made beds out of twigs and moss and wrapped bandages around her doll's arms and legs and spent hours nursing the dolls back to health. Perhaps she gave them the care she never got from her mother.

Don't start this, she tells herself. *No pity parties allowed.* She forces herself to stand straighter.

Near the carriage house, someone moves out of the deep umber and forest green shadows. Rose emits a slight gasp, but when the man smiles—looking pleased to have startled her—she realizes it is her brother, Edward. His hair graying at the temples makes him look distinguished, and his clothes convey the same attitude. Even Edward's smile is a tool of intimidation.

"Should have known you'd show up," he says. Edward, who is six years older, puts his hands on his hips as if to reinforce his dominance.

Rose and her brother have never been close. The last time she saw him was two decades earlier at the Denver airport during a two-hour layover for a flight from Los Angeles.

"I suppose you've come back to make sure you don't miss out

on the inheritance," he says with a smirk. Even in middle age, he has managed to throw Rose off balance. But she has no intention of letting him know.

"Actually, I've come to pay my respects," she says.

"Right," he says. "I know exactly how much you respect our lovely mother."

His sarcasm sounds so much like their mother, he could be channeling her.

Don't let him get to you, Rose tells herself. She's only been back to Savannah for an hour, and already she's talking to herself.

When they were young, she did her best to avoid Edward. She wishes she could avoid him now.

"You haven't changed," Rose says.

He tucks his light blue oxford shirt into his tailored navy pants. Does he think her comment is about his boyish figure?

A ghost of a memory taps her on the shoulder, and she remembers another sword that has nothing to do with secrets. Rose glances at her left hand where the tip of her little finger used to be, severed at the first joint forty years before. She lost it when she was almost five years old, Edward ten. He convinced her to play Cowboys and Indians. Rose was the Indian.

"We had some good times in this garden, didn't we?" Edward's smirk changes to a smile that appears almost genuine.

Is he serious? she wonders. "I don't remember them as good times," she says to him. "You used to lock me in the garden shed."

"It was the stockade," he says. "You were an Indian. It was where you belonged." He smiles again.

Interesting that he would bring up belonging, she thinks. For the last twenty-five years, she hasn't felt like she belonged anywhere.

"You had no business getting Grandpa Edward's sword," Rose says. It has taken her forty years to address her brother's recklessness.

Their grandfather's collection of weaponry dated back to the Civil War. Elaborate cases for these weapons extended down a hallway in the back wing of the house. Old Sally always mumbled to herself when she polished the dark wood of the cases, saying incantations to protect her from the evil these weapons had been used for.

"Oh, come on, it was fun," he says.

"Fun?" she asks. *Since when is severing body parts—even small ones—fun,* she wonders.

"When you tattled to Mother, she smiled, remember? It was weird the things that would get her attention." He laughs as though it is a treasured memory. A treasured memory that gave Rose nightmares for years.

A scream replays in her mind. A scream that brought Old Sally flying out the kitchen door, and sent Edward running back into the house. She wrapped her hand tight in a kitchen towel and ran with Rose in her arms all the way to the doctor's office, several blocks away. Whenever her various therapists asked for her earliest memory, it was always this one she recalled.

Old Sally kept the fingertip wrapped in wax paper in the freezer. A week later, she and Queenie, with Violet still in a stroller, gave a funeral for it in the garden. Queenie sang a moving rendition of *Swing Low, Sweet Chariot,* while Old Sally unwrapped the wax paper to reveal the severed fingertip. Before its internment, she poured a black root concoction over it and said a spell. As far as Rose knows, the tiny bone is still buried under the live oak in between two of the most prominent roots.

"It wasn't that bad," Edward says, glancing at her hand. "Simply a casualty of war."

"We weren't at war, Edward," Rose says.

"Weren't we?" Edward asks. "Mother and Father pitted us against each other."

Now that she thinks about it, they did. Their parents were embroiled in their own version of the War Between the States, and Rose and Edward were required to take sides. It was like each parent took a hostage while they were growing up. Perhaps to take the focus off how unsuited they were for each other. Edward was her mother's favorite, and Rose was her father's.

The Temple women were never good at nurturing their offspring. Although her relationship with her daughter, Katie, is a healthy one, it is mostly due to Queenie and Old Sally's influence. It also helped that Rose refused to be anything like her mother.

Her father was the kind one, the gentle one, to the extent that someone pickled in bourbon could be. He died during her freshman year at Smith, and she skipped an entire semester to grieve. Yet her mother's pending death seems entirely different. Rose's grief at never having her mother's love has filled much of her life already. In fact, her mother's impending death almost feels like a relief. At the very least, it will mark an end to Rose's lifelong dubious hope that her mother might become a different person— someone who is kind, loving, and tolerant.

For as long as Rose can remember, Edward wanted their mother to be proud of him. Unfortunately, she valued ruthlessness in her males, and even as a boy, he tried to become what she prized.

"Don't think you can waltz in here after twenty-five years and get any of Mother's money," Edward says, his words pulling her out of the past. "I'm the one who stuck around and protected her interests."

In your endless pursuit of her approval, Rose thinks.

However, before Rose can respond, Edward exits the garden and gets into a silver Mercedes next to the carriage house. For several seconds she waits for her breathing to return to normal. She didn't anticipate seeing Edward, at least not right away, and it has shaken her. Facing her mother again was a big enough challenge already.

What will it be like to see her mother again? She was her daughter Katie's age when she last saw her, and now she is middle-aged. Rose can't imagine she will derive pleasure from her mother's vulnerability. When both parents die, you realize you are next in line.

Rose wishes her husband, Max, hadn't been needed at the ranch. Max is the antithesis of Edward. A solid, kind man who can make sense of things. Though she wonders if anyone can make sense of her family.

Rose takes another deep breath telling herself to relax. After all the therapy she's had, at least she's learned to breathe. When she's calm again, she continues through the garden to the kitchen door. It feels odd to knock at the door she used daily for the first two decades of her life. A woman answers, of early middle-age and with a glowing smile. At first glance, Rose thinks it is Queenie, but then she realizes it is Violet, who was four years younger than Rose yet a best friend for most of Rose's childhood.

"Should we do the Sea Gypsy handshake?" Violet asks.

"Oh my, I haven't thought of that for years," Rose says, returning the smile.

As girls, Rose and Violet created a secret society called the Sea Gypsies, complete with secret handshakes and rituals. Rose and Violet decided that Queenie was the Sea Gypsy *queen,* and they were princesses. Up until then, Queenie's name had been Ivy. One entire summer, they wore only blue clothing because it was the sacred Sea Gypsy color. For years she has added that color to everything she paints, if only a single brushstroke.

Old Sally made them all special swimming caps with sparkling blue, green, and silver sequins. She still has that old swimming cap back home in Wyoming. This is part of the past that she doesn't mind remembering.

Violet, a pretty child, has now blossomed into a striking woman. With skin the color of coffee with extra cream, she looks like a walking advertisement for the Coppertone perfect tan. In comparison, Rose feels old and leathery. The Wyoming dryness and long winters have done nothing to preserve the little bit of beauty she thought she possessed in her 20s and 30s.

In her early years, Rose spent hours in the kitchen with Old Sally, Queenie, and Violet. Old Sally seemed to be raising everybody in those days. Then Violet came to work for Rose's family shortly after Rose's father died, and it got a little strange. Plus, Rose went away to college to major in art and to avoid her mother. She soon figured out ways not to come home. Friends in New York and Boston invited her to stay for the holidays. Friends whose families impressed Rose's mother enough that she didn't complain. During that time, Rose and Violet somehow lost touch.

Violet ushers Rose into the kitchen, and the two women have an awkward moment of deciding whether or not to embrace. The embrace wins out.

"It must be strange to be back," Violet says.

"You don't know the half of it," Rose says, remembering Edward's appearance in the garden.

Rose glances around the kitchen. She has fond memories of this room. Except for newer appliances, and a darker shade of taupe on the walls, it has changed very little in the last twenty-five years. Her kitchen at home is chaotic. Dishes need washing, the mail is stacked to read, and groceries need to be bought. Rose forgets how smooth things run when someone else is in charge of a house—someone whose entire job is to maintain order and keep things running smoothly.

What a luxury, Rose thinks, although she lived with this luxury the first twenty years of her life.

"I spent most of my childhood in this kitchen," Rose says. "How is Old Sally? The last I heard, she was still going strong."

"Grandmother just turned one hundred," Violet says. "We had a birthday party for her last month. She lives in the same place on the coast."

"I'd love to see her while I'm here," Rose says. "Is Queenie around?"

Their conversation, though warm, feels hesitant, as if the past is scrambling to catch up with the present.

"She's in her room," Violet says. "She's been looking forward to seeing you."

"Any change with Mother?" she asks, realizing she has relegated her main reason for coming to an afterthought.

"I'm sorry, there's not," Violet says. "They're bringing her home from the hospital in an hour. She'll have a nurse, 24 hours a day until..." Violet pauses, as though concerned about being insensitive.

"Until she dies?" Rose asks.

Violet nods and lowers her eyes.

Should Rose tell Violet that the possibility of Rose's mother's death holds no emotional charge for her? In a way, it's like her mother has already been dead for twenty-five years. But Rose hesitates to reveal this to someone she is just getting to know again, even if she is a Sea Gypsy.

"Evidently, your mother left detailed instructions on how to conduct her final days," Violet continues. "She made lists of things to be done in the event of her incapacitation, as well as instructions about her funeral."

"She thought she might get decapitated?" Rose asks, confused.

Violet laughs. "No, silly. *In*capacitation, not *de*capitation."

Rose rolls her eyes at her mistake and laughs, too. It feels good to laugh at such a serious moment.

"I guess I'm more jet-lagged than I realized," Rose says. She set the alarm for four that morning so she could leave the house by six and get to the Denver airport by eight. Weary doesn't begin to describe how she feels.

"I saw Edward in the garden," Rose says, her pinkie vibrating with the memory.

"What was he doing in the garden?" Violet asks. "I didn't even know he was in town."

"He's good at lurking," Rose says. "He probably appointed himself as head of my welcoming committee."

The look on Violet's face confirms that no love is lost between her and Edward.

"Your mother's stroke has been bad enough," Violet says. "Edward sure doesn't help things. He's like a vulture circling."

Footsteps approach, the kitchen door swings open, and it's like the sun breaks through thick clouds.

"I thought I heard you," Queenie says, her smile aimed right at Rose.

Seeing Queenie is like coming home to the best part of Rose's past. Queenie wears a flower print dress of bright pink and orange. Colors so vivid it looks like they might attract hummingbirds.

I wouldn't dream of wearing something so alive, Rose thinks. But just being around Queenie again makes her wonder if she should try.

"Sweet Jesus, there's a cowgirl in the kitchen," Queenie says, slapping her thigh.

Rose welcomes Queenie's embrace—a woman who was more like a mother to her than anyone else. On her desk at home is a framed photograph of Queenie carrying her around after she was born, a twelve-year-old toting a baby. She is the one person in Savannah that Rose has kept in close contact with, having exchanged letters several times a year for over two decades.

When they end their embrace, Queenie pulls Violet into their circle, and they are all young again and inseparable. Yet as much as Rose wants to relax into their reunion, the closeness feels almost unbearable. It is too much of what she's missed. Too much of what will be hard to leave again.

"How's Mother?" Rose asks as if she knows the question will serve to separate them. It does.

"I talked to her doctor this morning," Queenie says. "He says she doesn't have much time left."

"Do they think she'll wake up again?" Rose asks.

"Unlikely," Queenie says. "But you never know with Iris. She's probably writing a letter to God on Temple stationery as we speak.

She hasn't given all that money to Catholic charities for nothing." Queenie lets out a cackle that makes Rose laugh. There was a lot of laughter in her childhood. She has missed that, too.

"I'm sure it's not the way Mother would have wanted to go," Rose says, serious again.

Queenie agrees. "To lose all control must be killing her." She lifts an eyebrow at her choice of words. "You know how much your mother likes to be in charge," she adds.

"That's the understatement of the century," Rose says, putting her purse on the kitchen table.

"Perhaps the millennium," Violet says.

They pause as if each realizes how much Rose's mother would disapprove.

"They're bringing Iris home this afternoon," Queenie says. "Her wishes were to die here, and it would be just like Iris to haunt me after she's gone if I don't follow her requests to the letter."

"The famous Temple deathbed requests," Rose says. "I'd forgotten about those."

"She wouldn't be the first apparition to live here," Violet says. She glances up like she's listening for confirmation.

Queenie clucks her agreement.

"I can't say that I've missed the ghosts," Rose says. "There's nothing quite like seeing your dead great-grandfather in the garden on your way to school. Of course, he seemed harmless enough, but it was always a little startling when he first showed up."

"He's the one with the surgeon's bag, right?" Violet asks. "He's always out by the oak tree."

"He was a doctor during the Civil War," Rose says. "When my mother was a little girl, he was ancient and told her stories about the war. He said he had sawed off more limbs than all the limbs on that live oak in the garden."

"That's why Iris refused to go near that old tree," Queenie

says. "She told me once that she always imagined amputated arms and legs dangling from its limbs."

It occurs to Rose that only in Savannah would the first real conversation she's had in twenty-five years include an update on the Temple ghosts. From Rose's experience, sometimes the living can be scarier than the dead. In a way, her mother has haunted Rose her entire life.

It's also been years since Rose thought of curses and spells and the magical Gullah arts. When she was a girl, Old Sally told her stories that intrigued her, about how Old Sally's grandmother was a slave owned by the Temples, as was her mother before her. Old Sally's mother was the first woman in her family born free, and she was very proud of that fact.

Rose has never told anyone that her ancestors owned slaves. Not even Max. It is Rose's secret. Growing up, she related much more to being owned than to being an owner. Sometimes she still feels like she's waiting to be liberated. Maybe that's part of the reason she's here.

"You look like you're a million miles away," Violet says.

"I was." Rose turns to look at her and Queenie. "Remember that time when I was six, and I covered myself with mud from the garden to darken my skin?"

Queenie laughs. "You wanted to be black like Mama and me," she says.

"I thought you were magical," Rose begins. "Old Sally knew all these Gullah potions and spells, and you had these deep roots that extended all the way back to Africa," Rose says.

"I'll never forget the look on Mama's face when you showed up in the kitchen," Queenie says. "She laughed until tears came and was still laughing when she put you in the bathtub. Remember that?"

"She was always so patient with me," Rose says, thinking of how much she looks forward to seeing Old Sally again. But first, she needs to play the dutiful daughter for one last time.

CHAPTER SIX

Violet

M iss Temple would not like that Rose is back home, standing in her kitchen, which makes no sense to Violet given how kind Rose is. Violet remembers why she and Rose were friends now. Unlike some in Savannah, she doesn't see color as a reason to reject someone.

"Have you told Rose about our latest drama in the newspaper?" Violet asks Queenie. Her aunt has been acting strange the last several days. She practically races Violet to be the first one to grab the newspaper off the porch. Then the rest of the day, she mumbles about who must be behind telling the secrets.

"You mean someone is still releasing secrets from that old book?" Rose asks.

"One a day," Queen says. "At this rate, whoever it is will be at it for years." Queenie's eyes widen.

"Mother must have had a fit when this first started," Rose says.

"Actually, she had a stroke," Queenie says, with a grimace.

Violet retrieves the newspaper from the counter and reads Rose today's entry:

Temple Secret: Downtown Jewelry Shop
Does Money Laundering for Millionaires.
Contact Reeves Bartow.

"Do the Bartows still live here?" Rose asks. "I was in school with the son."

"He's probably calling his attorney as we speak," Queenie says. "All of Savannah is standing in line to file lawsuits. And nobody can figure out who is doing it."

"God, I hope I don't have any secrets in there," Rose says, her brow creased.

"Me, too," Violet says, although her only secret is how much she hates working for Miss Temple, and she doubts that is news-worthy. "Would you believe I found a designer poop bag at the front door this morning filled with doggie you-know-what?" Violet says, wondering why she's using *you-know-what* for its actual contents.

"Who would do something like that?" Rose asks.

"No telling," Violet says. "But I just thought you should know in case someone approaches you."

"It's probably good Mother's in a coma," Rose says. "She couldn't bear to see the Temple family name tarnished."

"She brought it on herself," Queenie says. "That *Book of Secrets* was how she kept everybody in line. Including me."

"This morning, I pulled a couple of posters from the fence," Violet says, "with not very flattering pictures of Miss Temple."

"That's the least of it," Queenie says. "You should have heard some of the phone calls."

Aware of how tired Rose looks, Violet interrupts: "Let's get your things," she says, taking Rose's arm. "Unfortunately, our resident ghosts don't carry luggage from the car. But I can do that. Then you can settle in a bit before your mother arrives."

"I can get my own luggage," Rose says, but Violet insists.

Violet retrieves Rose's suitcase and then ascends the spiral staircase toward Rose's old bedroom. Violet has trudged up and down these stairs thousands of times. At least it keeps her legs in shape. She's also memorized every detail of the maroon carpet runners on the wooden steps, the polished banisters, as well as the Temple portraits lining the walls. As girls, whenever the Temples weren't around, Violet and Rose slid down the railings as the Temple ancestors watched in framed silence. They watch her now. Do they remember Rose?

Violet meets Rose at the doorway to Rose's room as Rose places her suitcase on the bed. Violet seems to always be standing in doorways these days as if tempting herself to exit from the Temple lives for good. Rose's bedroom is frozen in time from before Rose left for college. The dark antique furniture, too heavy for a child's room, makes Violet feel claustrophobic whenever she cleans in here. The furniture and heavy draperies over the windows do their best to suck the oxygen from the room.

"I'm surprised she kept my room intact," Rose says. "I noticed my portrait was gone from downstairs."

Violet doesn't tell Rose that when Violet started working here, Miss Temple forbid her to ever speak Rose's name. But she did keep the room as it was. Over the years, Violet has discovered that Miss Temple is as complicated as her meal choices.

"I forgot how dark this room is," Rose says. "I could never paint in here."

"Do you still paint?" Violet asks. Rose was quite good by the time she went away to college.

"I do still paint," Rose says. "Mostly Western scenes now, but I'd love to paint more of the landscape around here."

Violet's creative side comes out in her cooking and baking. She walks over to the window and tries to open it, but it won't budge.

A large crepe myrtle twists upward outside the second-story window. At least the blossoms offer a touch of cheerfulness to the drab room. As girls, they rarely spent time here and played in the kitchen or in the garden while her grandmother worked.

"It looks like a museum or something," Rose says. "No wonder I could hardly wait to leave home."

Violet resists confessing that she can hardly wait to leave, too.

"I'm surprised a security guard isn't stationed at the door to make sure I don't touch anything," Rose says.

"I can get you one if you want," Violet says, and they both laugh.

A small photograph of Rose and her mother at Rose's college graduation sits atop her antique bureau. Rose looks sullen in it, as she always did when photographed with her mother. Miss Temple doesn't look that thrilled, either, her chin tilted upward in typical Temple fashion. As teenagers, Rose talked to Violet about how she was a constant disappointment to her mother. That's also when their friendship began to fade.

Queenie calls from the foyer that the ambulance has arrived.

"Should I go downstairs and greet her?" Rose asks.

"It's up to you," Violet says. "She won't know the difference." *Or will she?* Violet thinks.

Violet follows Rose downstairs, where two men wait with a stretcher next to Queenie. Strapped onto the stretcher covered with a white blanket, Miss Temple appears small and vulnerable, the opposite of the critical force she usually is.

Violet, Queenie, and Rose follow the men carrying Miss Temple upstairs. It feels ceremonial, in a way, as if they are practicing for the funeral, not that Violet would be part of the procession. Violet never knew her own mother, so she can't imagine what this is like for Rose. She imagines it is like witnessing a fire-breathing dragon whose flame is going out. She is surprised her arm isn't hurting since it usually announces a death or injury. Does this mean Miss Temple isn't ready to die?

Two technicians join the crowd in Miss Temple's bedroom to set up the various machines. A hospital bed is where the four-poster antique used to be.

"Mother won't like this," Rose says to Violet and Queenie. "She would want to die in a Temple bed."

"I know," Queenie says. "But this is the only way her doctor would agree to let us bring her home."

Even the Temple beds have lineages. Miss Temple was born in the same bed in which her grandmother and grandfather died. Working for Miss Temple meant Violet had to know the history of every piece of furniture in the house as if it somehow might make her dust and polish everything with more care.

Why anyone would want to sleep where numerous relatives have died is beyond me, she thinks. At the very least, it verges on weird. But to Miss Temple, tradition trumps weird. Tradition trumps everything.

Stories about the Temples are given on every carriage ride tour that passes the house. Most famously, the story of Rose's great grandfather, one of the more eccentric Temples, who took to his deathbed, requesting a final visit from his pet pig, Salty. According to legend, Salty lived on the Temple family's plantation near Charleston and was transported the hundred miles between Charleston and Savannah and led up the stairs to say his final goodbyes.

Violet overheard Miss Temple tell Queenie one day about how much she liked that "dumb old pig."

Evidently the same evening the grandfather died, the grand-mother condemned Salty to their dinner table. *Revenge for his transgressions,* Miss Temple said, of which there were supposedly many. To this day, Violet is to never serve Miss Temple pork of any kind.

The front bell chimes. Violet goes to answer it. She spies another fancy doggy-do bag on the porch. A nurse arrives, a young woman who introduces herself as Ava. She wears a white uniform, her dyed black hair pulled back in a rubber band. A green lizard tattoo crawls up the middle finger of her right hand, a detail that hints at a different personality hidden beneath the young woman's professional appearance. Violet knows what it's like to wear a uniform that's meant to obscure your personality, but she's never considered a tattoo. Maybe she should. It would certainly surprise Tia and Leisha.

Just outside the door, Violet, Queenie, and Rose wait for the flurry of activity to cease. Rose's face drains of color, and Violet steps closer. On the hospital bed a few feet away is the person her former friend has spent the last twenty-five years of her life avoiding. Even Violet's chest tightens with the thought. She decides to stay close in case Rose needs her.

The ambulance drivers leave first. Then after several minutes of testing the various machines, the two technicians leave. Ava, the nurse, straightens the sheet over Miss Temple's body and then motions for them to enter.

"Miss Temple is ready for visitors," Ava says, sounding older than she looks. If she is aware of the secrets that have caused such a fuss for the last ten days, she doesn't let on.

Rose approaches the bed and Queenie and Violet file behind her. Queenie rests her hand on Rose's shoulder as if to offer emotional support. Queenie can be counted on in a crisis. She was the one Violet called upon when darker girls said hateful things to her at school because Violet was lighter-skinned. Queenie was also there the time Edward attacked her when he was home from college.

"She looks strangely peaceful, doesn't she?" Queenie says. "It's like the *Temple Book of Secrets* never existed."

Peaceful isn't a word Violet would ever use to describe Miss Temple. "I guess we'd all be better off if we hadn't heard of that book." Violet reminds herself to pick up the second batch of dog poop on the porch and wonders what might come next.

"Look at it this way," Queenie says, her eyes sporting a twinkle. "It only took a devastating stroke and a coma to achieve this serenity."

Queenie's humor helps compensate for the gravity of the moment. Violet is seldom close enough to study Miss Temple's face. Instead of the usual tight line of irritability, her lips are relaxed and droop slightly. A drop of spittle collects in the corner of her mouth. Rose pulls a red bandana from her blue jean pocket and uses it to soak up the drool.

"It's so odd to touch her again after so many years," Rose says. "I half expect her to snap out of the coma and slap my arm away."

Violet gives Rose's other shoulder a squeeze, aware that her own shoulder isn't reactive at all. She turns to look at Violet, and Violet wonders if she and Rose might someday renew their friendship.

"You know, I think this is the longest I've ever spent in a room with her without getting criticized," Rose says.

"Iris is one tough cookie," Queenie says. "That woman should have come out of the womb with a warning label."

"I hope she can't hear us," Violet whispers.

"We listened to her bellyache for years," Queenie says. "Now it's her turn to get a little of what she dished out."

Violet isn't so sure this is wise. The energy is shifting in the house. The Temple spirits seem to be waking up irritable after a long nap.

Across the room, Ava unpacks a small backpack and arranges different nurse-related items on Miss Temple's vanity. With this task complete, she steps over and checks the IV drip that flows into Miss Temple's hand. A thin line of black eye-liner accentuates Ava's small green eyes, the same shade of green used on the lizard tattoo on her finger.

Nice touch, Violet thinks. If she gets to know Ava a little better, she will ask her about the lizard. There has to be a story there.

Ava sits on a Victorian loveseat in the far corner of the room and pulls a *People* magazine from her purse. Johnny Depp graces the cover. A person admired by her younger daughter.

Power and money haven't protected Miss Temple from this moment. She is dying just like everyone else, and with a scandal afoot.

The telephone rings and Violet jumps. Until recently, the phone had been unplugged because of all the crank calls they were getting, but with Miss Temple this ill, they need a line out. As Violet answers the phone, Queenie gives Rose a brief hug and excuses herself. Violet is relieved to hear no death threats or cursing when she answers.

"It's for you," Violet says, handing the cordless to Rose.

Apparently, it is Rose's daughter Katie on the phone. Rose cuts the call short, but not before telling her daughter how strange it is to be here.

Without looking up from her magazine, Ava smiles, as if she is no stranger to strange.

Rose hands the phone back to Violet and sits by her mother's side. "You don't have to stay," she says to Violet.

Violet appreciates the offer to leave and excuses herself to go make dinner. Rose talking to her daughter reminds Violet that she has two daughters of her own she needs to get home to. She descends the grand spiral staircase with a fantasy of sliding down the banister like she and Rose used to do, but then Violet realizes how many decades it has been since the last time she pulled this off. Long enough for broken bones or traction to result.

Past and present mingle as she crosses the foyer to the dining room and then into the kitchen, her constant refuge as a girl when she came to work with her grandmother. Like a game of hide-and-seek, the kitchen was always the place to run to that was deemed "safe." Otherwise, she was to stay out of Miss Temple's sight. A talent she still relies on to get through the day.

When Violet enters the kitchen, she finds Queenie sitting at the large, oval oak kitchen table drinking a cup of coffee. The difference between the kitchen and Miss Temple's bedroom feels like the difference between life and death.

"How are you holding up?" Queenie asks, motioning for Violet to join her. "Can you believe Savannah's biggest tyrant might actually die?"

"Why limit her to Savannah?" Violet says and then apologizes. "Rose isn't anything like her," she adds, and Queenie agrees.

"They say an apple doesn't fall far from the tree, but in this case, it fell in a totally different forest," Queenie says.

Violet makes herself a cup of tea. She isn't much of a coffee drinker—she prefers the smell of it more than the taste and only drinks it if she adds enough half and half and sugar to mask its bitterness.

Rose enters and sits at the table with Queenie. "I'm not sure how long I can just sit there and watch," Rose says.

Violet pours her a cup of coffee, which she accepts and drinks black.

"Would you like to visit Mama tonight?" Queenie asks Rose.

"I'd love that," Rose says.

"We can go right after dinner if you're not too tired," Queenie says. "I was going to drive over anyway and bring her back. She says your mother's crossing is tonight, and she needs to be a part of the transition."

Violet has never witnessed one of her grandmother's end of life rituals.

"Crossing and transition aren't words I usually associate with death," Rose says. "They sound more fluid and less final. Although with Mother, the more 'final', it is the better, I suppose."

"I'm not sure the Temples know when to go," Violet says. She waits for the resident ghosts to agree or disagree, but they are quiet for now.

"Mama and Iris have quite a history," Queenie says. "It almost seems fitting that they would be together at the end."

"Does Mother still believe that Old Sally put a curse on her?" Rose asks.

"Good lord, yes," Queenie says. "Several curses, in fact. I'm not sure how much of it is true, but Iris is at the effect of something. As I've mentioned in my letters, the last place you want to be when your mother is having one of her attacks is downwind. It's enough to kill a moose."

"And then have it for dinner," Violet says, offering another quick apology. She is starting to sound like her Aunt Queenie.

"No need to apologize for something true," Rose says.

"Mama would say that laughter and misery go together," Queenie says. "They're flip sides of the same coin."

Violet wonders how Queenie can still laugh. It's no secret how badly Miss Temple treats her. Sometimes Violet wishes Queenie would stand up for herself more. This is the part of her lineage she doesn't understand. The part that thinks nothing of staying under the Temple's rule. If Violet gets her way, this will all come to an end with the next generation. Maybe even before that, if Violet can finally save enough money to realize her dream. She glances at the spare cookie jar, where she keeps her life savings. With the Temple security system, this is as safe a place to keep it as any bank. And definitely safer than Violet and Jack's apartment, which was broken into several summers ago.

In the twenty years she has worked for the Temples, Violet has saved fifteen thousand dollars. She just needs a little more money for a deposit on the modest storefront she found downtown and to buy the equipment and inventory she'll need. But first, she must say goodbye to Miss Temple.

CHAPTER SEVEN

Rose

The machines keeping her mother alive breathe and beep in an oddly comforting way, a lullaby of technology. Ava, who is stronger than she looks, scoots one of the Queen Anne chairs from the corner of the room to the side of the bed. Rose thanks her and sits stiffly next to her mother as if anticipating complaints about her posture. At first, Rose looks at everything else in the room except her mother: the lavish draperies, the expensive antiques, and a small gold clock ticking loudly on the nightstand near her bed. Then Rose turns her gaze to the body in the hospital bed.

Her mother must have been fifty-five the last time Rose saw her. She is old now. Etched with wrinkles, her mother looks more like Rose's grandmother, who lived in the house when she was a young girl. A woman who scared Rose and always smelled of camphor and mint. Sometimes the old woman would yell at Rose for no reason at all. Her grandmother Temple was a woman who possessed a coldness that made her mother seem full of warmth. Years after she died, the smell lingered in the hallways and in the corners of the rooms. She can almost smell it now.

At five o'clock, a woman named Lynette arrives to replace Ava. Rose is the only person in the room. Closer to Rose's age, Lynette is almost as wide as she is tall and wears a traditional white uniform. Her pantyhose rub together as she walks and creates a synthetic swishing sound. Because of her height and width, she resembles a linebacker in drag. Rose likes her instantly.

"I'm one of those people who believes people in a coma can hear everything that's going on around them," Lynette says.

Lynette's southern accent is as thick as her plentiful waist. To her surprise, Rose has missed hearing such a vibrant rendition of her native tongue. In the West, the language is crisp and to the point, seeing no need to waste its time. A southern accent, on the other hand, is in no hurry. Every syllable entertains the luxury of an afternoon stroll or a balcony evening on the front porch.

Lynette asks Rose if she would like to help give her mother a sponge bath. Rose doesn't answer at first. How can she tell kind Lynette, that besides the earlier spittle removal, she can't remember the last time she touched her mother? *Or Mother touched me, for that matter.*

Lynette encourages Rose to join her. She coaches her on how to move the washcloth gently down her mother's arms and hands and avoid the needles that force fluids into her aged veins. Washcloth in hand, Rose stands motionless, looking down at her mother's body.

How can she be kind to someone who she could never please? Someone who didn't know the meaning of kindness, perhaps because nobody ever treated her that way, either.

"Oh, sweetie, I know it's hard to see your mama this way," Lynette says.

Rose has never, in her entire forty-four years of life, called her mother *mama* or *mom*. The terms are too endearing. She always called her Mother or simply said, 'yes, ma'am,' like Old Sally and Queenie did.

Lynette swishes her way to Rose's side of the bed. "Just follow my motions, sweetie," she says.

Following her instruction, Rose glides the moist white washcloth down her mother's slender arms sequined in liver spots. Colors she's used in western landscapes. She makes a long, soft brushstroke of care across her mother's skin. Skin does strange things as it ages. It loosens, puckers, spots, and blotches. Rose notes the beginnings of this process on her own body. Thankfully, it doesn't scare her. She has always felt older than her years. Growing up in the Temple household required a certain amount of toughness.

As Rose mirrors Lynette's motions, she pretends she is someone like Lynette who genuinely cares about the person on the bed. To her surprise, the washing of her mother's unconscious body carries unanticipated emotions for Rose. Hidden within the folds of discomfort is a secret longing for her mother's touch. Perhaps this reaction is brought on by her fatigue, combined with the onset of hot flashes and all the memories that have been waiting for her here. Whatever it is, she is too tired to resist it. It's like she's been running away for twenty-five years only to end up at the same place.

Unexpected tears rush to Rose's eyes. *More needed moisture,* she thinks. Like the droughts out west, she has had a drought of tears over the years. She takes a deep breath and welcomes the rain. Yet with the quickness of a sword cutting through flesh, all emotions cease, as her brother, Edward, steps into the room.

CHAPTER EIGHT

Queenie

After Queenie adjusts the seat and air conditioning vents so they'll blow straight on her, she backs the Lincoln out of the carriage house and waits at the gate for Rose to join her. The drive up the South Carolina coast to her mama's house will take thirty minutes, twenty if she has good luck with the traffic lights and is generous with the gas pedal. In the past, in return for the use of one of the Temple cars, Queenie had to run an errand for Iris. Perks like cars and cash have always been at her half-sister's discretion. But Queenie has other reasons for putting up with Iris. Reasons that nobody else knows about. Not even Rose.

Toilet paper is wrapped around the garden gate and thrown into the trees. *Good lord*, Queenie thinks *we've become a college frat house.*

The secrets have brought all sorts of undesirables to their doorstep. When Queenie gets back, she'll remove the toilet paper, so Iris won't wake from her coma to complain. At least the crank calls have stopped. Calls plagued them all evening until Queenie finally called the phone company to have their phone changed to a restricted number. She taps the steering wheel, worn out from worrying that her biggest secret will end up in the classifieds, too. She's also tired from getting up so early to get a first glance at the secret of the day. So far, several Savannah adulterers have been revealed, as well as a cross-dressing oil tycoon and a mentally ill banker. All deceased, and mostly forgotten, but still. Whoever is doing it likes to throw in secrets from the present-day every now and again just to keep people interested.

Meanwhile, not a single one of Iris's so-called society friends visited her in the hospital. Not one. For a week, Queenie has spent every day at the hospital with Iris. Her only visitors were Violet— who stopped by every evening on her way home— and Spud Grainger, who stopped by twice a day, once in the morning before going to the Piggly Wiggly and then afterward to relieve Queenie. Although she has a hard time understanding it, she appreciates Spud Grainger's loyalty to Iris.

Rose walks out of the house and latches the gate behind her. She looks tired. In an earlier conversation, Queenie and Violet discussed how difficult this trip back to Savannah must be for Rose. To come home after an absence of twenty-five years, her mother in a coma—a woman too stubborn to show any love— must be hard. Not to mention, seeing Edward again after all these years.

Queenie can't believe he showed up at his mother's bedside. When she called her half-nephew after his mother's stroke, he seemed indifferent and inconvenienced. At least tonight, he didn't stay long. Just enough time to give Rose a prolonged sinister look before rushing off to meet someone at the country club. Queenie has never liked Edward. He acts more like a spoiled brat than a man. Edward and Rose are about as different as two siblings can be.

Rose gets into the car and buckles herself into the passenger seat, giving Queenie a faint smile.

"Seeing Mama will be good for you." Queenie pats her hand. "You two have a special bond."

"I've missed her," Rose says. "I don't think I realized how much until now."

"She's missed you, too," Queenie says. "You're family."

Twelve years separate Queenie and Rose in age, but because of her mama's influence, they have similar sensibilities flowing through them.

With Rose silent next to her, Queenie lets her mind wander. She has driven this route thousands of times and never tires of it. The Talmadge Bridge stretches across the Savannah River, a ribbon of concrete reaching toward the horizon. The water fans out in every direction, and the late afternoon sun glistens across the grassy marsh.

Crossing this bridge suspends time for Queenie as if the bridge itself is a timeline for her family. Her ancestors made this crossing, at first in boats, and her descendants will make this crossing long after she is gone. At the highest point, where the bridge arches upward, she feels weightless, a water bird soaring up and out on a heavy wind. She wishes this part could last longer. But then the bridge delivers her to the land on the other side, as waterways skirt off in different directions.

Her mama never learned how to drive a car. Her entire working career, Old Sally caught rides into Savannah with different maids and housekeepers who worked the same hours. A wide assortment of family and friends are available to call upon whenever she needs a ride. But for Queenie, learning how to drive a car was a statement of independence.

Daughters need their differences, even if their mamas are wonderful, she tells herself.

As they near the ocean, Rose sits straighter. "So many memories," she says. "You used to drive us out here all the time."

"Mama loved bringing you and Violet to the beach," Queenie says. "I think it gave us all a break from your mother."

"Do you remember how we used to sing while we crossed this bridge?" Rose asks. Her eyes sparkle with recollection.

Queenie hums the melody of *Michael, Row Your Boat Ashore*. Her alto voice resonates, tickling her cheeks. Her hum becomes words, and to Queenie's surprise, Rose joins in on the chorus. After they finish, Rose smiles.

"That was wonderful," Rose says. "I forgot how well you sing."

"Violet is the real singer in the family," Queenie says. "A few years back, the preservation society in Beaufort did a recording of her singing some of the old Gullah songs Mama had taught her."

"I never knew that," Rose says, her tone thoughtful.

For several seconds they ride in silence until Queenie breaks the quiet. "I have a confession to make."

Rose turns to look at her. "You know I love confessions," she says.

"Well, sometimes I do more than sing when I cross this bridge," Queenie says.

"Like what?" Rose asks, sounding intrigued.

"Sometimes I do a kind of primal scream," Queenie says. "It's a technique I read about in the *Psychology Today* magazine while waiting on your mother to finish a plate of yak."

"Weren't primal screams big in the 80s?" Rose asks.

"They're still big for me. I do it whenever the frustration of living with your mother becomes too much," Queenie says. *Or whenever the shame and pressure of keeping secrets become too great*, she thinks.

"I'm convinced if everybody screamed while crossing bridges, the world would be a better place," Queenie continues. "Maybe we'd all break free of whatever holds us back. Maybe people right here in Savannah could break free of the past."

It occurs to Queenie that maybe whoever is leaking the secrets to the newspaper is trying to break free, too, and get out from under Iris's thumb. Once all your secrets are out in the open, nobody has power over you. She wonders if maybe it's time for her to tell hers, too. Her lips tighten as if they've already decided this isn't a good idea.

"If I started screaming, I might not stop," Rose says, leaning into the door.

"That's everybody's fear," Queenie says, "but from my experience, you do it for a while, and then you just get all tuckered out. It's like sprinting to a finish line. Not that I know anything about sprints." Queenie smiles and pats her thighs. "These old gals wouldn't know what to do if I took off running somewhere." Her giggle turns to a laugh.

"Has anyone ever seen you scream?" Rose asks.

Queenie grins. "Lord yes, honey. Sometimes a car full of people will pass me while I'm yelling my lungs out, so I just smile at them and wave. If they're from Savannah, they probably don't think anything of it. You're allowed to be crazy here, as you well know. And if it's tourists from out of state? Well, I figure I've just given them a good story to tell their friends when they get back home." She gives Rose a wide smile.

"You are so much braver than I ever could be," Rose says.

"It's not about bravery. It's about not caring what people think," Queenie says. "Besides," she begins again, "I may be responsible for Savannah being considered one of the premier tourist destinations in the South. Maybe everybody's heard of that crazy woman down in Savannah screaming her head off in her car while crossing that bridge, and they come here to see it for themselves." Queenie cackles her signature laugh. "Hell, for all my efforts, I may be getting a key to the city any day now," she adds.

When she opens her mouth and pretends to scream, Rose doubles over in the front seat to catch her breath. Her story has worked. Rose looks rejuvenated. Laughter does that. It's like a secret elixir Queenie uses whenever life gets too heavy. And it gets heavy a lot.

After their laughter fades, they settle into a comfortable silence. The bridge is now in Queenie's rear-view mirror. She likes the idea of having Savannah behind her, at least for a while. The road to the barrier islands gives her breathing room. She doesn't have to worry about what rich white people think of her out here. Different rules apply. You are judged by the quality of person you are, not by big houses and fancy cars.

Rose sniffs something in the air. For a second, she looks like Iris on the scent of a rogue fragrance. "Do you smell fried chicken?" Rose asks.

Queenie laughs a short laugh. "Well, I don't see any harm in telling Iris's secret now," she says.

"Mother has a secret?"

"Your mother has lots of secrets. Too many to get into right now. Of course, your mama's secrets never made it into that stupid book. That would defeat the whole purpose. That book is all about having power over prominent families in Savannah. But if they knew some of Iris's secrets? Oh my. Now that would cause a stink." Queenie chuckles, enjoying her pun.

"Tell me the one you're thinking about," Rose says, her eyes are bright with what could be mischief.

"Well, it seems your mother has a thing for Kentucky Fried Chicken," Queenie says.

"Mother eats junk food?"

"Uh-huh." Queenie smacks her lips together as if the secret is delicious.

"I thought she was on this strict diet and couldn't eat anything except water buffalo or something."

"The jury is still out about your mother's special dietary needs," Queenie says. "But it seems the Colonel's secret recipe is the exception."

"Are you saying Mother has been faking it all these years?" Rose asks. "What about the Gullah curse?"

"I'm not sure anymore," Queenie says. "Mama doesn't talk much about her spells. But if Iris is sneaking around eating KFC, she may be causing some of it herself."

"It's hard to picture Mother going to a fast-food restaurant," Rose says.

"Let me just say, I found a bucket of bones crammed under the front seat week before last. Picked clean like a buzzard had eaten them."

Rose's soft giggle grows into a full-fledged laugh, and before they know it, Queenie and Rose are laughing so hard Queenie has to pull over to the side of the road.

"For the first time in my life, I wish I wore Depends," Queenie says, which causes more laughter.

Smiles linger on their faces when Queenie pulls back onto the highway and drives east toward the ocean, to an area where her mother's family has lived for seven generations. She signals to turn and then drives down an unpaved road. Pine trees line the right side with an open field on the left. Sand billows behind the Town Car like choppy waves made by a motorboat.

"I've never known anyone who is a hundred years old," Rose says.

"Sometimes I think Mama's winding down. She spends hours looking out over the ocean now. Perfectly content."

"I owe her a lot," Rose says. "I don't know how I would have survived my childhood without her."

"Well, she loves you like you are her very own child," Queenie offers.

"I never asked if that bothered you," Rose says.

"Of course not," Queenie says. "Mama has enough love to circle the globe twice. I never felt cheated. Not for one instant."

Early on in life, Queenie learned to share her mother. People always needed her. If not for spells and cures, then for advice on everyday things. She has frequent visitors, some of them total strangers, and some of them the people her mama looks out for. *She is a mother hen with a lot of chicks.*

The ocean waits in the distance—the blue-gray water fading toward an invisible horizon. Rose rolls down her window and leans out to smell the salty air. Seconds later, Queenie parks the Lincoln in the backyard of her mother's house. Flowers are every-where and overflow their makeshift containers: large truck tires, a child's rusty red wagon, a washtub filled to the brim with purple, white, and yellow petunias.

Queenie and Rose take the wooden walkway to the house. Her mama sits in her rocker on the front porch and smiles as if she's been expecting them. Over the years, her mother's skin has dark-ened from the sun. Queenie has always been lighter-skinned than her. Every generation of her family seems to have a little more white mixed in.

As they approach, Old Sally claps her hands with joy. She looks weathered but strong, her gray hair clipped short, an inch from her scalp. The creases of age on her face make her look wise, an elder of their clan. A strong presence, even in her advanced age, she reminds Queenie of a lighthouse lighting the way for weary travelers, steering them to safety.

Queenie can't imagine her mother not being there anymore, and even now, she forces the thought away. Yet her mother's death is as certain as the ocean's ebb and flow. She squeezes Rose's hand and leads her up the steps, as though bringing her mama a long-awaited gift. One of Old Sally's daughters has come home.

CHAPTER NINE

Old Sally

"She be getting closer," Old Sally says aloud. "I can feel her."

Old Sally stands and faces the sea. The knowing starts out as a vibration in the center of her chest that grows in strength as Rose nears. It won't be long now before she can see her sweet Rose again.

Children get unlucky sometimes with who their parents are, and it creates bad medicine, like chemicals that shouldn't be mixed. As soon as Old Sally realized how bad the medicine was between Rose and her mother, she knew Rose was hers to watch after.

Old Sally glances out over the ocean that feels like an old friend, its waves racing to pound the shore. The rhythm of the tides is etched in her. To Old Sally, the land is living. The waterways and marshland along the coast are living. The oak trees are living. For Old Sally, everything she touches, everything she sees is alive. Even her Gullah ancestors, who some would say have gone out with the tide of time, are still alive and talk to her.

A memory is carried in on the breeze. Her grandmother, Sadie, was a slave for the Temple family until freed in 1865. Old Sally touches the small broach pinned to her simple dress that used to be Sadie's. Sally was only twenty when she learned the Gullah spells and potions from her grandmother, who was well into her eighties at the time.

"I be remembering what you taught me, Granny Sadie," she says.

The Gullah ways are as much a part of Old Sally as her heart that ticks away inside of her. She mixes medicines to protect the people she loves from bad things that might happen to them.

On the porch of the house she grew up in, Old Sally rocks in her wooden rocker. She lives twenty miles north of Savannah on a small island off the South Carolina coast. A place where the Atlantic Ocean bathes the islands and coastland, where waterways work their way inland like fingers grasping to hold onto the edge of the coast. A place where pungent marshes are home to shrimp, crab, and alligator and where oysters grow in terraced colonies like pearl necklaces scooped along the neck of the land. A place where osprey and cranes search the brackish water for their supper while seagulls squawk and hover above shrimp boats heading out to sea. The beauty here is seductive. It is deep and sometimes dark. Just like the Temple secrets that have begun to float up from the depths and come to light.

A melody comes to her. She hums a song taught to her by her grandmother about the crossing between this life and the next. A bridge we all cross, some early and some later.

"Iris Temple be making that crossing soon, and I been called on to help," she says as if her grandmother Sadie is sitting right next to her. "I remember everything you taught me, Granny, and it would please me if you could help, too."

For centuries, the Gullah people have carried the mysteries of

life. In addition to being guides between the two worlds, her ancestors wove sweetgrass baskets. They made medicine from herbs and
grew all their own food. When it came time to give birth, they
delivered their own babies. They fished the surrounding waters
with nets they made themselves. They lived off the ocean and land.

Another memory comes. Memories visit Old Sally often these
days so she can review her long life. This memory is from thirty-
five years earlier, in 1965, a time when certain things were set in
motion that are about to be made complete. The scene sweeps
over her like a warm ocean wave, and she closes her eyes to
receive it. The voices of children come.

*"Let's go, children," Old Sally says. She ushers Rose and Violet into the
back seat of the Temple car.*

*Around the age of sixty, the 'old' was added to Sally's name. She
never complained. Having worked as a housekeeper all her life and
raised three children of her own, there are days she feels older than the
land she lives on. Her youngest, Ivy, still lives with her. Lately,
everybody calls Ivy, Queenie, a nickname given to her by Rose and
Violet that has stuck like the Savannah humidity.*

*Queenie drives them to the island. Mister Oscar is good about
letting her use one of their cars if she needs it. He has a fondness for
Queenie that Old Sally and her daughter don't talk about.*

*Just like her mama was and her mama before her, Old Sally is the
Temple maid, housekeeper, and nanny. Iris Temple and Mister Oscar
have two children. Edward is nearly grown and away at boarding
schools most of the year, and Rose is ten years of age. Rose is Iris
Temple's only daughter. A child handed over to Old Sally to care for
when she was days old.*

*Today, Iris Temple is busy with meetings, and Old Sally has the time
to bring the girls to her house on the shore. She loads her ironing into
the trunk, so as not to get behind in her chores. The drive is familiar and
comforting, like putting on slippers after wearing shoes all day. As they*

approach the island, she feels her breath deepen. This coastline is where Old Sally feels the most connected to her ancestors.

After they arrive, the girls run to the beach to build sandcastles, and Old Sally opens the doors and windows of her house to catch the ocean breezes. In the kitchen, she refills a coke bottle with water and twists the sprinkler cap on the top so she can moisten the wrinkled sheets before ironing them. A portrait of Dr. Martin Luther King Jr. shares a wall with photos of her children, grandchildren, and great-grandchildren. She greets him, calling him Martin.

"I miss you, Martin," Old Sally says, making the leap from then to now. "A lot of people do."

As she rocks, the boards of the porch crackle to the beat of the rocking chair, adding background noise for the memory. Her eyes remain closed as she travels back to the past.

Old Sally turns on a burner on the stove and stirs the roots soaking in a pan. The water has already turned as black as the swamps where she collects them. She is conjuring up a new batch of a protection spell for Rose. Protection spells were one of her mother's specialties. Old Sally's mother lived past the age of 90 as an independent woman, still chopping her own firewood, washing clothes in a tin tub, and cooking on a cast-iron stove. Old Sally has this same sturdiness.

From the front porch, she keeps an eye on the three children in her charge—two brown and one white, one older and two younger—while they build a sandcastle on the beach. Although Queenie is no longer a child, she is still hers to protect.

Violet, the youngest, is six years old. She is Old Sally's granddaughter, with a complicated history, who Old Sally has agreed to raise. Old Sally will raise up whoever needs rearing. It is in her nature. It doesn't matter if they are her own blood or not.

Without warning, tears come as she remembers her daughter, Maya, who died the same year Violet was born. It doesn't matter how long it's been, the pain is still there. The only thing that made that year bearable was Violet's birth a few months before.

Earlier that morning, Old Sally braided Violet's hair and added colored beads to the end of the tightly woven rows. Despite her circumstances of coming into this world, Violet is a happy child. She often sings or hums, the beads in her braids keeping the beat as she moves her head with made-up melodies. Old Sally often finds her with her head back, eyes closed, feet stomping and hands clapping as she hums and sways with the music. Someone much older resides in her. Someone who has stories to tell.

Rose Temple might as well be an orphan, the way her mother treats her. If Old Sally lives to be a hundred, she will never understand how somebody like Iris Temple, given so much in this world, can be so stingy with her love. The ancestral line of Temple mothers be like a drought that changed the landscape from the lush low country marshland into a desert.

Queenie, Old Sally's grown daughter, her waist and hips already thick with good eating, helps the girls carry buckets of seawater to fill the moat around the sandcastle. In some ways, Queenie is like a girl herself, though grownup things have happened to her. Secret things.

Old Sally turns off the boiling roots on the stove and makes egg salad sandwiches and sweet tea. From the front porch, she waves and calls the girls to lunch. It is spring and the perfect temperature with the sea breezes blowing. Something sweet is in the air, blooming in the dunes. She closes her eyes to identify the flowers, but it is gone before she can catch it.

Hearing the call, the girls run through the dunes and up the steps to Old Sally's small beach house painted white with its blue trim to scare off evil spirits. The girls' bodies and bathing suits are covered with sand. Queenie follows them, her sleeveless cotton dress blowing in the sea breeze as she brushes sand off her brown arms and legs.

"Queenie, please wash the girls off before they come inside," Old Sally says.

"Yes, Mama," Queenie says. She uses the green garden hose at the *side of the house to rinse them off, and the girls squeal in ecstasy as Queenie covers the end with her thumb and sends water spraying in all directions. She can count on Queenie to get them giggling.*

Old Sally returns to her ironing in the front room.

If I hurry, I can get one more piece done before lunch, *she thinks.*

The sound of Rose's laughter makes her smile. She is much too serious for a child, nagged by her mother for every little thing—the way she walks, the way she talks, the way she should always be doing something other than what she's doing.

At least out here she be getting a little peace today, *Old Sally thinks.*

The two younger girls wrap themselves in towels hanging on the porch railings and come into the living room where Old Sally is ironing her fourth full sheet of the day. She has four more to go. At home, she irons in front of her three large windows, where she can keep an eye on the sea. She sprinkles the wrinkled sheet with the sprinkler bottle. Her iron sizzles as it hits the damp sheets. Steam rises. Sweat dots Old Sally's brow.

Rose leans into Old Sally's wide hip. Birthing hips, she likes to call them, perfect for bringing children into the world. She smoothes Rose's wet hair with her hand and notices again how thin she is. Old Sally is always trying to fatten Rose up. Yet Rose could eat chicken and dumplings every day of her life and stay skinny. She's tall for her age, too, most all legs. Her mother keeps her hair styled and permed like Rose is some kind of prize-winning poodle. Rose always tugs at it to try to make it straight.

"Baptize me," she says. Rose stands nearly as tall as Old Sally's shoulder and looks up at her, her eyes filled with playful pleading. She asks Old Sally to do this every time she irons like it is the food she needs most.

Old Sally nods, and Rose turns toward the sea and bows her head about to receive a sacred anointing. When Old Sally sprinkles the water on Rose's head, the child's laughter rides on the salty breeze that sweeps through the house.

Violet begs to be next. Old Sally repeats her christening ritual, and Violet and Rose collapse in giggles on the sofa. Queenie shakes her head as if she is too old for such nonsense, so Old Sally aims a few sprinkles in her direction, too. Her daughter, who also seems much too serious these days, laughs a little.

"Lunchtime," Old Sally announces.

The four of them enter the kitchen where the food is set out on her round wooden table. The girls and Queenie each eat two sandwiches that Old Sally has cut into triangles like finger sandwiches at the fancy parties Iris Temple throws. Big slices of watermelon are piled high on a plate in the middle of the table, and they devour these, too, collecting all the seeds in a bowl for Old Sally to plant later. The thirsty girls drink a gallon of sweet iced tea to go along with lunch, a slice of lemon perched on the lip of each glass. Meanwhile, Old Sally reheats some shrimp and grits from her dinner the night before and then joins the girls.

"What's that smell?" Rose asks. She wipes her mouth with a napkin all proper as if her mother might be watching.

"That be something your Old Sally conjuring up," Old Sally says.

She walks over to the stove, her bad hip already stiff from a few moments sitting, and gives the root mixture on the back of the stove a stir with a wooden spoon. Then she spreads the roots on towels on the kitchen counter and pours the black brew into a brown bottle with a stopper. The spell will be complete when she goes back to the Temple house and adds some of Iris Temple's hair to the mixture pulled from Iris's hairbrush while cleaning her bathroom later on this afternoon. This is one of Old Sally's most potent protection spells. Without this protection, Iris Temple will do more damage than she already has. She is worse than the Temple men when it comes to forcing her way. In fact, she has all of Savannah scared of her for one reason or another. Mostly because of that Book of Secrets that the different Temples have kept for over a century.

If I had my way, I'd destroy that old book, she thinks. Then the

Temple reign over Savannah could end. But she doesn't have her way. Without work at the Temple's, she couldn't survive.

"Grandma's spells get rid of evil spirits," Violet says to Rose. Her eyes widen as she says, 'evil spirits.' Then she shakes her head to get her beaded braids to agree.

Old Sally gets a saltine cracker tin from the cabinet that is now filled with homemade oatmeal cookies. She gives the girls two each and Queenie three.

"Mama's medicines help people get rid of ailments and such," Queenie says to Rose. She wraps her cookies in a napkin and puts them in the pocket of her dress. "Back in the old days, illnesses were cured with roots, herbs, and teas," she adds.

Queenie looks at her mother like she's proud of how much she knows. What she doesn't say is that illnesses caused by hexes or spells can only be cured by magic. And in the Sea Islands, those islands and coastal regions along the Georgia and South Carolina coast, magical medicines are created using feathers, bones, fingernails, hair clippings, and sometimes blood. Materials that are mixed with other natural elements such as roots, sand, and leaves. Since the white slave owners feared the use of Gullah magic, these conjuring practices were kept secret, although Old Sally has never kept anything hidden from Rose. Old Sally doesn't believe in secrets. They just give the darkness something to feed on. She'll tell anybody anything they want to know.

Violet puts her plate and glass in the sink, and Rose follows.

"Can we go back to our sandcastles?" Violet asks Old Sally. "We still have work to do." The girls exchange a look as if their 'work' is of the top-secret variety.

Old Sally nods, and Violet challenges Rose to a race, the finish line being their sandcastles. It is inevitable that Violet will lose. She is a foot shorter than Rose. Yet the two girls throw their towels across the porch railing and make a mad dash through the dunes as if equally paired.

While the girls play, Old Sally and Queenie sit on the top step together, looking out over the Atlantic Ocean. The sun is just beyond the house, and the porch is shady now. It feels good to rest a minute before Old Sally has to get ironing again.

Violet and Rose build a new sandcastle in the distance right next to the old one. If not for the differences in the color of their skin, they might pass as sisters.

"They call themselves the sea gypsies," Queenie says. "They've decided they want to live together when they grow up."

Old Sally laughs. "Imagination, it be a powerful thing," she says.

"I get to be their Queen," Queenie adds, rolling her eyes.

Old Sally puts an arm around her daughter and squeezes a dose of love into her. "You be a queen to me, too."

Queenie lowers her head. Her hair is clipped short. Otherwise, it will take over her entire head. She wears colorful headbands that Old Sally makes from fabric she finds. Today's is bright yellow. The color of a bright, shiny lemon. Queenie has always liked bold colors. The bolder, the better. Old Sally gives her another squeeze like the lemons she uses to make lemonade.

"So, what be on your mind, baby?" Old Sally asks. "Not like you to be so quiet."

Queenie's brow furrows. Whatever she's thinking about has steered her into deep waters that she's not so sure she can navigate.

"I need to make a decision, Mama. Mister Oscar wants me to move into the house and be Iris's companion."

Now Old Sally is the quiet one. Mister Oscar has other reasons for wanting Queenie there. But she can't think about that right now. Sheets are waiting, and her memories of Maya weigh heavy on her today.

"You have to make a living some way, baby, and since he be offering room and board." Old Sally's voice trails off.

Queenie huffs and pulls away. No one in their right mind would want to be a companion to Iris Temple. Old Sally can barely stand working for her as it is. But Queenie hasn't found work yet, and Old Sally hardly makes enough to support Queenie, Violet, and herself.

Silence stretches in front of them like the long stretch of beach along the coastline. Old Sally searches for the truth inside her. When she *thinks she has found the words to say, she takes a deep breath, and her words come out soft.*

"Daughter, I be a strong woman in many ways," Old Sally begins. "I be good at cooking, cleaning, and raising children. And I be especially good in the invisible arts of our people."

Old Sally pauses, asking for courage from her ancestors to keep going. The truth isn't always an easy thing to see, much less speak. Queenie, patient in her waiting, stares out at the ocean that is so quiet it looks like a sheet of dark blue glass.

Old Sally takes another deep breath and wrings her hands together to calm herself.

"Something else be true, though," she begins again. "I still be just a colored woman whose whole life been spent taking care of white people and their children just like my mama did and her mama before her." She pauses, thinking through what she'll say next. "Sometimes history and the times be bigger than a single person," she continues, her voice softer. "And I think this be one of those times. Honey, I don't know how to tell you to do anything different than I did with my own life. I wish it weren't so, but it is, and I'm sorry I can't do better."

Queenie is the daughter of Iris Temple's father, Edward Temple, III. The fact that she has a different father than her older siblings has never been a secret to Queenie. Edward Temple was a powerful man and used to getting whatever he wanted—this included Old Sally. No love involved. Old Sally needed to keep her job so she could support her family since her husband was long gone.

Children fathered by landowners and servants were not that unusual in those days, and in some ways, the old days are still going on. The Temple blood has been mixing with Old Sally's ancestors for centuries now. Her grandmother, Sadie, carried and raised a Temple child, too, although this secret was swept into the shadows because he was a boy child. This is what Old Sally means when she tries to explain to Queenie about fighting the tides of history. Sometimes those currents just run too deep and too strong. And sometimes those tides even have an undertow.

Yet Old Sally has been getting the message for a while now that something is about to change. She's not sure when. She's not sure how. But change is coming. The tea leaves say it. The wind whispers it. And the voices of her ancestors confirm it.

When Old Sally opens her eyes, the scene fades. She goes inside to get a shawl and pauses in front of her large picture window. A worn, comfortable chair sits next to her front window overlooking the sea. Old Sally spends more and more time in this old chair praying over the collection of souls that are hers to look out for. Usually, they are people who have been handed a challenging life, like Rose. The sensitive and creative ones often need her the most.

Every object on Old Sally's large window seat stands in for one of these people. Pieces of coral sit next to eyeglasses, alongside two blue robin's eggs, as well as other things. Each object has a story.

At the center of the window seat sits the most special object of all: a small sculpture of a sandcastle. Old Sally thinks of Rose as she holds it. Rose is one of her exceptional cases that could have gone either way. The dark side wanted her just as much as the light. Every day of Rose's life, Iris Temple sent a message to that child that she wished she had never been born. Nothing you can do to a person is worse than cursing their existence.

The vibration grows stronger in Old Sally's chest. "I waiting for you, baby. It won't be long now," she says to Rose.

Old Sally shivers and pulls her shawl close. Earlier that day, her ancestors told her that Rose is in danger again. Her return to Savannah has made her vulnerable. Old Sally's work is not yet finished. She walks out onto the porch again. These days she feels every single one of her hundred years. Her bones creak and talk to each other like they are saying, *Can you believe this old woman still be alive?* Old Sally talks back to her old bones sometimes and tells them to hang on, that it won't be long now, that they still have work to do. Thankfully, her old body and the good lord have listened.

Old Sally smiles and taps the center of her chest as the hum grows louder. The salty air fills her lungs with whispers from the sea. The night is clear. The moon will be full as Iris Temple makes her passage. That means the dark forces will be at their strongest. She must prepare for what's coming. The change she predicted thirty-five years ago is finally here.

"Whenever a cycle begins or ends, it be a powerful thing," she says to the ocean breeze. "I must stay awake to what be next and not be lulled to sleep."

In the distance, two figures approach the house. She has lived a long, rich life, and when her time comes, she will be ready to go. But first, she must finish what she set out to do for Rose, as well as protect Queenie and Violet during the transition to come. Then Old Sally's work will be complete. Then she, too, will get to rest.

CHAPTER TEN

Rose

A warm breeze pushes Rose and Queenie down the path. The beach lays out her sandy skirt in front of them. Rose stops in the middle of the path to greet the landscape. It will be dusk soon, and the sky takes on brilliant shades of orange and red to the southwest. Rose wishes she had her paints with her. Something this beautiful begs to be captured. She and Queenie walk arm in arm, as the wind playfully whips at their clothes. It is high tide. The ocean crashes on the shore a hundred feet away. Water birds squawk and run along the front edges of the waves, like small, winged children daring the water to catch them.

Rose and Queenie take the walkway through the dunes. Rose has spent many happy hours on this stretch of coastline. It feels like an old friend she hasn't seen in twenty-five years. A flood of memories comes with her reunion. Memories of entire days spent by the shore.

The salt spray hits her face. Moisture. Something the dry air in Wyoming doesn't possess. A substance prayed for during years of drought, given freely here. Her skin tingles as if thanking her for coming back to her moist homeland.

Even though she feels like rushing, she stops to take in the scene. The horizon stretches into the distance joining the sky with a thin gray line. Seagulls hover close like beggars asking for coins. Four pelicans soar on the breeze, away from the setting sun, their wings nearly touching. Why has she waited this long to return? She could have always come here without her mother's knowledge. Or perhaps she knew the effect it would have on her to be here again.

Queenie squeezes Rose's arm as if to remind her who awaits. It was good to laugh with her in the car. The whole of Savannah seems tense, including Queenie. It can't be easy to deal with the uproar those secrets have caused. She can't imagine what good could come from collecting secrets to begin with.

They continue up the path to the house. Unlike the reunion with her mother, the anticipation of seeing Old Sally again holds great sweetness. The grand woman sits in the corner of her front porch, overlooking the ocean. She appears regal, an African goddess reigning over the sea. Goosebumps rise on Rose's arms, confirmation that she is participating in something mysterious, perhaps even sacred, although Rose has rarely thought in those terms for the last twenty-five years.

Meanwhile, nothing about Old Sally seems tense. If anything, she is a messenger of calm. Rose wishes she could be more like her. This trip home has been difficult. Nothing having to do with her mother is ever easy.

Wearing a cotton dress the color of sand dollars, Old Sally stands as they approach. Creases of age flow like soft rivers down a brown landscape. Her skin is taut as the finest leather, and she is barefoot. For some reason, this makes Rose smile. In the West, she wouldn't dream of not wearing shoes. The parched earth of the high plains produces plants with prickly spines. Not to mention rattlesnakes. Yet in this setting, Rose wants to toss her shoes in the dunes and feel the sand between her toes. Instead, she hesitates with the awareness that she is only passing through. She will need these shoes again.

Despite the fact that all the other small houses on this stretch of coast have been bought up by developers and replaced by multi-million-dollar properties, Old Sally's house has not changed. It is just as Rose remembers it: a small, old, yet spirited force, just like its owner. Over a decade ago, she tried painting it from memory and couldn't capture it.

What must it be like to live on the edge of the sea, she wonders, *instead of on the edge of the Great Plains.* She imagines all the storms Old Sally has seen and that this little house has weathered. Old Sally has probably weathered personal storms, as well. Although at that moment, Rose realizes just how little she knows about her.

A momentary shame colors Rose's face. She should know more about this woman who took care of her for the first twenty years of her life. Her wishes. Her dreams. Her challenges.

I've done what every little rich white girl has done, she thinks. She's taken Old Sally's care for granted. Never giving a thought to the fact that she was a woman with a family of her own that she went home to every evening. A woman with needs and sorrows, as well as joys. If she were going to be there for more than a couple of days, she would make an effort to get to know her better.

After climbing the dozen or so steps to the house, Rose pauses at the top. Every window of the house is open to let in the sea breezes. Three large windows reveal a living space filled with things brought in from the outside: driftwood, large shells, roots left drying on the ample window sills, as well as the eclectic collection of objects on the window seat that have grown in number since the last time Rose was here. Objects she studied with fascination as a girl. Rose recognizes the small sandcastle sculpture she gave Old Sally before she left for college.

Queenie walks over first and hugs her mother. Although keeping an eye on Rose, Old Sally exhales a laugh, as though seeing Queenie gives her immense pleasure.

"Oh, child, I do love them hugs," Old Sally says to Queenie. Old Sally then turns her gaze to Queenie alone and holds her face between her hands while looking deep into her eyes. "How you be, child?" she whispers. "In your heart of hearts."

"I'm well, Mama," Queenie says, and then gives Rose a wink.

Old Sally looks into her eyes again as if to confirm what Queenie says. "I guess you be telling the truth," the old woman says. She kisses her daughter on both cheeks before returning her attention to Rose.

"I've missed you, girl," Old Sally says and laughs like her happiness can't be contained.

Rose's face grows hot as they embrace, and she receives a gift she's not so sure she deserves. At the same time, Old Sally's strength surprises her. She is thinner than Rose remembers as though her body has intentionally shed some weight to make it easier to carry.

As she did with Queenie, Old Sally holds Rose's face in between her wrinkled hands. They are soft and cool, despite the heat of the day. Rose looks away as Old Sally looks deep into her eyes. Although this loving attention is probably what Rose longs for the most, to receive it in such abundance causes her awkwardness to come out in a brief laugh. Not even Max looks at Rose with this level of intensity. He still notices when she makes an effort to look nice for him, and he seems appreciative of her body, but he has never looked into her eyes for any length of time. Nor, to be honest, has she looked into his.

"Oh my, child. You not be doing too well," Old Sally says to Rose. "It be your mama, I think, haunting you again." Then she whispers to Rose, "You be all right pretty soon, though. Just wait and see."

Old Sally kisses Rose lightly on each cheek, as she did with

Queenie. Rose can't remember the last time she was kissed on the cheek. Perhaps it was the last time she saw Old Sally when she was leaving Savannah to move to Wyoming. Old Sally's lips are as cool and soft as her touch. Her gesture brings tears to Rose's eyes. Returning to the Georgia coast has brought unexpected moisture into her life again.

"Good girl," Old Sally says when she sees Rose's tears. "Now, don't be brushing those away. I need to capture them."

Old Sally reaches for a dark brown bottle sitting on a small wooden table bleached white by the wind and sand. She unscrews the top and uses the eyedropper to suck up the tears on Rose's cheek and put them into the bottle. Having lived with Old Sally the first two decades of her life, Rose doesn't question any of it. Back then, Old Sally was always gathering roots or collecting tears or strands of Rose's hair to be used for one of her spells. Looking satisfied, Old Sally screws the cap back on the bottle and puts it in her pocket.

"Sit down, you two. Let me look at you," Old Sally says.

Queenie and Rose, though mature women, do as they are told. From the other end of the porch, they pull up two rocking chairs that have seasoned to the color of the dunes. Meanwhile, Old Sally sits and takes in every nuance of them, nodding as if taking an inventory of their every movement and emotion. It's almost as if Old Sally is about to paint their portrait.

"Yes, there's still work to do," Old Sally says, more to herself than to them. "But it's nothing I can't handle." She smiles and rocks in her chair. "Would you girls like some lemonade and pound cake?" she asks.

"We'll get it, Mama," Queenie says.

Rose follows Queenie inside, noting how little the living room has changed with its one worn sofa and two side chairs. On the way to the kitchen, they walk down a hallway that contains a wall of family photos. As a girl, Rose stared at these photographs for vast periods as if the brown faces and bright smiles might reveal the secret of happiness to her. The pictures at her mother's house weren't photographs, but portraits of long-dead white people with serious looks on their faces, as though interrupted from counting their money. She knows much less about Old Sally's family.

"I'd forgotten how powerful she is," Rose says, once they are in the kitchen. "But in a good way," she adds. Rose touches her check, remembering Old Sally's kiss.

Queenie laughs. "Yes, Mama is a force to be reckoned with, that's for sure," she says.

Old Sally's attention is the opposite of anything Rose's mother would have offered, even if she weren't in a vegetative state. No judgment resides in Old Sally's gaze, only love, and concern. The mystery to Rose is how love given so freely can feel more threatening than criticism.

Old Sally's kitchen is a celebration of primary colors and is painted the color of lemonade. Ample windows overlook the dunes and coastal grasses. Treasures rest on the window sills: shells of all sizes, small pieces of driftwood that look like earthen sculptures, a variety of stones, as well as fossils of the most intricate creatures, their spirals imprinted in history. Her mother would never dream of bringing the outdoors inside, except for expensive flower arrangements. However, Rose wonders if her own desire to collect stones, fossils, and bones at the ranch is Old Sally's influence.

Queenie uncovers the old cake tin that has been in Old Sally's kitchen since Rose was a girl. She cuts three pieces of pound cake while Rose pours the lemonade. Slices of lemon twirl inside the glasses as she stirs the sugar in the bottom.

"Homemade lemonade is a lost art," Queenie says.

"Old Sally is a lost art, too," Rose says. "I don't know anybody else like her."

Queenie agrees.

When they return to the porch, Old Sally rocks her chair

slowly as if keeping time to the waves. Evening is coming on, and a hint of coolness floats on the breeze. The three women eat cake, drink lemonade, and watch the ocean like it might reveal its secrets at any moment. The water's grayness extends to meet the evening sky. The sea churns up memories for Rose that she can almost taste. Old Sally always had a snack ready whenever she came home from school: oatmeal cookies, chocolate pudding, cheese and crackers. No matter where Rose returned from, the kitchen was always the first place she went. It never occurred to her to find her mother.

Back then, Old Sally, Queenie, and Violet were Rose's life preservers in the choppy Temple seas. They were safe. They listened when she spoke and responded. They laughed, told stories, and included her. Those moments in the kitchen taught Rose everything she knows about love and relationships.

In contrast, Rose's parents were Savannah society. Dressed in formal attire, they attended dinner parties and events full of people parading like show dogs to display their breeding. Ultimately, Rose decided that they were the poor ones, with their insincere friends and emotionally bankrupt marriages. Their children were commodities, possessions. Their value measured by their return on investment.

Rose shudders with the awareness that her mother will never know who Rose really is. To her credit, she walked away from that world twenty-five years ago and hasn't looked back. But what Rose also walked away from was Old Sally, Queenie, and Violet. Now she realizes how big a loss that was.

As night falls, Old Sally lights two large candles protected by hurricane globes. The quality of the light is intimate and warm. The floorboards of the porch creak with three melodies as the three women rock into the evening. Rose breathes deeply, filling her lungs for the first time in years. Her shoulders relax.

"That be good, child, that be good," Old Sally says. "This pain be over soon," she adds. "Your mother be about to make her transition." The reflection of candlelight dances across her face.

Rose sighs. Her mother's approaching death elicits only a vague sense of regret. After being sober for nearly two decades and having had what feels like a lifetime of psychotherapy, she has reached a point where she has made peace with her life. Nobody escapes unscathed. Some people have easier lives, some have harder. Rose takes life one day at a time, as the AA motto goes. The woman sitting on the porch next to her played a profound role in her early life, and for this, she feels thankful.

Waves surge and crash in the distance. Rose relaxes into her tiredness, embraced by sea breezes and the moonlit night. Candles flicker yet hold their light. Rose, Queenie, and Old Sally don't speak. It is as though their conversation is just below the surface, dipping and diving with the carefree motion of the dolphins often seen offshore.

CHAPTER ELEVEN

Violet

At least the phone calls have stopped, Violet thinks as she dusts the phone in the sunroom. For the last few hours, Violet was answering calls every ten minutes. At first, she answered, saying, *Temple Residence*. Then later, she responded with: *Just say what you need to say*. Unfortunately, most of the calls involved people cussing her. All the calls were anonymous. Made by cowards. Miss Temple would hate what people are saying about her. Who knew a bunch of old secrets could cause such a mess? And how in the world did someone get their hands on a book locked in a bank vault?

After Violet returns to the kitchen, she prepares a fresh cup of coffee and a bowl of strawberry shortcake for Lynette, the nurse upstairs. She cooks whenever she doesn't know what else to do, and with Miss Temple so gravely ill, she is definitely at a loss.

What will her job entail after Miss Temple dies? Will she even have a job?

Violet hums, as she often does when the house is quiet. A tune comes to her from a long time ago. It has a melancholy tone, somehow linked to the past.

Violet's mother was a nurse, and something about the uniform always causes Violet to entertain the *what if's* of life. *What if* her mother hadn't died when her tire blew out on the island, and she crashed into a three-hundred-year-old live oak tree? *What if* she had grown up knowing her mother, instead of only seeing pictures of her? How might her life have been different? Unfortunately, she will never know. And the one ghost she would hope to see is totally absent.

When Violet returns upstairs with a piece of shortcake, Lynette lifts a fork and takes a bite. "Oh my, this is wonderful." She moans and takes two more bites. "The Temples are very lucky to have you," she adds.

At least for now, Violet thinks. Both turn to Miss Temple like she might have something to add to the conversation. But there is no movement, only the sound of the ventilator pushing air into her lungs.

Earlier that evening, Queenie asked Violet to stay later than usual so she and Rose could pick up Old Sally and bring her back to the Temple house. Tonight is the night Jack teaches a class, and the girls have basketball practice, so she can be flexible. Although it is nice to see Rose again, Violet wishes it were a happier reason for her to visit.

Every family has broken places, but the Temples seem to have more than most.

Violet has never known Miss Temple to be content, and because of this, Violet has sometimes felt more fortunate. She pauses to assess the different vibrations in the room and thinks how interesting it is that someone unconscious can still radiate such a chaotic buzz.

Miss Temple's force is like static from a radio station not quite tuned in. It reminds her of that Peanuts character, Pigpen, who has a cloud of dirt that follows him everywhere he goes. Miss Temple is similar, except her cloud is chaos.

Lynette finishes her shortcake and pats her vast stomach, complimenting Violet again. She walks over to the window as though the view might aid her digestion.

"Why are those people gathered in front of the house?" she asks Violet. "Two groups have come by in the last two hours."

Violet joins her at the window. "We're on Savannah's ghost tour," she says. "The Temple Mansion is the main event."

"Ghost tour?" Lynette says. "Oh my. I had no idea." She glances around the room like she's searching for evidence.

Violet doesn't mention that the secrets in the newspaper have caused the groups of tourists and gawkers to swell to three or four times their usual numbers. While Miss Temple has always craved attention, she would not be pleased with this level of scrutiny.

"Every night around dusk, tour guides show up with their groups to watch the house for signs of the ghostly Temples," Violet says.

In Violet's experience, this is precisely when apparitions go away. Ghosts never show themselves when people want them to.

Lynette's eyes widen. "You really have ghosts?" she asks.

"We have our fair share," Violet says, though, in truth, the Temple house probably has more than their fair share.

"How do you know?" Lynette asks, looking uneasy.

"Footsteps on stairways," Violet begins. "Things moved an inch or two from their original positions. Blasts of cold air sending shivers up your spine when entering certain rooms. Things that can just as easily be attributed to an overactive imagination, if not for the sensations that accompany them."

Lynette's eyes have changed from full moons to crescents as if squinting might reveal the hidden entities in the room.

"Miss Temple's dead husband, Oscar, likes to rattle bottles at the bar in his study," Violet begins again. "Her mother always brings a camphor smell when she's around and often lingers in the upstairs bedroom that was hers. Miss Temple's father prefers to communicate by heavy footsteps on the stairway like he's just home from one of his business trips. Or he'll come into the kitchen to look for my grandmother who used to work here."

Lynette's white face turns even whiter.

I shouldn't enjoy shocking people this much, Violet thinks.

Yet she has to admit, as the mother of teenagers and the wife of a busy husband, she doesn't always have the gift of a captive audience.

When the doorbell rings, Lynette jumps as if goosed by Oscar himself. Before excusing herself to get the door, Violet reassures Lynette that everything is fine. On her way downstairs, she glances at her watch long enough to wonder who would be visiting after nine o'clock.

Violet opens the door, and a very-much-alive Edward Temple brushes past her, entering with so much authority that Violet is surprised that he even rang in the first place.

I prefer spirits to men like Edward any day, she thinks.

"I want to see my mother," Edward Temple says.

"Weren't you just here this afternoon?" Violet asks, wondering what Edward is up to now.

"Did you see this?" Edward asks. He holds a placard he found in front of the gate that has a big red X over a photograph of Miss Temple taken at a fundraiser.

"No, I didn't," Violet says, although she and Queenie have been busy for days taking down dozens of signs with even stronger sentiments.

Edward towers over her and has a habit of always standing too close. Although Violet hasn't seen him in several years, he looks the same, except his dark hair has begun to gray. He wears a look of superiority he's had since adolescence. His gray suit—

probably worth six months of Violet's salary—is accessorized with a charcoal gray shirt and a tie that matches to perfection.

Edward twists a large gold ring on his right hand that contains a red stone.

He cools his gruffness and flashes a smile that Violet believes is intended to charm her. Instead, it makes her more uneasy.

"I just thought I'd give the old broad a proper send-off," Edward says as if crassness is the only language she might understand. "Bet you'll be glad when she finally kicks off."

Violet debates whether to tell him that nobody should talk about their mother this way. From her perspective, people are fortunate to have mothers at all, even if that mother is Miss Temple.

When Violet doesn't respond, Edward rolls his eyes and adds a smirk at the end, as though to say, *we can play it that way if you want.* He isn't usually this crass, and she wonders if he is worried about the *Temple Book of Secrets* going public.

Edward steps into the living room and glances around as if taking a mental inventory of the antiques in the room. Inheritance, in families like these, means a great deal. But he isn't giving any clues as to what he might be scheming.

"The old place hasn't changed much. It still has as much charm as a funeral parlor."

Edward smiles and twists his ring again.

Is he nervous? Violet wonders if he might lose his fortune if all these threatened lawsuits come to pass.

She tries to remember the last time Edward visited. It was probably Mother's Day, three or four years ago. Before that, he came more often. Now he's here for his third visit of the day. A record by any means.

While Violet stands in the center of the large Oriental rug in the hallway, Edward surveys his father's study and then walks into the dining room. On the dining room table is a stack of photographs Rose brought of her ranch in Wyoming. He picks them up and studies each picture as if to assess the ranch's net worth.

"Surely you realize she's shown up again just in time to cash in," he says.

"That doesn't sound like Rose," Violet says.

"She's not who you think she is," Edward says, his tone soft now as if this softness might convince Violet of its truth. "She's taking advantage of the situation."

"Not everyone is like you, Edward," Violet says.

"Have you forgotten who you're talking to?" he asks.

She has never had much patience with him or anyone who looks at her like a landowner overlooking his property. This is precisely why she will never let her daughters do domestic work.

"Miss Temple is my boss, Edward, not you."

"At least for now," Edward says with a grin.

It occurs to Violet that if Edward inherits the Temple mansion after his mother dies, she'll for sure be looking for a new job.

Seconds later, he moans and bends over.

"Damn ulcers." He takes a bottle of antacid tablets from his jacket pocket and pops two into his mouth. He crunches them while Violet waits. She seems to always be waiting these days, and she's not sure why.

"Tell Rose I know what she's up to," Edward begins again. "And tell her she won't get away with it. She gave up her right to any Temple money when she moved to that Godforsaken place." He tosses the photographs back on the table before going into the sunroom. Then he opens a drawer to the wicker table Miss Temple uses as a desk and shuffles through his mother's papers as if looking for something he's lost.

"I don't think you should be doing that," Violet says.

"Who's going to stop me?" Edward asks. "You?" He winks at her.

A cold chill ignites a memory that haunts Violet as surely as the Temple ghosts. At fourteen, she was making a little money helping her grandmother during one of the Temple's charity events. Edward was home from college, and she had stepped outside to take a break from serving. It was hot. The peepers were croaking their little hearts out in the fountain on the other side of the garden. She didn't even realize Edward was there until he grabbed her and pulled her into the garden shed. When she screamed, he covered her mouth, and she bit him hard until she tasted his blood in her mouth. Edward pushed her aside and cussed her all the way to the kitchen.

Violet inhales sharply and reminds herself that the event was twenty years ago.

"What is it?" he asks, stepping back into the foyer.

"Ghosts," Violet says. She forces herself to look him in the eye. She will bite him again if she needs to. All the way to the bone.

"Call an exterminator," Edward says with a laugh. He goes into the study that was his father's office. She can hear him going through the desk drawers and wonders if she should tell Queenie.

That night, twenty years ago, was the first time Violet realized the role women in her family played with the Temples. Edward acted entitled to her and seemed surprised when she fought back. In a way, it was like they were both actors playing the roles their ancestors played.

Right after, her grandmother had known what happened without Violet saying a word. She's always been like that. She knows things without being told. That night her grandmother doctored the bite on Edward's hand and used an ointment that she laced with chili pepper. Edward's scream was just as loud as Violet's had been in the garden shed. He left Violet alone after that. She always wondered if her grandmother put one of her spells on him to keep him away. If so, she hopes the spell is still working.

Clearly agitated, Edward returns to the foyer. Whatever he is looking for, he hasn't found it. He smells of expensive musky cologne. Has Edward forgotten about his mother's aversion to scents? Or perhaps he doesn't care.

"I guess I've put off seeing her as long as I can," Edward says. He makes a grimace that seems almost boyish.

Edward follows Violet upstairs, and they enter Miss Temple's bedroom.

"Hello, Mother, how are you feeling today?" he asks cheerfully.

Does he not realize she's in a coma? Violet wonders.

Edward walks past Lynette like she is invisible and kisses his mother on the forehead before sitting at the foot of the bed. He crosses his hands on his lap as though a position honed and polished at a school for deathbed etiquette. Violet feels certain Edward will play the good son until he gets what he wants, which seems to be whatever he was looking for downstairs.

"Mother, are they treating you all right?"

He glances at Violet and talks to his mother like they are having a polite dinner conversation. He fills Miss Temple in on his work and tells her how horribly busy he has been. He asks if she received the flowers he sent to the hospital and waits a beat for her to answer.

A crowd has gathered that has nothing to do with a ghost tour. Someone rattles the gate. Who knew secrets could get people so riled. Violet wonders if she should call the police, and she and Lynnette exchange concerned looks. The ad in this morning's paper questioned the wrongful conviction of a long-ago murder. None of the parties are still alive, except for a few descendants who seem to want revenge.

Edward describes to his mother in detail about what is going on outside. Something Queenie had suggested they never mention to Miss Temple in case she can hear. Every few minutes, Edward reaches over and pats his mother's hand with four quick taps, as though patting the head of a bunny at a petting zoo.

Surely, even comatose, Miss Temple can see through her son's perfor-mance, Violet thinks.

Meanwhile, Lynette hovers over Edward like he might turn off the life support machines while she isn't looking. She also peers occasionally out the window where the crowd is building.

"Well, Mother, I must be going," Edward says finally. "I need to go outside and deal with the rioters. They're very upset about those secrets in the newspaper. Whoever is doing this must be very angry with you," he adds. "There's certainly plenty of people that fall into that category." He leans over and kisses Miss Temple on the cheek.

As soon as Edward steps away from his mother's side, Lynette double-checks the machines.

"Would you like me to show the gentleman out?" Lynette asks Violet, sounding like one of the bouncers at the jazz clubs she and Jack went to before the girls were born.

Edward turns and looks at Lynette like he's just now noticing her. He wastes no charm on her. "I can show myself out," he says. "I used to live here." He then stops in front of a full-length antique mirror to straighten his tie before leaving, perhaps to irk Lynette. Violet and Lynette follow him to the second-floor landing where they watch the door to make sure he goes. Without looking back, Edward crosses the foyer, walks out the door, and then slams it.

"Who died and made him king?" Lynette stands with her hands on her ample hips.

"That was Edward Temple, Miss Temple's son," Violet says.

"I know," Lynette says. "When he was in here before, he was absolutely rude to his sister. Didn't even speak to her. He just laughed and stared." She scoffs. "Forgive me for saying so, but I don't think he cared one bit about his mama laying there. I think it was all just a show for us."

"I couldn't agree with you more," Violet says.

The lights in the old house flicker as if the ghostly Temples agree, too.

"Is that them?" Lynette asks, looking more than a little alarmed.

Violet nods.

All day the house has been more psychically alive than usual. Like the people outside, the former Temples are riled. Violet glances at her watch again. She is ready to be home, where the only spirit in their apartment is a bottle of rum in the kitchen cabinet used to mix with honey, garlic, and lemon whenever she and Jack are getting colds.

The noises outside grow, as Miss Temple's energy builds. The whole house is humming along like a Hoover vacuum cleaner. In the meantime, Violet's shoulder confirms that something big is about to happen.

CHAPTER TWELVE

Old Sally

Old Sally stops her rocking and listens to the message on the wind. Except for the light of the full moon, the beach is dark.

"It's time," she tells Rose and Queenie. "We best be going now."

Old Sally stands, ignoring the pain in her hip, and walks inside. Urgency accompanies her movements as she gathers items in the cloth bag she uses to tote ingredients for her spells.

"What is it, Mama?" Queenie asks, following her inside.

"You two wait in the car. I'll be right there," Old Sally says. She needs to not forget anything. Every ritual requires certain sacraments.

Queenie and Rose return to the car. A few minutes later, Old Sally joins them.

"Tonight, Iris crosses over into the next world," Old Sally says to them, "and I'll do my best to help her."

As they drive into Savannah, Rose is quiet in the back seat. Even Queenie isn't talking much. When death is close, people often get quiet. Life's biggest mystery requires respect.

Rose leans forward with a question Old Sally has been expecting. "Have you used Gullah magic on my mother?" she asks.

"Mostly protection spells, so others don't get hurt," Old Sally says. She always knew she would never lie to Rose. "Whenever your mother gets puffed up with meanness, it doesn't sit right in her belly."

"You mean Iris could have stopped all that stomach upset herself if she'd just been nice?" Queenie asks.

Old Sally nods.

"Lord, have mercy," Queenie says. "I wish Iris had figured that out. Then Violet wouldn't have to carry those tinctures around."

"What most people don't know," Old Sally begins again, "is that Iris has her reasons for being the way she is. Your mama was a sweet thing at first," she says to Rose. "She was a good girl and tried to do everything right, so her mama and daddy might praise her. But they be too busy to even notice her. The only thing that got their attention was meanness," she continues. "That's when they sat up and noticed because they be worried that Savannah's rich folk might judge them. Edward inherited this meanness, too, just as sure as if it had passed down like the Temple family china."

"I forget Mother has her reasons for being the way she is," Rose says.

"That be true," Old Sally says. "But just like any of us, your mama could have chosen to be something different if she wanted. She had a heart of gold, too. She just lost track of it."

"Is that the only spell you used on her?" Rose asks.

Heaviness sits in Old Sally's chest. Sadness older than her and passed on from an earlier time. "There be another spell," she begins, her tone softer. "This spell be started by my grandmother, Sadie, against the old slave master Temple for sending away the children of the slaves to work other places, never to be seen again."

"Oh, that's horrible that he did that." Tears sparkle in Rose's eyes, but Old Sally has no time to capture them. "That would be my great-great-grandfather?" Rose asks.

Old Sally nods and pulls a burlap doll from the pocket of her dress to show Rose and begins again. "This spell requires a special root that can only be found deep in the swamps of southwest Georgia. The root is ground up and put inside this doll."

Rose takes the doll and looks at it for a long time, and then sniffs it. "It smells like molasses and marsh water," she says. Rose starts to pass it to Queenie, who holds up a hand and says *no, thanks.*

"Every year, I put new roots in the doll to keep the spell fresh," Old Sally begins again. "This is a revenge spell, pure and simple. It makes any Temple sick to their stomachs when they are the master over people. That's why you've never had a stomachache in your life, Rose, and why your mother has more than most."

"I don't think it ever occurred to Iris that life had anything to teach her," Queenie says. "Or that she may be the cause of her own discomfort."

"That be right," Old Sally says.

The messages Old Sally has received from the other world confirm that Iris Temple's time on this earth has ticked down to a matter of hours instead of days. For decades Old Sally has known that she would be present for Iris's death. Her family and the Temple family have been entwined for generations like a sweet-grass basket woven and bound tight enough to hold water. Old Sally's family carries the secret elixir to cure the dark parts in the Temple's history. Centuries have passed where Old Sally's family has mingled with the Temple bloodline. Old Sally's mother was a result of this mixing, as was Queenie.

The closer they get to Savannah, the more Old Sally feels

pulled into the agitation of Iris Temple. It confirms that this crossing will not be an easy one. Some souls are ready to leave this earth and embrace the transition feeling their work is complete. Others fight it with everything they have. They are the ones who have unfinished business.

And if anyone has unfinished business, it be Iris Temple, she tells herself.

Within a mile of the Temple home, Iris's edginess makes Old Sally clutch her cloth bag and pray for the strength she'll need for the battle ahead. She hopes there is enough strength in her hundred-year-old body to do her part in the ritual.

When they enter the house through the kitchen door, the Temple spirits rush forward, clamoring for Old Sally's attention. In the center of the room, she stops and waits. To Old Sally, the Temple ghosts are like youngsters that can't sit still and get into mischief all the time. When she worked in the house she was always telling those ghosts to behave. They listened, for the most part. But now it seems those youngsters—with the help of the Temple secrets—have grown into something much older and darker.

"What is it, Mama?" Queenie asks. "You look frightened."

"The spirits. They all riled up," Old Sally says. Shadows dance in the room, but with no precise shapes. Old Sally points to a note on the kitchen table. "That be for you," she says to Queenie.

Queenie reads the note from Violet aloud:

Dear Queenie,

Edward was here again tonight. Creepy, as usual. There was a crowd at the gate earlier, too, but the police came and made them leave. I've gone home for the night, but Lynette is upstairs watching after Miss Temple. I hope all goes well. V.

Old Sally feels the imprint of Violet's earlier distress. She is glad that her grandchild went home to be with Jack. Jack will never let anything bad happen to her. Like Rose, Violet is a special child, too, but in a different way. After Old Sally is gone, Violet will make sure the Gullah traditions don't get lost. The safer she stays, the better.

"Why was Edward here again?" Rose asks.

"Sometimes, the spirits of the living get riled up with the spirits of the dead," Old Sally says. "That's why so much happens on a full moon. The veil is thinner between the two worlds."

"I forgot there's a full moon tonight," Queenie says.

"A blessing and a curse," Old Sally says. "There be no turning back now."

The color leaves Rose's face.

"You'll feel better once your mother passes," Old Sally says to her. *We all will,* she thinks. She squeezes a bit of reassurance into Rose's hand.

Old Sally isn't surprised that Edward has shown up three times today. Everything happens in threes right before a significant change. He's been waiting a long time for this moment. Once his mother is out of the way, Edward gets to do whatever he wants with the Temple estate. But Old Sally will have to deal with him later. For now, it is his mother that requires her full attention.

Rose and Queenie follow Old Sally through the dining room and into the foyer. She spent sixty years of her life working in this house and could walk through the rooms with her eyes closed and never run into anything. Her mother worked here before her, and her mother's mother before that. As a girl, she explored it when the Temples weren't around. In some ways, she knows the Temple house better than her own. She certainly cleaned it many times over. And though she hasn't been here for twenty years, she hasn't missed it one bit.

The ghost of the third Edward Temple stands halfway up the stairs as if waiting to greet her. Old Sally sees him clear as a sunny day, though Rose and Queenie don't appear to. This is Queenie's father. Wooden arms and legs used to hang on various hooks in his office in the Temple home. The sight of them always shocked Sally. Sometimes he would make the wooden limbs dance for her like he was a puppeteer, and they were his puppets.

The second Edward Temple, in specter form, stands at the top of the stairs. A surgeon in the Civil War, he was said to have lost his mind as a result of the mountain of arms and legs he amputated. He still wears his officer's uniform. Even as a ghost, his eyes are open wide, still witnessing the horror. Old Sally's grandmother, Sadie, had a boy child by him who was sent away before the war to a plantation in Virginia. They never knew what happened to him, and they never saw him again.

Old Sally's family tree is so gnarled she can barely keep it straight herself. Patterns have played out for two hundred years like they have all been puppets to the same puppeteer. In the past, she's thought of their intertwined history as a Gullah spiritual with different verses.

But now it be time for a new song, she tells herself.

For over three decades, Old Sally has known a change was coming that would end the dark pattern. The other world has sent messages foretelling the change for years, in dreams, tea leaves, and inner knowing. All speak a language Old Sally understands. Yet the messages lately all point to danger.

The *Temple Book of Secrets* showing up makes sense, too. All sorts of darkness releases before the light comes, that's why people always say it's darkest before the dawn. Old Sally caught sight of that old book many years ago. Before Edward the 3rd died, it was kept in a desk drawer in his office.

Once when it was on the top of his desk, she looked inside. It was a fancy ledger, covered in leather, where each wealthy family had a page with a list of bad things they'd done. Pages filled with different inks made from different pens, the dates going back to when her Grandmother Sadie was a girl. Some families had died out or didn't even live in Savannah anymore. But others still lived here.

Notations of who beat their wives or had mistresses. Notes about fathers who messed with their children. Heavy drinkers. Barren wives. Addicted sons and daughters. Slaves who disappeared. Illegitimate children. Secrets that even generations down the line make a family look bad. Old Sally had never seen anything like it.

It be like the devil keeping track of all his people's evil deeds, she thinks. Nothing at all about anything good.

Queenie offers a hand, and Old Sally holds it as she climbs the spiral staircase. Rose follows a few steps behind. Old Sally rarely climbs steps anymore. Her house is on one level.

"White people just keep building up and up," Old Sally says, "reaching for the sky instead of earth." *Makes no sense,* she thinks.

The second Edward Temple laughs like what she said is ridiculous. They don't want her to succeed. They want Iris to stay with them. As long as Iris stays behind, the past has more power and keeps people down. She pauses, and Queenie asks if she's okay. She says she is.

"Are the spirits still active?" Rose asks.

Old Sally nods. "Like a fancy party where everyone is in attendance."

The Edward Temples in the past were not especially mean men, but they chose women who carried their meanness for them.

"Is my father here?" Rose asks.

The question from Rose doesn't surprise her. It broke Rose's heart when her daddy died so young. Though feeling rushed, Old Sally turns and touches Rose's cheek.

"Mister Oscar be a better man than several Temples combined," Old Sally begins. "Your daddy's ghost doesn't hang out with the other Temples. He stays in his office on the main floor."

Rose glances in that direction.

At the top of the stairs, Old Sally holds Queenie's arm to steady herself. It feels like she's walking into a strong wind. A wind that wants to steal her breath. The closer Old Sally gets to Iris's room, the more Iris's spirit shoves her away.

When Old Sally enters the bedroom, Iris Temple laughs from the in-between world. She will not go to the other side without a fight. The forces are stronger than Old Sally expected. Her head lowered, she pauses and asks Queenie and Rose to give her a moment to think. Her mind races like a general putting together a plan before going into a battle where the enemy is twice as big as anticipated. All the crossings she attended have been tame compared to this wildness.

Queenie and Rose both carry Temple blood and will be useful in their fight. But based on Iris's resistance, Old Sally needs more help than she thought. She debates whether to call Violet, but it seems her granddaughter has dealt with dark forces enough for one night. Another presence in the room calls for her attention, and Old Sally raises her head. A large white woman in a nurse's uniform stands next to the bed. In that instant, Old Sally knows this stranger is the additional help she needs.

Lynette smiles at Old Sally like somehow she recognizes what they will do together. Her ancestors have chosen her. A hard-earned kindness surrounds her, as someone strong enough to overthrow the dark and claim the light.

As Old Sally approaches Iris's bed, she senses Iris gathering strength in the in-between world. Being back in the Temple house is giving Iris power. For the longest time, Old Sally thought everyone heard voices from the spirit world. The first time dead people talked to her, she was still a girl and thought she was making up the voices in her head. But the older Sally got, the more she realized that she could communicate with people in the spirit world. What she didn't know is that people in a coma are in this in-between world, too. She thinks of it as a waiting room where people are waiting to be called. Except it isn't a room, it's a way of being.

A conversation commences between Old Sally and Iris that no one else can hear.

I'm here to help you transition, Iris.

I'm not ready to go, Iris says. *I need to set something right.*

The spirit world thinks you be ready now, Old Sally says.

You and your stupid voodoo magic, Iris says. *You're nothing but a fake.*

Then how am I talking to you? Old Sally asks.

Iris pauses like Old Sally may have a point. *What's she doing here?* Iris asks, her words aimed at Rose.

Old Sally glances at Rose, who has regained some of the color in her face. *She's come to say goodbye to you.*

It's just like her to crawl back on her hands and knees, Iris says. *All she wants is my money.*

Iris's stomach revolts in a loud grumble, revealing to Old Sally that her spell is still at work.

You did this to me, didn't you, Iris says to Old Sally.

You did it to yourself, Old Sally says.

Shut up, old woman. Iris laughs.

Within seconds, Iris's smugness changes to weeping, now a helpless child. Whenever a spirit is threatened, it takes on many disguises.

You don't fool me, Old Sally says.

Come close and comfort me, Iris says, in-between bouts of crying.

But Old Sally refuses to fall for Iris's trick. This childlike part is the most dangerous. It will do anything to get its way. Not stopping until it wraps its arms around Old Sally's neck and chokes the life out of her.

Lynette pulls a chair close to the bed and encourages Old Sally to take a seat. Old Sally thanks her, sits, and places her cloth bag on her lap. The room is quiet except for the sound of the machines.

"Mama, do you need anything?" Queenie asks from behind her.

"A glass of water, please," Old Sally says. "And a clove of garlic from the kitchen," she adds.

Queenie leaves for the kitchen, and Old Sally turns to Rose, "Gather me a piece of your mother's hair."

She pulls a pair of kitchen shears from her bag and hands them to Rose, who walks over to her mother. Rose's hand trembles as she holds the scissors.

"You can do it, Rose," Old Sally says. "Your mother needs your help."

I don't want her touching me. Iris says. *She deserted me.*

While ignoring Iris, Old Sally encourages Rose to cut her mother's hair.

Iris screams at Rose and forbids her to touch her.

Unable to hear her mother's pleas, Rose clips a small strand of hair and then gives the scissors and the hair back to Old Sally. Old Sally thanks her, not letting on at how much her mother is cursing Rose in the spirit world.

From her bag, Old Sally pulls out a small black iron bowl that looks like a miniature cauldron. She places the hair inside, along with ingredients she gathered earlier that day. In the background, Iris pleads, sobs, and then insults everyone in the room.

When a person's spirit is disturbed, sometimes the best thing to do is to turn a deaf ear. Old Sally is good at hearing only the things she wants to hear.

Queenie returns with the garlic and glass of water. Old Sally takes the water and drinks it. Water always helps ground her.

"I thought garlic was to keep away vampires," Queenie says, handing her mother the bulb.

"Oh, I don't need it for a spell," Old Sally says. "I need it for a recipe tomorrow."

The women laugh, which serves Old Sally's purpose. Laughter clears fear out of a room. However, Iris isn't laughing.

"I need your help with the transition," Old Sally tells the three women. They stand at attention, three soldiers enlisted in Old Sally's army.

"What can we do, Mama?" Queenie asks, speaking for all of them.

"Iris Temple be putting up all sorts of resistance," Old Sally begins, "because she knows she hasn't done right in this life. But she won't take care of that old business, either. She needs to go fully into the spirit world. Right now, she's stuck in-between, and she not be going to the next world without a fight."

The three women exchange looks like they are wondering what they got themselves into.

"I think my grandfather had trouble transitioning, too," Lynette tells Old Sally. "I wanted to help him, but I didn't know how. That's part of the reason I became a nurse."

"You be right, honey," Old Sally says. "And your grandfather wants you to know you did all the right things back then. He appreciated the help."

"How do you—" Lynette begins.

"Your Old Sally just knows," she says. "Now, let's be getting down to work."

Iris's right hand shakes like she's pointing a finger to condemn their actions. Rose and Queenie take a step back, while Lynette steps forward and holds Iris's wrist.

"Her pulse is fast," Lynette says.

"That's because she be putting up a fight," Old Sally says.

Worry creases Rose's forehead like she's already had one too many battles with her mother.

"Nothin' to be afraid of, child," Old Sally says to Rose. "This be a good thing. Not only for you, but for your mother, too. Unfortunately, she not see it that way. Not yet, anyway."

"Just tell us what to do," Queenie says. She holds her head high, ready for the task.

Even though Queenie has never studied the healing arts on

Old Sally's side of the family, she has never questioned it, at least not to Old Sally's knowledge.

As Old Sally stands, her bad hip sends a shooting pain down her leg and into her foot.

Most people don't realize that there's an invisible world that is just as real and complicated as the visible one. Old Sally has a foot in both worlds.

"First, we need to form a circle and hold hands," Old Sally says to the women. They do as they are told and form a half-circle around Iris's bed.

"What I be telling you tonight will sound crazy," Old Sally says, "but even if you question it, I need you to pretend you believe." She looks each woman in the eye to get their agreement. "We need to use our imaginations now," Old Sally begins again. "That be one of the languages used in the other world. We need to imagine a circle of light surrounding the bed. This light be creating the opening for Iris to leave."

Of the three women, Rose looks the most uncertain. Soon, Old Sally will know how much Rose trusts her. Meanwhile, Queenie knits her brow as though intent on creating the light while Lynette's efforts sit heavy on her broad face. Old Sally waits for Rose, who inhales deeply and finally nods.

"Your job be to make the light so attractive and filled with goodness that Iris can't resist going toward it," Old Sally says to them. "Then imagine an opening at the top of the ball of light that Iris's soul can go through and leave this world."

Old Sally thinks of herself as a midwife, except she helps people leave this life instead of enter it. She's helped dozens of people make this crossing, and though everyone is different, many things are similar. People who have a peaceful passage are usually the ones with no regrets. These people feel complete, and even though some have had hard lives, they have made peace with what their lives have been. It is the ones with resentments and disappointments who go kicking and screaming into the next world. In Old Sally's experience, the ones who resist life in all its fullness of light and dark also resist death.

"It be over soon," Old Sally says to the women, at the same time reassuring herself. After this, Old Sally can finally rest, and Queenie and Rose can carry forward a new legacy as the next generation of Temple women.

Iris laughs as if amused by Old Sally's thoughts. *You'll never get to relax, old woman,* Iris says. *You're nothing but a servant. My servant. Who worked for sixty years for my family for next to nothing.*

Iris's words are meant to weaken her, so she won't be able to fulfill her task.

I've come to set you free, Iris, Old Sally says in the spirit world. *You've been locked into being a Temple, just like those secrets have locked people into doing your bidding. You never tried to get free of this prison, except for that one time with Mister Grainger. That boy was sent to set you free, too. But you were too scared and stubborn to go with him. If you had gone with him, your ending would be totally different. Life is like that, Iris. Sometimes it comes down to a single choice.*

Iris's struggle grows stronger. *You don't know what you're talking about,* she says.

The spirits on both sides are in a tug-of-war as Iris tries to pull Old Sally into her world. Yet Old Sally stands firm. To anyone walking into the room, it might look like an ordinary gathering of a family around a deathbed. But it is much more than it appears. Many years before, the stage was set for this final scene to play out.

Death calls Iris Temple to the journey we all must make. Old Sally is a witness to this call. Iris's life energy wanes. Her soft moan grows to a scream, loud enough for Old Sally to want to cover her ears. After several seconds, the screaming fades to a quiet weeping. Iris refuses to give up easily. Old Sally calls on her ancestors for more help. After a few moments, her grandmother Sadie appears in spirit form and stands at one shoulder and her mother at the other. In the far corner of the room is an old black woman in tribal dress she has never seen before. Is this Sadie's mother, who never left Africa? Old Sally closes her eyes to concentrate on the task at hand. Her past must not distract her.

To Old Sally, death is the next great birth, and it is the grandmothers who are needed for this task.

Death be women's work, Old Sally thinks, *just like birth be women's work.*

Rose's gaze drops, as though her mother's latest surge of anger has weakened her. Queenie puts her arm around Rose, keeping the circle intact. Old Sally can count on Queenie to watch after Rose. Just like she did when Rose was a girl. At the same time, Lynette stands steady, her large legs like the trunk of a live oak anchored to the ground. Her attention hasn't wavered.

Never underestimate the power of a large woman, Old Sally thinks, and then thanks the spirit world for sending Lynette to help.

Old Sally speaks, her voice growing in power with each word. "It won't be long now, children. She be almost ready to go." She says what the women need to hear.

Three generations of Temple women have carried the darkness that Old Sally's grandmother experienced first, back in the slaveholding days. After her son was sold off, her grandmother wept nearly every day, crying out to God to make it right. Grief bound them to the Temples for all these years. Tonight, if Old Sally succeeds, that grief will finally stop, as the ancestors foretold. If she is unsuccessful in helping Iris transition, then it will have to be healed in the next generation. Or the generation after that. Like those secrets in that old book, someday the grief will find a way to come out.

Only Old Sally hears the torment coming from Iris's unmoving lips. The machines continue to breathe for her and monitor her heartbeat. Nothing, as far as anyone else can tell, has changed. However, an invisible war is playing itself out in a final battle.

At Old Sally's suggestion, they hum to make their bond stronger while still holding hands. Iris's resistance grows like a hurricane coming ashore. A roar fills Old Sally's ears. Chaos crackles in the spirit world. Old Sally's body quakes in the storm. For the first time in all her years of doing this, she feels all might be lost. Instead of Iris dying, it is she who might die.

Like a vessel at sea riding the giant waves, Old Sally and her ancestors rock with the current. She reminds herself that she is not alone. Queenie asks if Old Sally is okay. She says she is, and at the same time, wonders if this might be her transition, too.

"Keep holding hands," Old Sally says, "and hum louder."

The women hum and sway as the hurricane passes through them and between them. Seconds later, they stop humming, and a calmness spreads over the room. They have stepped into the eye of the storm. Then to the complete surprise of the four women standing hand-in-hand, Iris Temple opens her eyes.

CHAPTER THIRTEEN

Queenie

"Good Lord in heaven!" Queenie shrieks.

The four women stare at Iris like she is Lazarus walking out of the tomb.

Queenie had thought for sure they were successful in helping Iris to the other side. She'd never concentrated so hard in her life. But it appears that all they've helped her do is open her eyes.

Too bad the newspaper isn't here to take photographs for the society section, Queenie thinks. She imagines the headline: *Savannah's Grandmother Cheats Death!*

All this while amid the biggest scandal in Savannah's history. A secret a day hasn't kept the doctor away, it is making her sicker. Every day Queenie wakes and wonders if today is the day that all of Savannah knows her most tender confidence.

Iris's eyes take in the room, but the rest of her doesn't move. Her lips tremble as she tries to speak, and she emits something like a frustrated groan. Rose's mouth drops open, and even Old Sally looks surprised. Lynette picks up the telephone and has an animated discussion with someone, probably Iris's doctor. Evidently, Iris has done something miraculous by waking up. According to Lynette, Iris should be dead now. Even the machines say so. But Iris is as alive as any of them.

Iris opens her mouth, but nothing comes out.

Queenie thinks of all the times she longed for Iris to shut up. Yet as awful as Iris can be, Queenie wouldn't wish this helpless fate on anyone.

Old Sally leans close to Iris's ear and whispers something. Iris's eyes blink and then blink again. Queenie doesn't begin to know how her mama talks to spirits or even near-spirits, in Iris's case. All she knows is this is weird.

Lynette gets off the phone and steps over to Iris. "Hello, Miss Temple. I'm Lynette Fielding," she says, a little too loudly. Does she think Iris's muteness has also made her deaf? "I'm an RN, and I need to check you over a little bit, okay?"

Lynette, who makes Queenie look petite in comparison, shines a small penlight into each of Iris's pupils and then checks her reflexes.

When Iris looks down at her body, her eyes widen. Queenie can only imagine her half-sister's horror at wearing a light blue backless hospital gown, the ultimate in bourgeoisie.

"The doctor will be here in about an hour," Lynette says. "I can't believe he wants to come out. Doctors don't do house calls anymore. Can I get you anything?" Lynette offers a toothy smile and pats Iris on the hand.

But as Queenie can attest, doctors do make house calls for Iris. They always have. And they will continue to do so as long as she might dedicate a new wing to their hospital.

Old Sally nods like Iris is giving her an ear full. Everyone turns to Old Sally, waiting for a translation of the unspoken conversation.

"She's asking for Edward," Old Sally says.

"Do we know how to get in touch with him?" Rose asks.

"Only Iris would know that," Queenie says.

Iris looks at Rose as if to push her out of the room with her gaze. Queenie has never understood why Iris hates Rose so much. Perhaps even Iris doesn't know. A whisper of gas escapes into the room, evidence of Iris's unspoken thoughts. Queenie wishes she had some of Violet's essential oils.

"Oh my, did you have a little accident in your diaper, Miss Temple?" Lynette says in a whisper as she pats Iris's hand. "Don't worry, sweetie, I'll take care of it."

Iris's eyes ignite in a primal—yet silent—scream.

Lynette rolls Iris over and pulls open the back of Iris's gown. She peeks inside. Queenie imagines Iris would rather jump off the widow's peak of her house than wear adult diapers.

"Nothing there," Lynette reports. "Maybe it's just gas. That seems to happen to you a lot." Lynette turns to the others. "We had a phrase for that when I was a girl," she whispers with a wink. "'Silent but violent.'"

Lord, in heaven, Queenie thinks, *Lynette's lucky Iris can't move, or she'd be in traction before she even knew what hit her.*

Old Sally stands close to the bed as if listening to Iris's thoughts. "What's she saying now, Mama?" Queenie asks.

For Iris to have to rely on Old Sally to convey her wishes must feel like Iris's version of hell.

"She be agitated," Old Sally says. "She keeps saying to contact Bo Rivers. Something about a key to a safe deposit box."

It must have something to do with the Book of Secrets, Queenie thinks. Yesterday the newspaper ran another secret accusing a prominent family finance company, led by an equally prominent patriarch, of embezzlement. His wife is one of Iris's so-called friends at the Junior League. If Iris had been awake to read it, she might have had another stroke. And if Queenie's secret ever shows up, she may have to take a bed next to Iris.

"Does she have anything to say to me?" Rose asks Old Sally.

Old Sally listens for a long time, her face unable to mask her disappointment. Iris must be telling her things she can't or won't repeat. In response, Old Sally begins to hum an old Gullah melody to calm Iris.

But Queenie can't imagine anything calming her half-sister while in this paralyzed state. Seconds later, the machines in the room scream out in alarm. Lynette rushes toward the machines but then stops. She looks at Iris and then back at them.

"Do something," Rose begs Lynette.

Lynette's expression reveals her helplessness. "I can't. Miss Temple has a *do not resuscitate* order."

"She does?" Rose asks. "That doesn't sound like Mother."

"Edward had her sign some papers a few months ago," Queenie says. "I delivered them to Bo River's office myself."

At the time, Queenie wondered why Edward would make his mother sign such an order. Perhaps he was preparing for a moment exactly like this, so his mother's death wouldn't drag out.

Iris's eyes dart around the room as if finally realizing what is going on. The women join hands again without Old Sally saying a word. They circle the bed and hum again. Queenie imagines a circle of light and goodness calling her half-sister home. When that doesn't seem to work, Queenie imagines a bucket of the Colonel's secret recipe chicken in the center of the circle. To her surprise, Iris begins to calm. Queenie smiles briefly and wonders what would get her to go toward the light. She imagines Denzel Washington calling her home to the Promised Land and smiles. Although Oprah would be tempting, too.

Old Sally sits at Iris's side holding her hand. Perhaps her mama is encouraging Iris to let go and telling her that everything will be okay. Rose has tears in her eyes. Queenie leans closer to Rose. She can't even imagine having to say goodbye to her own mother and pushes this thought away. Finally, Iris closes her eyes. Queenie waits for them to pop back open, but they don't. Then just like on the television shows where the patient flatlines, the urgent sounds of the machines become a single tone.

After Lynette turns off the machines, the room goes silent. She looks at her watch. "Time of death, 11:54 p.m.," she says.

Old Sally releases Iris's hand and moves to a chair in the corner. She rests her head in her hands.

"What is it, Mama?" Queenie asks. "Iris has crossed over, right?"

"It didn't work," Old Sally says.

"What do you mean?" Rose asks.

"Iris's transition," Old Sally says. "I wasn't able to help her complete it."

"You mean she's not dead?" Queenie asks.

"She be dead all right," Old Sally says. "But her spirit be stuck in the in-between world."

"Does that mean I still have to run errands for her?" Queenie asks. The other women turn to look at her. "Just asking," she adds.

Iris's body gets the last word with a final, triumphant hiss.

CHAPTER FOURTEEN

Violet

M iss Temple *would want me to use the silver serving dishes instead of the China,* she thinks.

Violet has worked since six a.m. preparing food for the funeral reception and still has things to do. Every edible sea creature known to Savannah is spread out on the kitchen counters in serving dishes that she is now covering with cellophane to store. A knock on the kitchen door pulls her away from the task, and she opens the door to find Spud Grainger holding a plastic bag full of fresh scallops.

"I couldn't have done this without you," Violet says, giving him a quick hug.

"Happy to help," Spud says, but he doesn't look happy at all. In the other hand, he carries several posters pulled from the ornate ironwork surrounding the house.

"You look exhausted," Violet says, feeling worn out herself.

She hasn't had time to consider how Spud might be affected by Miss Temple's death.

"I've been up all night," he says.

In a suit and bow tie, Spud is already dressed for the funeral later this morning. For his sake, she hopes there isn't a scene. If polled by Savannah's upper class, Miss Temple's approval rating would be in the negative numbers. However, popular opinion appears to be changing. At least a little. Two posters she pulled off the gate yesterday had a different message and portrayed Miss Temple as a kind of folk hero.

Spud helps Violet carry the serving dishes to the spare refrigerator next to the laundry room. In the last bit of space, she stores the scallops to prepare later.

"Would you like a cup of coffee?" Violet asks, putting the posters in the trash.

Spud accepts her offer. "Iris would hate all those terrible signs on the fence. Does anybody know who's putting those secrets in the newspaper?"

"We have no idea," Violet says. "We were hoping it would stop after Miss Temple died, but they haven't."

Spud takes a seat at the table. "Iris would be so disappointed about how the Temple legacy is being tarnished," he says.

Thirty minutes before, Rose and Queenie left the kitchen to get ready for the funeral, and Violet was looking forward to some uninterrupted time. She has a thousand things to do, but she can tell Spud needs to talk.

Ten years ago, Spud began delivering Miss Temple's exotic meat—bringing only the best cuts, trimmed to perfection, carefully wrapped in single servings—as if Miss Temple herself might receive these gifts. But since her employer rarely stepped into the kitchen, Spud began coming to see Violet. Not in a romantic way. He is old enough to be her father. Perhaps that was part of the initial draw since Violet never had one.

After pouring him a cup of coffee, Violet cuts two slices of banana bread, a small one for her, a bigger piece for Spud. She sits at the kitchen table, almost expecting her chair to still be warm from when Queenie and Rose were there.

Violet has often thought that more healing goes on around kitchen tables than in churches. At least it always felt that way at her grandmother's kitchen table when Violet was a girl. Meals were celebrations that not only included good food, but laughter, tears, singing, love, and conflicts—all aspects of life. To Violet, kitchens are where community happens.

In a way, it makes sense that her dream is to open a tea shop and bakery in downtown Savannah for an even bigger community to enjoy. But her dream can wait. She returns her attention to Spud.

"What did you think about all night?" Violet breaks off a piece of banana bread and eats it. It's delicious if she does say so herself.

"Mostly memories," he says. "The time when Iris and I were together."

"How did you meet her?" Violet asks. She's curious why she never thought to ask this before.

Spud smiles and pauses like he's gathering his thoughts.

"I played saxophone in a small jazz band called the Grainger Quartet," he begins. "We played local clubs and wedding receptions and various engagements with the Savannah Historical Society."

Violet has never heard this story, and it seems important for Spud to tell it.

"I first laid eyes on Iris in the mid-seventies at one of our gigs for the Historical Society." He looks out the window into the garden as if reliving the moment. "Her presence captured my imagination, the part that's prone to improvisation. She was older, of course, and a privileged member of Savannah. Iris was everything I wasn't supposed to want or have. Perhaps that was part of the attraction." He turns away from the window and smiles at

Violet. "Love doesn't always abide by the rules of social order," he concludes.

"My grandmother worked here then. Did you ever meet her?" Violet asks. "She goes by the name Old Sally."

Spud narrows his eyes as if searching the past. "I do remember her. She was very regal looking."

Violet likes to think of her grandmother as regal.

"Whenever my quartet played one of Iris's events, and we were on a break, we went to the kitchen, and your grandmother fed us," Spud says. "She took a liking to me. One time she asked if she might have something of mine to add to some kind of collection. *Something small,* she said. I didn't really understand why she wanted it," he continues. "But I didn't want to refuse her. She was quite persuasive if you know what I mean."

You have no idea, Violet thinks. And if her grandmother's personality isn't persuasive enough, there are always her spells.

"The only thing I had on me that night was a box of brand new saxophone reeds," he says.

Violet remembers a small rectangular box with gold lettering. "Oh, that's where those came from," Violet says with a laugh. "My grandmother collects things. I always wondered what those were."

"I'm sorry, I'm confused," Spud says.

"It means she chose you," Violet explains. "She kind of watches out for certain people. People that she feels need her for one reason or another."

"Well, I was always struggling in those days," Spud says. Then it seemed my luck changed. Maybe that was your grandmother's doing," he adds with a chuckle.

"Maybe," Violet says.

"Is she still alive?" Spud asks. "That must have been forty years ago."

"Alive and well," Violet says. "We just celebrated her 100th birthday last January."

"Impressive," Spud says. He pets his mustache. "Next time you see her, please tell her how much I appreciate her looking out for me."

Violet promises she will as Spud straightens his tie again.

Several years ago, Violet counted how many times Spud straightened his tie over coffee. The result was seven, but today he seems to have doubled his efforts.

"My quartet played for Iris's daughter's wedding reception," he begins again. "I can't remember her name."

"Rose?" Violet asks.

"Yes, Rose," he says. "We played 50-minute sets, with a 10-minute break to rest our lips and grab a smoke. Rose was marrying a young man from somewhere out West. I remember this detail because it was the first and only wedding my quartet played where the groom wore a cowboy hat. I don't think Iris liked that. She always worried about appearances in those days."

Violet doesn't tell him that Miss Temple probably died with the same concerns, the *Book of Secrets* being her biggest worry. She glances at her watch. Violet won't have time to go to the church now, with all she has left to do, but maybe the graveside service.

"Oh my, Iris was beautiful in those days," Spud continues. His gaze drifts. "I wasn't so bad-looking myself. People used to say I looked like James Dean."

He turns his profile for Violet to see the resemblance. She nods, even though she has no idea who James Dean is.

"I never deluded myself into believing that I had anything to offer Iris," he says, sadness showing in his eyes. "I've been replaying the past for days now, ever since you called to tell me that Iris had passed. The news hit me hard, Violet. I couldn't even work the next day."

She reaches over and squeezes his hand, and he returns the squeeze.

"What I keep remembering is that first time we got together,"

Spud says. "Can I tell you about it? I've never told anyone before."

"Please do," Violet says. She has to admit she's curious. She can't imagine her former employer in the throes of a passionate love affair. It's hard to imagine Miss Temple passionate about anything except perhaps elevating the Temple's social status.

"It was after her husband, Oscar, died. Iris was planning a charity house tour, and I came here to talk about the music. She asked if I wanted tea and when I said yes, I was surprised that she went into the kitchen and made it herself. For some reason, your grandmother was gone."

"I didn't think Miss Temple ever stepped foot in the kitchen," Violet says. *Except for leaving her critiques,* she thinks.

"Well, I'd never had anything other than sweet iced tea in my entire life," Spud says. "So when she served me a cup of hot tea from a silver tea service, I had no idea what I was doing. I'd watched enough British movies to know how to hold up my little finger when I drank from the fancy cup," he says, with a laugh. "Can you believe I was that naïve?"

Violet touches his hand again. "I can relate to being naïve. It took me years to get used to the day-to-day excesses of the wealthy," she says. "Especially while Jack and I watched every penny."

Spud nods as though he's watched a few pennies himself.

Violet imagines what a handsome man Spud must have been earlier in his life. Photographs of a younger Miss Temple always surprise her. At times, even Miss Temple looked softer and prettier.

Spud continues with his story. "Iris and I were in the sunroom when she asked me if I was familiar with the free love movement. I can't say I had any idea what she meant. It's not like Savannah had hippies in those days. But that was the first time I realized that Iris wasn't just a Temple, but a woman with desires."

His eyebrows rise as he lowers his head. "Since I was much

braver back then, I asked if I could kiss her. Keep in mind I was a musician. Who was I to think I could kiss someone like her? Savannah bowed at her feet."

Violet's face grows warm with the thought that Miss Temple would not like her housekeeper and cook knowing something so intimate about her.

"Afterwards, she led me upstairs to her bedroom," Spud says without looking up. He stops here, as if, as a gentleman, he has gone far enough. Then he looks at her. "She refused to call me Spud, you know. She called me Henry. She said the name Spud, sounded common, like a French fry."

They laugh. Violet can imagine Miss Temple's inflections while saying this, the emphasis on *French fry*. However, her actions are much harder to visualize. In a way, Violet wishes she had known this side of Miss Temple. The side that allowed herself to be swept away by a jazz musician.

Violet touches his arm. "How long did it last?" she asks.

"Several months," he says. "To keep it private, we spent week-ends on Hilton Head. Those times were some of the happiest of my life."

His eyes redden, and he pulls a handkerchief from his suit jacket.

"Why did it end?" Violet asks, genuinely curious.

"Iris called it off," he says, blowing his nose. "I'll never forget the day her letter arrived, telling me that our love affair was over. She threatened to sue me for everything I had if I ever told anyone, and I haven't told a soul until now."

"I'm so sorry, Spud."

"Me, too," he says. "But the most difficult part was that attached to the letter was a check for 180,000 dollars. I think Iris was reimbursing me a hundred dollars for every day of our six months together. I still have the letter," he adds.

Spud blows his nose with vigor now, as though all these years later, he is still insulted by Iris's actions. "I never cashed that check."

"Oh, Spud," Violet says, "love is hard no matter what the circumstances, but this sounds devastating."

"What I want to know is, why do rich people always think money is the solution to everything?" Spud asks.

"I have often wondered the same thing," Violet says, thinking this is one thing she'll never have personal experience with.

"Iris changed after that," Spud begins again. "She was always proper but never cutting. I changed too," he adds. "I disbanded my group, and I took a full-time job at the Piggly Wiggly as their butcher." He neatly folds his handkerchief and puts it in his breast pocket. "Then years later, she started coming to the Piggly Wiggly to order her exotic meats," he continues. "I knew it was more than that. I knew she wanted to see me. To see how I was. You don't travel across town to get something you could have delivered from anywhere in the world right to your doorstep. You don't do that unless you want to see someone and want to let them know that you still care. Right?"

"I wish she could have told you how she truly felt," Violet says. "We all deserve that much."

He sighs and agrees. "I think the most hurtful thing was that Iris required that it be kept a secret," he says. "She was convinced our affair would ruin her."

"What is it about the Temples that attracts so many secrets?" Violet asks.

"I know. It's such a mess, isn't it?" Spud says. "By the way, I saw the *Book of Secrets* once that everybody's talking about. Iris showed it to me. She said that whoever had that book could bring Savannah to its knees."

"Well, I'm not so sure about bringing Savannah to its knees, but it has certainly brought Savannah to our gate."

Spud gives a brief smile. "You know, now that I think about it,

Iris mentioned that there was a second book that nobody else knew about."

"A second book?" Violet doesn't know if she has the stamina to withstand the fallout from more secret books.

"She didn't say much about it," Spud continues. "Just that it could be dangerous if it fell into the wrong hands. Where do you think that one is?"

"I have no idea," Violet says, and she doesn't want to know.

Spud thanks Violet for listening, glances at his watch, and says he'd better get going. They hug again and say their goodbyes.

The house returns to quiet, except for the unseen entities that offer an occasional bump and rattle. Cold air brushes past her. She rubs goosebumps on her arms.

"Is that you, Miss Temple?" Violet asks as she looks around the kitchen. "He still loves you, you know."

A heavy sadness descends. A sadness that feels more like Miss Temples than her own. She shivers again and reminds herself that she doesn't have time to be a counselor for ghosts. At least not right now. She has a reception to prepare for.

Violet retrieves the scallops from the refrigerator and thinks again of Spud. Miss Temple's time with him was like a *Get Out of Jail Free* card.

"Too bad you didn't take advantage of that," Violet says, in case the newest Temple ghost can hear her.

How would Miss Temple's life have been different if she'd made decisions based on what her heart wanted instead of her head? How would any of our lives be different?

"This is what happens when books of secrets are more important than relationships," she tells her deceased employer. But it seems Miss Temple is gone. Perhaps to make it to the church on time for her own funeral.

CHAPTER FIFTEEN

Rose

M*other would like this,* Rose thinks.

The street in front of the Catholic Church has been blocked off for her mother's funeral, which promises to be well-attended. Do people want proof that the grand matriarch of Savannah is finally dead?

People gather outside to chat, and some even smoke. A cacophony of smells rises from the crowd, as though every fragrance ever denied them at her mother's insistence is being worn on the day of her funeral.

Talk of secrets is everywhere as she overhears several people suggest that this will be the end of the daily reveal in the newspaper. But isn't that assuming her mother was responsible for them? That just doesn't make sense. Besides, Queenie told Rose the secrets showed up in the classifieds every morning the entire time her mother was in a coma. Rose wonders if the person or persons responsible are in the crowd of mourners. She surveys the guests and decides that they all look guilty of something.

It is a sweltering day, even for Savannah. The air is thick with humidity as if the clouds might burst at any moment, releasing the rain. The thickness holds the scents close to the ground like a cloud of toxic waste hovering near the earth's surface.

As Rose walks through the crowd, she receives a few nods from old family friends, who are at least pretending to mourn. Most everybody else appears to hide their glee. Inside the door of the church, Rose grabs a program and uses it to fan the fumes. The church reeks of a hundred years of incense, which seems tame compared to what is outside.

The obituary in the newspaper that morning applauded her mother's philanthropy over the years, as well as her commitment to the betterment of Savannah. Though her mother was generous to specific organizations, to Rose it sounded like a press release written by her mother. The announcement only mentioned her brother, Edward, and spelled out in several paragraphs the Temple lineage. A lineage that made no mention of Rose and Queenie.

Rose thinks of Old Sally. Given the predominance of Temple ghosts already "stuck" in the house, Rose hopes that Old Sally is wrong about her mother's transition being incomplete. Perhaps her mother's spirit made a belated exit after all. Or maybe she's here right now.

"Rest in peace, Mother," Rose says aloud as she enters the empty sanctuary. She wears a simple black dress and heels she pulled from her closet at home and threw in her suitcase before leaving Wyoming, an outfit she hasn't worn in the seven years since Max's uncle died. Ranching seldom calls for formal attire.

Rose walks down the same aisle of the church that she walked down when she and Max were married. A platinum casket with gold handles sits in front of the altar, where her father's casket sat many years before. It didn't matter that he wasn't Catholic and may have preferred another church. Her mother was in charge of everything and—in her usual way—used the event to showcase the Temple family.

Should she view her mother's body before people arrive? Rose debates this issue while Queenie and a younger priest enter the sanctuary through a side door. Wearing a black dress with a large yellow sash and a yellow hat, Queenie waves as she and the priest discuss lighting and sound as though preparing the stage for a Broadway production. They stop momentarily to reposition several containers of flowers—full of their own scent to rival the incense—that might impede the flow of traffic. Then Queenie and the priest exit stage left.

As if stepping to the edge of a precipice, Rose inches closer to view her mother in repose. The top half of the casket is open, revealing a plush white lining dotted with gold stars sewn into the fabric, as though the person in the coffin was a president or one of the heads of state.

A bit over the top, Rose thinks, *but this is just the kind of thing Mother would have picked out for her exit scene.*

Her mother's lips form a stern, thin line like she is bound and determined not to rest in peace. Her makeup is minimal, something she must have specified in her funeral arrangements, and her white hair is perfectly styled the way her mother has worn it since Rose was a girl.

Rose's mother is dressed in an elegant black dress, as if a mourner herself, and wears a double strand of pearls, the creamy-white in perfect contrast to the black. Proof that you can take it with you, at least until after the service.

While viewing her mother's body, Rose studies her like a possible portrait subject. She notes the line of her mother's brow, the slope of her nose, her wrinkled jaw—the skin all drooping southward in a tribute to her Dixie roots.

A door opens in the back of the church, and Rose jumps like she's been caught stealing the pearls from around her mother's neck. Queenie strolls down the aisle. Despite the sobering occasion, her eyes sparkle.

Sweet Queenie, Rose thinks. *What would I do without you?* This moment would be much harder if it were Queenie in the casket or Old Sally. A thought which makes her feel guilty.

"How are you holding up?" Queenie asks as she joins Rose.

"To be honest, she seems like a stranger," Rose says.

Queenie squeezes Rose's hand. "I doubt anyone really knew Iris," Queenie says. "Including Iris."

"Do you think she was ever happy, Queenie?" Rose's voice catches on a snag of emotion.

"For a brief period years ago," Queenie says. "But it didn't last for long."

"It's like privilege robbed her of any ability to be real," Rose says. "I wonder who she might have been without the Temple money. What might she have done if she had to venture out and forge a career?"

"I guess we'll never know," Queenie says.

They gaze into the casket, as though peering into the vastness of the Grand Canyon. On the ranch, death is a mystery that reveals itself quite often. Nature makes sense in the way it takes care of things. The weak die. The strong survive. But it is harder to put humans into that model. She would have thought her mother was too strong to die.

As Rose contemplates the meaning of life—a hazard of attending any funeral—Queenie pulls a tissue from her purse and covers her mouth overcome with emotion. Rose does her best to console her but then realizes that Queenie isn't weeping at all. In fact, she is doing everything she can to keep from laughing.

"What's going on?" Rose whispers. Her eyes widen with the question. She doesn't know whether to be alarmed or intrigued.

"Can you keep a secret?" Queenie whispers, her hand still covering her mouth.

"Of course I can," Rose whispers back. She has been bred to

keep secrets. In a way, secrets are the family business. Just ask anyone in Savannah right now. But what could be so funny on such a solemn occasion?

Queenie pulls Rose toward the closed end of the casket and taps the top of the lid with a fingernail. It makes a slightly hollow sound.

"The secret's in there," Queenie says. Her voice remains a whisper.

Rose's face registers her confusion. "The secret's in Mother's casket?"

Queenie nods. Rose's thoughts jump to a letter or something of sentimental value. Perhaps a locket or a trinket. Or maybe the infamous *Temple Book of Secrets*. But this doesn't make sense. Why is Queenie fighting so hard not to laugh?

"I don't understand," Rose whispers.

Queenie leans toward Rose and whispers back, "I put something in the casket."

Rose studies Queenie's face, and she gives Rose a grin that can only be described as sheepish.

"Don't be mad," Queenie says.

"Why would I be mad?" Rose whispers.

Queenie pauses as though weighing the consequences of her confession and then announces: "I put a bucket of Kentucky Fried Chicken at your mother's feet. Or between her knees, actually."

Queenie's whispered confession carries the strength of a Shakespearean actor projecting to the back row of the empty church. Her eyes glisten with tears and not tears of grief.

"You did what?" Rose says in full voice.

"I wedged a bucket of Kentucky Fried Chicken between your mother's knees," Queenie says in a quasi-whisper. Then she shrugs, as though disbelieving of the news herself.

Rose's shock slowly warms to a muffled laugh. Her face turns red and hot.

"It seems only fitting," Queenie whispers in conclusion. "It was, after all, her favorite food. And not the least bit exotic, I might add."

Two sets of double doors fling open in the back of the sanctuary as if orchestrated by well-trained theater ushers. The first wave of aromatic mourners enters the church. Queenie takes Rose's arm and steers her into the family pew. Rose refuses to look at Queenie in case the glance might cause a snicker to escape. Rose anticipated her mother's funeral might be difficult, but she never expected that it might be difficult for this reason. She begs Queenie to be quiet and then grits her teeth to stop the laughter that threatens to burst past her lips into the room.

Do not laugh, she tells herself. *Do. Not. Laugh.*

Rose forces herself to think of tragic things like world hunger and puppy mills. Nothing is working. Then a more urgent problem presents itself. Rose locks her knees together to stop her bladder from releasing. She reminds herself that she is at her mother's funeral, not the best venue for hysterical laughter or menopausal bladders.

"Are you angry with me?" Queenie asks.

Rose shakes her head. Queenie's defiant gesture seems mild, considering everything she put up with over the years. It is the element of surprise that has put Rose at risk of losing it on more than one level.

Luckily, Rose and Queenie's squelched laughter sounds close enough to the sounds of grief that the stares they receive are out of sympathy instead of shock. The organist, soft-pedaling their grief, begins to play one of her mother's favorite hymns, *Onward Christian Soldiers.* In response, Rose imagines an army of fried chicken legs marching off to war led by a miniature Colonel Sanders.

A snort of laughter escapes that she segues into a cough. She forces herself to count the panes in the stained glass window in the side chapel. Perhaps if she engages the mechanical side of her brain, it will override her desperate need to laugh. In the meantime, the perfumes, colognes, and aftershaves of two hundred mourners—who have undoubtedly dabbed on extra portions on her mother's behalf—consume the musty, incense-laden, flower-filled church. Refusing to go down without a fight, the aroma of fried chicken joins the other smells. The cumulative effect makes Rose's eyes water. It also makes her nauseous, which proves the most effective tool in stopping her need to laugh.

A door squeaks open in the side chapel, and Edward steps inside. He looks straight at Rose and gives what could be mistaken for a sneer. Suddenly, laughing is the last thing she feels like doing. Encounters with Edward always prove to be a bit harrowing. First, there was the brief, bizarre meeting in the garden and then Edward's macabre visit to their mother's bedroom later that afternoon.

Queenie nudges Rose and motions in Edward's direction. Rose nods that she has seen him, too. The nub of her missing pinkie throbs.

The young priest enters from behind the altar and begins the service. According to Queenie, he has stepped in at the last minute to replace the older priest, who has been ordered bed rest because of a mild cardiac infarction the day before. The young priest is probably thirty at best and is a Sunday school Jesus look-alike with shoulder-length brown hair. Her mother would not be pleased.

Will he pull out a guitar and lead the mourners in Kumbaya? As an afterthought, Rose leans into the aisle to see if he is wearing sandals. If her mother were still alive, his informality would prompt several letters to the Vatican. Long hair and guitar singing are for the lower classes. As is anything else that might hint at liveliness.

Throughout the next hour, several people from the community get up to eulogize her mother. If not for their familiar faces, Rose would think they were paid actors endorsing a product. Iris Temple was *generous to a fault*, says one. *Thoughtful*, says another. *Selfless*, says yet another. The woman described in the eulogies is not Rose's mother. No one speaks of secrets, either, yet she imagines that is precisely what is on everyone's mind.

Glancing at her mother's casket, she decides that it is ingenious product placement. Then her stomach growls. Maybe it is the smell of chicken, but she is suddenly borderline ravenous. Why didn't she eat at the house before they left? At the time, she wasn't hungry. Now she salivates as she envisions the banana bread Violet made that Rose turned down. The current speaker looks over at her, an older gentleman wearing a bow tie. Did he hear her stomach growl?

Spud Grainger gets up to eulogize her mother and introduces himself. The name sounds familiar, and Rose wonders where she's heard it before. His dark suit is accented with a pale yellow shirt and a bow tie that looks like the wings of a monarch butterfly. He has kind eyes and seems like the type that would take in stray animals, yet paradoxically he mentions he is the head butcher at the Piggly Wiggly.

Rose nudges Queenie's arm. "Who is he?" she whispers.

"Long story," Queenie whispers back. "I'll tell you later."

Rose nods.

As Spud Grainger speaks, he stops several times to blow his nose into a white handkerchief he pulls from his jacket pocket. Of all the mourners, he is the only one who appears genuinely bereaved. Rose wishes she had known the woman he grieves.

Meanwhile, the front of the church smells more and more like a fried chicken franchise. Rose fantasizes about tiny Styrofoam containers holding mashed potatoes with gravy, as well as small white dinner rolls. It doesn't help that Spud Grainger is going on and on about exotic meats. Her stomach growls again, louder than before. Sound carries quite well in the sanctuary. Unfortunately, smells do, too.

The reptilian part of Rose's brain plots out different ways to scavenge food. She fantasizes about creating a diversion so that she can make her way to the altar and grab a chicken breast from between her mother's knees. Perhaps she could do it under the guise of revealing one of the biggest Temple secrets. However, she's not sure what that would be.

She glances at her watch. Katie, Rose's daughter, is due in from Chicago any minute for the graveside service. Rose busies herself with worrying about the synchronization of Katie's different flights and landings as the next speaker rises to eulogize her mother, offering more praise for the saint-like Iris Temple.

This is overkill, Rose thinks, regretting her word choice.

Rose looks over the large crowd of Savannah's elite gathered to pay their last respects. Some of the same people attended Rose's wedding. She didn't know them then and doesn't know them now. The wealthy do this for each other. They throw parties and donate to each other's charities and attend weddings and funerals. But other than that, they are strangers. Except these strangers, who are wearing Rolexes and designer fashions, seem poised for a revolution.

The young priest steps forward to end the service, asking one final time if anyone has anything they want to say. Edward rises from the shadows and walks over to their mother's casket. He rests a hand on the top as if a gesture of ownership.

"Thank you for your heartfelt acknowledgment of the Temple family's contribution to our fair city," Edward begins as if to remind the angry mob of their manners. His words are as polished as his shoes. He exhorts the Temple brand, reminding everyone that Savannah wouldn't be Savannah without the Temples. And despite any hard feelings of late, because of a few unfortunate secrets, they should be grateful that it wasn't worse. He looks at Rose as he speaks as if to remind her who is now in charge. His hubris, like his suit, seems perfectly tailored to fit the event. His presentation would have probably made their mother proud.

THE SERVICE FINALLY OVER, Rose avoids Edward and steps into the first black limo she comes to outside of the church. Queenie follows her, a splash of color among all the black. Rose rifles through her purse and pops three cinnamon Altoids into her mouth, hoping the curiously strong mints will count as sustenance. She has a headache now.

"I'm starving," Rose says to Queenie, her mouth on fire from the mints.

"Hold on," Queenie says. "Let me see if I have something."

Queenie drapes her large purse across her even larger lap and pulls things out of her bag that look like they might belong to some kind of southern survival kit: lipstick, billfold, two different types of bug spray, a crumbled box of tissues, a paperback mystery, four crumpled packets of Splenda, a small roll of twine, a red Swiss army knife, and enough colorful headbands to set up a store display in the corner of the limo.

Queenie finally offers Rose a handful of orange Tic-Tacs that are loose in the bottom of her purse. Rose picks off the biggest pieces of fuzz before popping them into her mouth, along with two aspirin and the cinnamon Altoids. Her mouth puckers in disgusted satisfaction. As Queenie loads everything back into her purse, Rose chews the aspirin and Altoids, leaving only small pellets of orange Tic-Tacs to suck on.

"Edward was in rare form today," Queenie says.

"This is an awful thing to say about my own brother, but I don't trust him," Rose says.

"I would worry about you more if you did," Queenie says. She straightens her hat that nearly touches the roof of the limo.

"He always stays at the country club when he's here," Queenie says. "In the past few years, he's come to Savannah and not even told your mother. I would see him in town when I ran errands. I never told her, though. That would be just the thing to get your mother on the warpath."

"Why would he not tell her he's in town?" Rose asks. She crunches the last of the Tic-Tacs.

"I don't think he could stand to be around her," Queenie says. "Lord knows she would test the patience of Job."

The limo leads the procession to the graveside. At the entrance, people hold placards that say things like **Good Riddance** and **The Wicked Witch is Dead.** Queenie and Rose hold hands as if to fortify themselves against the scene.

"Why are they so angry?" Rose asks.

"They think she's a snitch," Queenie says. "They thought she was the one releasing the secrets. Now they don't know who it is, but they're still angry."

The limo passes through the wrought-iron gates leading to the section of the cemetery where the ornate Temple mausoleum stands. The last time Rose was here was when they buried her father, over two decades ago.

Thick clouds gather and block the sun. Though a bit cooler, the humidity seems to be rising. Within minutes, an afternoon drizzle begins. Edward stands on the other side of the priest. Even though it is only three o'clock, his five o'clock shadow is pronounced. He seems alone, even in a crowd, which causes Rose to wonder if her brother ever gets lonely.

As far as she knows, he has lived in the same penthouse in downtown Atlanta for the last thirty years and has never married or lived with anyone. His firm specializes in helping corporations handle scandals—another form of dealing with secrets. Rose can't even imagine the wealth he has amassed while she and Max have struggled to keep the ranch afloat. Being a Temple in the southeast can have its advantages. He probably doesn't have to work at all, but just wants to have something to do.

Despite the rain, there are smiles on the faces of several mourners. Do they think the *Temple Book of Secrets* is being buried with her mother? *Along with a bucket of chicken, thanks to Queenie,* Rose thinks. She resists smiling.

A few minutes into the graveside service, a taxi arrives. In the distance, Rose's daughter, Katie, gets out of the cab with another woman. They share a large rainbow pride umbrella as they approach. Rose smiles at the thought of her mother turning cartwheels in her grave as her lesbian granddaughter makes a flamboyant entrance.

Rose and Queenie part to make room for the two women on the front row. Rose notes Edward's instant disapproval as his glare now includes raised eyebrows. As the *Kumbaya* priest leads them in prayer, Katie leans into her, and Rose pulls her close. The rain increases. Rose briefly greets Katie's latest girlfriend, Angela, a woman Rose has never met and has actually heard very little about. Angela's hair is short, almost shaved, and she appears to be ten years older than Katie, maybe more. Multiple piercings make Rose wonder if she wants to look younger than she is. One piercing is on the side of her nose, another through her bottom lip and yet another through her tongue. Three holes on each ear are filled with silver studs. And these are only the ones Rose can see.

How in the world did she get through airport security? Rose wonders.

Wearing a tasteful gray dress, perhaps a little too short, Katie has even donned a bit of makeup for the occasion, making Rose think that maybe she has some Temple blood in her after all.

Her daughter looks like a Catholic school girl in comparison to Angela, who could just as easily be dressed for an equality rally in Washington, D.C. She wears black leggings and black loafers with a pink oxford shirt, shirttail out.

She must be baking in this heat, Rose thinks. If her mother were still alive, she would write Angela a handwritten letter to educate her about proper funeral attire.

Katie stands next to Rose, their shoulders touching. The four of them, including Queenie, now share the large colorful umbrella as the rain increases in intensity once again. All stare at the coffin posed in front of the family crypt.

Through the years, Katie has asked very few questions about Rose's mother, and Rose hasn't volunteered the information.

Twenty-five years before, Rose moved out West with Max and started a new life. Now that the reason for her staying away is gone, will she feel the need to visit more often? She hasn't realized how much she missed Queenie and even the old house, as well as Old Sally and Violet. Not to mention the ocean and the moisture, intent on baptizing her at every opportunity, now with rain at her mother's funeral. Maybe the question now is how she is going to go back to Wyoming.

The various fragrances of the mourners have mellowed into a smell resembling an over-ripe banana wrapped in a magnolia blossom. As the misty rain continues to fall, the dry-eyed mourners now look a little bored. Violet stands at the back of the crowd in a red raincoat, her posture erect like a dancer. It feels generous of her to come to the funeral at all, given the stories Rose has heard about how difficult her mother was.

By the time the priest has finished his remarks, the rain has grown in intensity to a mild tropical storm. The skies open up and produce raindrops the size of small tree frogs and just as hard to avoid. Black umbrellas spring open with a touch, one after another, as if choreographed for a Gene Kelly musical. Quick, awkward handshakes are exchanged as everyone disperses for their cars. The wind grabs at their umbrellas and creates a spattering of muffled expletives from the mourners. A loud rumble of thunder accelerates their departure as if her mother is warning them that they haven't heard the last from her.

Rose and Queenie run for the black limo, followed by Katie and Angela. The four of them scramble into the back, laughing from the exhilaration of the run. They dry off as best they can with the box of pink tissues from Queenie's handbag. Their funeral attire makes them look like water-logged crows. Formal introductions are made all the way around, and they exchange damp handshakes. Rose has forgotten that Katie and Queenie have never met. It seems these two important women in her life should somehow already know each other.

Angela's streaked eye-liner adds to the crow effect. Katie dabs at Angela's rogue eye-liner, a gesture that reveals a level of intimacy that surprises Rose. She thinks back to an earlier girlfriend, also named Angela, when Katie was a freshman at Smith. While home for Christmas during her freshman year, Katie announced over eggnog that she had fallen in love with her roommate—the first Angela—who at the time of the announcement was sitting in Rose and Max's living room. Rose and Max tried not to overreact. It was Smith, after all, and this could possibly be a four-year phase. But the phase did not end after Katie graduated. After many hours of discussion about the matter, Rose and Max came to a simple conclusion: they loved Katie and wanted her to be happy and would stand by her no matter what the world thought of her lifestyle choice.

Now that Rose is getting a better look at her, the current Angela looks at least forty. According to Katie, Angela is a writer of feminist fiction and has won a Lambda Literary Award, an award Rose is embarrassed to say she has never heard of.

"Who was that man standing next to the priest?" Katie says. "He looked familiar."

"That was your Uncle Edward," Rose says. "You met him once when you were very young. He had a layover in Denver, and we drove over to meet him for coffee."

"Oh," Katie says as if discovering long-lost relatives is a regular occurrence.

"We've never been close," Rose says. "He's six years older than me."

A new tattoo peaks from underneath the cuff of Katie's sheer gray blouse as she reaches to hold Angela's hand. It is a thin vine of roses around her wrist.

"What is it with young people and their tattoos these days?" Rose asks, ready to change the subject.

Her relationship with Edward is too complicated to explain on an empty stomach.

Katie pulls up the sleeve of her blouse to show her latest prize. Katie collects tattoos like charms on a charm bracelet. They all have meaning to her. Rose tries not to reveal her worry that when Katie is elderly and getting sponge baths in the nursing home, she might regret having a skull and crossbones tattoo at the base of her spine.

"They don't mind if you have those at work?" Rose asks.

Right out of college, Katie, somehow miraculously, acquired a job in Chicago working for Harpo, Inc.

"No, Mom, they encourage self-expression," Katie says. "And they're not called tattoos anymore. They're called body art. You should see Angela's."

Her daughter's new girlfriend's tattoos don't rank high on her list of must-sees. Yet Rose smiles and nods as though she will schedule it on her calendar. Angela looks at Rose like she sees straight through to her thoughts. They exchange a moment of understanding, both agreeing to suspend judgments during this initial meeting.

When they leave the cemetery, the protesters are still there, their signs now smeared with rain. To distract herself, Rose contemplates what symbol she might imprint on her aging body. Given her name, a rose would be the most obvious. Although when it comes to flowers, she actually prefers lilies to roses.

"Is this your first time visiting Savannah, Angela?" Rose asks, all the while thinking, *it can never be said that I don't make an effort.*

"It's my first time anywhere in the South, actually," Angela says. "It's, uh, interesting," she adds, as though searching for something nice to say and coming up empty.

Will Rose's birthplace ever outgrow its stereotypes? Northerners often make conclusions without ever spending time here.

Katie has a new girlfriend every six months. At this point, Rose tries to not get too attached to them, especially the ones she likes, because those are usually the ones that come and go the fastest.

"It's my first time in the South, too, Mom," Katie says.

Rose turns to face her. "Of course you've been here before, sweetheart," she says. Then she thinks back to their infrequent family vacations. Yosemite one year, the Grand Canyon, Monument Valley, then for Katie's graduation from high school, Santa Fe. "On second thought, I guess you haven't," Rose adds.

Katie gives Rose a look like *duh* should be tattooed on Rose's forehead.

"Well, you're in for a treat, too," Rose says to Katie, patting her daughter on the knee. If she doesn't get food soon, her social skills may deteriorate even more.

WHEN THEY RETURN to the Temple house, an elaborate buffet has been set up in the dining room. Violet has pulled off what Rose could never have managed. Even Rose's mother would find little to complain about given the grandeur of the presentation—a spread that has Rose salivating like one of Pavlov's famous dogs.

Fresh, local seafood is the fare of the day. Mounds of shrimp and oysters on the half-shell sit next to steaming seafood casseroles and luscious fruit plates, without a single serving of exotic meat in sight.

CHAPTER SIXTEEN

Queenie

W *hite people sure do know how to suck the life out of a funeral,* Queenie thinks.

She looks around at the elaborate reception. She has never seen this many white people wearing this much black and sipping this much booze. Most of them are hypocrites, as it is. They hated Iris, especially after those secrets started to leak. Queenie still has no idea how those forbidden tidbits got in the newspaper in the first place. If they were meant to hurt Iris only, then she thought they would have stopped since Iris is obviously no longer around. But even this morning, the day of Iris's funeral, there was a secret in the newspaper about a Savannah banker in the 1890s who bought his mistress a hotel in Paris where she lived with their illegitimate son.

Queenie sighs, feeling tired in her bones. Dealing with all the secrets, and now Iris's death, has been harder than she realized.

Not to mention that burials and receptions were never intended to be this dreary. When people die on her Gullah side of the family it's sad, of course, but also a celebration. They wear clothes with some color to them. At funerals they tell stories, dance, and clap. Queenie taps her foot as if hearing a song coming on. But even her foot knows better than to rock a boat with this much money in it.

Queenie thinks back to Iris's gravesite service—an event duller than dirt despite the fact that more than one attendee probably wanted to search the casket to see if Iris was taking that stupid book with her. A few rioters might have made the event more interesting, but they were kept at the gate. She wonders if they'll show up here now that the rain has stopped.

In the Gullah tradition, cemeteries are sacred ground. Often they enclose a grave with a small fence to protect the soul of the person who died, and they adorn the graves with conch shells to ward off evil spirits. On the tombstone, they leave a jar of water for thirst, a bag of rice for hunger, a candle and matches for light, and a collection of herbs and roots in case any spells need to be created in the afterlife.

None of that happened at the Temple mausoleum. If Queenie had thrown a conch shell across Iris's grave, it would have hit a dozen millionaires before it hit the ground. She rolls her eyes with the thought.

All that matters in this grand send-off is that all the right people attend. All the right food is served. All the right things are said. And an enormous amount of alcohol is consumed. Meanwhile, not a single story surfaces that might shake the body with laughter to release some of the boredom.

"Violet has outdone herself on the reception," Rose says to Queenie.

Queenie agrees. Violet is a gem.

However, since they returned to the house, Rose—usually uninterested in food—has been on a mission to divide and conquer the enormous amount of seafood on the dining room table. An impressive pile of shrimp carcasses rests on her plate as she goes in to load up on scallops, and then moves into the corner of the room to feast on them.

Katie stands next to her mother and nudges her girlfriend, who watches as if witnessing a lioness devouring a gazelle.

"You look surprised by your mother's appetite," Queenie says to Katie.

"For sure," Katie says. "At home, she usually nibbles."

"There's probably a lot you don't know about your mother," Queenie says.

"You've got that right," Katie says. "I feel like I just found out that she's been in a witness protection program for the last twenty-five years."

Queenie laughs, thinking: *Finally, some life is coming to this wake.*

Katie leans close to Queenie and whispers, "No wonder she's watched the movie *Steel Magnolias* over a dozen times."

A cackle comes out of Queenie that she has been holding in for hours. The crowd turns to look. Angela, no stranger to stares, turns to Katie.

"I can't believe the accents around here," Angela says. She gives Queenie an awkward smile, as though realizing that Queenie is one of these people, too. "I want to use this experience in my next novel," she continues. "Maybe a storyline about a transgender southern belle."

That should go over well, Queenie thinks, not really sure what 'transgender' means. It sounds complicated.

Angela excuses herself and goes into the foyer where she stands behind a prominent couple from Savannah and pulls a notepad from her back pocket to take notes. She should get an earful about Savannah's secrets.

"So, your mother never told you about any of this?" Queenie asks Katie.

"Oh, I knew she grew up in Georgia," Katie says. "But I thought her folks were probably rednecks or moonshiners or something. It never crossed my mind that they would be Ted Turner with old money and extra flash."

Queenie laughs again and then hushes herself when the mayor shoots her a dirty look. "We all have our secrets," she whispers to Katie, wondering if the current mayor also has connections to the mafia like the one revealed in Iris's book.

"Are you two talking about me?" Rose skewers a scallop, dips it in a crater of Violet's homemade tartar sauce, and swallows it in one gulp.

"Absolutely," Queenie says.

Violet brings another serving bowl full of jumbo shrimp, and Rose's eyes widen as if intrigued by the challenge.

"People must tell you that you look just like your mom," Violet says to Katie.

"All the time," Katie says. "I'm okay with it. Of course, I would have preferred voluptuous, instead of tall, lean, and flat-chested." Katie rolls her eyes and Queenie can see the family resemblance there, too. Violet returns to the kitchen.

"Do you want some seafood?" Queenie asks, noticing that Katie hasn't eaten anything.

"I'm a vegetarian," Katie says. "Vegan, actually, I don't eat seafood."

"Oh," Queenie says. "Violet can make you a cheese sandwich if you'd like."

"No, that's okay," Katie says, after a slight hesitation. "There's plenty of good stuff here."

Katie picks up a strawberry along with several pieces of cantaloupe and eats it as if to appease Queenie.

Queenie isn't sure what a vegan is, either, and wonders if it has anything to do with being gay. Katie is the first lesbian she has ever met, and Angela is the second.

Live and let live is my philosophy, Queenie decides. She knows what it's like to be judged. Plus, Oprah loves the gays.

Queenie excuses herself and goes into the kitchen. "You've

outdone yourself, Vi," she says.

Violet thanks her but looks tired.

"Do you need any help?" Queenie asks. She's asked this question a dozen times today. But even as a little girl, Violet wasn't the type to ask for help.

"Not really," Violet says, loading the dishwasher. "I think I've got everything under control."

Queenie steps into the laundry room off the kitchen and takes an empty laundry detergent box off the top shelf to retrieve a hidden pack of cigarettes and a pack of kitchen matches from inside. She slips them into her dress pocket.

"Come get me if you need anything," she tells Violet. "I'm going to step into the garden for a minute."

Queenie smokes only on rare occasions, usually after Iris has trampled on her last nerve. This is definitely something Oprah would never do. But today, for some reason, she feels like she could smoke an entire carton. After lighting the cigarette, she blows out the match and waves the smoke away.

Although most of Savannah was waiting on Iris to die, it still seems strange to have her demanding half-sister finally gone. Managing Iris was a full-time job. Now, she needs to decide what to do with the rest of her life. All Queenie knows how to do, really, is take care of people. She also knows Rose will be leaving again and who knows how long she will stay gone this time.

However, now that Iris is gone, Queenie is free to visit Rose. She also wants to try to convince Old Sally to move in with her here in the Temple house when it passes to Queenie, as Iris said it would.

But death has a way of reshuffling the card deck in unexpected ways, Queenie thinks. *Nothing is set in stone. Except maybe Iris.*

The rain has stopped. Mist rises from the pathway in the garden. Water drips from the leaves of the live oak and magnolia trees as steady as if it were still raining. Queenie stands near the fountain in a sunny spot to avoid the droplets that can drench someone in seconds. The stone face at the center of the basin glares at Queenie to reprimand her for smoking.

"Mind your own business," she says and flicks ash at him.

At least the protestors have left them alone for now. Queenie never imagined they would show up at the cemetery. It seems like people would have better things to do than stand in the rain and watch a hearse pass by.

From the far corner of the garden, Katie's girlfriend approaches. Water droplets christen her pink shirt like polka-dots. Queenie searches her memory for the woman's name. *Alice? Abigail? Oh, yes, Angela,* she determines.

Queenie greets her, and Angela asks Queenie if she can bum a cigarette. After lighting it Angela inhales and rolls her eyes with pleasure before a long exhale.

"I quit ten years ago," Angela says. "But I still need one every now and again. Especially today for some reason."

"This crowd could intimidate the Queen of England," Queenie says.

Angela smiles. "I thought it was just me."

"No, honey, it's not just you," Queenie says. "If we confiscated all the Rolex watches at this reception, we could feed a third world country for a year."

The two women laugh. The more uncomfortable Queenie is, the funnier she gets. But the two grow quiet. She has run out of lines.

"This is a beautiful garden," Angela says as she glances around.

"I played here when I was a little girl," Queenie says. "My father was Edward Temple. Katie's grandfather."

"Oh," Angela says as she blushes her surprise.

"It happens sometimes," Queenie says.

"For what it's worth, my father had an affair with his secretary," Angela says. "He sold insurance. I don't think any children came of it," she adds. "Although I guess it's entirely possible."

"Humans are complex," Queenie says.

"And stupid," Angela says.

"Amen, Sister." Queenie giggles.

Angela offers a cautious smile as if Queenie might be one of those Bible-thumping Baptists she's heard about. But Queenie isn't a Bible-thumping anything, and she has nothing against Baptists. Lord knows, we are all God's children, whatever we call ourselves.

"So, what do you think of Katie's family?" Queenie asks, thinking it best to leave the subject of religion alone.

"I can honestly say they are not at all what I expected," Angela says.

"What did you expect?"

"I was thinking *Deliverance*, not *Gone with the Wind*," Angela says.

They laugh again.

Queenie is curious about Angela and Katie's relationship. Love fascinates her, especially since she has minimal experience in the art. Actually, Queenie is probably the least experienced person in Savannah in regard to intimate relationships.

A persistent ray of sunlight dances off the piercings on Angela's nose and bottom lip.

Those piercings must have hurt like hell when they went it, Queenie thinks. She is too cowardly to even pierce her ears.

Queenie flips over a stone under the magnolia tree to reveal a tiny graveyard of cigarette butts. They add two more that sizzle in the wet earth.

"Our secret?" Queenie says, looking at the butts.

"Our secret," Angela agrees.

Secrets like this Queenie can handle. The ones that don't involve lawsuits or death threats. However, there is one secret that Queenie fears will make people hate her. That secret would be best left buried under a rock with a bunch of cigarette butts.

The side gate squeaks open. Queenie and Angela turn to look.

Edward walks into the garden surveying the outside of the Temple property like he does the inside. Every time he is in the Temple home, he acts like a landlord trying to catch renters doing something wrong.

What will Edward do if Queenie gets the house like Iris promised? She doesn't anticipate that it will go over very well, even if he inherits the lion's share of property and investments. It doesn't matter that he hasn't lived in the Temple house for over forty years; his sense of ownership is undeniable.

When he sees them, Edward lifts his eyebrows as though a judgment rides on his thoughts. She has never forgiven him for what he tried to do to Violet years ago. But even without that, she would still think he was an ass.

Without saying a word, Edward strides past them and walks through the back door into the kitchen.

"We'd better see what he's up to," Queenie says.

Queenie leads the way into the kitchen, where Edward has begun to quiz Violet on her qualifications for running the Temple household, as though conducting an impromptu job interview.

"I've worked for your mother for twenty years," Violet says. "I think that more than speaks for my qualifications."

Good for you, Queenie thinks. She's proud that someone in her bloodline has the gumption to stand up to Edward.

"I think I'll go find Katie," Angela says to Queenie. "I've seen way too many egotistical white men for one day."

Edward and Angela exchange looks as if they have summed each other up and are still in negative numbers. Meanwhile, Queenie keeps an eye on Violet and wonders if Edward even mourns his mother. He doesn't appear to.

"Can I help you with something, Edward?"

He huffs, as though Queenie's help is the last thing he needs. Without answering, he exits the kitchen into the dining room. A blast of frigid air follows him out the door, and Queenie can almost swear she just heard Iris let out a short laugh.

CHAPTER SEVENTEEN

Rose

Rose mingles in the living room, receiving condolences, hearing more perfunctory comments about how wonderful her mother was, knowing full well that nobody believes it. Her mother was not sweet or caring, nor will she be greatly missed. She was, as Queenie would say, a royal pain in the backside, to friends and foes alike.

In fact, it wouldn't surprise Rose if there were an after-party following the reception where these same mourners celebrated having her mother finally gone. But in the meantime, Rose thanks them for their condolences and tells them each how fondly her mother spoke of them, proving she can lie as well as anybody.

At the same time, it strikes her as one of the few times her mother might have been proud of her for being a Temple. Rose is acting. She is onstage. She is playing the good daughter, the gracious hostess. And her mother, the foremost critic in her life, is not around to judge her for her performance. Or is she? All after-noon, she has had a distinct feeling of being watched.

Edward enters the living room, and goose flesh crawls up Rose's arm. He greets several men from the country club and shakes hands like a politician trying to win votes. He is acting, too. A slight smile remains plastic on his face, mixed with an appropriate tinge of grief. He turns and walks in her direction.

"Shit," she says, under her breath.

Her first instinct is to duck into the kitchen, but it's too late. She doesn't want to give Edward the pleasure of seeing her retreat. Not that she could make a quick exit anyway after all the food she has eaten. Her stomach feels like a shrimp trawler after a big haul.

"Hello, little sister," Edward says. His smile holds firm through capped and gritted teeth.

"Hello, Edward," Rose says with a shiver. *Is it suddenly colder in here?*

"How long do you plan on staying in Savannah?" Edward asks.

"I'll be taking an early flight out tomorrow," she says.

Edward sips his drink. Rose has forgotten how freely the alcohol flows in Savannah.

One day at a time, she tells herself. However, this is turning into a very long day.

"So, were you with our dear mother when she passed?" Edward asks. He glances around the room.

"As a matter of fact, I was," Rose says.

"I hope I didn't miss anything." Edward's gaze turns to Rose, an eyebrow raised.

"Not a thing," Rose says, without expression.

"By the way, where's that cowboy husband of yours?" Edward says.

Does he even remember Max's name? she wonders. "He's back at the ranch," she says.

Edward extends his smile as though he finds someone working on a ranch amusing. The less information Rose gives her brother, the better. Otherwise, he will find a way to use it against her. It is a gift he has. Edward even blamed Rose for the accident with the sword when they were children. He told her parents that it was Rose's idea that they play Cowboys and Indians and also her plan to get the sword from the weapons case.

Like a five-year-old would come up with such an idea? she thinks.

Goose flesh rises on Rose's arms again, and a shot of cold air brushes past her. She wonders if their mother is eavesdropping.

"Did you ever get married, Edward?" Rose asks. Her question comes out more pointed than she intends, but she offers no apology.

"I'm married to my work," Edward says. "She's a sweet bitch of a wife, too." He narrows his eyes as if to say: *Is that the best you've got?*

Ever since they were young, everything was a contest. Edward can put a spin on anything so that he comes out the winner. It doesn't matter what the truth is. It is all about winning the game.

The smell of rotten eggs causes Rose to cover her nose. Her olfactory sense is worn out from the day. Edward doesn't seem to notice the smell.

"Well, enjoy your trip home," Edward says. "I've got to do more damage control around those damn secrets. Nobody seems to have a clue who's doing it. Is it you?"

"Me?" Rose asks, taking a step back.

Edward smiles again as if Rose's defensiveness gives him the advantage.

"I'm surprised you don't have possession of the book yourself, Edward. You always were the most likely heir of the Temple weapons, including the *Book of Secrets*."

Before he has time to respond, a brick flies through a window in the sunroom. Rose ducks and covers her head. She looks for Katie. Somebody screams. Chaos follows. The crowd gathers in the hallway, forming a semi-circle around the lone brick. Whoever threw it had a good arm. The sunroom juts out from the house but is still a good twenty feet away from the gate.

Edward runs outside, but whoever did it is long gone. Several people take this disruption as an opportunity to leave. Katie finds Rose, and Angela takes notes like her new book has morphed into a crime novel. As Queenie disposes of the brick, Violet sweeps up the glass, the only real danger of anyone getting hurt. The brick was clearly a message, not a threat. The message, Rose imagines, is that people are pissed.

A man around her age, tall and impeccably dressed, approaches Rose. He asks if he can speak with her. She excuses herself from Katie and notes that one side of his mustache is shorter than the other as though his aim was slightly off while shaving that morning. He introduces himself as her mother's attorney.

Despite the recent crisis and the humidity of the day, Bo Rivers' handshake is cool and dry. He has the tan of someone who plays golf daily or spends a great deal of time on a sailboat. His aftershave is expensive and understated—one of the few fragrances in the room that isn't intentionally overdone. Unlike the other men attending the reception, he hasn't removed his suit coat, as if to further prove his inability to sweat, even after a brick is thrown through a nearby window.

"Can you come to my office next Monday, say around one o'clock?" he asks. His accent reeks of old Savannah. "We have some things we need to discuss."

"Next Monday?" Rose's return ticket is booked for tomorrow. Monday extends her stay by three days, and she is ready to be home. "Can't we do this over the telephone?" she asks. It seems a bit old fashioned to do things this way. But if Savannah is anything, it is old fashioned.

Bo Rivers takes one step closer and lowers his voice. "I think you'll want to be there in person."

"What's this about?" Rose asks.

Directness is practiced infrequently in this part of the country, but she'd like to know if it is bad news or good before she extends her stay.

"I don't think this is the time to talk about it," Bo Rivers says, his answer predictable. His glance around the room stops at Edward, who is watching them. Bo Rivers tips his chin upward as if refusing to be intimidated. "So it's settled then, Monday afternoon, one o'clock?" he asks, turning to Rose.

She nods her consent.

"My condolences again for the passing of your lovely mother," Bo Rivers says, making Rose's mother sound much lovelier than she actually was.

Within seconds of his leaving, Katie returns to Rose's side.

"What was that about?" she asks. "You looked so serious."

"Mother's attorney wants to meet with me Monday afternoon."

"Monday? I thought you were leaving tomorrow."

"I was," Rose says. "But he seemed adamant that I attend."

"Do you want me to stay, too?" Katie asks.

Her daughter has always been protective of her, and she isn't sure why. However, she now wishes someone had protected her from all this food she's eaten.

"No, honey. There's no need to stay," Rose says. "You need to get back to work, and so does ..." Rose pauses, unable to think of the name of Katie's latest girlfriend.

"Her name is Angela, Mom, and she's very important to me," Katie says.

"Sorry, honey, it's been a big day," Rose says.

"For us, too." Katie yawns, revealing a silver ball pierced into her tongue.

"You got one of those?" she asks, with a moan.

Katie smiles as if she enjoys shocking her mother. "You're so predictable, Mom."

"And *unpredictable* is better?" Rose says. She thinks again of the brick.

"Don't start," Katie says, giving Rose a playful nudge. "If you're okay, I'll go mingle again," she adds. "Everybody's talking about some book your mother kept and a bunch of secrets. Do you know about it?"

"Unfortunately, I do," Rose says. "The Temples are infamous for collecting secrets of the wealthy here in Savannah. It's how my mother always gets her way. Or 'got' her way, I should say."

"Wow, Mom, your family is fascinating," she says. "I've never been to a funeral where there were protestors, and people threw bricks through windows."

"It's your family, too, sweetheart," Rose says, her smile glib.

"I keep forgetting that," Katie says.

Despite a few minor differences having to do with current cultural trends, Rose prides herself on how well she and Katie get along. They have always been close, and as an only child, Katie seemed to get along better with adults. The closest she's come to a teenage rebellion is with her latest body art and tongue piercing.

Rose glances at the familiar strangers in the room, the ones who couldn't be dissuaded by a brick. It occurs to her why they are here. Is her mother really dead? Before the funeral, she surprised herself with a good cry. In fact, she still feels a bit hungover from the emotion, although she feels better now that she has finally eaten. *Or overeaten,* she thinks.

Regardless, she is grateful to have Katie here. Like Max, Katie helps her stay calm and reminds her of her present, rather than her past. However, there are parts of her past—Queenie, Old Sally, Violet—that she has genuinely missed.

While she hasn't missed the drama, what surprises her most is how much she has missed the land—the tidal pools and tributaries, the meandering marshland, the live oaks, the Spanish moss that graces nearly every tree. She's missed the azaleas, the vibrant green moss that grows in every garden, the people rich with secrets and gossip. Rose has missed people of color most of all. People in all their many shades.

Thomas Wolfe says you can't go home again, but Rose finally feels free to do just that. It is much more than being back in her old room, or back in the house she grew up in. It is like sliding back into her skin and becoming one with the rich, moist low country of Georgia. This landscape is in her soul.

Queenie approaches with a glass of red wine in her hand. Rose is struck again by that feeling of having someone glad to see her. Fortunately, she can return her affection.

"I'm glad your mother wasn't alive to see someone throw a brick through the window," Queenie says. "And to think I was complaining earlier about how dull the event was."

"Hopefully, that's the end of the excitement for the day," Rose says.

"We'll see," Queenie says.

Within seconds a soft chanting can be heard coming from outside. Rose listens carefully to make out the words: *Secrets, no! Book's gotta go! Secrets, no! Book's gotta go!*

"I'll drink to that," Queenie says.

Rose holds up her glass of tonic water and salutes. They clink glasses. Twenty years before, there would have been vodka in her drink. But drinking for Rose was never about celebration. It was about forgetting. And she isn't willing to forget anymore.

After entering the dining room, Violet straightens various serving trays and then picks up empty glasses and used napkins. Rose asks if she can help, but Violet declines her offer. On the way back into the kitchen, Violet stops and glances out toward the street to see the chanters and then shrugs like nothing surprises her anymore.

"By the way, did you turn up the air conditioner?" Rose asks her. "It's freezing in here."

"It's Miss Temple," Violet says, turning to face Rose and Queenie. "She's crashing her own wake."

"That sounds like something Old Sally would say," Rose says. Queenie agrees.

"I take that as a great compliment," Violet says.

"By the way, I smelled rotten eggs earlier," Rose says. "At first, I thought it was Edward, but maybe you're right. Maybe it's Mother."

"Oh my, this is just what Mama was afraid of," Queenie says with a tsk.

"Ignore Miss Temple if you can," Violet says. "That's what I do. Try to ignore the chanting, too."

Rose has tried to ignore her mother for the past twenty-five years, and she's not sure what good it's done. Earlier today, she finally felt free. But it seems her deceased mother isn't exactly cooperating. As if to offer commentary, another current of cold air slides across her arm. She rubs away a new crop of goosebumps.

"Well, I think Iris would be pleased with the reception," Queenie says to Rose. "I followed all your instructions to the letter. Didn't I, Iris?" She glances up as if expecting an answer from the chandelier.

"Violet did an amazing job, too," Rose says.

As they applaud, Violet gives an exaggerated curtsy. Meanwhile, the chanting outside grows louder.

"Do you really think Mother's here?" Rose asks, with a quick glance at the same chandelier. Perhaps her mother is protesting the protesters.

Violet and Queenie nod, and Rose can see a bit of family resemblance between the niece and aunt. Rose doesn't have experience with extended family. The Temple line has dwindled over the years. Her mother was an only child, as was her mother before her. Rose has often thought she was an accident and that her mother would have preferred to have just had Edward. It is obvious Edward would have preferred it, too.

Late afternoon sun breaks through the sheer curtains sending brushstrokes of light into the dining room and hallway. The

Temple house always seems dark to Rose so any outside light breaking through is a welcomed change. Plus, it makes it warmer, given her mother's intent to chill.

"I'd better get back to work," Violet says, balancing dirty dishes. "I don't want to find a note in the morning from you-know-who." She smiles before returning to the kitchen.

"Did Bo Rivers approach you about a meeting on Monday?" Queenie asks Rose.

"He did," Rose says. "I hadn't planned to stay that long. But he made it sound important."

Another blast of frigid air makes them pause.

"That woman was never very subtle," Queenie says and directs a sneer at the chandelier. "It's just like Iris to be the center of attention at her own funeral reception," she continues. "She is already, of course, being that she is the deceased. But probably not in a fully satisfying way." Queenie grins.

"It must be killing her that people are protesting outside," Rose says.

"No pun intended," Queenie says with a laugh.

Meanwhile, the reception has flat-lined. Even the different scents in the room seem to be dying away. The people who are left check their watches as though counting the seconds before they can make a mass exodus after staying the obligatory hour.

"Do you know what this meeting is about on Monday?" Rose asks Queenie.

"Probably the will."

"That's fast," Rose says. "What about probate and all that?"

"Somehow, your mother arranged it. You know how she hates to draw things out."

The chanters repeat in the background: *Secrets, no! Book's gotta go!*

"It should be pretty simple, right?" Rose asks. "I'm sure Edward gets my share of everything. I have no idea why I would be required to be there. I certainly don't look forward to watching him gloat."

"I'm sure your mother had her reasons," Queenie says in a quasi-whisper. "That woman had more secrets than anybody in that cursed book, although I'm sure she never wrote them down. She wouldn't have taken that chance. Of course, I've been known to have a few secrets myself."

Queenie's face looks playful, even devilish. Is the wine getting to her?

"Out with it," Rose says. "Did you put a quart of coleslaw at Mother's ankles? Baked beans at her feet?"

Queenie guffaws, insisting her latest secret isn't even remotely related to fast-food. Heads turn in their direction. Edward, now schmoozing with a councilman, narrows his eyes in disapproval at Rose and Queenie, who, it turns out, are dangerously close to enjoying themselves, despite the rabble-rousing outside.

"It seems we've broken the cardinal rule of white folks at a funeral reception. No laughter allowed," Queenie says to Rose. "Darker folks don't mind a good laugh, no matter what the occasion."

Before now, Rose has never heard her speak about differences in race. She has never thought of her as black or white. In her mind, Queenie transcends color. Yet it appears she hasn't felt this transcendence. Rose wonders if the people outside are white or black. Does it even matter?

Queenie pulls Rose into a corner of the dining room as if wanting privacy. "Would you like to know one of your mother's secrets?"

Secrets, no! the crowd answers.

"Absolutely," Rose says, ignoring the voices outside. She nibbles on some fruit. All these secrets are making her hungry again. Not to mention the resident ghosts in attendance and not being able to drink.

Queenie leans in and lowers her voice. "Did you meet Spud Grainger earlier today?"

"I didn't officially meet him," Rose says. "But isn't he the butcher? The one who went on and on about exotic meats?"

"Uh, huh," Queenie says. She cuts her eyes from door to door.

"What does Mother's secret have to do with a butcher at the Piggly Wiggly?" Rose asks, putting a cocktail shrimp in her mouth.

"After your daddy died, Spud Grainger had an affair with her," Queenie says. "From what I hear, it was quite passionate."

The shrimp shoots across the room and lands in a large ficus plant. Guests from the back of the foyer turn to look as if to determine the credibility of the crustacean UFO.

"I thought you'd like that one," Queenie says with a smile.

Rose asks in a whisper, "Really?"

"Your mother told me one night when she had a little too much sherry," Queenie says. "You know how she gets on holy days."

Queenie leans over the buffet table and fills a clean plate with crab legs. The chanting fades. It is raining again. While Rose attempts to process this latest piece of news, Queenie cracks one of the spindly legs and sucks the white meat from inside with the deftness of an orthopedic surgeon.

"Mother had an affair with the butcher at Piggly Wiggly?" Rose asks.

Passion is not something Rose has ever associated with her mother. It is hard to imagine her being intimate with her father, much less the butcher at the Piggly Wiggly.

"This from a woman who could make Antarctica seem warm in comparison," Rose says.

"Tell me about it," Queenie says. With a fingernail, she fishes out a piece of crab meat from one of the legs and then sucks her nail. She savors the crab like a delicious secret.

For the first time, it is Rose who feels like chanting, *Secrets, no!* This day has already been too much, but her curiosity wants more.

"How long did it last?" Rose asks.

"Six months," Queenie says.

"Are you kidding me?" Rose says. "Next you'll tell me that Mother wasn't really a member of the Daughters of the Confederacy and that our family fought for the Union."

"Now that really would be a scandal," Queenie says. "But the confederacy was definitely supported by many, if not all, of the Temples, as the family on my mother's side can unfortunately attest." She cracks another crab leg as if to add an exclamation point to her words.

Rose sometimes forgets that Queenie has lived both sides of the Temple story, and in fact is from both sides.

Violet enters the dining room again, refreshing different plates of food and then returns to the kitchen with Queenie's discarded crab legs.

"Violet's staying on, right?" Rose asks Queenie.

"Unless she decides she can't take the boredom of a house without your mother's drama," Queenie says. "Of course, if your mother decides to haunt the place, it may be like she never left."

Queenie excuses herself and goes into the kitchen, and the reception dwindles to a small collection of her mother's oldest acquaintances, most of whom treat Rose with a certain amount of caution. What story has her mother told the old guard as to why Rose hasn't been around for the last twenty-five years? When it comes to her mother, a storyline that involves mental illness or prison can't be ruled out.

Most of her life, Rose has been cast in the role of the ungrateful daughter—the child born with a silver spoon in her mouth who spit it out just to spite her generous, benevolent mother. Very few people, other than Queenie and Old Sally, know the truth behind the disconnection.

Rose looks around for Edward, who is nowhere in sight. If he isn't still snooping around, he has left without saying goodbye, which is okay with Rose. For all she knows, Edward has probably perpetuated these lies and may have renewed his campaign to discredit her at this very reception. Or maybe he has joined the protestors. *Secrets, no!* Lately, she has had enough contact with her brother to last another decade or two, perhaps even a lifetime.

BY LATE AFTERNOON, the last of the mourners exit. The crowd outside finally disperses, too, leaving the five women alone in the dining room. Queenie, Rose, Katie, Angela, and Violet finish up the last of the food. Rose takes off her shoes, her feet much more accustomed to boots these days than heels. She releases a long sigh. Her mother's funeral is complete.

Katie puts her head on Angela's shoulder and looks so much like Max, at that moment, it makes Rose miss him even more than she already does.

"Angie and I have a flight back to Chicago in three hours," Katie says to Rose. "Are you sure you don't want me to stay?"

"I'm sure," Rose says. "I'll drive you to the airport, so you don't have to take a cab."

"Where are you staying?" Katie asks.

"Here, of course."

"You mean you're staying here at the house?" Angela asks.

Katie and Angela exchange concerned looks.

"Why wouldn't I?" Rose says, thinking Angela's question a bit odd. Although truth-be-told, Angela is a bit odd, too.

"Mom, this house is so, like, haunted," Katie says. "Earlier, when I was standing in the hallway, I kept getting these blasts of cold air that had nothing to do with the air conditioner vents. I checked."

"And when I was in the garden," Angela says, "someone put a hand on my shoulder. But when I turned around, nobody was there."

Rose looks at Queenie who shrugs as if deferring the secret-telling to Rose.

"I guess it's time for you to learn one of the many Temple eccentricities," Rose says to Katie. "It seems your grandmother made an appearance earlier. But there's nothing to be alarmed about. This is what Temples do. They haunt."

After two decades of watching her offspring, the look on Katie's face is one Rose hasn't seen before—a cross between horror and exhilaration. Angela appears a bit unnerved, as well, and glances at her watch as though ready to make an exit.

"It wouldn't be the first reception the spirit Temples have attended," Queenie tells them. "But they're harmless. Honest."

Is Queenie crossing her fingers behind her back with that promise? Rose wonders.

"Was it that way when you were growing up, Mom?" Katie asks.

"It's Savannah, honey. Every house has its ghosts."

"I don't understand how you can be so nonchalant," Katie says. The look on her face is: *who is this woman and where have you taken my mother?*

"This kind of thing happened my entire childhood," Rose says. "Every family in Savannah has crazy uncles and cousins or a few ghosts."

"And its secrets," Queenie interjects.

"And definitely its secrets," Rose says. The danger lies in both worlds and seems to have only just begun.

CHAPTER EIGHTEEN

Violet

What is Miss Temple up to? Violet wonders. She searches through the clothes in her bedroom closet to find something to wear for the meeting downtown later that afternoon. Miss Temple's lawyer sought her out after the funeral and insisted that she attend a meeting in his office the following Monday. All week she has wondered why.

"I thought you'd left already," Jack says. He carries his morning coffee into the bedroom and sits on the bed.

"I'm the last person I thought would be invited to the reading of Miss Temple's will," Violet says. "Unless she wants to embarrass me in front of a bunch of rich, white people and tell me I'm out of a job."

She pulls three dresses from her closet that are possibilities and holds each in front of her as she stands in front of the full-length mirror on the back of the closet door.

"You worry too much, sweetheart," Jack says. "Who knows, something good could come out of it."

"Must you always be so optimistic," she says, realizing how crazy this sounds. "We need this income, Jack. Your teaching job doesn't bring in that much money, and the girls will be going to college soon. It's never a good time to lose one of our incomes, but especially right now."

"Take a breath, Vi. We'll figure it out."

Violet knows he's right, but this meeting has her on edge. To her surprise, however, her shoulder hasn't warned her of anything horrible about to happen. She feels perfectly fine.

"If I do lose my job, I can probably find something else. But seriously, Jack, how much call is there for someone who specializes in how to cook rattlesnake, buffalo, and kangaroo? Not to mention the other wild things that have come through my kitchen over the years." She laughs a short laugh and Jack smiles.

"Maybe it's time to follow that dream of yours," he says. "I can get a second job or a third one if I have to. Then you can open your tea shop."

She pauses, thinking how much she loves this man before her fear clicks in again.

"Oh, Jack, people like us don't get to follow our dreams. We're too busy taking care of people who can afford to have them."

This is gloomy, even for her. Violet needs to get this meeting over with so she can think straight again. She holds up two dresses, and he points to one. She slides it on before stepping into her low heels.

"You look beautiful," he says.

"At least I don't have to wear my uniform today," she says.

"You look beautiful, even in that."

She shakes her head, thinking he should be more worried. Although it seems she carries enough worry for both of them.

· · ·

LATER THAT MORNING when Violet arrives at the Temple house, Queenie is already downstairs making coffee. Everyone assumes the house and property will revert to Queenie, who has basically taken care of Miss Temple for almost 40 years.

Not a task for the faint of heart, Violet thinks.

Even Violet has heard Miss Temple's promise, telling Queenie the different things that need to be done to keep the Temple mansion in pristine shape.

Savannah owes Queenie a lot. If not for her, Miss Temple might have aimed all that spite at other people.

Above all else, Miss Temple valued loyalty, and Queenie has been more than loyal. Not only to the Temples but to Violet, too. After Violet lost her mother so young, Queenie always found time for her. Not only is she Violet's aunt, but a friend.

"Why are you so dressed up?" Queenie asks.

"The meeting later," Violet says.

Queenie gives a slow nod. She seems distracted, but Violet can't quite put a finger on why. Sometimes she can read live people, as well as dead ones, but this isn't one of those times.

"I lost sleep worrying about it," Violet says.

"Rose must have, too," Queenie says. "I heard her up early this morning."

Violet straightens her linen summer dress bought ten years before when Jack received the Teacher of the Year award at the community college. It pleases her that she can still fit into it, but the heels feel ridiculous. She excuses herself and slips them off in the laundry room before putting on a pair of her work shoes.

Not the best look, she thinks, but at least she'll be able to still walk by the end of the day.

After returning to the kitchen, she opens the fridge to look for something to make for dinner. With Miss Temple gone, she's relaxed her strict menu planning and now takes a more spontaneous approach.

"Don't be surprised if Iris drops a bombshell today," Queenie says. "Mama called this morning and predicted it."

"Then I don't doubt it's true," Violet says. She pulls two chicken breasts from the freezer to thaw.

"Coffee's ready." Queenie pours herself a cup as Violet makes some English Breakfast tea.

Queenie refuses to be waited on, and it was only after Violet's insistence that Queenie allowed her to prepare her evening meal. They trade sweetener and then half-and-half before sitting at the kitchen table. For decades now they've sat at this same table together long before Violet even began drinking tea. She tilts her head to check in on the psychic energy in the house. The haunting has calmed over the last few days, the ghosts abandoning their usual patterns. Since her death, Miss Temple's energy has come and gone like power surges flickering the lights during a storm.

Thankfully, the protestors haven't returned. Queenie doesn't know if she could take another day of that chant.

"I've been thinking about Iris all morning," Queenie says. "It's strange to not be bossed around anymore. It's like having a toothache for thirty-five years that suddenly disappears."

"You were kind to put up with her for so many years," Violet says.

"I'm no saint," Queenie says. "I had good reasons for sticking around."

"Like what?" Violet asks, her curiosity genuine. Her aunt has been acting strange lately. The more secrets that get released, the more secretive she becomes.

Queenie takes a gulp of hot coffee and then runs to sputter it into the sink.

"Are you okay?" Violet asks.

Queenie wipes coffee from her blouse that blends in with the colorful jungle pattern. "Do you want eggs this morning?" Queenie blows her coffee with gusto now, like she's trying to blow off Violet's question.

"Wait a minute. What just happened?" Violet says. "It's not like you to avoid a subject."

"I guess I'm worried about what Mama said. She's usually right with her predictions."

Violet decides to drop it for now as Queenie takes eggs from the fridge and breaks several into a bowl. A hand on her hip, Queenie scrambles the eggs in the skillet. Why won't she answer such a simple question?

"It's just so quiet without the old gal," Queenie begins again as if they were talking about Miss Temple. "By the way, I'm wearing *scented* deodorant today," she says with a wink.

Violet laughs and then looks around the kitchen for things she should be doing. Until now, she didn't realize how all-consuming taking care of Miss Temple was. For years Violet had a set routine. First thing in the mornings, after she arrived at work, she read the critique from the day before and made adjustments to the day's meals. Between cooking, she cleaned the house, a never-ending process.

"I don't think any of our neighbors will miss her," Violet says. "I've gotten an earful from every housekeeper in Savannah. None of their employers liked Miss Temple, though most everybody feared her."

"Nobody escaped those letters of hers," Queenie says. "If she disapproved of anything you did, she wrote whoever she thought was your superior a letter, whether it was the Governor, the President of the United States or the Pope. Iris took being a tattle-tale to an international level."

Queenie delivers the scrambled eggs to the table.

"Did you get the newspaper this morning?" Queenie asks. "It wasn't there when I looked."

"The delivery boy seems to have missed us," Violet says. "Either that or somebody took it."

"Are things still disappearing off the front porch?" Queenie looks concerned.

"Three potted plants yesterday," Violet says, "but they left two very full doggy poop bags. Their dogs must be Dalmatians."

Queenie grins. "Is this ever going to stop?" she asks, turning serious again.

"I hope so," Violet says. "The whole neighborhood seems effected. I've heard from more than one housekeeper on the block that arguments have increased since the newspaper started running those secrets."

The door opens, and Rose comes in from a long walk. She looks wilted, like an azalea blossom cut from the main bush and left to languish in the heat.

"An old lady in a purple bathrobe just called me a traitor," Rose says, her face flushed.

"That's nothing," Queenie says, "I've been called the a-word, the b-word, and the c-word, all in one sentence."

"Wow, that's creative," Rose says.

"I guess we're all in this together," Violet says. "In fact, this may be the perfect time to do the sea gypsy's secret handshake."

Without hesitation, the three women gather in the center of the kitchen and begin the handshake: two claps, three arm rolls, a hip bump, and then ending with arms akimbo while shaking their heads up and down. They laugh.

"Not bad after thirty years," Rose says.

"Not good either," Violet says, but the silliness is what she needs on such a serious day.

"Come to think of it, there isn't even a handshake as part of it," Queenie says. "I never noticed that before."

"I don't know how I would have survived growing up without you girls," Rose says.

"Me, too," Violet says. "Even without parents around, I felt like I had a family."

"I need Mother to show up with one of those cool blasts of air." Rose fans herself.

"Be careful what you ask for." Queenie smiles.

"Miss Temple hasn't made an appearance since the reception," Violet says. "I think she's saving up for something big."

They agree that this can't be good.

THAT AFTERNOON, Violet and Queenie ride together to Bo Rivers' law office in downtown Savannah. Violet has never been in this building before. With equal amounts of white marble and glass, it is one of those places built by rich white people to impress other rich white people. On the ground floor, they get into the elevator, the doors close, and they take a slow ride to the third floor. A secretary lets them wait in Attorney Rivers' office. They are the first to arrive.

Portraits of old white men adorn the walls in dark wooden frames that match the furniture.

"Just once I'd like to see black men and women on the walls," Violet whispers to Queenie, even though nobody else is in the room. But it is Savannah, after all, and despite its problems, she loves this city.

"I know what you mean about the white faces," Queenie says. "Sometimes I have fantasies about asking Rose to do my portrait so I can put it in the foyer of the mansion. Then my smiling face will greet everyone who enters."

"You should do that," Violet says, with a smile.

"I would, but I'm afraid Iris might do more than roll over in her grave. She might send me to mine."

Violet and Queenie sit together on a large leather sofa in front of an entire wall covered with floor to ceiling bookcases holding law books.

"Those must be hell to dust," Violet whispers again.

Queenie agrees and picks up the newspaper on the coffee table to read since theirs never arrived.

Being in Bo Rivers' office is like stepping into that walk-in cooler Queenie talked about earlier. Violet crosses her arms over her chest to hide her body's reaction to the cold. She should have known better than to dress for summer. Air conditioners in Savannah could keep an igloo from melting. The thermostat at the Temple house was guarded religiously by Miss Temple, who kept it set at 76 degrees. But this office must be set in the low 60s. Violet half expects to see her frosty breath in front of her.

Despite the frigid temperature, Violet breaks into a sweat. She doesn't want to be here. "If I'm going to be fired, I wish someone would just tell me," she whispers again. "Why make such a big production out of it?"

"You're not going to get fired," Queenie whispers back. "Iris had a wicked mean streak, but she wasn't that horrible."

Queenie turns to the classifieds and within seconds, lets out a muffled scream. "Oh, my living God." She points to the newspaper as Violet reads:

Help Wanted: People of Color,
Housekeeper willing to Slave all day
and Sleep with the Master of the House.
Call Iris Temple: 912-944-0455

"Who the hell is doing this?" Queenie says.

Violet assures her that she doesn't know, but it doesn't help that the ad is for a housekeeper. Perhaps whoever is planting these secrets knows her job is in jeopardy. Or maybe she's reading too much into it. She's been known to do that, too.

It's now weeks since the first secret was released, and they are still clueless as to who is behind it. Whoever is doing this, not only has access to the *Book of Secrets* but to the newspaper, too. Otherwise, why would they ever agree to run them? Although, she imagines those secrets have sold more than a few papers.

The door opens, and Spud enters. They exchange looks of surprise. He leans over and hugs Violet and then shakes Queenie's hand. Oddly, his outfit matches hers. Queenie's jungle motif goes with his white suit that looks like it might be a leftover from the 80s, and his shirt is lime green. They look like they are both on a safari and want to blend in with the jungle. Spud stands against the wall and except for the periodic straightening of his purple bow tie, looks about as uncomfortable as Violet feels. She has never seen him this nervous.

Queenie shoves the newspaper under a stack of *Georgia Now* magazines like the will is all she can deal with for now. Violet feels the same. This time last year, her life was totally predictable, and more than a little boring. Now, she can't imagine what might happen next.

"Where in the world does he get all those ties?" Queenie whispers to Violet. "Do they even make those things anymore?"

"They must," Violet says, thinking how Queenie and Spud are much more alike than they are different in their preference for bold colors.

"Does anyone know why we're here?" Spud asks, his voice full amid their whispers.

"Evidently for the reading of the will," Queenie says.

"Then why am I required to be here?" Spud straightens his tie, looking perplexed now, as well as uncomfortable.

The question goes unanswered. Silence fills the room while the discomfort settles.

What if her grandmother is right about Miss Temple dropping a bombshell? If so, they are all standing at ground zero.

Rose enters, says her hellos, and sits in a leather chair to the left of the desk. Since she was running late, she told them to go ahead and drove herself. Her short, thick hair still looks wet from her shower. She shakes Spud's hand and introduces herself before silence settles in again. She gives Queenie and Violet a wink as if she is familiar with their secret code.

Minutes later, the door opens again, and Edward Temple steps inside.

"Creep alert," Queenie whispers to Violet.

Violet smiles. "Let me guess. You got that from Tia and Leisha?"

Queenie nods. Violet loves the effort Queenie makes with her daughters. Not that many great aunts would be so doting.

Edward eyes the collection of people, aiming his intense gaze for several seconds on Rose as if surprised she's there. He takes a seat close to the lawyer's desk. Is it possible that the room got even colder with Edward here? Violet's teeth begin to chatter, and she clenches her jaw to stop them. She doesn't want Edward to mistake her coldness for fear. But even Edward seems agitated. Perhaps the latest secret has him on edge, too. Meanwhile, the Temple drama seems far from over.

In a trait that reminds Violet of his mother, Edward sits perfectly straight. After he crosses his legs, he runs two manicured fingernails along the crease of his pants as though wanting to perfect the perfect line. There are few people Violet dislikes, but Edward Temple tops her list.

Seconds later, the lawyer enters the room, papers stacked in hand. His smile looks fake, and he gives a nod to Edward, the other rich white guy in the room. Violet's only dealings with Bo Rivers were answering the door on the two occasions when he joined his father, who was calling on Miss Temple. He always wanted his coffee black and made comments about watching his waistline. He flirted with Violet, too. But not enough that she could actually call him on it. She imagines his preference for women to be younger and blonder, like the secretary who showed them into the office.

"Please make yourselves comfortable." Bo Rivers' accent has the smoothness of one of Violet's meringues that always get compliments.

Yet comfort is the last thing Violet feels. Not only is she in danger of freezing to death, but other than Queenie, she is in a room full of people much lighter-skinned than her. Of course, she is used to this kind of thing by now, but somehow being in a lawyer's office makes being outnumbered more unnerving.

Every chair in the elaborate office is made of leather, and whenever somebody moves, the leather makes a raspberry sound, as if the cows themselves are getting the last laugh. If Violet wasn't so cold, she might find this funny. Unfortunately, as soon as she sat down, her bare legs adhered to the leather, anchored in place by a healthy crop of goosebumps, so she couldn't make a raspberry sound if she tried.

"Someone may have to pry me off of this sofa at the end of the meeting," she whispers to Queenie, who assures her that she will help.

Seconds later, Miss Temple's prickly presence enters the room, as if rushing in late for the meeting. Her chaotic energy hovers around Spud and has a particular pitch to it, almost like a minor musical chord. But instead of a sound, it registers on a feeling level in Violet's chest.

Sometimes Violet wishes she could return this "gift," as her grandmother often calls it. It's not like she asked for it. One day it was just there—and without a return receipt.

While waiting for the lawyer to begin, she remembers the day the weird vibrations started. She must have been six and Rose around ten. It was winter, and they were playing in the attic because all of Rose's old toys were stored there. An old white man with solid white hair appeared. Rose couldn't see him, which was strange given Rose always saw her great-grandfather out by the oak tree. But maybe that was because a tiny piece of Rose's finger was buried out under that tree.

Violet looks at Rose now, and she can see the girl Rose used to be. She wonders if Rose sees her the same way.

The ghost in the attic that day scared Violet because he didn't go about his business like most ghosts do. He kept asking her questions. Not every spirit is harmless, yet they do share some common traits. Most ghosts do the same things over and over again, like they are locked into a pattern. They walk the entire length of a hallway before disappearing. They rattle a few glasses as if pouring themselves a drink. They move through the same rooms at the same time of day. Their routine doesn't vary. But the guy in the attic didn't have a pattern. To this day, she avoids going up there.

What's unusual with Miss Temple's ghost is that she isn't locked into staying at the house. She's here this very minute. Violet scans the room, but her former employer refuses to be pinned down. She is everywhere and nowhere at once.

Grandmother always told her that the dead don't move on if they have something incomplete in their lives. If this incompleteness has nothing to do with you, you just wish them well and tell them to move on along. After Miss Temple's death, Violet has tried to move her along, but she refuses to go anywhere.

The lawyer stands behind the large mahogany desk and opens a leather-encased folder. After taking out several sheets of paper, he pauses. Is he trying to build the suspense? He clears his throat but doesn't appear the least bit nervous. If anything, he comes across as overconfident. It occurs to Violet that they are in his territory and have to play by his rules. It is a game he appears to relish.

"As you all know, you are here at the request of Iris Temple, who specifically asked that the five of you be brought together as the will is read. It should be noted that the will was updated June 4th of this year."

"Isn't that the day she had the stroke?" Edward asks.

"Yes, it is," Bo Rivers says. "But I assure you, Edward, the updated will is perfectly legal. There's no question that your mother was of sound mind when I saw her that afternoon."

The two men exchange a look that Violet has trouble reading. Are they friends or enemies?

The lawyer puts on a pair of dark-framed reading glasses that look like they'd be sold at a specialty shop that carries lawyer accessories. He begins to read the document. Most of it is legal jargon. Violet glances at Queenie, who winks at her and gives a slight roll of the eyes that Violet translates to mean, *Don't worry*.

While Edward studies her, Rose crosses her legs and leans back in the chair, as if determined to relax. Growing up, Violet would have given anything to have a brother or sister, even a half-sister, like Queenie had Miss Temple. But having Edward as a sibling would be worse than not having one at all.

Spud straightens his bow tie again. Grief hangs around the corners of his eyes. He is the only one in the room who seems to remember why they are all here. Violet's mind wanders. Now that Miss Temple is dead, she hopes Spud will meet someone new. He deserves to be happy.

Even though Violet listens to every word, she understands only half.

Rich people make things so complicated, she thinks, *especially when it comes to their money.*

There is a trust for this, a trust for that. Trusts rest on top of trusts, housed in multiple banking institutions, along with assets of corporations and land contracts dating back two hundred years. In contrast, she and Jack have one checking account, and a savings account opened for the girls' college fund that they rob for household emergencies. They don't even have credit cards, just a debit card. Life is a struggle sometimes, but the payoff is a simple life.

As he reads the document, the lawyer's voice falls into a steady rhythm like a washing machine on the wash cycle. Already tired, Violet daydreams about the chores left to do at the Temple house, as well as the ones to do at home. The next time she looks at her watch, minutes have passed in what feels like seconds. Opening her eyes wider, she forces herself to pay attention. If her position is about to be terminated, she doesn't want to be caught unaware.

Miss Temple's energy spins across the room and distracts

Violet from what is being said. Is her former employer trying to tell her something? Maybe she's worked up over the latest secret, although it never occurred to Violet that ghosts might read the newspaper. But perhaps they read the vibes of people who read the paper.

I wish Grandmother were here, she thinks. Her skills are better than Violet's when it comes to dead folks.

Meanwhile, everyone else in the room appears oblivious as Miss Temple's power grows. The vibration makes Violet's head hurt like all the air is being sucked out of the room. Then her shoulder begins to ache for the first time that day. Whatever has Miss Temple furious is also threatening to Violet. A blast of cold air confirms that whatever game Miss Temple is playing is about to begin.

CHAPTER NINETEEN

Queenie

Queenie glances around the office furnished with dark antiques and law books and then takes a quick stab at her hair, wishing she'd worn one of her hats. *If for no other reason than to add some color to this dreary room,* she tells herself. The office space is enveloped in beige, deep browns, and burgundy. The color of wealth.

Queenie chews on a fingernail and thinks about the latest secret. Is it someone in this room who is releasing them? No, she decides, this would make no sense. It has to be someone who wants to see the Temple status in the community fall. That first day that an ad appeared, she and Iris had gone straight to the bank. According to Iris, the book was right where it should be and hadn't been moved.

As Bo Rivers reads Iris's will, Queenie grasps for an understanding of the document. She has devoured enough courtroom dramas in books and on television that the lingo isn't wholly foreign to her. But still, it seems that some of the words are obscure on purpose, to sneak things by.

Last fall, Bo Rivers came to the house to visit Iris with his father, Rutledge Rivers, who was so out of it at the time that Queenie wondered if dementia had set in. Queenie, of course, was never included in any of their meetings. As Edward Temple, III's *bastard* daughter, she was treated with indifference by Rutledge Rivers, who she heard died last winter. At the time, she had to resist saying, *Good Riddance.*

Iris and Rutledge were Catholic school chums, and she confided in him quite a lot. Could he have had access to the *Book of Secrets*? If so, what would he gain from it? More lawsuit battles for Iris? With her being his most prominent client, perhaps he would have a motive for releasing them, but how would he have gotten to that ledger in the first place? Queenie hates that she hasn't been able to solve this mystery.

Secrets aside, Queenie took it as a good sign that after Bo Rivers initially entered the room, he shook her hand first. Perhaps he realizes that when the Temple house reverts to her, they will continue to have dealings together. Or maybe she was simply sitting closest to his desk.

As controlling as Iris could be, for the last decade she has turned most house-related things over to Queenie and always talked of when the house would be left to her. Hopefully, Iris filled Edward in on her plans, too. Whenever Iris spoke of the future, she referred to her eventual demise as a kind of extended vacation. Never actually using the word death.

When I go away, she would say, *you need to do* this and that.

Well, you've gone away now, haven't you Iris? Queenie thinks. *Although maybe you haven't.*

She glances around the room. Violet is shivering, and she wishes she had a sweater to give her.

Meanwhile, Edward taps a finger against the arm of the chair as if both irritated and inconvenienced. However, Queenie knows nothing short of a total apocalypse would keep him from this meeting. Edward is the oldest son—the male heir—here to collect his legacy.

Even though Queenie wouldn't dream of threatening Edward's inheritance, the house should be hers. Not just because of Iris's promise all these years but because Queenie has taken care of the mansion like it was her own for decades now. No small feat, given how obstinate Iris was about every little detail.

Her mother's warning from earlier that day causes Queenie to sit straighter, as well as feel a little queasy. If anyone knows what Iris Temple is capable of, it is her mother.

But if anyone knows how to hit curveballs thrown by Iris, it's me, she thinks. "Bring it on, Iris," she says under her breath.

While the Temples have their share of eccentricities—the males with their penchant for bedding the servants and the females with their controlling yet delicate constitutions—Rose has somehow escaped that fate, as well as Queenie. As for not being a "true Temple," as Iris reminded her daily, she responds with a hearty *halleluiah* that she isn't. It is her mother's DNA, after all, that keeps her sane.

Queenie focuses when Bo Rivers reads a clause stipulating that anyone contesting the will loses all rights to any of the monies. He glances at Edward when he reads that part. It is just like Iris to not want any talking back, even in death.

"This could get interesting before it's over," Queenie whispers to Violet, who nods her agreement, her arms folded across her chest. She hears a chattering and leans closer. "Is that your teeth?"

Violet nods again.

When it comes to the bequeathing part of the document, her name is read first: Ivy Temple. She hasn't heard her real name in so long it sounds unfamiliar to her. Remembering her mother's warning, Queenie braces herself for Hurricane Iris.

"Ivy Temple will receive a stipend of $20,000 a year for the remainder of her natural life," Bo Rivers reads.

"Say what?" Queenie says. Rose and Violet gasp. All Iris has done is extend her allowance.

Edward Temple laughs. "You were expecting more?"

Queenie looks at Edward, thinking: *You are damn lucky I don't have one of Mama's spells at my disposal*. Then she wonders how much damage she could do if she sat on him. At the very least, it might mess up his crease.

She turns her attention to her present dilemma. In the twenty seconds it took to read the part of the document that pertains to Queenie, her world has shifted into something unknown.

"Mama was certainly right about this one," she says under her breath.

Violet looks concerned.

Never mind that there is no mention of the house or other properties or any of the Temple millions hidden away in stocks and bonds. This news sticks in Queenie's throat like a wedged chicken bone. She coughs to dislodge it. Iris not only gets the last word, but she also has her revenge. Queenie has been put in her place from the grave.

A hand touches her shoulder. Queenie jumps, thinking it is just like Iris to take a moment to literally rub it in. But it is only Spud Grainger.

"Miss Queenie, are you all right?" he asks.

"I've been better, Mr. Grainger," she says, "but thank you for asking."

Queenie and Spud have never talked that much, even though they often find themselves in the same room. For different reasons, they were both bonded to Iris, and his reason was undoubtedly the more genuine one. Iris was a difficult woman and not easy to love, but Queenie had grown accustomed to her lifestyle. She is the first in her family to not scrub floors, dust antiques, and make endless meals for the Temples.

Iris never had any intention of leaving me the house, she thinks, looking up at the light fixture. It was all just an act to keep me loyal. Her face grows hot with this awareness. Queenie is not easily duped. But duped, she has been.

While Violet and Rose express their bewilderment at Queenie's meager inheritance, Edward's eyes sparkle as if her defeat means he is one step closer to his divine destiny. Her mind scrambles to keep up with what just happened. For the first time in thirty-five years Queenie worries about where she will live. And who will the Temple house go to? Edward?

Over my dead body, Queenie decides. Living with Edward isn't even a remote possibility. Not that he would ever suggest it. For all she knows, he will probably evict her later this afternoon, and where will she go then?

Even though Queenie has spent the last three decades of her life doting on Iris, Savannah's matriarch has her revenge. Her guilt over the casket prank disappears. She wishes now she had soaked Iris's casket in chicken grease and thrown in a match. Their acts of retaliation hold no comparison. The last word is given to Iris.

Bo Rivers reads Rose's name next, and Rose crosses her legs, the leather chair responding with a sound that Queenie thought only Iris could make.

"Rose Temple will be given a one-time amount of two thousand dollars," Bo Rivers says.

Edward laughs and claps his hands like a child opening a delightful gift at Christmas. To be given such a small amount is more insulting than being totally written out of the will. In an instant, Queenie forgets her own distress and turns her attention to Rose, who has become as white as one of the monogrammed Temple sheets.

Bo Rivers holds out a hand as if a school-crossing guard at a dangerous intersection. "Wait. There's more," he says. "The will stipulates that if Rose moves back to Savannah to live, that amount will increase to twenty million dollars. However, if at any time she moves away from Savannah, the money will go to the Iris Temple wing of the Daughters of the Confederacy building."

More gasps and murmurs fill the room. The vein on Edward's forehead bulges like an alien creature might burst through his skin. They are all on a roller coaster ride that Iris has designed. Queenie can almost hear the *click, click, click* of the metal car as they ascend the next steep climb. Meanwhile, Rose's face turns from ashen to red. A tear rolls down her cheek. Queenie reaches into her purse to get Rose a tissue and hands it to her.

"I'm so sorry, sweetheart," Queenie says to her.

Conflicted feelings are written all over Rose's face. It is Iris's final manipulation. How can Iris expect Rose and Max to move to the east coast? Their whole life is out West.

As if awakening from his stupor, Edward says to Bo Rivers: "Wait a minute, that can't be right. Rose was written out of the will years ago."

"In the latest revisions, she was written back in," Bo Rivers says.

"Mother was very troubled at the end," Edward says. "Those damn secrets getting out made her insane. Plus, I think my sister may have manipulated her. She's always been after the Temple money."

Bo raps on his desk as if to call order to the room. "Edward, this isn't the time or place—"

A gust of frigid air sweeps through the office, a current so strong that papers flutter on Bo River's desk.

"Did y'all feel that?" he asks, turning to see if one of his permanently closed windows is open.

"Iris is weighing in," Violet says matter of fact, as though ghosts attending the reading of their wills is commonplace.

Bo Rivers' gaze darts around the room.

Is he looking for his *dead* client?

"We need to finish this up," he says. Bo continues to read, now a little faster. The name, Henry Grainger, is read next.

Henry must be Spud Grainger's legal name, Queenie thinks. She finds herself relieved that his parents didn't intentionally name him after a root vegetable. Queenie grips the chair arm to prepare herself for the next surprise.

"Henry Grainger will inherit three beachfront properties on Hilton Head Island," Bo Rivers says.

From the shock registering on Edward's face, this real estate must be worth millions. Queenie covers her smile. *What a hoot,* she thinks. Iris has left one of the Temple jewels to a jazz musician turned butcher. At the same time, Edward looks like he might take a cleaver to him.

"For God's sake, that can't possibly be right," Edward insists. "He's nobody."

Even Bo Rivers looks offended. "I assure you, Edward, your mother was quite explicit in her wishes," he says.

Meanwhile, Spud Grainger has a hand across his heart like he might recite the Pledge of Allegiance to Iris Temple. Seconds pass as his hand moves from his heart to his tie as if this single action might somehow help him pull himself together. He clears his throat.

"I think there's been some kind of mistake," Spud says.

"No mistake, Mister Grainger." Bo Rivers thumbs through the rest of the will and looks at his watch as if needing happy hour to start earlier today.

The vein on Edward's forehead appears to be throbbing now. If he strokes out, Queenie knows how to administer CPR like she did with his mother. She cringes at the thought of giving Edward mouth-to-mouth.

"Mother wasn't of sound mind," Edward says. "She had trouble with her health for years. Hell, everybody can attest that she smelled like a sewage plant."

A thin layer of sweat aligns itself above Edward's top lip as he twists the ring on his finger.

"This will is airtight, Edward," Bo Rivers says. "Your mother didn't leave any wiggle-room. Besides, everyone in this office can attest that Iris Temple would never do anything she didn't want to do."

"But what I'm saying is that Mother wasn't well," Edward says to Bo. "For all we know, she was releasing those secrets herself."

"No chance," Queenie says. "You weren't with her the first time she saw them. Iris wasn't that good of an actor."

"Why else would she give millions in property to a damn butcher?" Edward asks. He turns his glare to Queenie and then back at Bo. "She was manipulated, Bo, and for all I know, you may have been in on it."

They meet each other's gaze. "Careful, Edward," Bo says as if to remind him whose turf they're on.

Their exchange reminds Queenie of a game of H-O-R-S-E in basketball, where each player tries to make a shot from the same location. Except with Edward playing, a better name for the game might be J-A-C-K-A-S-S.

Even though everyone in the room appears visibly shaken, Bo Rivers is intent on finishing the reading of the will. Edward's name is read next. He repositions himself in his chair like his coronation requires proper posture. He takes a deep breath, and the vein relaxes on his forehead.

Queenie anticipates that Edward will receive the Temple mansion. In which case, she might have to move in with her mother at the beach tonight, considering what $20,000 a year buys these days.

But instead, Bo Rivers reveals that Edward will inherit a collection of real estate properties in Atlanta.

"Wait a minute," Edward says, his look disbelieving. "Those are junk properties. They aren't worth anything."

"Sorry, Edward," Bo Rivers says, in a tone that reveals he isn't sorry at all.

But what about the house? Queenie wonders. Maybe she gave up too soon.

Edward's face is an unnatural shade of red. She waits for his head to explode. Instead, he folds his arms tightly against his chest and looks like he did as a little boy whenever he didn't get his way, which wasn't very often.

Except for Violet—who appears to have slipped into hypothermia—they all wait to hear who gets the central jewel in the multi-jeweled Temple crown.

The reading continues. Large dollar amounts pass to several different charities, the Daughters of the Confederacy and the Junior League being the biggest winners in that category. Then Bo Rivers announces the last item of business, the Temple mansion.

Queenie leans back as Edward leans forward. The only thing missing is a drum roll as the winner is announced.

"The historic Temple house in downtown Savannah, Georgia," Bo begins, "is to be left in its entirety to Violet Stevens."

The news hits Queenie like a cymbal crash at the end of the drum roll. She does what comes naturally and giggles.

Everyone turns to look at Violet. "What did I miss?" Violet asks as if shaken from a daydream.

Bo Rivers rereads the news for Violet's benefit.

Iris, I never knew you had this in you, Queenie thinks, barely unable to contain her glee. Meanwhile, Edward strides out of the office, his fists clenched. A blast of cold air follows him out, along with an invisible contrail that smells strongly of rotten eggs.

"Edward's true legacy," Queenie says, covering her nose with her handkerchief.

Queenie turns to congratulate Violet, who suddenly keels over on the sofa in a dead faint.

CHAPTER TWENTY

Violet

Violet opens her eyes to see several people standing over her. Spud, on his knees, gently pats her hand and tells her everything will be all right. To counteract her dizziness, she focuses on his tie.

"Welcome back," he says. "We lost you there for a while."

"Thank goodness you're okay," Queenie says to Violet. She's on her knees, too—something Violet has never actually seen her do—and she looks relieved to see her awake. She fans Violet with what looks like Miss Temple's will, evidently grabbed from the lawyer's desk. The breeze makes her even colder than before.

"Did I imagine it, or did I just inherit the Temple house?" she asks Queenie.

"You didn't imagine it," Queenie answers. "Iris has surprised us all." Queenie smiles as though not the least bit upset.

"You mean I'm not fired?" she asks.

"Not by a long shot," Queenie says.

Violet remembers the seconds before she fainted: the collective gasp, everyone looking at her, Edward Temple's face frozen in controlled fury. Then she remembers feeling warm for the first time in Bo Rivers' office right before the light-headedness hit, like the time she tried to stand up too soon in the hospital after giving birth to her daughter, Tia. The room became a washing machine on the spin cycle and then faded to black.

While Spud continues to pat her hand, Queenie leans over and asks if she's okay. For a second, Violet imagines what it must be like to have parents. Meanwhile, Rose takes on the role of the first responder and helps Violet sit up. She holds three fingers in front of Violet's face.

"How many do you see?" Rose asks, her expression serious.

Violet answers the correct number. She's never seen Rose act like this before.

"Who is the president of the United States?" Rose asks. She widens her eyes as if to offer a clue.

"Rose, I haven't lost my mind. I just passed out." Violet still feels a little light-headed and definitely confused, but she doesn't think her current state is a result of a concussion, only the shock of a lifetime.

In the background, the lawyer is on the phone to the paramedics. His secretary stands in the corner, videotaping the entire event as if to cover him if a lawsuit arises.

With the help of Rose and Spud, Violet stands. Her knees feel shaky, and for the first time since Violet fainted, she notices the energy in the room has shifted. Iris isn't there anymore.

"Are you sure you're okay?" Rose asks.

"It was just such a shock," Violet says. But, in reality, 'shock' doesn't begin to describe what she feels.

Violet assures Bo Rivers that she is okay and that paramedics are unneeded. "I just fainted," she says. "Wouldn't you if you just inherited a mansion in downtown Savannah?"

He chuckles and agrees he probably would. Then he tells his secretary to turn off the video recorder, and everyone returns to their seats. Without Edward and Iris, the room feels different. Almost peaceful. They could be a party of friends, except no one seems to know how to proceed, including Bo Rivers.

"Now, where were we?" Violet says with comic flair, which sounds like something Queenie would say instead of her.

"You had just inherited the Temple mansion," Queenie says with another smile.

A new blast of cold air brings chill bumps to Violet's arms. Miss Temple is back. The vibration registers in Violet's solar plexus. It accelerates and grows more chaotic. New frequencies emerge, and Violet doesn't understand what these new energies mean.

Her grandmother has offered to teach Violet more about the Gullah tradition. But with Violet's full-time job and caring for Jack and the girls, she just hasn't had time to pursue it. But maybe she should make time for it. After all, her grandmother won't be around much longer. Weirdly, Violet feels her presence in the room, too, as if here to protect her.

Miss Temple's energetic charge bounces around the room like a four-year-old after drinking a 16 ounce Mountain Dew.

But why would Miss Temple be angry about something she put in her own will? This doesn't make sense. Violet tries to detect what's going on below the surface of the meeting, but there are so many layers of chaos she can't get a clear reading.

"Did Miss Temple give any explanation for why she would leave the house to me?" Violet asks Bo Rivers. "Because I think there's been some kind of mistake."

He looks at Queenie and then back at Violet. "I thought you knew," he says to Violet.

"You thought I knew what?" Violet says. She looks at Queenie, too, who is somehow in on this.

"What is it, Queenie?" Violet asks.

Without answering, Queenie bows her head as if the moment calls for earnest prayer. Violet looks back to the lawyer for an explanation. He hesitates. He doesn't strike Violet as someone who is at a loss for words very often.

"Well, since I'm the Temple family attorney, it isn't a breach of confidentiality to tell you, Violet," Bo Rivers begins. "Can I call you Violet?" he asks, turning up the volume of his southern charm.

"But I'm not a Temple," Violet says.

"Actually, you are," he says. He speaks softer as if wanting to avoid another call to the paramedics.

"I don't understand," Violet says. "How could I be a Temple?"

Spud takes her arm as if also anticipating the worst.

"Let me explain," Bo Rivers begins. "My father, Rutledge Rivers, was the Temple attorney for many years, which included Iris Temple's husband, Oscar Bell. After my father's death earlier this year, the client files passed to me. Upon reviewing the files a few weeks ago—when all those lawsuits started showing up because of the secrets in the newspaper—I found a letter written by Oscar Bell in the back of one of the files," he continues. "I immediately called Iris Temple to the office to view the letter, and she confirmed that it was indeed from Oscar Bell. In this letter, Violet, he confirmed that you were his biological daughter."

"But that's not possible," Violet says. "My mother didn't even work for the Temples."

Rose and Spud look just as confused as she is. Everyone looks at her except Queenie, who is digging in her giant purse as though making room to crawl inside

"Someone, please tell me what's going on," Violet says to the group. "If this is true, why am I just now finding out?" Violet hates that her voice is shaking.

Silence.

"I have no idea why the letter came to light so late," Bo Rivers says, "except that it was simply misplaced all these years. It's amazing that we found it at all. Like I said, if it hadn't been for all the fallout over the *Temple Book of Secrets*, I might never have found it."

Violet remembers Mister Oscar coming into the kitchen when she was a girl and him bringing her small gifts after he returned from business trips. Sometimes it would be a pink diary with a lock and key or a book. She never questioned why she might receive a gift. She just thought he was a nice man.

"But this doesn't make sense," she says, to no one in particular. She wishes Jack were here. She could use some of his ceaseless optimism right now.

"Certain facts and requests were revealed in the letter that Iris Temple took to be true," Bo Rivers continues. "It seems that Oscar Bell is your biological father. And upon Iris's death, he specifically wanted the house to go to you. Per his deathbed request, Iris Temple changed the will that day."

Violet rubs her forehead to help her brain take it all in. "Oscar Bell was my father?" she asks. "But that still doesn't make me a Temple."

"There's more," Bo Rivers begins again. "The letter also reveals your biological mother."

"But I know who my mother was," Violet says. "She died in a car crash on Tybee Island when I was a baby."

"Not according to Oscar Bell," Bo Rivers says. He pauses and glances at his watch as if happy hour cannot come soon enough.

"According to Oscar Bell, my real mother didn't die?" Violet asks. She's never felt so confused. Bo Rivers glances at Queenie again, who has given up on her purse and is staring into the palms of her hands on her lap as though reading her fortune and the news isn't good.

"Violet, *I'm* your mother," Queenie says, finally looking at her.

For the second time that day, Violet feels like she might faint.

CHAPTER TWENTY-ONE

Rose

R ose lingers in the hallway of the attorney's office after Violet leaves in tears.

"I had no idea the secret was going to come out like this," Queenie says, also close to tears. "I feared that it would show up in the newspaper some morning. I never dreamed it would come out this way."

"Queenie, why didn't you tell Violet you were her mother?"

"It's complicated," Queenie says. She pulls a box of tissues from her purse. She offers one to Rose, who declines.

Rose is confident Queenie must have had her reasons for sitting on this secret. She isn't the type to be cruel.

"Oh, Rose, I'm such an idiot," Queenie says.

At this moment, Rose is inclined to agree. "Violet's very upset," Rose says. Should she be comforting Violet instead of Queenie?

"She has every right to be upset." When Queenie blows her nose, it sounds like the honk of the Canada geese that migrate to their field back home. Rose wishes she was on her way there right now.

The events of the last hour have shaken her. Her father is also Violet's father? Queenie is Violet's mother? Not to mention the biggest shock of the meeting. Is she really being offered twenty million dollars to move back to Savannah?

One crisis at a time, she tells herself, as her thoughts return to Violet.

"I always wanted a sister," Rose says, deciding to look at the positives. "But you have to admit, you don't usually find out that you have one after forty years."

"I need to find Violet and explain," Queenie says, biting her bottom lip. "There are reasons for all of this."

Rose has never seen Queenie this off-balance. Her mother always had a knack for making a mess of things. What Rose didn't expect was that she could create such a mess after her death.

"I've got to make this right," Queenie says, giving Rose a quick hug. She takes the elevator in search of Violet.

Alone now, Rose thinks to call Max but then decides to wait. It is still early in Wyoming, and he will be out checking the cattle. Besides, she needs time to think about what just happened.

She walks through the parking garage, grateful that she was running late this morning and drove her rental car. Riding home in a vehicle with Queenie and Violet and all this drama is the last thing she needs. But what to do next? Her flight is later tonight. She has hours to wait before she can make a proper escape. Since she doesn't know when she'll be back on the coast again, Rose decides to take a walk on the beach to clear her thoughts.

Her heels click across the concrete parking lot. She can't get the look on Edward's face out of her mind. His cold expression makes her shiver in the Savannah heat even now. It isn't news that her brother hates her. She just didn't realize how much.

Mother must have been livid when she found out about Daddy and Queenie, Rose thinks.

If her mother had known beforehand, she would never have let Queenie live in the house, nor would she have ever hired Violet. Not to mention that if her father had been faithful to her mother, none of this would be happening anyway. She tends to forget his culpability in all this. Yet, if she's honest with herself, she must have known something was going on. Once, when she was around twelve, she walked into her father's office and found him and Queenie there. Nothing was going on, but they were startled by her intrusion.

After pulling the rental out of the parking lot, Rose drives toward the shore. Even though she drives the speed limit, her mind races to process the last hour. She stops at a convenience store to get a cup of coffee and grabs a newspaper to read on the plane. It's too hot for coffee, but it's what Rose drinks when she really wants a glass of wine.

"How's life treating you?" the cashier asks, who is barrel-chested and middle-aged. A space between his teeth offers a view of his pink and gray tongue.

Rose forgets how friendly people are in the South, even strangers, and decides to answer truthfully. "Well, my father's been dead for twenty-seven years, but I just found out that he had an affair with our housekeeper's daughter and fathered the girl that became my best friend while I was growing up. So I now have a half-sister that I never knew I had."

"I've had days like that, too," he chuckles and hands Rose her change.

She thanks him, thinking how nobody in Cheyenne would have been so understanding. Things happen in the south that don't happen anywhere else. This is one of the things that makes her birthplace interesting.

With no idea of where she wants to go, Rose returns to her car and just drives. Before long, she finds herself on the way to Old

Sally's house. Even though it is hot and humid and the coffee is making her hotter, she has the windows down so she can smell the sea.

The island has changed dramatically since she was a girl, but when she turns onto Old Sally's road, everything looks the same. Rose parks at the back of the house and gets out of the car. She isn't dressed for the beach—she's wearing the same dress she wore to the funeral—but being here feels right.

Despite all the history, Rose has come to the conclusion that her time back in Savannah has been good for her. She hasn't realized how much she missed the coast. After Rose married Max, she left all that was familiar to start a new life. She succeeded in that part, at least. Moving from Savannah to Cheyenne is about as different as a person can get without leaving the country. Until now, it never occurred to her that she might not spend the rest of her life in the West.

Rose leaves her black pumps in the car and walks barefoot through the dunes to Old Sally's house. She didn't anticipate that her quick trip to get closure with her mother would stretch into a week. Rose needed more clothes for a more extended stay, including shorts and sandals. At the same time, she's ready to be home. Ready to be with Max.

The Atlantic Ocean stretches into the horizon. Rose stands at sea level, as opposed to roughly 6,000 feet in the high plains of Wyoming. The sun feels much softer here than on the plains. The temperatures in Wyoming can easily hit one hundred degrees for several weeks every summer. But it is a dry heat, where a hundred degrees feels very different due to 10 percent humidity, not 90 percent. Coastal summers are sticky and steamy. The winters are chilly, yet mild.

When she turns toward the house, Old Sally is waiting at the door. Though this should surprise her, it doesn't. Old Sally gives a brief wave, and Rose returns the greeting. For some reason, this simple welcome makes Rose's eyes mist.

"I was expecting you," Old Sally says, as Rose climbs the steps.

"I know you were," Rose says.

She opens her arms, and Rose lets Old Sally hold her. Her embrace is as solid and strong as ever, and Rose sobs as if it is the most natural response in the world to all that has happened. Old Sally rubs Rose's back like she did when Rose was upset as a girl and says Gullah words that Rose doesn't understand, but that comfort her nonetheless.

Finally empty of tears, Rose pulls out several unused tissues she stuck in the pocket of her dress for her mother's funeral. She blows her nose. "I'm a mess," she says.

"You be a beautiful mess," Old Sally says as she smoothes Rose's hair.

Old Sally directs Rose to sit on the top step and then joins her, her body slower and more careful. For several seconds, Rose stares at Old Sally's bare feet—her long, brown wrinkled toes. Sturdy feet that have served Old Sally for a hundred years.

What must it be like to be this old, in a culture where people half her age are given senior discounts?

"I've just come from the attorney's office," Rose says. "Mother's trying to get me back to Georgia. In her will, she offered me a lot of money if I live here again."

Old Sally listens like this is no big surprise.

"I would dismiss her offer just on the principal of the thing," Rose says, "if I hadn't noticed these last few days how much I miss Savannah."

Old Sally leaves plenty of room for Rose to talk.

"The last time I was here, it was just so awful," Rose continues. "Mother and I had this horrible fight, and she accused me of only visiting because I wanted her money." Rose sniffs back new tears that threaten to come. "Then she said that she wished I'd never been born. Can you believe that?" Rose asks. "What kind of mother wishes their kid had never been born?"

"A bitter one," Old Sally says, her voice soft. "But you need to know that no matter what kind of person you turned out to be, your mother would have felt the same way about you."

"But she wasn't hateful to Edward," Rose says. "She worshiped the ground he walked on."

"Edward paid a high price for that," she says. "He still be paying."

Rose pauses while her shoulders slowly relax. "I guess I never thought of it that way," she says.

"Let's take a walk," Old Sally says. "The wind be good for blowing away muddy thoughts." Her toes wiggle as if ready to go.

Rose helps her stand and holds her arm as they go down the steps. Old Sally is frailer than Rose wants to admit. When they reach the beach, Rose continues to hold her arm, not knowing if it is Old Sally who needs support or her. As they walk, Rose tells Old Sally the details of what happened in Bo River's office, although she doesn't seem surprised by any of it.

When Rose tells her about Violet finding out about her real parents, Old Sally stops walking and turns to look at the sea, like she sees something play out in the past.

"Secrets be no good for anybody," Old Sally begins, still staring at the horizon. "It's the truth that sets people free. I just wish I'd been brave enough to tell the truth when I could."

She lowers her head as though disappointed in herself. For a second, Rose wonders if it is Old Sally who is releasing the secrets to the newspaper. But the thought seems so far-fetched, she doesn't entertain it for long.

"I lied to Violet," Old Sally continues. "It was wrong to let her think that my daughter Maya was her mother. But Queenie be convinced we'd all lose our jobs if people knew."

"You mean you knew, too?" Rose never thought Old Sally capable of lying.

"I'm not proud of going along with it all these years," Old Sally continues. "I left it up to Queenie to say whatever she thought was best, and I stayed out of it. But I owe Violet a big apology, and I hope she can forgive me."

"Violet needs an apology from Queenie, too," Rose says.

"She and Queenie got some mending to do, for sure," Old Sally says. "We've all got mending to do."

Betrayals are commonplace in the Temple lineage. In fact, you could almost say they are a Temple family trait. Yet it seems that Queenie, as well as Old Sally, were not without their reasons.

"We humans be on this planet for about a minute and a half," Old Sally begins again. "And all that time we be struggling with ourselves and each other, trying to be something that we're not. Even this old, I still don't understand why we do that," she continues. "It seems like we spend our whole lives sleepwalking. Not noticing the love and beauty all around us."

Old Sally continues to look out over the sea, like the answers to her lifelong questions might ride in on the waves. The old woman takes a deep breath, and Rose does, too. They stand in silence for a long time, Rose digging her toes into the moist sand of the rising tide. Even though she has never been comfortable with the quiet, something about this moment feels different. Rose always thought silence was empty and lonely, but while standing next to Old Sally, she realizes how full it is.

Old Sally begins to walk again, and Rose joins her. "What do you think you'll do?" Old Sally asks.

Rose almost regrets the end of the silence. "I can't imagine how Max will react to all of this," she begins. "We're always worried about money, but he isn't the type to be bought. The ranch is his life. Besides, we're too old to start over."

Old Sally laughs. "Nobody ever be too old to start over," she says. "I may just start over myself one of these days." She laughs again as if the idea tickles her.

Their walk is snail-paced compared to the vigorous walks Rose has done for exercise since she's been here. Yet this rhythm feels more natural. It occurs to her that if she walked this way every day of her life, she might finally arrive at contentment.

The ocean breeze blows in her face. The grasses among the dunes wave at her in the breeze. Rose stops and picks up a sand dollar in perfect condition. She runs a finger along the raised petal-like design on the shell's back.

"Violet and I used to collect these as girls, do you remember?" Rose asks.

"Like it was yesterday," Old Sally says. "You hid them in the roots of that old oak in the garden. You thought I didn't know your hiding place, but I did."

Memories clamor for Rose's attention. "Do you remember that day we tied our entire collection onto the lower limbs of the oak with white kitchen string that you gave us?"

Old Sally smiles. "It looked like a Christmas tree covered with beautiful white ornaments," she says.

Rose smiles. "Violet and I lay on our backs looking up at that tree for hours until Mother told us to take those tacky things down. Of course, we shot up like rockets," Rose continues. "Violet got scared and ran into the kitchen to find you and left me standing there to face Mother alone. That woman scared me to death."

"Nobody be forcing you to take anything down now, baby. You free," Old Sally says.

Rose looks into Old Sally's eyes, the brown having more flecks of gray than she remembers. "Am I really free?" she asks.

Old Sally nods. "The door to the jail cell be open. Now you just got to walk through."

Rose picks up a pebble and tosses it into the ocean. How many times has she walked this same coastline with Old Sally? She wishes now she'd kept count. As a girl, one of the biggest treats of her life was getting to spend the night at Old Sally's house. Old Sally would move all her special trinkets and make a bed for Rose in the window seat where she could watch the ocean in the moonlight. Sometimes Rose awoke at dawn, and dolphins would be playing on the waves. Later, she would wonder if she'd dreamed it.

After wandering down the beach, they turn around and walk back over their own footprints. An unexpected calm flows through Rose.

"I've missed this place." She breathes in the sea air.

"This place has missed you, too," Old Sally says.

Rose feels ready to come home to Savannah now. She's tired of running from the past. Tired of pretending that she doesn't miss the people and the land here. Her mother's bribe has helped her take an honest look at where she really belongs. It has everything to do with who she is at this moment and what she needs in life.

But Max will never leave the West, she tells herself. It is his home just as surely as the Georgia coast is hers.

CHAPTER TWENTY-TWO

Queenie

"Holy heaven, what a disaster," Queenie says to herself. She places the keys to the Town Car on the hook in the kitchen. Her secret is out and not at all how she wanted it to be. After Iris died, she gave herself a month to tell Violet. The plan was to take her out to dinner some night and spill the secret she'd bottled up all these years. She has to admit, though, it will be helpful to get some sleep again. She's been worried for weeks that this very secret would show up on people's doorsteps all over Savannah and everyone in town would know. Not that anybody would even care, except Violet.

The drive home from Bo River's office with Violet was the longest ride of her life. Violet's silence proved fertile soil for Queenie's shame. Queenie apologized, but her apology was met with more of Violet's silence. She then attempted several more apologies with the same result. Once they were home, Violet insisted that Queenie stop apologizing. Then she got out of the car, slammed the door, and ran inside.

The moment called for something more than Queenie had. A better reason. Better words to explain. In all honesty, it felt inevitable that she would have a child by Iris Temple's husband. Wasn't that what history expected of her?

The phone hasn't stopped ringing in the foyer, even though she had it changed to a private number. It is unreal how many people have called looking for a job after this morning's ad. Did they really think it was real? Queenie unplugs the telephone and goes upstairs. She doesn't have time to worry about phone calls or the handful of protestors outside. She seeks refuge in the green armchair in the corner of her bedroom. She pulls out her journal and pen from the side table drawer where she keeps it hidden. The last thing she needed while Iris was alive was Iris finding all her private thoughts. They might fill a whole other book of secrets.

Journaling is something Queenie picked up from watching Oprah, and she is faithful to the practice of documenting her feelings and thoughts. In the margins, she writes the three things she's grateful for every day. But she is not ready for gratitude yet. Too much is in the way. Queenie picks up a pen and begins to write the story she never shared with anyone until now, not even her journal.

I was sixteen when Mister Oscar first invited me to his study. I hated him for suggesting it, but another part of me liked the attention since I'd never really had a daddy. Not having a parent is like having only half of a road map in life, one torn right down the middle, so you never fully know where you're going or where you've been. Of course, I always knew that Iris and I had the same father. But he never acknowledged it. Not once. Sometimes I would sneak looks at him to see if I could recognize parts of me that came from him. As far as I could tell, we had the same nose, but other than that we could have been total strangers.

He was tall and thin and very white. Did I mention he was very white!?
Maybe the most significant thing we had in common was how well we
could keep a secret!

What secret, you may ask, dear journal? Well, when I was a girl, my
mama would disappear from time to time into his bedroom, and I knew
not to ask where she'd been. It was just the way things were. Other girls
I knew had mothers who did the same thing. All housekeepers for
Savannah's upper class. Afraid to lose everything they had if they
refused to do what the Misters wanted.

So, actually, going into Oscar's study that first time when I was
sixteen was like being initiated into the secrets that my mother knew.
But unlike the Sea Gypsies that Rose and Violet created, I never enjoyed
being a member of this secret society.

Don't get me wrong. Oscar was a nice enough man. He wasn't
cruel. Sometimes Oscar was even sweet. But I hated the way he smelled,
a combination of liquor and cigars. To be honest, I think we were both
playing at a game we hated, but a game that was expected of us.

Queenie pauses and recalls the smell of Oscar's cigars and his
bittersweet breath and thinks: *Funny how smells can bring back*
memories so strongly. It's as if Oscar stands right next to her this
very moment. She looks around like maybe he is. At this point, the
dead outnumber the living in the Temple mansion.

More than once, Iris accused Oscar of making her sick to her
stomach with all his smells. He let Iris use him as a doormat on
more than one occasion. At times, her harsh treatment made
Queenie feel sorry for him. Didn't he know that men—white men
—ran the world?

It never occurred to her that Iris didn't know about the affair,
just as it seemed that Iris's mother must have known what Queenie's father was up to. *How do you deny children running around the*
house who are a light brown version of your husband?

The Temple features are distinct: a nose just a bit too pointed,
eyes just a bit too small, yet with kindness around the creases that

don't necessarily match up to the personality—facial features that most people would find hard to miss. However, the denial in the Temple family is powerful enough it could power all of downtown Savannah. Denial that's served up in their shrimp and grits every morning, as if to fortify them to keep the secrets. Secrets that are now showing up all over Savannah.

It feels good to confess, even if it's only to her journal. She begins to write again:

When I was fifteen, Oscar would come into the kitchen all the time. I wasn't a great beauty—I was already what you might call FULL figured—but my complexion often got me compliments. Of course, Oscar was no spring chicken and was already worn around the edges. He liked to make me laugh, and made jokes about boys beating down the Temple door to get to me.

"Don't be silly, Mister Oscar," I remember saying to him. "That door's too old and heavy."

Then he'd say how he'd break a door down to get to me if he had to.

At the same time that I hated the attention, I also craved it. Mama watched his subtle advances and didn't say a thing. Not one thing. She just stayed busy, refusing to look up from her work. I waited for weeks for her to say something. I kept thinking she would stop Oscar from flirting with me and tickling me right under her nose. Maybe Oscar was waiting for that, too. But when Mama turned a blind eye to it, I hated her with every bit of my teenage vengeance.

Since then, I've learned that nobody's mama is perfect, but this was the first and only time she ever disappointed me. And I think she disappointed herself, too.

Then over the years, I resigned myself to what was expected of me. I wasn't proud of what I did. But there were consequences to saying no, and who knows, I may have loved Oscar a little bit, too.

Queenie puts down the pen. "How could Violet possibly understand how things were back then?" Queenie says aloud.

History pulled at Queenie from every direction and created a dangerous undercurrent of shame in which she thought she might drown. She didn't have the strength to choose anything different from what her mother and grandmother had done. *Hadn't we been taught our whole lives to take care of the needs of white people? And didn't that include the bedroom needs, too?*

If her mother had stood up to Oscar, she might have been fired and never worked again. That's how things were. One word from the Temples, and you could be blackballed forever. Blackballed from Savannah, the whole state of Georgia, and maybe the Carolinas, too. Then how would her mama support herself?

Today, keeping servants in their place is much more covert. Messages are sent by innuendo, a wink, a glare. Yet they are just as potent. She thinks of Violet downstairs and wishes she could go to her. But Violet made it clear she isn't ready to talk.

W.W.O.D? she writes in her journal. What would Oprah do?

She thinks for a few seconds and decides her hero would give Violet the time she needs. Then take responsibility for the pain she's caused. Queenie sighs. Sometimes making Oprah proud isn't the least bit easy.

Thanks to Oscar, Queenie found an alternative to spending her life in a kitchen and cleaning until her shoulders froze up, and her knees went bad. For years, she's been saving up the puny allowance Iris gave her so that Violet can stop working here and finally open that business she's always wanted.

It was Oscar's idea for Queenie to become Iris's companion. But even this so-called luck came with a price tag on it. She was never to tell anyone that Violet was their child, especially not Iris. And when her older sister, Maya, tragically died a short time after Violet was born, Oscar dreamed up the story to go with their deception, saying that Violet was her sister's child. Maya was several years older and was already married by the time Queenie was in grade school.

"Just so you know, Iris, I don't miss you one bit." Queenie

points her finger at the overhead light fixture. "I don't miss your bitterness. I don't miss your constant criticism. Nor do I miss your not-so-subtle reminders, every day of my life, that I was servant stock and not a true Temple. And those errands you used to send me on? What a ridiculous waste of my time. All I've got to say is that you sure didn't trouble your imagination very much."

Queenie huffs and remembers all the times she was told to mail a letter at the downtown post office, even if their regular postal carrier was expected to deliver and pick up within minutes. Then an hour after Queenie returned from the post office, Iris would decide she needed stamps.

Her huff is followed by a yawn. *This delving into the past is quite exhausting,* Queenie thinks.

After hiding her journal again, she puts her feet up for a quick snooze. Within minutes, she settles into a sweet dream about Denzel Washington giving her a sexy foot rub and then is startled awake by a knock on her bedroom door. In her imagination, she asks Denzel to come back later and then shuffles toward the door to find Rose.

"Sorry to disturb you, but I have to leave for the airport in a couple of hours," Rose says.

Sometimes Queenie can see the young girl Rose used to be. Shy. Awkward. Serious. "Did you have a nice walk on the beach?" Queenie asks.

"I spent some time with Old Sally, so yes, it was wonderful," Rose says.

At Queenie's invitation, Rose sits on the end of the bed. "Have you thought about what you'll do?" Queenie asks. She's been so into her own crisis she hasn't even thought about Rose's.

"I'll have a long talk with Max, I suppose," Rose says. "I haven't told him yet. I left a message that I had something to talk to him about once I got back. I guess I want to think about it more and decide how I feel. Mother sure knows how to shake things up, doesn't she?"

"Your mother was a force of nature," Queenie says, "and in some ways she still is." She looks at the chandelier again, as if daring Iris to disagree.

"I doubt Max will have anything to do with Mother's black-mail," Rose says. "This whole day has just been unreal, hasn't it?"

Queenie nods, her thoughts returning to the meeting in Bo River's office. She expected surprises from Iris, but not from Oscar.

Why did he write that stupid letter? she wonders.

Queenie was prepared to go to her grave without anybody knowing. Except that after Iris died, it just didn't make sense to keep it a secret anymore. What she didn't expect was that finally telling the truth would feel like such a huge relief, despite the fact that Violet may never forgive her. It reminds her of those girdles she tried to wear in the 60s. Her ample body pinched and contained until finally released in the evening, so grateful to be unencumbered. Having that secret out feels a little like that, too. Like finally she can breathe again.

"How did I not know that you were Violet's mother?" Rose asks.

"I'm very good at keeping secrets," Queenie says. "But keeping this one was selfish. I know that now." She joins Rose at the end of the bed. "What I want to know is how I could have been such a coward? For years I convinced myself that Violet was better off not knowing the truth. She had this image of her dead mother that comforted her. A perfect mother who died too soon. How could I compete with that, Rose? I'm not a perfect anything, and I thought that if Violet found out the truth, she'd be disap-pointed."

Rose takes Queenie's hand and squeezes it. "When are you going to talk to her?" Rose asks.

"As soon as she'll listen. Although I'm not sure what I'll say."

"You need to explain what it was like for you and why you felt the need to keep the secret," Rose says. "She needs to hear the truth, Queenie. In AA they call it making amends."

Queenie remembers Rose's attempt to make amends with Iris twenty years before. After the letter arrived at the house, Iris read it aloud to Queenie. It was a lovely letter. Heartfelt. Sincere. But Iris dismissed it. Then she marked the letter *return to sender, recipient deceased,* and ordered Queenie to return it to the post office. Even for Iris, the response was especially mean-spirited. Her whole life Iris never knew how to apologize. To her, apologies were a sign of weakness, not of strength.

"Promise me you'll talk to Violet today," Rose says. "I don't want what happened between my mother and me to happen with you and Violet."

"I promise," Queenie says and rests a hand on the shelf of her bosom to offer a solemn swear.

Rose squeezes Queenie's hand again and stands. "I've got to pack," she says.

"Can I take you to the airport?"

"I'd appreciate that," Rose says. "I need to drop off the rental car, but if you want to wait with me in the terminal, we could have a little more time together."

For the first time that afternoon, Queenie feels like everything might be okay again. She has amends to make, but maybe Violet will forgive her.

"If you're hungry, we can stop by Kentucky Fried Chicken on the way," Queenie says with a grin. "I haven't been back since the day of the funeral."

"I still can't believe you put a bucket of chicken in Mother's casket," Rose says.

"Original recipe," Queenie says. "You know how your mother had a thing for tradition."

Rose laughs, as Queenie turns serious again.

"I have no regrets, Rose. Especially after that stunt your

mother pulled today." Her head upturned, Queenie waits for Iris to comment, but the room is quiet.

"I don't think she's been around since the reception," Rose says. "Maybe that's a sign that she's finally ready to go."

"We should be so lucky," Queenie says. "Truth be told, I've had enough of your mama to last at least two lifetimes, maybe three."

Rose leaves to pack, and Queenie goes downstairs. When she enters the kitchen, Violet jumps. "You scared me," she says with a frown.

"I didn't mean to scare you, baby, and I certainly didn't mean to hurt you either."

Violet's face softens, and she bites her bottom lip as though willing herself not to cry.

"I was wondering if we could talk about all this after I get back from taking Rose to the airport," Queenie says.

Violet looks away and doesn't answer.

Queenie's shame feels full-bodied now as if a literal person standing in the room. She doesn't like this person.

"I need to tell you what happened," Queenie says. "You deserve to hear the facts."

Violet wipes a single tear from her cheek and then agrees. At this point, nothing can keep Queenie from telling the truth. She owes Violet that much. This secret has stayed hidden way too long. Unlike people, secrets never die. Look at that stupid book. Just when you think two hundred years of confidences will be buried in a bank vault forever, it resurges, refusing to be forgotten. It's in their nature for secrets to surface in one way or another, and Queenie is counting on it being in Violet's nature to forgive her.

CHAPTER TWENTY-THREE

Violet

Once the house is empty again, Violet looks at the kitchen ceiling and calls Miss Temple's name. It's not like spirits to come when called, but she wants to know if Violet getting the house is what Miss Temple really wants. After all, the note on Miss Temple's nightstand said she was going to change the will, and then her agitated spirit showed up at the will reading.

Violet leaves the kitchen and stands in the foyer listening to the tick of the grandfather clock, the heartbeat of the house. Having no time to process anything, she isn't sure what she feels. It is a mixture of shock, sadness, and exuberance. None of which she has much experience with.

As if moving through a dream, Violet walks from room to room. Could this house really be hers now? She walks out the front door and down the front steps, something she rarely does since she always uses the side entrance. The Temple house is one

of those mansions with a gold plaque on the front giving the date
it was built.

A house with a pedigree, she thinks.

Violet has often thought that their apartment would fit into the
Temple carriage house with room to spare.

After opening the gate, she steps onto the wide sidewalk,
looking back at the house. She covers a smile, embarrassed by her
good fortune. For years she's wanted to get away from this house
—specifically from her duties as a housekeeper and cook. Libera-
tion was her goal. Yet even as a girl, she loved this place. While
Rose complained about its formality, Violet always thought it was
like a castle in a fairy tale. A castle that would never, ever be hers.

Further down the sidewalk, posters are taped to the tall
wrought iron fence, their messages scrawled in dark markers. **Iris
Temple is a Traitor**, says one. **Keep Your Secrets to Yourself!** says
another. **Who Do You Think You Are?!** says a third. Miss Temple
worked so hard to make the Temple name mean something. She
would hate how ordinary folks are reacting to the scandal.

A black Buick with darkened windows is parked at the end of
the block. It has sat there for several days. She can make out the
figure of a man inside. It reminds Violet of a scene from one of the
crime novels Queenie loans her. A suspicious-looking character
lurks in the shadows, though you don't find out who they are
until the end of the book. The smoke from the stranger's cigarette
exits out of a one-inch gap at the top of the window. The car is
running, probably for the air conditioner. A soft beat of bass comes
from the car radio. Rhythm and blues. She likes the music but not
the stranger.

Violet shudders, adding fear to her list of mixed emotions. She
lowers her eyes as she passes, and then walks through another
gate to a stone pathway that leads to the side entrance. The
kitchen entrance is typically the servant entrance, although nearly
everybody uses it to come and go, except for Miss Temple. While

the front entrance is formidable, the garden entrance is open and inviting.

To rid herself of the fear, she focuses on her surroundings. The courtyard and garden always have a magical feel for Violet. She spends her breaks out here whenever she can. A large oak dominates the center of the garden, the ground nearby covered in a carpet of moss. It is the kind of spot that invites a picnic, or perhaps a nap, no matter what season or time of day. Not that she ever has time for such a thing. Except her grandmother used to make picnics for her and Rose to have under this tree when they were girls. Sometimes she would join them and tell them stories about their ancestors. Queenie was nearby. Always.

What did she think about when she watched me? Violet wonders. She can't imagine standing by and watching Tia or Leisha and not claiming them as her own. It would break her heart to do so. She pushes away the betrayal she feels. It is too big to face. Too dangerous.

A wooden bench sits under an arbor next to an ivy-covered wall of the house. Blooming flowers are everywhere. In the far corner, a twisted crepe myrtle tree stands, its blossoms scattered on the ground, releasing the last moments of their scent. The breeze pushes the aroma of the blooms in Violet's direction. She drinks in the garden's perfume, feeling intoxicated by the events of the day, as well as nauseous.

Will she keep the gardener? But how will she afford him? She has heard of people who are house-rich and cash-poor. This is definitely her now. Although, she can't believe she's even thinking this way.

A warm breeze rattles the leaves of the crepe myrtle tree. Even though it is only April, the evenings are already hot and will continue to bake them to the end of October.

The squeak of the garden gate alarms her until she sees it is Spud. Now dressed in casual clothes, he is without his bow tie.

Violet has never seen him without a tie. He carries an armload of posters he's pulled from the fence.

"What kind of people do this?" He rips the posters into pieces.

"People with nothing better to do, I guess," Violet answers. "Which reminds me, did you see that black Buick out there?"

"I did. Who is that?" Spud asks.

"No idea," Violet says. "Queenie walked up to rap on the window yesterday, and he drove off when he saw her coming. At least we assume it's a 'he.' With those dark windows, it's hard to tell."

"Do you want me to talk to him?" Spud asks, sounding braver than he looks. Something about being able to see the tiny tuft of gray hair at the V of his polo shirt makes him seem overly exposed. It occurs to Violet that earlier today, they were regular, hardworking people, relying on a weekly paycheck to get by. Now, they are wealthy. All because of Miss Temple. A woman he obviously loved. And a woman Violet worked hard not to hate.

"I think if you try to talk to him, he'll just drive away again," Violet says.

"Have you called the police?"

"We did," Violet answers, "but since he isn't breaking any laws, they can't do anything."

"Doesn't it scare you?" Spud asks.

"I guess I have a higher scare quotient since I deal with ghosts every day," Violet says. With that, she gets Spud to finally smile. "Besides, the Temple mansion is like a fortress with all the security systems on," she adds, thinking she probably needs to learn how to operate them. Of course, Queenie knows how, but she doesn't want to talk to Queenie right now.

Violet invites Spud inside, and he takes his usual place at the kitchen table. "We both got quite a shock today," he says.

"I think I'm still reeling," Violet says. It strikes her odd that an older white man would be such a good friend. A friend she can say almost anything to. A friend that if not for Miss Temple's eccentricities, she might never have met. "Jack keeps calling to see when I'm coming home," she adds, "but I can't seem to leave."

"How do you think he'll react?" Spud asks.

"I honestly have no idea," Violet says. "He'll probably be in shock just like I am." She pauses. "Is it alright with you if we don't talk about that right now?"

"Whatever you need is fine with me." Spud starts to straighten his tie, but his hand hangs there a moment when he realizes it isn't there. An awkward grin crosses his face, as though going casual will take some getting used to.

"I was in the middle of making turnovers," she says.

While he pours himself a cup of coffee, she turns her attention back to the biscuit dough she left on the countertop when Rose and Queenie left. She rolls out and cuts several pieces—shaped like the sail of paper boats—and folds the strips of dough over sliced peaches before placing them on a baking sheet.

"You're as good as Julia Child," Spud says.

Violet thanks him. She always gets compliments on her cooking. At church socials, people line up in front of whatever she brings, so they don't miss out. With Spud watching, she makes a dozen peach turnovers, one after another.

"I bake when I don't know what else to do," Violet says.

"Lucky for me," Spud says.

Violet smiles. Flour dots her arms and forehead, and she wipes it off. Silence follows.

"Here we are together, a butcher and a baker," Spud says. "All we need is a candlestick maker." He pauses like he's waiting to see if she thinks he's clever.

Violet smiles. She used to read the nursery rhyme to Tia and Leisha. When Violet was young, Queenie read them to her. She claps the memory away, along with the flour. It seems she has to rethink her entire life.

"Tell me something I don't know about you," Spud says as if wanting to fill the silence until she's ready to talk.

Violet looks at him, reminded of how often she appreciates his kindness.

"Well, let me think," Violet says, glancing out the kitchen window that overlooks the garden. "In 1980, I was a runner-up in the Miss Georgia pageant." Her face tingles with warmth. She hasn't told anyone this fact in twenty years.

Spud reacts like this news requires a standing ovation. "Well, it doesn't surprise me one bit," Spud says. "What did you do for talent?"

"I sang Amazing Grace," she says. "A blues version. It was my grandmother's idea."

"I bet it was beautiful," he says.

"I don't know about that, but for years people walked up to me on the street and told me how moved they were by my performance. One of the judges even confided that if I'd been a little lighter-skinned, I would have won the title."

"Will you sing it for me someday?" Spud asks.

"I've kind of given up singing," she says, "but maybe someday." She pauses, wondering why she gave up singing. Did she just get so busy working she didn't have time anymore?

The smell of turnovers calls her back to the oven where she takes them out and places them on a cooling rack, their perfectly browned crusts glisten with a light sugar glaze. Despite her recent windfall, she still wants to open her Tea Shop and Bakery. She wants to have something to pass along to her girls. Of course, a mansion might be a nice thing, too.

With a peach turnover on a plate for each of them, she adds a scoop of vanilla ice cream. Then she refills Spud's coffee and makes a cup of tea for herself. Although Spud and Violet have sat together many times, this moment feels different.

Spud takes a bite of turnover, and his eyes close. This pleases her. Her own turnover sits untouched. Vanilla ice cream forms a moat around the pastry to create an island of sweetness.

"I can't believe dear Iris left me real estate," Spud says. "I feel like I won the lottery."

"Me, too," Violet says. "But I can't help wondering if there's been some huge mistake."

"It wouldn't be like Iris to make mistakes," Spud says.

"But she gave you up," Violet says.

Spud pauses, as though his peach turnover is trapped behind the lump in his throat. He swallows, and she can hear his gulp. "I think that's the kindest thing anyone has ever said to me," Spud says.

Violet rests a hand on Spud's arm. "It's the truth," she says, watching him blush.

"Have you talked to Queenie yet?" he asks like there's truth to be found there, too.

"We're supposed to talk later tonight," Violet says. "I don't know whether I'm angry or sad or relieved. Rose seems to think that Queenie had to keep it all a secret so I wouldn't lose my job, and she could still live here and be close to me. It makes sense, in a way. But, honestly, I don't know what to think."

"That's why it's important to talk about it," Spud says.

As if summoned, the door opens, and Queenie walks into the kitchen. "Sorry for the intrusion," she says.

Violet pretends interest in the soggy turnover.

"Would you like some coffee and dessert?" Spud says to Queenie. "Violet has outdone herself with the peach turnovers."

Queenie thanks Spud and serves herself. The tension in the room feels like a tightrope stretched between two Savannah mansions. When Queenie takes a seat at the kitchen table, Violet has to resist leaving the room. Her muteness accompanies the tension.

"Shall I leave you two alone?" Spud asks.

"No!" Violet and Queenie answer in unison. Their awkward laughter waits for a beat before filling the room. The tightrope quickly relaxes.

The last six hours have felt like a roller coaster ride at Six Flags. Violet's emotions have ranged from intense anger to confusion, with moments of compassion thrown in. On the one hand, she wants to hear what Queenie has to say. On the other hand, she'd prefer never to speak to her again.

"Rose will get to Denver around ten tonight," Queenie says. "Max is driving from Cheyenne to pick her up."

Is she hoping the small talk will rescue her from the big conversation we need to have? Violet wonders.

"I guess they'll have a lot of talk about," Violet says. *Like we do,* she wants to add. Which one of them will have the courage to speak first? Meanwhile, she's tired. Her day started early, and now it's eight o'clock. The hurt she feels lies just underneath her skin like a splinter that refuses to work its way out on its own. She wants to scream: *How could you lie to me all these years?*

"I'm so sorry I lied to you," Queenie says as if she's read Violet's thoughts. They have this kind of connection sometimes. A connection where they know what the other is thinking. Now Violet knows why. In the womb, she nestled just inches from Queenie's heart. With this thought, her breath catches in her throat. She refuses to cry. She's cried enough for one day.

Violet stands and puts her uneaten turnover into the kitchen sink. She wants to go home but stands frozen.

"Just listen to what she has to say," Spud tells Violet, his voice soft.

Despite his awkwardness, she is glad Spud is here. "I'm willing to listen for a little while," Violet says to Queenie. She leans against the kitchen counter to anchor herself in place. "But if I say 'stop,' I need you to stop."

"Absolutely," Queenie says. But then she hesitates as though her courage flounders.

Violet and Spud exchange a look. His eyes open wider. Is he reminding her to stay open to what Queenie has to say?

"At first, I thought that if the Temples knew, they might try to take you away from me," Queenie begins. "Then later, I thought they might say I couldn't live here anymore." She looks into Violet's eyes, who turns away. It is too much to deal with her pain, as well as Queenie's. "Perhaps it's not a good enough reason to live with a lie all these years," Queenie continues, "but it's all I knew to do. To complicate things, Oscar made me swear that I would never tell. He was convinced that nothing good could come of it. But it seems that nothing good has come from keeping the secret, either."

A long pause follows. Spud taps his coffee cup as if to remind Violet to speak. But she hasn't a clue what to say. *Go to hell? Get out of my house? I forgive you?*

Queenie bows her head. If she's waiting to be forgiven, she's going to have to wait longer. Violet isn't the type to give angry outbursts, but sometimes she wishes she were.

"I've been afraid that you would hate me, not that anyone could blame you," Queenie begins again.

"I don't hate you," Violet says, her voice raised. She doesn't want to let Queenie off this easy, but she is telling the truth. Violet doesn't hate Queenie. Maybe if she did, it wouldn't hurt so much.

Queenie's relief comes out in a rush of words. "You don't know how good that is to hear."

"Well, I'm glad one of us feels good," Violet says, her voice elevated again. "How could you lie to me every day for the last forty years?" Her voice breaks with emotion.

As Queenie takes a step closer, Violet holds out her arm to stop her. Queenie lowers her eyes. "I've done unforgivable things," she says, her voice contrite.

Violet can't believe how messy life sometimes gets, even when people mean well. "I need some time to get used to this." She steps back like even a few inches might help create the time. "What would you do, Queenie? What would you do if you thought your mother had died when you were a little girl, and now you're told that your real mother has been sitting right across from you all these years?"

"I honestly have no idea." Queenie stands and puts a light hand on Violet's shoulder that Violet shrugs away. "Please don't touch me. Don't speak to me and stay out of my sight," Violet says. She looks straight into Queenie's eyes that fill with tears. Perhaps she is the type for angry outbursts after all.

Queenie's lips tighten as if trying to hold back the sobbing. She leaves the room to give Violet what she wants. Now it is Violet's tears that begin again.

AFTER A GOOD CRY, Violet goes home to their small apartment. She's put off telling her family as long as she can. Tia and Leisha are watching television in the living room as Jack walks out of their bedroom.

"I was getting worried about you," Jack says. "How was the meeting with the lawyer?"

She turns away from his kiss. "I need to call a family meeting," she says, loud enough for the girls to hear her in the living room. Both girls moan. Family meetings usually mean there's a problem, and something needs to change.

Reluctant, the girls turn off the television and sit at the table. Jack does, too. All three look worried that they've done something wrong, but she is too tired to reassure them.

"Something really big happened today," she begins. "Something really, really big." In the moments that follow, she tells them about the meeting at the lawyer's office and what she learned while she was there. When she finishes, all eyes stay on her. She can't remember the last time she had her family's full attention.

"Queenie is my grandmother now?" Leisha asks. "How come we're just now finding out?"

"I think Queenie was afraid I might lose my job if Miss Temple knew." Violet's voice trails off. She is so tired of thinking about all this.

"Well, I don't think people should lie," Leisha says.

At sixteen, Leisha makes all A's and is one of the youth leaders at their church.

"I don't think she felt that she had a choice," Violet says.

She surprises herself with her willingness to defend Queenie. It helps that they've been so close over the years. But isn't this what makes the betrayal hurt even more? Violet wonders again why Queenie never told her the truth.

"I love Aunt Queenie," Tia says. "She's funny and cool."

Tia is fourteen and looks just like her father. Tall and lean, she plays center for the girl's basketball team in high school. Unlike her outgoing sister, she is shy.

"I love Queenie, too," Violet says.

"So, are we going to live there?" Tia asks. Tia and Leisha share one of the bedrooms in their two-bedroom apartment.

"Yes, I suppose we will," Violet says, "if your father agrees."

She has thought about this possibility all afternoon. She can imagine the Temple house full of teenagers and life, where homework is done on the large dining room table, enough room for both girls to have at least six friends over.

"All of this will be up for discussion," Jack says. "Let's not go counting chickens," he adds.

"Your dad's right," Violet says. "None of this is a done deal."

Violet imagines how Jack's life might change, too, if he finally has a home office to do his class preparation, instead of taking up the whole kitchen table. He can have two offices if he wants. Not to mention the thousand square foot workshop located at the very back of the property that currently serves as a garden shed of sorts, but could easily be converted. The biggest question, of course, is whether or not he minds sharing an office with the ghost of Mister Oscar. *My father*, she reminds herself. She remembers as a little girl riding on his shoulders in the garden. She blinks away more tears that threaten to come. It is still too much to take in.

"I can't leave my high school," Leisha says. "All my friends are there."

Despite their phenomenal good fortune, Violet's older daughter looks upset. Geographical changes don't sit well with teenagers. So much change is going on in their bodies that to throw in a literal geographic change, even if it is only a few miles away, is too much to ask. Leisha's best friend moved to Atlanta over the Christmas holidays, and it's been hard on her. Violet reassures Leisha that everything will work out. It's too soon to make any decisions, anyway. The house isn't officially Violet's yet, and maybe it won't ever be. *Especially if Edward Temple has any say about it,* she wants to add.

For the first time that day, she realizes Edward is her half-brother. The thought makes her queasy. Violet was Leisha's age when he attacked her. She never told Jack about the incident, and now she wonders why.

Violet yawns. It is after midnight by the time she and Jack crawl into bed.

"God works in mysterious ways," Jack says.

"Do you really think this is God's doing?" Violet asks.

"You never know," Jack says.

Jack always has more faith than Violet that things will work out and that God is watching out for them. Violet isn't so sure.

"I don't even know how to think about Queenie being my mother," she says.

"I've always liked her, though," Jack says. "If you were going to have a surprise relative, she's a great one to have."

Sometimes Jack is so easy-going, Violet wishes she could get a rise out of him. He looks like a giant teddy bear, and he acts like one, too.

"You're not upset that she lied to me for all these years?" Violet asks.

"It sounds like she had her reasons," Jack says. "Besides, she's been so generous to you and me and the girls over the years. Now it all kind of makes sense."

"So, what's your reasoning about Miss Temple leaving her house to me?" Violet says. "Even if her dead husband, *my father*, did leave a letter telling her to do it, that's just too unreal."

"Maybe she grew a conscience," Jack says. "Your family has been working for her family forever. Let's face it. You haven't been paid what you're worth the whole time you've been there, and it's doubtful anybody else did, either. Maybe it was time for her to give something back. Maybe, at the end of her life, she realized that."

"But this just doesn't happen in real life, Jack. No matter how many maybes you throw in."

He gives her a quick kiss on the lips and rolls over. "Just accept it and be grateful," he says.

Her anger at Queenie threatens to bleed over to Jack. She stops herself from voicing it. Besides, she doesn't have the energy to fight.

Within minutes, Jack begins his low snore. Violet questions briefly how he can sleep with all that has happened, but that is Jack. He's unflappable. He won't let this windfall go to his head. It simply goes in the blessing column, and a requirement of accepting blessings is to have gratitude. But Violet hasn't made her way to the gratitude column yet.

Her thoughts return to Queenie. She'll need a place to live. Violet can't imagine throwing her out. If anything, it's more Queenie's home than hers. Despite her anger and hurt, she has to admit that Queenie's reasons for withholding the truth make sense. Miss Temple could be vindictive. If she found out the truth, she might have thrown Queenie out of the house and probably Violet, too.

But why give Violet the house? Did she really feel that strongly about honoring the last wishes of Mister Oscar—Violet's father?

Something doesn't add up. Unfortunately, it seems, everybody who could clear up the mystery is dead.

I might as well give up on sleeping tonight, she thinks. Violet rolls over in bed and for the first time that day, her shoulder throbs. Edward. The last thing she needs is to have him seeking revenge for something she didn't even ask for. If she's right about him, and she's almost certain she is, he will do anything to get back whatever he feels belongs to him. Her shoulder confirms the danger. But there is already something suspicious going on. Someone in a black sedan is watching the Temple house. Not to mention that long-buried secrets are popping up everywhere.

CHAPTER TWENTY-FOUR

Rose

The landing at the Denver airport is bumpy. Wind currents dance along the Front Range of the Colorado Rockies like bucking broncos refusing to be tamed. Rose gets off the jet and has to resist getting on her hands and knees to kiss the azure blue carpet at the unloading gate. She makes her way through the familiar airport feeling a combination of fatigue, hunger, and shell-shock from the reading of her mother's will.

At the baggage claim, she looks for Max. He is probably parking the truck by now. At least she hopes he is. Rose feels weary from the day and wants to see him. It's hard to believe a few hours earlier, she was in the office of her mother's attorney. Yet Savannah feels a world away now. She wants to be home. She wants to sleep in her own bed. And tomorrow morning, Rose will get back to her regular routine and check in on the new calves that were born while she was away.

As she waits on Max, she tries to adjust to being back in the West. She remembers when she first arrived here. After growing up on the east coast, relocating to Cheyenne was like moving to another planet. The average rainfall is 13 to 15 inches in Wyoming. Savannah receives fifty inches or more. Cheyenne is high plains, semi-desert—Savannah is low country, sea level, and marshland. The first few years, it felt like the wind on the edge of the Great Plains nearly lifted her off the ground. She made jokes about being Dorothy in *The Wizard of Oz*. Now, like Dorothy, she wants to find her way back to Kansas, but in Rose's story, that is Savannah. She clicks her heels together three times but is too tired to smile.

A man next to her announces it is snowing outside, as he retrieves his skis from a second baggage area. Winter in Cheyenne has an element of life and death to it. Becoming stranded on the highway in an unexpected blizzard in April or May can be dangerous. A woman she knew from the co-op froze to death during a May snowstorm. Her body wasn't found until the snow-drift finally melted in mid-June. It is April now, one of the most unpredictable months of the year. It can be raining one minute, hailing another and snowing heavily the next. The Rocky Mountains create their own weather system, and the Front Range has a front-row seat to the drama. Meanwhile, Rose isn't even wearing a coat. It is packed in her suitcase.

"Where are you, Max?" she whispers, scanning the crowd for a familiar face.

"Are you from around here?" a young man asks, perhaps college age. If not dressed in blue jeans and a sweater, Rose might think he was a Hare Krishna. He seems much too friendly and peaceful to be an average guy. *Do Hare Krishnas still hang out in airports?* she wonders.

"I've lived in Wyoming for twenty-five years," Rose says.

"Wow, that's a really long time," he says. Rose is grateful he doesn't add that he wasn't even born yet or one of those comments that the young say to accidentally bring attention to how ancient she is. "I'm from D.C.," he adds. "Is it true that it's still wild here?"

"In Denver?" she asks.

"The West, in general," he says.

"It's true," she says. "We have coyotes that roam outside our ranch and pronghorn deer, descendants of the African antelope."

"Wow," he says again with a grin.

Rose doesn't really have the energy to be friendly, but in a way, it's a nice distraction while she waits on Max. On the ranch, there aren't many opportunities to *wow* people. "Of course, our biggest worry out here is the rattlesnakes." She adds this part solely for the shock effect.

"Really?" the young man says. His smile has not wavered.

"We find them in the garden all the time and under the house and in the barn, and sometimes they'll just be sunning themselves out on the road or next to the mailbox."

No wonder I miss Savannah, she thinks. The Georgia Coast has its own species of rattlesnake, as well as water moccasins. But in all the years she lived there, she never actually saw any. The wildness in the South has an easier time keeping itself hidden in the undergrowth than creatures in the stark, open plains. The people on the coast keep their wildness mostly hidden, too. Especially when it comes to their secrets.

Rose remembers the look on Edward's face when her part of the inheritance was read. If he had been holding a sword, he might have lopped off her head instead of a little finger.

The luggage conveyor springs to life. Everyone turns to watch luggage surge out of the terminal's inner bowels and circle on the baggage carousel.

"Hey, nice talking to you," the Hare Krishna says, with an even bigger smile to go with his blond hair and peaceful blue eyes.

"You, too," she says with what she decides is a western wave —quick and noncommittal. Rose and the young man are separated as people in the back move forward to get their bags.

As usual, Rose forgot to tie a red ribbon around the handle like Max always tells her to do, so that her common-looking black bag can be more easily recognized. She grabs one off the conveyor belt, sees it isn't hers, and then hoists it back. Too tired to be coordinated, Rose bangs her knee in the process. Wincing with pain, she eyes another.

"There you are," Max says, arriving at her side. He grabs Rose's bag off the conveyor belt just as it is about to pass and sits it at her feet. Help has arrived.

Rose hugs him and takes in his smell, his shape. At six feet, two inches, he is a half a foot taller than her, and when he's wearing his cowboy hat, it seems even more. Max has cleaned up for the occasion. He wears the shirt she loves and his best pair of blue jeans. His face is also clean-shaven. Rose hasn't realized just how much she missed him until this moment.

"You look good," he says.

"You're lying," Rose says. "I caught a look at myself in the airport bathroom and nearly scared myself to death. But thanks for saying so anyway." She squeezes him again. These days, her face always reveals her tiredness. She can't rely on the resiliency and elasticity of youth any longer, the only help she gets is from Revlon.

"How was the flight?" Max asks.

"Bumpy, as always," Rose says with a grimace.

Rose hates turbulence. It ranks right up there with stomach flu and a pinched nerve in her back. Except for the quickness of getting places, there isn't anything about flying that she actually enjoys. By car, the trip from Wyoming to the Georgia coastline would take 28 hours of nonstop driving. She would still be somewhere in Tennessee.

"Let's get you home, little lady," Max says in his faux western voice. His attempt to sound like John Wayne isn't even remotely close, but Rose plays along as his damsel in distress.

"Why, thank you, kind sir," Rose says in an exaggerated southern drawl she reserves only for him.

Max reaches for her carry-on full of books and magazines for the trip—she always takes enough to read for a year—and swings it lightly over his shoulder. Life feels easier whenever Max is around. Rose wraps her arm around his as they walk in a comfortable, welcoming silence to the parking garage.

After Max puts her things in the back of the truck, he pays the parking attendant, and they hit the open road. Despite her weariness, she resigns herself to the two-hour drive home.

Even though it is dark, Rose can feel the vastness of the landscape stretching out in front of them. It is snowing hard now. Max has his wipers on high. On I - 25, they have a straight shot home to Cheyenne. Rose's thoughts drift to where normal life awaits her. The next morning she will make her favorite coffee and glance at the morning newspaper before diving into the bookkeeping for the ranch that is undoubtedly piled up on the desk in the den. Then as soon as the sun is up, she will go out to the barn. *If I can make it to the barn,* she thinks, as they pass a snowplow.

The windshield wipers take frantic swipes to keep the glass clear. Her shoulders are tense. The weather is a topic of daily conversation at the ranch. Part of Rose's job is to monitor the cable weather channel, so nothing storm-related catches them by surprise.

"Do you want to tell me what happened?" Max says, breaking the silence. He keeps his eyes on the road.

Rose called him earlier that day and told him there was big news, but that she wanted to tell him in person. This also bought her time to decide how she felt about it. Max, in his infinite and sometimes maddening patience, hasn't pushed it. Now she feels too tired to go into it.

"You've kept me in suspense all day," he says as if sensing her hesitation.

Rose pauses, pulling forward what feels like her last bit of energy. "Well, it seems Mother has an interesting proposition for us," Rose says, "and I don't know if you'll even consider it for a second."

Max gives an inquisitive grunt, cowboy-ease, for *'what might that be?'*

"If I move back to Savannah, I inherit twenty million dollars," Rose begins. "If I stay here, I get two thousand."

This time, Max's grunt has more energy to it—a kind of nuanced *'what the hell?'* A long pause follows as he takes this news in. He doesn't talk much, but when he does say something, it is usually worth waiting for. Rose waits. She and Katie used to make jokes about Max being E. F. Hutton, from those stock brokerage commercials that aired with the slogan: *When E. F. Hutton talks, people listen.*

Max takes off his cowboy hat, worn on even the darkest of nights and the cloudiest of days. The lights on the dashboard reveal the crease from the brim that always brands his forehead, along with the rancher's version of a golfer's tan. Max grunts again.

A three-grunt conversation, Rose notes. *That's a new record.*

Rose doesn't know how to tell him that she'd like to go back. Maybe after she's rested, she'll have the energy to bring it up.

The wipers keep to their task and begin to drag against the glass. The snow slows. Max turns down the wipers, and Rose relaxes her shoulders.

"How soon can we pack?" Max says, finally.

Even in her tiredness, Rose's gasp is full volume. "Excuse me?" she asks.

This isn't the response she expected at all. She never considered that Max might actually give up the ranch. Four generations of his family have lived in Wyoming. Most of his extended family are still here, except for one wild cousin—considered disloyal by the rest of the family—who moved to Austin and works on radio.

"I say, let's do it," Max repeats, sans grunt.

"Are you serious?" Rose asks although she knows Max isn't the type to kid around.

"For twenty-five years, I've watched you try to fit in here," he says. "You've tried. You've really tried."

"But this is our home," she says.

"I know." He goes silent again like he's giving the possibility more thought.

For several minutes Rose is hypnotized by the wipers pushing the snowflakes to the edges of the windshield. She doesn't want to get her hopes up. If they stay in Cheyenne, she'll be fine. They have a good life here.

Max clears his throat and pulls her out of her daze.

"It's not a decision to take lightly, Rose, but I turn fifty this year. Before I know it, I'll be seventy, with no one to turn the ranch over to."

"What about Katie?" Rose asks.

"You know Katie doesn't want to come back here. She's not the ranching type."

Max is right. Katie wasn't happy in Cheyenne. She survived high school by pouring all her energy into making good grades so she could be accepted at a college back east.

The evening after the funeral, Rose gave Max a detailed description of Angela on the phone. Their daughter's lifestyle has not caused Max to waver in his devotion to Katie in the slightest. Their only hesitation—the fear of any parent, especially in Wyoming after the Matthew Shepherd tragedy—is that they don't want Katie to have a difficult life.

"Besides," Max begins again, "we're practically bankrupt. So twenty million dollars sounds very attractive at the moment."

They pass Fort Collins, an hour from home. The snow has slowed even more. A full moon emerges from behind the clouds. It fills the entire side view mirror and looks enormous. It suddenly occurs to Rose that if they move, she will miss seeing the moon and stars with such clarity on the open plains. But there is also something magical about seeing a full moon through trees laden with Spanish moss accompanied by the smell of magnolia blossoms wafting through the air.

"I can't believe you're even considering this," Rose says to Max.

"I can't believe I'm considering it, either," Max says. "But I think I'm ready for a new adventure. I'm definitely ready to stop working so damn hard. But mostly, I want you to be happy, Rose. We've lived for the last twenty-five years where I wanted to live. Let's live the next twenty-five years where you want to."

Emotion catches in her throat. She has never loved Max more than she does at this moment. Like every couple, they've had their issues, but nothing they didn't work hard to get past. She reaches over and takes his calloused right hand and presses her love into it.

"Are you sure?" she asks.

"I'm sure," he says.

Their eyes meet briefly, and he squeezes her hand again before returning it to the steering wheel.

The weariness around Max's eyes is as tangible as the calluses on his hands. She has spent hours of her life trying to rub the pain out of his back and shoulders after a long day. Ranching is hard on an almost fifty-year-old man. It's hard on anyone. She's had her share of aches and pains, too. But this is the first time she's heard him voice his willingness to walk away from the ranch.

Rose tries to imagine Max in Savannah. He's only been there twice. Once for their wedding and then a second time at Christmas, a year after that. Rose pauses to let this new possibility seep into her tired body. She thought moving back to Savannah was not even an option. She thought that Max wouldn't want to leave their home, nor be manipulated by her dead mother. But evidently, Rose thought wrong.

As they pass the last exit for Fort Collins, the snow begins again in earnest. She hopes they don't close I-25 down before they get home. She thinks back to her walk on the beach earlier that day. It was nearly 80 degrees in Savannah. She doesn't have the heart to tell this to Max.

Snow drifts form along the highway. Max isn't talking now. He's putting all his attention into getting them home before the road closes. Even though Max seems certain, they will probably need to have many more conversations about her mother's proposition before they sell the ranch. But Rose feels a spark of possibility come alive inside of her. Can she really go home again?

CHAPTER TWENTY-FIVE

11 Months Later
Queenie

The one year anniversary of Iris's death is a month away, and the *Temple Book of Secrets* is still in the news. Reporters have joined the crowds out front, and Queenie has even dealt with paparazzi while doing her errands. Paparazzi—Savannah style— which consists of a couple of acne-faced teenagers taking snapshots of her picking out lettuce in the produce aisle of the Piggly Wiggly. Why anyone in the world would want a picture of Queenie threatening to throw produce at her stalkers is beyond her.

After a court injunction stopped the newspaper from printing the secrets, they began to show up on flyers delivered to downtown mailboxes and stapled to light poles and trees. Not to mention community boards in almost every grocery store and coffee shop. The mystery continues as to who is planting the secrets, and Queenie has heard that there are even bookies who are laying odds as to who it might be. Queenie, Edward, and Rose are suspected. Even Violet has been named. But what would they have to gain from all this? If she had to guess, she thinks that whoever is planting the secrets is someone outside of the immediate family, but also someone who knows a tremendous amount about the Temples and somehow got access to the book. But how?

Queenie is usually good at figuring out *who done it* in the murder mysteries she reads, and it is often the last person you would ever suspect. But this is one mystery that has her totally stumped. She is even starting to wonder if it is the deceased Temples who are doing it, to somehow free themselves.

Whoever is doing it has not tired in their quest to expose every last secret. It doesn't matter if a secret is two hundred years old and contains information about a family that has long since died out, it shows up somewhere and is reported upon. Savannah is getting a history lesson about its past.

However, Queenie prefers to focus on the present. Earlier that day, she received a phone call from Rose that they sold their ranch and were now in the process of packing up everything to move to Savannah. At Violet's insistence, they will live in the Temple house with Queenie, as well as Violet and her family, who plan to move in as soon as school is out in June.

"How do you like that, Iris?" Queenie looks up at the light fixture in the sunroom. "This old mansion is becoming a halfway house for recovering Temples."

As always, Queenie's laugh comes out as a cackle, but then she stops herself with the thought: *No need to rub it in.* Even dead, Iris can still make Queenie regret it. For months now, she has carried a sweater with her everywhere she goes to combat the icy blasts of Iris's disapproval. But at least the odor has gone away.

For Queenie, life without Iris isn't what she expected. As much as she yearned not to be ordered around and criticized, she has yet to find something to fill the yawning gap that Iris left behind. In her weaker moments, she even wishes Iris was still here.

For months, Edward kept things interesting with his team of lawyers contesting the will like a team of Georgia bulldogs fighting for a touchdown from the one-yard line on a fourth down. However, Bo Rivers assures them that Edward doesn't have a case and that the entire dispute should be settled in the next few weeks.

Queenie walks into the dining room and looks out the window to see the black sedan parked in its usual place. It shows up as regularly as a Temple secret. She wonders if they are somehow related. Queenie goes into the kitchen where Violet is polishing the silverware at the kitchen table.

"What are you doing?" Queenie asks. "Nobody's going to fire you if you want to relax for a change."

"The silver still needs to be polished," Violet says. "What am I going to do, hire someone?" She laughs.

Queenie tells her she has a point and takes a polishing cloth and starts on the knives.

A day doesn't pass without Queenie writing in her journal about how grateful she is that Violet forgave her. It took several months and many talks and tears on both parts, but they reached the conclusion that they needed to forget the past and focus on the future.

Now, if these damn ghosts would just do the same, Queenie thinks. "Rose called this morning," she says to Violet. "They'll be here this time next month."

"I'm so glad they'll be living here, too," Violet says, going to town on a gravy boat. "At least then, the ghosts won't outnumber the people anymore."

"It's about time," Queenie says.

Violet's girls, her granddaughters, as Queenie is now finally free to call them, have already claimed two bedrooms at the east end of the house. Queenie and Violet have been getting them ready for weeks. Not only have they taken down draperies and cleaned windows, but they have also moved furniture from other parts of the house to accommodate two teenage girls.

"I like that this old house is coming alive again," Queenie says.

"I'm not sure the rest of the Temples like it," Violet says. "Have you noticed how quiet it's been on the ghost front lately?"

"Come to think of it, I haven't needed my sweater all day," Queenie says.

"It's like when children get quiet," Violet says. "It means they're up to something."

"It wouldn't be the first time," Queenie says. "By the way, Mama called with another warning. She says to be careful around the anniversary of Iris's death. Evidently, anniversaries create openings between the visible and the invisible worlds."

"That's the last thing we need," Violet says.

"Tell me about it." Queenie polishes the salad forks, wondering how many of her ancestors have done this same thing. Except now, these salad forks belong to her daughter. She smiles her glee.

"I think Rose and Max should have the back two bedrooms," Violet says. "They look out over the garden, and they can convert one of the bedrooms into a den."

"That's a great idea," Queenie says, "those rooms will be perfect for them." She remembers a summer when Violet and Rose were girls. The older she gets, the more vivid her recollections. "Do you remember saying as a little girl that you wanted to live with Rose when you grew up? Mama and I just rolled our eyes. But it seems you got your wish."

Violet smiles. "I'd forgotten all about that," she says. "Maybe the seed got planted then, and the possibility has been growing all these years."

"In that case, I should have planted the seed that I'd be wealthy in my old age," Queenie says with a wink. "But, I guess there's still time."

Queenie has talked to Violet about Old Sally may be living here, too, someday. Not that it will be easy to convince her to leave her house. Violet was totally open to the idea. Old Sally is getting frail—something she didn't think was possible a few years ago—and Queenie worries about her.

"By the way," Violet says. "Spud is coming over later to help with some things."

"He's been coming around a lot these days," Queenie says. She's not sure how she feels about this. In a way, she hates sharing Violet, now that they get along again. But she doesn't want to be selfish.

"I think he's lonely," Violet says. "That's our good luck because he's incredibly helpful, too."

"I'll see him today," Queenie says. "I've continued Iris's tradition of going to the Piggly Wiggly every Wednesday. He always seems glad to see me." What Queenie doesn't admit is she likes seeing him, too.

"Spud is a real sweetheart," Violet says. "Maybe you should get to know him a little better. How long's it been since you had a man in your life, Queenie?"

She pauses long enough to count back the years.

"Would you believe in 1973?" Queenie asks. This shocks her as much as it appears to shock Violet.

"Time to get back on that horse," Violet says.

"That horse turned into a jackass and died a long time ago," Queenie says with a chuckle.

"I have an idea," Violet says. "Why don't you invite him over for dinner? He's a vegetarian, you know, so how about picking up some Portobello mushrooms at the store, and I'll make Portobello burgers."

"I could never be interested in a man who doesn't eat meat," Queenie says, her tone dismissive.

"Don't make excuses," Violet says. She hands Queenie the car keys and gently pushes her toward the door.

. . .

As Queenie walks down the aisle toward the meat section, she remembers following Iris down this same aisle. At the counter, Spud Grainger wraps a package of ribs for a customer. When he sees Queenie, he smiles, and she nods in return. Lips pursed, she studies him from the back of the line.

He's a tad scrawny, as men go, she thinks, *yet still handsome.* It doesn't seem to matter that he's about a dozen shades lighter than Denzel. But how does he feel about full-figured women? Iris was scrawny as a Q-tip. Queenie puts her hands where her waist used to be. A waist that disappeared sometime in the 1970s. *Lord, have mercy,* she thinks, *if things ever got amorous, I might accidentally crush him.* She smiles at this thought and catches Spud Grainger smiling back.

When it is her turn, Queenie tells Spud of Violet's invitation to come to dinner that night, all the while trying not to gag at the thought of mushroom burgers.

Yet Spud accepts the invitation and then straightens his tie, which prompts Queenie to straighten the red wrap she's wearing around her hair. Instead of two peas in a pod, they are more like a zucchini and a watermelon growing on different vines altogether.

A flash goes off near the dairy section, and she rolls her eyes at the same kid who got a photo of her getting out of the Town Car. Does he think she's delivering a Temple secret to the butcher?

"If it's okay with you, I'll bring some shrimp," Spud says, unaware of the camera. "We just got in some beauties this morning. Do you like shrimp and grits?" he asks. "I make a mean shrimp and grits."

"I thought you were a vegetarian," Queenie whispers, in case he doesn't want his customers or the paparazzi to know.

"Not a strict one," he says. "I also eat seafood."

Queenie smiles, thinking there may be hope for him after all.

"Six o'clock?" Queenie asks. She flutters her eyelashes,

wondering who she's trying to fool. She hasn't flirted with a man since Elvis Presley wore blue suede shoes.

"Is something irritating your eye?" Spud asks. "I have some eye drops in the back."

Queenie assures him she's okay and swears off flirting for another forty years, as they say their goodbyes.

While in the area, Queenie gets her hair done at the Gladys Knight and the Tints beauty parlor, as she always does. It feels strange to drive on these outings, instead of being Iris's unwitting passenger. However, she likes the thought that pedestrians are safe in Savannah again. She half expects a public service announcement to run at the bottom of her favorite television programs to document this change. Along with the latest Temple secret.

In Iris's honor, and because she's hungry, Queenie goes through the pick-up window at Kentucky Fried Chicken. Another acne-clad teenager—minus a camera, yet with an Adam's apple the shape of a chicken gizzard—sticks his head out the window.

"Hey, isn't this the car of that rich old lady who used to come through?" he asks.

If I needed further proof there it is, Queenie thinks. "I'm afraid Iris Temple died almost a year ago," she tells him.

The teenager sniffs as if genuinely saddened, and starts to pick at one of his pimples. "She was kind of interesting, you know?"

"Yes, Iris Temple was definitely interesting," Queenie says.

He leans further out the window and whispers, "She used to tip me. Can you believe that? Nobody ever tips."

Queenie smiles. Iris could be generous when she wanted to be.

After he takes her order, the teenager gives Queenie a free side order of slaw as condolence. After parking at the back of the lot, she eats three chicken strips and a biscuit, along with the bereavement cole slaw. It is still a mystery to her how Iris could devour an entire bucket all by herself. As delicate as Iris's digestive system appeared to be, she must have had an iron stomach.

Queenie thinks back to the bucket of original recipe she placed in Iris's casket the morning of her funeral. *Not my finest moment,* she thinks, realizing that with all the preservatives they put in things these days, the chicken will probably stay crispy for the next thirty years.

She pauses with the regret that sweeps over her occasionally, but it's not like she can take it back. Queenie's feelings for Iris have softened over the last months, like a mother who forgets the pains of childbirth. Although she has a vivid memory of giving birth to Violet at her mother's beach house in the middle of the night on the 13th of August. Violet was a perfect baby, and it broke Queenie's heart to not claim her as her own. It was a death of a sort, too.

After she finishes the chicken, Queenie drives back to the Temple house, where the black Buick remains at the end of the block. On this particular day, the driver has changed shirts from the one he wore earlier. At least the sleeve sticking out of the window is different. The windows are tinted so she can't see his face.

"I'm going to get to the bottom of this once and for all," she tells herself.

Queenie parks the Town Car in the carriage house next to the big house and then sneaks back toward the gate so the anonymous driver won't see her in his rear-view mirror. She tiptoes down the sidewalk, wondering when she might have last tiptoed anywhere. Hiding behind a forest of pink azalea bushes, Queenie then scoots along the edge of the hedge. Finally, about twenty feet from the sedan, she begins to half-run, half-pounce toward the driver's window.

"Who are you?" she demands. "Why are you watching our house?"

The driver jumps and says, "Holy shit! Where'd you come from?"

The element of surprise has worked in her favor. She looks into the sunglasses that shield his eyes and sees her own reflection. She has to resist fixing the bow in her hair.

"What are you doing here?" she asks.

The driver turns on the car and quickly closes the window. She pounds on the dark glass. "Tell me who you are," she insists. "Are you the one releasing the Temple secrets?"

He guns the motor but waits until she is a safe distance away before he races off.

Her heart racing and still huffing from the exertion, Queenie retrieves her groceries from the car and goes inside to find Violet, who, despite her windfall inheritance, works every day as she always has. With everything in limbo until probate is over, Queenie has been paying her salary from her own savings, although she told Violet that she is using some money Iris left behind for household expenses.

"What's up with you?" Violet asks. "Why are you panting?"

"That guy's still out there," Queenie says. "I walked right up to his window this time, and I think I scared him to death."

"Did he say anything?"

"Nothing," Queenie says.

"It's not like we're doing anything worth watching," Violet says.

"Exactly," Queenie says. "But that makes twice I've tried to get a look at him and haven't been able to."

They agree that maybe Queenie should leave the sleuthing to someone else.

Everything from the refrigerator is on the counter, and Violet is wiping down the shelves. For the last couple of weeks, Violet and Queenie have done the spring cleaning of a lifetime. After taking down the heavy, lined curtains that covered every window of the house, they donated them to one of the black funeral homes in town. Every day the rooms get brighter. Queenie and Violet have also cleaned the inside windows, hiring a man to help with the outside. As her lower back can attest, they have scoured everything that can be scrubbed. She likes to think that they are cleaning out all the secrets that were ever hidden in the Temple house.

"Oh, I almost forgot, Spud will be here at six," Queenie says. "He's making shrimp and grits." She hands Violet the Portobello mushrooms.

"I'll marinate these and make some fresh collards," Violet says.

Collards are one of her mama's specialties, and her mouth waters just thinking about them. For some reason, Queenie has been thinking about her Gullah ancestors more than usual lately. She has a few ghosts to deal with on that side of the family, too. She thinks again of the man in the sedan. Even though she saw only a sliver of him through the window, there was something about him that seemed familiar.

LATER THAT EVENING, Queenie sets the kitchen table with regular plates, stainless steel cutlery, and worn cloth napkins—the ones the servants always used when she was growing up. No bone china. No silverware polished to a high gloss. No crystal water goblets. While incredibly casual in comparison to the fancy dinners Iris insisted on, Queenie loves the informality of her meals now. She has not missed the exotic smells that always hovered around the dining room one iota—including the ones coming from Iris.

From the kitchen, they hear a crash in the foyer. They exchange surprised looks before Queenie rushes into the dining room toward the noise, with Violet a second or two behind. A sizeable tropical plant in the hallway has fallen on its side with dirt scattered everywhere.

"Maybe our toddlers have shown up again," Violet says. "This kind of thing happened a lot right after Miss Temple passed."

Together they right the container, sweep dirt onto a dustpan and return it to the pot.

"Maybe she isn't happy with the changes we've been making," Violet says.

"Iris never did like change," Queenie offers.

Violet stops in the foyer and tilts her head to listen. "Oh my, Miss Temple is definitely worked up over something."

Will Iris ever be at peace? Queenie wonders. It's sad to think of her half-sister rattling around this old house, dragging her unfinished business through the rooms like an invisible steamer trunk, knocking over whatever gets in her way.

"We should tell Mama about it," Queenie says. "I hate to worry her with stuff like this, but maybe there's a Gullah spell that's like Valium for ghosts."

"Or maybe she can conjure up something for the humans who have to put up with them," Violet says.

Queenie smiles. "Now there's an idea," she says.

Violet pauses. "You know, Queenie, I've been thinking that it's time that I learned the Gullah secrets. Old Sally's been offering to teach me for years."

"She'll be thrilled to hear that, Vi, provided she doesn't already know through her tea leaves or something," Queenie says. "The minute you were born, she was convinced you had the family sensitivity. She even thought your gift might be stronger than hers. And, as you know, that's saying a lot. She'll be thrilled to hear your decision."

As far as Queenie is concerned, the family 'sensitivity' skipped a generation, leaving Queenie with a tone-deaf instrument. Not that she minds that much. Having the family gift seems as much a curse as a blessing. If she were as sensitive as Violet is to the entire goings-on in this house, she would probably be popping Xanax like after-dinner mints.

They scoop the last of the dirt back into its ornate pot, and within seconds someone bangs on the front door. They jump.

"Maybe it's that man watching the house," Queenie whispers.

"He's kept his distance for months," Violet whispers back.

"Why would he knock on the door now?" The knocking continues harder and louder.

"Or maybe it's someone pissed because their secret got out," Queenie whispers again. "Did anything show up in the mailbox today?"

"Not that I know of," Violet says.

They exchange a look. Thankfully, the protesting out front has all but stopped. But they've received packages of rat poison in the mail. A brick through a carriage house window closest to the gate. Not to mention, they pull enough posters off the fence every week to build a bonfire. But who knew that that crazy *Book of Secrets* contained enough confidences to release one every day for over a year.

Violet approaches the door with Queenie close behind. As she passes the ornamental stand by the door, Queenie grabs one of the large black umbrellas.

"I'm not afraid to use this," she says. "In fact, I welcome the opportunity."

Queenie pulls back the umbrella like it's a bat, and she's winding up to hit a baseball out of the ballpark.

"Let me in," a voice demands.

Every muscle in Queenie's body tenses as she recognizes the enraged voice of Edward Temple.

CHAPTER TWENTY-SIX

Violet

Violet's shoulder throbs as Edward Temple pounds the ancient beveled glass. If he breaks the glass, it will be next to impossible to replace. She and Queenie hide behind the door. Edward is furious, and Queenie looks about as terrified as Violet feels.

Before opening the front door, Violet takes a deep breath and tells herself to stay calm. Edward's face is red, and he smells of alcohol. Behind him, Spud has arrived for dinner and strides up the walk, looking alarmed. Violet appreciates his timing. They could use reinforcements.

Unfortunately, Edward has at least twenty pounds on Spud, but Edward's anger makes it seem like even more.

Spud asks Violet if she's all right. She says she is, but in fact, she's been better.

"Can I help you with something?" Spud asks Edward.

Edward narrows his eyes at Spud as if attempting to focus. "Oh, it's you," he says, "the family butcher. Making another delivery?" Edward smiles as though he finds himself funny. Then he turns and glares at Violet like she has something he wants.

"I suggest you calm down, Mister Temple," Spud says from behind him.

"I suggest you go screw yourself, Mister Grainger," Edward answers, not taking his eyes off Violet.

A sharp pain shoots through Violet's shoulder, and she grabs the door jamb to steady herself. Meanwhile, Queenie holds up the umbrella like she's ready to swing for the fences if Edward takes another step forward.

Weeks ago, Violet heard that Edward's case against Miss Temple's will wasn't going in his favor. This is the part about having money that Violet doesn't like. It can make people greedy and not think clearly. She has no idea why Miss Temple didn't take better care of Edward in her will, but she is certain she had her reasons. Miss Temple always had her reasons.

"Perhaps we should speak about this in the lawyer's office," Violet says. She crosses her arms, getting a ghost of a chill.

"Those asshole attorneys don't know what they're doing," Edward says, as a spitball of saliva hits her cheek.

Violet hates cussing as much as she despises Edward.

Edward's eyes are red like he's had too many martinis. A piece of toilet paper clings to a small dot of blood on his neck.

"I need to look for something in the house," Edward tells Violet. "It's imperative."

Even if he is her half-brother, Violet isn't about to let him in and resists telling him it isn't his house anymore.

Seconds later, a police car arrives, flashing lights twirling but no siren. Edward cusses under his breath. In Violet's and Jack's neighborhood, the police would have sirens blasting and two or three squad cars. Yet here they don't seem to want to disturb Savannah's wealthiest citizens. For the first time Violet realizes that because of inheriting this house, she is now part of the wealthy, too.

One of the police officers walks up to the front door, and Edward straightens his clothes like he's getting in character. He turns to greet the cop.

"Are you sure you're all right?" Spud asks Violet and Queenie.

"A bit shaken, that's all," Violet says.

Violet and Queenie hold hands, and Spud looks at them like he's seeing the family resemblance for the first time. It is still odd for Violet to think of Queenie as her mother. But she looks forward to getting used to it.

"Who called?" one of the police officers asks. He looks barely old enough to shave. A drop of mustard christens his shirt to the right of his identification tag. Violet's first inclination is to grab the spot remover from the laundry room and get that stain out before it sets.

Violet looks at Queenie, who shrugs, her umbrella still poised. "I'm not sure who called," she says.

"Ma'am, I need you to put that down," the officer says to Queenie.

Queenie glances at the umbrella she forgot she was holding. Then she returns it to the stand just inside the door, and the officer thanks her.

Edward steps forward and introduces himself, holding out his hand for the young officer to shake. The officer puts his hand on his holstered gun instead.

"Step over here, sir," the second officer says. He is older, with a substantial middle-aged paunch.

"Don't you know who I am?" Edward asks the officer, his voice raised. "Who is your commanding officer? I could have you fired, you know."

Edward may know how to talk to a high society crowd, but you don't speak this way to regular people. Especially if they work for law enforcement.

"Yes, sir, I'm sure you could get me fired," the officer says. "And my wife would be all for it, too." The officer leans next to Edward and sniffs. "Is that alcohol I smell on your breath, sir? Did you drive here?"

"For God's sake, go catch some real criminals," Edward says.

Within seconds, the officer has Edward walking a straight line and touching his nose. A test he appears to fail. What prompted Edward to lose control like this? In the distance, he points at Violet and Queenie like they are the real criminals.

"Those women have something I need," Edward says. "They are thieves. They are living in my house under false pretenses. They must be removed immediately."

Edward holds his stomach and releases a burst of gas like a warning shot over the bow of a ship. Violet cringes, feeling mortified for Edward. But Edward doesn't seem embarrassed by it at all.

"Good heavens, man." The older officer covers his nose with his sleeve.

Edward points his finger at Violet and Queenie. "It's my house. Not theirs. Look at them," Edward continues. "Do they look like they belong here?"

The older officer looks at Edward, then at Violet and Queenie. He shakes his head like he's sick and tired of dealing with people like Edward.

"I think we'd better take them all downtown," the older officer says to his partner. The younger officer agrees.

Edward turns toward the house. "But I need to find the key," he says.

Violet's shoulder throbs again. The younger officer takes Edward to the squad car as Edward keeps yelling about needing to find a key. Does he mean a key to the front door? Then the older officer walks up to the porch to escort Violet and Queenie down the walk.

"Excuse me, officer," Spud says. "Do you mind if I drive these women to the station? We could follow you."

The officer hesitates but then agrees.

"It's just a formality," Spud says to Violet and Queenie, as he opens the door of his small Toyota. Queenie eyes the back seat like she's wondering if she can fit.

"Would it still be a formality if we weren't a darker color than them?" Violet asks.

Spud says he doesn't know, but he hopes that isn't the case.

Meanwhile, Queenie falls into the back seat of the Toyota and says, "Heaven help me, this car is made for midgets!"

Violet laughs and gets in on the passenger side.

"Why was Edward making all that noise about a key?" Spud asks.

"This is the first I've heard anything about a missing key," Violet says. But her shoulder confirms that it is something important.

"Maybe he's trying to find the key to the safe deposit box," Queenie says from the back seat. "That means there's probably a whole lot more in there besides the *Temple Book of Secrets*. For all we know, there may be secrets about people that don't even have ties to Savannah. Senators. U.S. Presidents. Iris's grandfather dealt with foreign heads of state," she continues. "The possibilities are endless as to what the Temples—what *we*—have lorded over people."

It is still strange for Violet to realize she is even remotely related to the Temples.

"But I thought this last year of being in the spotlight would be the end of it," Violet says.

"We may be closer to the beginning than the end," Queenie says.

The pain in Violet's shoulder intensifies, confirming that whatever has Edward worked up has placed them all in grave danger.

CHAPTER TWENTY-SEVEN

Queenie

"Happy Anniversary, Iris."

Queenie addresses the chandelier in the dining room, which always shakes with the cold blast of Iris's presence. She and Violet clear dinner dishes from the dining room table, which hasn't been used since Iris's stroke. But they wanted to have a special dinner to celebrate Rose and Max's arrival earlier that afternoon. They had driven for three days and have already retired to a guest room upstairs to get some rest. The moving trucks are scheduled to arrive next week.

"I'd forgotten how handsome Max is, in a rugged cowboy sort of way," Queenie says. She follows Violet into the kitchen and wonders if Denzel Washington has ever made a western.

"Max seems quiet but nice," Violet says. She stacks dishes next to the sink.

"He certainly loved your roast," Queenie says, "and the apple pie."

Violet smiles and then rubs her left shoulder. "Something isn't right," she says.

"It's bothering you again?" Queenie asks.

"Maybe I'm just getting old," Violet says.

"Nonsense. I've got pantyhose older than you. Besides, that shoulder is better than having a crystal ball."

Violet frowns. "The last time it did this was the night Edward showed up at the door, and we ended up at the police station," she says.

Queenie and Violet spent nearly an hour explaining their relationship to the Temples to a police sergeant who took notes like he was writing a screenplay. Finally, Queenie thought to call Bo Rivers, who showed up in the middle of the night to clear things up. As much as she tries to resist it, there is something about him that she likes. Bo asked for a temporary restraining order against Edward, which she is sure didn't go over very well. Edward wasn't charged with anything, and luckily neither were they.

After that night, Queenie and Violet began a diligent search for the key to the safe deposit box that holds the *Temple Book of Secrets*, and no telling what else. So far, they've found nothing.

"Surely Edward won't show up tonight," Queenie says, addressing the concerns of Violet's shoulder. "He doesn't even know Rose is here. Plus, we've got a cowboy in the house, and I don't think Max will let Edward get away with anything."

Violet doesn't look convinced. "All I know is that as soon as Rose and Max arrived, Miss Temple's ghost started throwing fits," she says. "Then the others got on the bandwagon. I've never heard them this high-spirited."

"Maybe it's because of the anniversary that Mama warned us about," Queenie says.

Anniversaries of deaths don't usually bother her, but for some reason, this one has her biting her nails. Queenie is nowhere near as sensitive as Violet, but even she can feel a tension in the air.

"I guess it could be a false alarm," Violet says. It sounds like she's trying to convince herself, as well as Queenie.

"*I guess* I could be a size six," Queenie says with a laugh, thinking the last time she was a size six was probably when she was about six years old.

Violet rolls her eyes, and it reminds Queenie of how Violet did this as a girl.

"Well, I'm going to leave the dishes until the morning," Violet says. "I've got to get home. Jack will be wondering what happened to me. Will you be okay?" she adds.

"Don't worry about us. I'll keep an eye on things," Queenie says. "And tell my son-in-law hello."

As they hug, Queenie feels grateful again for Violet's forgiveness. Life is much more enjoyable—not to mention simpler—without so many secrets to keep. Although she has a feeling the Temples have a few more hidden away.

After Violet leaves, the house is quiet. Almost too quiet. The kind of quiet that makes people use clichés like *the calm before the storm*. It doesn't help that Queenie has been reading a new murder mystery in the sunroom, now dark except for a single Tiffany lamp near her chair. The room itself looks staged for a murder, and it helps to remember that Rose and Max are upstairs.

The sound of rattling glassware comes from Oscar's old office. Queenie gets up and walks toward the noise.

I'm acting like every nitwit in every horror movie I've ever seen, she tells herself, but this awareness doesn't stop her.

She opens the door to his study and turns on the light. Nothing is out of place. No shadows grace the corners. Except for Iris, who doesn't seem to mind being blatant with her gusts of cold air, it's hard to catch the Temple ghosts haunting the place. She pulls her sweater closer. Her attention is drawn toward the leather couch against one wall, the scene of more than one secret.

"Are you getting in on the excitement, too, Oscar?" Queenie asks. She looks at the large leather chair behind the desk, where he often sat nursing a glass of bourbon. A photograph of Iris glares at Queenie from the desk. "You stay out of this," she says, pointing at Iris's framed stare.

Violet is right, Queenie thinks, *the knocks and creaks in the old house are turned up on high tonight.*

Maybe, without her knowledge, a family reunion of dead Temples has been called. Queenie shivers with the thought, then returns to the sunroom to get her book before going upstairs. Despite the extra noises, Queenie anticipates sleeping better tonight with Rose and Max nearby. She hasn't liked sleeping in the house alone since Iris died. Violet didn't want to move her family until it was clear Edward would lose his legal challenge. She also didn't want to disrupt Tia and Leisha's school year, which Queenie could understand.

In bed now, Queenie finishes another chapter of her book. A murderer stalks within the pages of the novel she's reading, and she can't help feeling that someone is stalking here, too. Certainly not Rose or Max, but it is a big house with plenty of room for murderers to hide. Not to mention, most of Savannah has it in for them right now.

Queenie reaches into her nightstand to retrieve a hefty stack of letters. She hasn't told Violet how many death threats she's received in the last eleven months. At first, they were all addressed to Iris, but since her death, they aren't sent to anyone in particular. They arrive anonymously. No return address. The threat typed on plain white paper as if they all watched the same television mystery. Some say they are watching, and when we least expect it, they will get us. Others say to stop telling secrets, or we'll live to regret it. Threats are rarely very creative. At least the lawsuits have been dropped since Iris's death.

Queenie takes comfort in the fact that the Temple mansion is practically a fortress with its security alarms and locked gates. She also knows that most threats are simply that—threats. It is a bold move for a bully to actually take action on what they say. She sighs, too tired to entertain her fantasies. It takes forever for her to fall asleep, yet when she does, it is deep.

THE TELEPHONE RINGS several times before Queenie is awake enough to answer it. When she picks up the phone, she hears her mother's voice: "Get out of the house, baby. Bad things be happening."

Queenie, in that fuzzy place between wakefulness and dreaming, keeps wondering which world is real. She opens one eye and glances at the digital clock by the bed. It is 4:34 in the morning.

"You hear me, baby? You be in danger," her mama says. "Get out of the house!"

Old Sally's frantic message finally breaks through the fuzziness. Queenie sits straight up, and her eyes pop open like she's just had a double espresso. It's not just her in danger, but Rose and Max, too. She sniffs and smells smoke.

"Mama, call the fire department!" Queenie tells her before slamming down the phone.

A crackling comes from downstairs that sounds like bacon frying. Hundreds of strips of bacon. The whole downstairs is the pan. Queenie sniffs and smells smoke. She remembers a recurring nightmare from her childhood where the same thing happened: a frantic call from her mother, the crackling fire, the desperate need to get out of the Temple house. She has an odd feeling of going through the same motions. The dream always ended before she got out, as though the real ending is being left up to her.

Queenie stands and throws on her yellow bathrobe. She pauses long enough to wonder what she should take with her as she flees. She thinks of her dozens of journals, too heavy to carry out. Then her gaze falls on the framed photograph on her bedside table taken years before of a young Violet and Rose on the beach.

Clutching it to her chest, she runs to her bedroom door. She unlatches it and then stops. Like she saw in a movie once, she touches the outside of the door to see if it's hot. The door is cool to the touch, so she opens it. Smoke wafts up the stairs. She coughs and pulls her bathrobe over her nose to keep out the smoke.

Queenie makes her way to the bedroom where Rose and Max are staying. The smoke hasn't reached here yet. Yelling their names, she bangs on their door. Max opens the door wearing boxer shorts and his cowboy hat.

"Fire!" Queenie manages to yell, which sounds like something a prankster would yell in a crowded movie theater.

Max turns and yells to Rose to wake up. Within seconds, they have thrown on clothes and shoes as if they've practiced this scenario before. Then the three of them set out for the stairs. The darkness is illuminated with a nightlight of flames. In the shadows, Queenie sees someone fleeing downstairs. Fearing Violet may have returned to the house, she calls out. But the figure is too tall to be Violet. Whoever it is runs through the dining room and into the kitchen, disappearing so quickly Queenie wonders if she imagined it.

The crackling of the fire increases as they descend the stairs. The flame's intensity dwarfs any heatwave Savannah has ever experienced. The nightgown underneath her robe is soaked with sweat. They descend the spiral staircase and Queenie hesitates at the bottom, long enough for Max to yell out that they can't stop.

The inferno roars and swallows his words as soon as he shouts them. Rose's eyes are wide with terror. Max takes both of them by the arms and leads them toward the door, yelling at them to keep moving. All of a sudden, dark smoke billows out of the kitchen. The door between the kitchen and dining room is now covered in flames crawling toward the ceiling. Queenie doesn't see how anyone could have escaped through the wall of fire.

"Shouldn't we try to save something?" Queenie yells, but the flames swallow her words, and no one hears her.

Priceless artwork and antiques fill the house, as well as Temple memorabilia dating back to the Revolutionary War. She glances at the extinguished Civil War torch in the Temple foyer and wonders if the ghost of one of those Union soldiers—or perhaps General Sherman himself—has shown up to finish the job. She hears her mama's voice tell her to keep going, to get out of the house. It's like a secret passageway has opened between their minds, and Queenie hears her mother's thoughts. She tells Queenie to run and then orders Edward out of the house, too. Is Edward here? Could that be who she saw in the house?

Smoke billows across the high ceilings, unwilling to waste any time. The whole back of the house is already engulfed in flames. A smoky orange glow illuminates the contents of the house.

Two thoughts occur almost simultaneously: *How has the fire spread so quickly? And why haven't the alarms gone off?*

They move now as if in slow motion. Everywhere they turn, there are more flames. The floor grows hotter under her bare feet. She wishes now she'd thought to grab a pair of shoes. Sweat drips into her eyes and stings. They pause in the foyer. The floor gets hotter, as though the cellar underneath her has turned into a furnace. Queenie sidesteps the embers that begin to pop and fly from the walls. With Max's help, they make their way to the front of the house and he flings open the heavy wooden front door. The moist air of the Georgia coastline fills her lungs as they run toward the street.

"The dogs are in the carriage house," Max yells over the noise of the flames. He runs in that direction as Queenie and Rose wait on the sidewalk in front of the house. Queenie puts an arm around Rose, who appears stunned, as anyone would. She glances down the street for the black sedan, but it isn't there.

"I'm going to go next door and call the fire department," Queenie says.

Rose nods, her gaze transfixed on the burning Temple house.

Since Queenie hasn't run anywhere since Jimmy Carter was in

office, her awkward jaunt across the street to the Bennett house takes her breath away. Pebbles stick to the bottom of her feet. Every few steps, she stops to brush them away. Mister Bennett lives there with his new wife, who moved in two years before. They are an American cliché. The new Mrs. Bennett is thirty years younger than her husband and used to dance in a chorus line on Broadway. Soon after she moved in, Iris dismissed the woman as *trailer trash* and wrote a letter to the head of the historical district to insist that they weed out the riffraff. Queenie isn't even sure what *'riffraff'* is, but Iris would probably put her into the same category.

From the looks of things, I'm homeless riffraff now, Queenie decides.

As she pounds on the Bennett's door, she remembers Edward's pounding from weeks before. Was he the one who started the fire? Is Edward the type to burn down a house out of spite? She pounds on the door again and tries to remember if the Bennetts have had any secrets revealed about them. If so, they might slam the door in her face. She can't remember. Maybe something about his first wife, who was addicted to painkillers and went to the Betty Ford clinic? She realizes how silly secrets are when it comes to life and death issues like fires.

The *riffraff* dancer answers the door in a red teddy that pushes her ample breasts toward heaven.

Mercy, Queenie thinks, *those things will have every heterosexual man in Savannah puckering up.* Queenie has to remind herself not to stare.

"Our house is on fire!" Queenie yells. She turns and points to the illuminated skyline. The teddy-clad dancer runs back inside and calls for her husband to telephone the fire department. Before Queenie has time to thank her, the first fire truck rounds the curve that her mama must have called.

The teddy-clad dancer invites her inside. Queenie thanks her, but then explains that she has to check on Rose, Iris Temple's estranged daughter who has moved back to Savannah with her cowboy husband and their two dogs. Sometimes when Queenie is stressed, she gives too many details.

"It would be helpful if you could call my daughter, Violet, and tell her what's happening," Queenie says to the new Mrs. Bennett. Queenie writes down the number on a piece of paper Mrs. Bennett provides.

Violet will be heartbroken that her surprise inheritance is going up in flames. But what if the fire had broken out while they were all living there? Maybe not all of them would have gotten out.

Sirens pierce the night air as red and white lights bounce 360 degrees around the square. Firemen jump off trucks and run with hoses toward the house. It is exhilarating, in a way, to watch such heroic actions. Flames climb the outside of the building like red wisteria vines. Within seconds, two of the dining room windows burst outward, causing the firemen to duck and cover their heads. Just as another fire truck arrives, flames surge out of the broken windows like a dragon whose fury has been unleashed.

From the Bennett's driveway, Queenie watches the scene in disbelief. She has always enjoyed fires in fireplaces. Fires with carefully confined blazes that take the moisture out of a room on the handful of cold days in Savannah when the temperature nears freezing. But this blaze is a different beast. It roars its power and jumps from one surface to the next while eating everything in its path. Yet miraculously, it stays contained to the Temple house. Multimillion-dollar mansions on either side remain untouched.

A small crowd gathers as Queenie rejoins Rose and Max a hundred yards away from the burning Temple home. Their two border collies, Lucy and Ethel, howl to the chorus of fire trucks. Queenie stands barefoot on the sidewalk, her feet aching from her flight across ash and ember. Flames shoot out of Iris's bedroom window and stretch into the sky. For a split second, Queenie sees the figure again in the window. She squints to make out who it is.

"Did you see that?" she asks Rose.

They stare at the window. "Maybe it's a Temple ghost," Rose says.

"Or maybe it's Edward," Queenie says.

"Edward?" Rose asks. "You think Edward might be in the house?"

Rose runs to a nearby fireman. "I think my brother may be in there," she calls to him over the noise of the fire and spraying hoses.

With a look of alarm, the fireman runs to his superior. Both men study the flames. Seconds later, the inferno explodes outward. Everyone cowers to avoid flying debris. The front of the house is now engulfed. The fire chief directs the hoses to address the latest surge and walks over to Rose and Queenie. "I'm sorry, but I can't send my men in there. It's just too dangerous," he says.

Rose and Queenie look back at the house.

"What was Edward doing in there?" Rose asks her.

Queenie tells her she doesn't know.

Meanwhile, a crowd has gathered in front of the house. Some of them are people she recognizes from protesting the secrets being released. At least they aren't chanting while the house burns. She doubts any of them would have had the nerve to start the fire if it was arson.

Max returns and holds Rose in his arms, two leashes in hand. The dogs are quiet now. Everyone is.

CHAPTER TWENTY-EIGHT

Old Sally

"It be time," Old Sally says. The dream woke her out of a sound sleep. In it, the ancestors told her that today is a day of reckoning. It is also the anniversary of Iris's failed crossing. This told her that Iris may be trying to go again.

Old Sally believes dreams are always a step or two ahead. Sure, they speak in riddles most of the time. But they are riddles that Old Sally takes the time to decipher. After more than a half-century of listening to her dreams, Old Sally believes they have wisdom deep as a gold mine, but only if you take the time to dig out the gold. These days, they come to her crystal clear. She will make her own crossing soon enough.

In this most recent dream, the Temple house was on fire. Edward wore his great grandfather's Confederate uniform and set fire to the draperies in his mother's room while all the Temple spirits urged him on. Iris laughed as the flames increased as if this was the only way to take back her power. Edward acted out his mother's bidding.

Awake, her heart still races while she calls Queenie and then the fire department. Then she calls Kenny, the son of a friend of hers who lives nearby, to get a ride into Savannah.

As she gets dressed, Old Sally remembers the night Iris died and how Iris cursed her as Old Sally tried to help with her transition. She's been waiting to see how that curse plays out. Being on the other side, all mysteries are revealed, so Iris Temple knows the spells she's put on her over the years. This knowledge, no doubt, fueled Iris's need for getting even. Now it seems her revenge is to put Queenie in danger. The worst way to hurt a woman is to harm her children.

Old Sally goes out of the kitchen door and down the back stairs to wait for Kenny. The moon is so full it makes her eyes widen. Its power pulls the tide high, as the waves crash on the other side of the dunes. She's seen many storms on this beach and a hurricane or two, but tonight feels much more dangerous. Old Sally asks again for their ancestors to intercede and keep Queenie, Rose, and Max safe. Headlights turn off the main road, and she makes her way to the end of the walk.

Kenny stops the car and runs to the passenger side to open the door for Old Sally. He is in his thirties now, but he was in some trouble as a teenager. Nothing that serious, but he stayed with Old Sally until he got his life back on track. Kenny is the color of night and is sweet as an angel if you treat him nice. He drives a bit reckless, and as soon as they take off, Old Sally grips the door. She puts up with Kenny's driving because her child is in danger. It doesn't matter that her child is in her sixties.

"I left there around midnight, and everything was quiet," Kenny says.

Kenny is out of work right now and agreed to keep an eye on Queenie and Violet after Old Sally saw in the tea leaves that Edward and Iris might try to hurt them.

"This not be your fault, Kenny," Old Sally says. "Bigger forces at work."

The world blurs by Old Sally's window as they ride in silence. *That's what it's like to get this old,* she thinks. You look up one day, and your whole life has rushed past so fast you barely caught a glimpse of what's passing. Then before you know it, you're at the end of your life and wondering how you got there.

Old Sally shivers with the awareness that Queenie and Rose are still in danger.

"Can you get there any faster?" Old Sally asks Kenny.

"Are you sure?" he asks.

Old Sally nods.

"Well, hang onto the Jesus bar," he tells her.

"The what?" Old Sally asks.

"The handle above the door. You hold it and say, *Oh, Jesus!*" Kenny laughs.

"You was always a cut-up, Kenny, even when you was a little boy." She grips the handle, thinking *I'll take all the help I can get.* Then as Kenny accelerates, she closes her eyes.

WHEN THE CAR finally comes to a stop, Old Sally opens her eyes again and waits for her stomach to catch up. A block away, the Temple house is in flames. The sight makes her want to close her eyes again, but she reminds herself that sometimes total destruction is the only hope for things to change.

Kenny comes around and opens her door. Ash flies through the air and is all she can smell. When Old Sally gets out of the car, she realizes how tired she is. Not just from being up in the middle of the night, but from all the years of battling the dark side of the Temple family. She is ready for this to be over. It started this time last year when all those secrets got released. It was the beginning of gaining power over the darkness.

Her heart pounds as she finally sees her daughter. Queenie

crosses the street and walks into Old Sally's arms. Old Sally hangs on tighter than she usually would. Only she knows how close she came to losing her daughter.

"Are you okay, baby?" Old Sally asks.

"I've been better," Queenie says. "It looks like I don't have anywhere to live anymore."

"You know you can always live with me," Old Sally says.

"At sixty, moving back in with my hundred-year-old mother isn't that appealing." Queenie's laugh dies quickly like an ember shooting from the house.

While Queenie holds her arm, Old Sally watches the fire.

"A dream woke me up," Old Sally says. "I saw the flames, and I saw you and Rose and Max still in the house. I be so frightened," she adds. "I thought the Temples had finally won."

"They almost did," Queenie says. "But I don't think Edward was as lucky."

Old Sally looks up at the burning house.

Sacrifices are often required before things can change, she thinks. She lost her daughter Maya way too young. Now there is Edward.

"Shame on you, Iris, for poisoning your son and creating this mess," she says aloud. Iris poisoned Edward with bitterness just like she tried to poison Rose. But unfortunately, Edward liked the poison.

Old Sally turns away from the fire. The way she sees it, all those years when Rose was out of the picture, Edward was glad. It meant more for him. But when he heard that Rose was coming back, he plotted on how to get his way. Just like he cut off a piece of Rose's finger when she was a little girl, he thought nothing of cutting her out of the picture forever.

Yesterday, Old Sally spent all day putting together another protection spell for Rose on her return to Savannah, using the tears she collected when Rose came to visit her at the beach. She renewed a protection spell on Violet, too, since Edward already came after her once when she was young.

There was another Edward, Queenie's father, who Old Sally wasn't strong enough to resist, so she got pulled into history repeating itself, as did Queenie. But Violet was unwilling to go down that road. Old Sally is proud of her granddaughter for that. She may be the strongest of Old Sally's line yet.

"I want to see Rose," Old Sally says.

Queenie helps her cross the street. "Mama, who brought you here?" Queenie asks, glancing back at the black sedan.

"That be Kenny," Old Sally says. "You remember Kenny, Evelyn's boy? He was away for a long time but came back a year ago."

"That tall black man is little Kenny who used to come to the house with Evelyn?"

"He's not so little anymore," Old Sally says.

"All this time, I thought he was one of Edward's goons," Queenie says.

"No, he be one of my goons," Old Sally says, the word 'goon' giving her pleasure. "Did I ever tell you about the time Iris accused me of being part of the Gullah mafia? I said to her, 'Iris, I not part, I be the head!' Iris didn't know what to say to that, but I think she kind of believed me."

"I guess nothing should surprise me anymore," Queenie says. "I certainly never expected you to have Kenny spy on us for nearly a year."

"I needed to protect you from Edward, and anybody who might be upset about their secrets being told," Old Sally says. "But the one time Edward did show up a few weeks ago, Kenny had gone to take his mama to church. He felt awful about that, too. Of course, Kenny has to sleep, so he goes home around midnight every night."

"But how could you afford to hire someone to watch the house?" Queenie says.

"It not cost a thing," Old Sally says. "Maybe you don't remember, but I helped his mama heal her cancer a few years back."

"Why didn't you just put a spell on Edward?" Queenie asks.

"I have two spells on him already," Old Sally says. "But since his mama died, she joined forces with him, so I needed a little extra help."

"I'm glad you called when you did, Mama. You saved our lives."

Old Sally and Queenie join Rose and Max in front of the house, and she gives Rose a big hug.

"Edward was in there," Rose says, her voice shaking with emotion. "Was he waiting for me to come back to do this?" Rose asks. "How did he even know?"

"He probably had someone watching the house, too," Old Sally says.

Max extends his hand, and Old Sally shakes it. The last time she saw him was the Christmas after he and Rose married. *Some men be afraid of them hugs*, she thinks. *But give me time. I'll win him over.* Regardless, she can tell he is a good man.

"Mama, when we were fleeing the fire, I heard you talking to me in my head," Queenie says.

"I know you did, baby."

"But how is that possible?"

"There be all sorts of mysteries playing out all the time," Old Sally says. "Besides, you may have more of me in you than you think."

"Maybe I do," Queenie says.

Violet and Jack arrive, winded from running from where they parked their car. Violet gasps when she gets close, as though swallowing a scream. Then tears begin, and Queenie pulls her close. To see Violet hurting makes Queenie cry, too. Old Sally is so happy they get to be mother and daughter again.

"It be alright, Violet," Old Sally says. "Important things can't be destroyed. They be yours forever." Now it's her turn to give Violet a hug. The four women stand witnessing the sacred flames, while the men talk.

"My shoulder predicted this was going to happen," Violet tells Old Sally. "After I got home, it got so painful I walked into the emergency room. But the doctors couldn't find a single thing wrong, and now it doesn't hurt at all."

"That shoulder kept you safe and sound," Old Sally says.

Violet agrees.

"I'm sorry about the house, sweetheart," Queenie says. "But Mama's right. We haven't lost the important things."

Meanwhile, Old Sally pictures all those secrets going up in flames with the Temple ghosts and the Temple house. The fire purifies and wipes clean all the sins and secrets of the Temple family.

A blessing can often be found in the center of a tragedy, she thinks.

Despite the firefighters' efforts, the blaze continues to burn through the early morning hours, fueled, she imagines, by a century's worth of lemon oil massaged into the ancient wood of antiques. Some of that polishing came from her. She can still smell that lemon oil on her hands sometimes, like a ghost at her fingertips.

A fire always draws people to it. It seems all of Savannah is here to watch the Temple house burn. Iris Temple spent most of her life trying to leave a legacy that people would respect, but she also saved secrets to threaten people with if she ever needed to get her way. With the Temple secrets purged and the house destroyed, the Temple family might be able to rebuild on a new foundation.

Old Sally senses her mother and grandmother watching the scene. Their spirits finally liberated from the past. Both women worked at the Temple house, their tears and sweat embedded in the history of this place. Meanwhile, the scene holds them all captive, as they are called to witness the end of an era.

"I think Edward was in the house because he was looking for the key to the safety deposit box," Queenie says, the first to break their silence. "Maybe he found it and started the fire. Or maybe the fire was an accident. But that safety deposit box held the *Book of Secrets,* as well as a bunch of other things that would make people nervous."

Old Sally startles at Queenie's words. Could there be more in that box than the *Book of Secrets*? Things Old Sally doesn't know about? She forces herself to believe that it is finished. She doesn't have the strength to do more. Either way, her part is over. She is certain of this. Only one ritual remains.

"Was the key somewhere in the house?" Rose asks.

"Nobody knows," Queenie says. "Iris died without telling anyone where she kept it. At least as far as I know."

Old Sally remembers where the key used to be kept. She found it one day while she was cleaning, probably thirty years before. Among the old objects on the dresser, there was a new box there. She had opened it to see what was inside. The key was there on a small gold chain.

"But why would a key be so important?" Rose asks.

"The keeper of the key has the power," Old Sally says. For everyone's sake, she hopes that the key is never found.

"Mama, did your dream show you how the fire got started?" Queenie asks. "The fire alarms attached to the security system didn't work, even though I just had them tested last month."

"It be Edward," Old Sally says. "With the encouragement of Iris."

"You mean on purpose??" Violet asks.

"Yes," Old Sally says. "I don't have proof, but I think Edward be a prisoner to the old ways, too, and needed things to change."

Old Sally stands between Violet and Queenie near the old oak that holds court in the Temple garden. Like the houses nearby, it remains untouched by the fire. A slight breeze blows from the east, carrying the smell of the sea. The crowd has dwindled, leaving only a few firemen and family behind.

"Old powers claim people every day," Old Sally says. "The Temple house burning to the ground be a fitting end to the old way. Now the cycle can be broken."

Her words are soft, and everyone leans closer to listen. It's times like this when Old Sally becomes the elder of her clan, chosen to pass on messages from the ancestors. As if anticipating the final ritual, Violet asks everyone to hold hands, and they form a small circle. Moonlight scatters at their feet.

"Now the dance between the masters and slaves can end," Old Sally tells them.

"May it be so," Violet whispers, and encourages the others to repeat it.

Old Sally feels no need to rush. She's waited a century to fulfill this task. The task of letting go of the past. "Now all that hurt between the Temples and us be turned into ash," she begins again. "That old way be gone. Now, something new be coming."

"May it be so," they say together, and it is Jack who adds an "Amen." She is glad Jack and Max are part of the circle, too. If they are uncomfortable in any way, they don't show it, which speaks well of her granddaughter's and Rose's choice of mates.

Silence follows. Still holding hands, Violet begins to hum a Gullah melody that Old Sally taught her and that her Grand-mother Sadie had taught Sally. The tune sounds sad and haunting at first, but then it rises and lifts on Violet's pure tone as if carrying a moment of grace for each of them. Old Sally rubs the goosebumps on her arms. Goosebumps tell her Spirit is close. As she sways with the rhythm, she looks up through the tree's branches. A lone star peeks through. She has waited a hundred years for this one moment—the moment when her life follows the full circle of the moon. Gratitude fills her. There is nothing more powerful than knowing that you did with your life what you were meant to do.

They stand together until dawn. An orange sun, the same color as the dying flames, rises behind the Temple house. The scene is oddly beautiful, as a new day rises above the smoking ruins.

CHAPTER TWENTY-NINE

One Year Later
Rose

Vibrant green moss grows where the Temple house once stood. Palm trees have been planted and dozens of camellias. A color palette of pastels spreads before her. Rose wants to come back and paint this scene. Sunlight pours through the garden, the only part of the Temple property that remained untouched by the fire. In the months afterward, Violet donated the land to the city of Savannah, and city planners extended the original garden over to where the house once stood. A gold plaque that reads *Temple Garden* hangs on the wrought-iron gate that opens into the small park in honor of the Temple family. No posters or protestors are anywhere to be seen. It is as if the burning of the Temple mansion satisfied everyone's need for revenge.

Rose opens the gate. She likes to think that all the Temple

ghosts are buried here, along with all the secrets. The investigation into the cause of the fire was inconclusive. Arson was not ruled out, but there were questions about some of the wiring in the basement. After the fire, the leaking of secrets from the Temple book stopped. Did the person releasing them take pity on the Temples? Or was there another reason?

Shortly after the fire, Rose remembered something from her childhood. When she was maybe seven or eight years old, she came home from school one day and Old Sally wasn't in the kitchen. When she went looking for her, she found her sitting at the Temple desk, a ledger in front of her that she had been reading for some time. Old Sally had told her that it was the *Temple Book of Secrets*. This was when it was still kept in the bottom drawer of her father's mahogany desk that had been Rose's grandfather's desk before that and her great-grandfather's desk even before that. Her mother would like that Rose remembers the history of it.

Old Sally hadn't scolded Rose when she found her but had said something peculiar that Rose can still remember because it was like a riddle she could never figure out. Old Sally said: *There will come a time, Miss Rose, when this old book will spill all its secrets and then the Temples will be free.*

Would Old Sally be capable of revealing those secrets if she thought it would release the past? For all she knows, Old Sally might have copied out every secret in that book in all those years she worked there. Yet this makes no sense either.

As Rose steps into the garden, her memory jumps to the night of the fire and the transformative moment with Old Sally under this same tree. The melody Violet sang plays again in her mind. That night marked a beginning for Rose. Although, if pressed to explain, she isn't sure she could express what she means by that. Perhaps it wasn't a beginning at all, but the ending of her exile from Savannah.

Something moves in the shadows. At first, Rose wonders if it might be her great-grandfather haunting the old tree, but it is someone else, someone alive. The well-dressed African-American woman is statuesque and is dressed like she might work on Wall Street. She stands underneath the live oak that has been in the garden for as long as Rose can remember. When the woman sees Rose, she looks away, but not fast enough for Rose to miss the sadness in her eyes.

Rose calls across the garden: "I didn't mean to disturb you."

"It's lovely here," the woman says as if this might somehow explain her sadness.

Rose agrees. The garden, now a mixture of new and old, has never looked more scenic. She wonders if it approves of its new purpose. The crepe myrtle that stood outside her bedroom window was scorched by the fire, but it came back the following season with the most astounding blossoms she has ever seen. Like the phoenix rising from the flames, the garden has risen to a new level of beauty. No longer in the shadows of the house, every plant and tree appears to have new growth.

Should Rose leave the stranger alone? To answer her question, the woman walks over to her and introduces herself as Regina.

"It's my first time in Savannah," she says, "though I've wanted to come for years."

Rose notices a gold ring with a red stone on her left hand. Her eyes widen as she stares at it because the ring is just like Edward's, except smaller.

"I'm wondering if you knew my brother," Rose says. "Edward Temple?"

The woman looks at her as if to determine her level of trustworthiness.

"I'm Rose," she says. "Edward's sister." She extends her hand, and they shake. The woman's handshake is firm, confident.

"Your brother and I were very close friends." Regina places the emphasis on *close*.

Rose tells her how sorry she is for her loss. "Were you friends for long?" she asks, although from the rings she thinks they are much more than that.

"Twenty years," Regina says. "We met on one of his trips to California, and then I moved to Atlanta." She pauses. "Actually, we've been married for ten of those years," Regina adds.

Rose tries to hide her surprise. Edward was married? The knowledge of her brother keeping someone he loved a secret for so many years, causes a poignant throbbing in her little finger. At that moment, she wonders if she ever knew him at all. She can only imagine what her mother might have done if she knew that Edward was married to a woman of color. She might have required Edward to get a divorce before he received his inheritance.

"We didn't know about you," Rose says.

"Edward insisted that we tell no one in his family," Regina says. "He was always afraid that his mother would disown him. I never even met her." She hesitates and offers an awkward smile like tears might come next. Tears she doesn't want to shed.

A breeze rattles through the Palmetto palms as Rose recalls Edward's insistence at their mother's funeral reception that he was married to his work. How sad it is that Regina wasn't included in the gathering.

"It's hotter here than in Atlanta," she says as she rolls up the sleeves of her blouse. "I didn't think that was possible."

"People like to say you get used to it, but I don't think you ever do," Rose says. "I suppose it's the price we pay for living in paradise."

Regina nods as if she likes the idea of paradise. "Oh," she says. "I almost forgot. Actually, I was hoping to find you." From her purse, Regina pulls out a small priority mail envelope and hands it to Rose. It is addressed to Edward and has their mother's name as the sender. "I found this the other day and thought you might like it."

Rose thanks her. She glances at the envelope and sees that it is postmarked the day before her mother's stroke.

"Well, if you don't mind, I think I'll go seek out some air conditioning," Regina says.

Rose turns toward her, not wanting their meeting to end. "We're in the process of moving, or I'd invite you over for dinner," Rose says.

"Oh, that's all right," Regina says. "I'm just passing through. I wanted to see, you know, where it happened and where Edward grew up. I had no idea the neighborhood was this lavish, but there was a lot I had no idea about." Regina pauses and steps closer. "By the way, I didn't think Edward should publish those secrets in the newspaper."

Rose gives a half-gasp, half-laugh. "It was Edward? But why would he release the secrets?"

Rose is genuinely confused. Her thoughts race. It makes no sense that her brother would want to tarnish the Temple brand. Yet she remembers how half-hearted his eulogy was.

"But why?" Rose asks again.

"A few years ago, when Edward went to visit his mother they were having dinner at a restaurant downtown," Regina begins. "Evidently, an interracial couple came in, and your mother was appalled and said some ugly things. Edward was furious over that for months. Then after she mailed him the key to the safe deposit box a few months before she died, Edward decided that releasing the secrets would be his way of destroying the Temple legend—the secrets, the racism, all of it. He has a lot of connections in Savannah, you know, and different old school buddies helped him arrange things, as long as he kept their secrets out of it."

Regina pauses as if remembering the sequence of events.

"In the letter from your mother that contained the key, she also mentioned a second safe deposit box and a second key," Regina begins again. "This was news to Edward, and evidently this second box contained secrets that stretched beyond Savannah to include the entire world. After that, Edward became obsessed with finding the second key," she continues. "That's why he made that last visit here. He wanted to find that key before anybody else did. I'm not sure what he was going to do once he found it. I guess now we'll never know."

Regina looks at Rose and begins to cry, enough tears that Rose embraces this stranger who is also her sister-in-law. After guiding Regina to a nearby bench, Rose pulls a clean tissue from the pocket of her shorts and hands it to her. If she were Old Sally, she might try to collect these tears. But perhaps the time for protection spells is past.

As quickly as they began, Regina's tears stop and she announces that she has to leave. She walks away, and Rose calls after her. "Regina, did Edward leave everything to you?" she asks, hoping she doesn't find her question rude. "I mean, I hope he did, you know?"

"Actually, I'm now the landlord of several Atlanta high rises in need of renovation," she says with a wry grin and turns toward the gate.

"I'm happy to have met you," Rose calls after her again. "Whenever you come back to Savannah, I hope you'll look me up."

"I will," she says, turning to wave. But Rose wonders if she actually will. "Good luck with your move," Regina adds, before exiting through the gate.

Rose can't imagine that her brother was easy to live with, but she likes to think that perhaps he found some happiness. Though in Temple fashion, it was all a secret.

ALONE IN THE GARDEN AGAIN, Rose digs in her purse and pulls out the sand dollar she found in a box of her childhood memorabilia while she was packing. After tying the shell onto one of the oak's lower branches, she stands back to admire it, remembering the day she and Violet laid in the grass looking up at the tree adorned with sand dollars. Like all childhoods, there was a mixture of good and bad, but she chooses now to remember the good.

Today marks the second anniversary of her mother's death. They purposely chose this auspicious day to move into their new place. According to Old Sally and Violet, who can see these things, her mother's spirit has been at peace since the fire. For her mother's sake, Rose hopes this is true. Her mother would like the idea of a park being created in honor of the Temples. In a way, it redeems the mess those secrets caused.

Before leaving, Rose bows to the garden of her childhood.

"Goodbye, Mother. Goodbye, Edward. Goodbye, old tree." She pats the rough bark of the live oak that watched over her all those years. Her best wishes extend to all her lineage, descendants, as well as ancestors, the best and worst of the Temple clan.

STOPPED at a traffic light on the way out of town, Rose opens the envelope that Regina gave her. Inside is a small key on the end of a gold chain. With the key, is a letter written by her mother on Temple stationery.

Dear Edward,

Enclosed is the second key to the second safety deposit box at the bank. For some reason, it feels wise to send it to you, now that the Book of Secrets is being released. You must use all of your resources to find out who is doing this and make them stop. Our family has always had enemies, but this is someone who is especially devious. You must make them pay.

Nobody else knows about this second key or the contents of the box, and it should stay that way. The Book of Secrets is nothing compared to the ledger in the second vault. Use it whenever you see fit, and by all *means, don't let Rose or Queenie get their hands on either of the keys. They don't understand the world the way we do.*

By the way, did you know that Violet Stevens is your father's child? I only just found out. Oscar left a letter saying he wanted her to have the house. Since it was his final request on this earth, I will honor it. My last request to you, which hopefully won't need to be followed for many years, is that you accept my decision.

Love from your devoted mother,

Iris Temple

P.S. I called earlier. Was that one of your servants who answered the telephone? I'm not sure why she was working so late, but I hope you didn't have to pay her extra.

P.P.S. This may come as a surprise to you, Edward, but I've been thinking a lot lately, and I wrote Rose back into the will. Please don't contest it. I've been so unforgiving of her over the years. Perhaps it is because your father was much fonder of her than me.

A CAR HORN honks behind her. The light is green. Rose drives but then pulls off the road as soon as she can and turns off the car. Two keys? Two safety deposit boxes full of secrets? Even for her family, that seems excessive. If her brother was in the house the night of the fire looking for the second key, was it merely his misfortune to be in the wrong place at the wrong time, as the saying goes? Or did he actually set the fire? These are questions that will never be answered.

Shaking, Rose rereads the letter while tears spring to her eyes. She has come to expect moisture these days, in its many forms. However, this final word from her mother is totally unexpected.

TRAFFIC IS light across the Talmadge Bridge and up the South Carolina coast. Rose anticipates the next chapter of her life. If two years ago, someone had told her that she would be living in Savannah again on Old Sally's property, she would have thought them crazy. But a lot can happen in two years.

The original structure of Old Sally's house remains, though it has been expanded and totally renovated in ways Rose never imagined. Before, it was like a tightly closed bud that now has blossomed into a spacious, lovely flower with many petals. Even Old Sally, who knows most everything before it happens, seemed surprised by the overall transformation.

During the construction, Old Sally lived near the renovation site in a Winnebago that Rose bought for her so she could remain near her beloved beach. Old Sally made friends with the construction workers, and they ate lunch with her every day on two picnic tables they set up outside her camper. For months, Violet cooked hamburgers and hot dogs on two large grills for the workers and made huge bowls of potato salad and baked beans. Other times, she made dozens of ham and cheese sandwiches with homemade sweet potato chips and gave them large slices of lemon meringue and peach pies. As a result, they finished the house in record time and promise to visit whenever they can. According to the workers, they have never known a project to go so smoothly.

Rose turns off the main road and takes the sandy drive to the beach. In the distance, their new home resembles one of the elaborate sandcastles Rose and Violet built when they were girls. There are enough bedrooms in the big house for Old Sally, Queenie, Violet, Jack, and the girls, as well as Katie and Angela. Rose and Max have the guest cottage in the back with a wrap-around porch that connects to a wooden walkway leading to the main house. In their new compound they have a combined total of three dogs—Rose and Max's two border collies and Katie's small mutt. In addition, Angela has two cats, and Violet's girls, Tia and Leisha, have a pet turtle but have already asked for a dog.

Nearly home, Rose pulls into the driveway of Spud Grainger, who now lives a quarter of a mile down the beach. He waves from the second story deck of his new house and heads down the steps to her car. Officially retired from the Piggly Wiggly, Spud has traded in bow ties for colorful Hawaiian shirts. As he opens the car door, she thinks how odd it still is to see him without a tie.

"You ready?" Rose asks.

"I'm always ready, now that I'm a man of leisure," Spud says. He smiles.

"It's nice of you to help with the move." Rose has enjoyed getting to know Spud over the last year.

"Did Katie and Angie make it in?" Spud asks.

"They arrived last night with a full U-Haul," Rose says. "We were up until midnight unloading it."

Katie and Angela are the most surprising addition to their complicated living situation. Six months ago, they had a commitment ceremony in Chicago that Rose and Max attended, and just last month, Katie announced she was pregnant. Rose doesn't question the details—a grandchild is a grandchild. Although what surprised her even more was Katie's announcement that she wanted to raise their child in Savannah among family. Luckily they have plenty of family—in a traditional and non-traditional sense—to go around.

"I was in Hilton Head last night, or I would have helped with the U-Haul," Spud says.

Spud converted one of his Hilton Head properties into a retirement village for jazz and blues musicians. Having taken up the saxophone again, Spud spends every Saturday night attending a jam session in the lobby. People from all over the Carolinas and Georgia come to hear them.

"Did Queenie enjoy herself?" Rose asks.

"Oh my, yes," Spud says with another smile. "That lady can really dance."

Over the months, a budding romance has developed between Queenie and Spud. She goes with him on Saturdays to hear him play the saxophone.

The Temple clan looks different these days, becoming inclusive instead of exclusive. A mixture of black and white, married and single, straight and gay. If her mother is somehow privy to these events, she is probably writing a letter of protest to God at this very minute. But Rose doesn't care. She is happy to let her mother have the last word.

Three moving trucks of various sizes are in different stages of unloading as Rose pulls her car into their new eight-car garage. Moving men carry boxes and furniture out of the different trucks like bees coming out of several hives. Rose and Spud dodge movers as they walk the wooden boardwalk to the front of the house. At one point, Spud takes her elbow and steers Rose out of the path of an overstuffed armchair.

Like she paused that day she first saw Old Sally again, Rose stops on the walkway to take in the ocean. It is high tide. Sandpipers skirt the edges of the waves, as they always do.

"I could look at this view every day for the rest of my life," Rose says to Spud.

"And the good news is, you will." Spud's smile is almost as bright as his shirt.

Rose laughs. "You know, Spud, you're absolutely right."

The renovated house is at least four times bigger than Old Sally's original dwelling. It has two stories now, with a large porch attached to the kitchen and a sunroom facing the ocean. A dozen wooden rockers rest on the front porch, and a large wooden picnic table is built in so they can eat outside if they choose. While Rose takes off her sandals at the top of the stairs to go barefooted, Spud excuses himself and goes inside.

Max stands at the ornate double wooden doors looking like a native. He no longer wears his cowboy hat and boots but opts instead for a ball cap, shorts, and flip flops. Having relaxed like a pro into their financial freedom and subsequent early retirement, Max gives Rose a quick embrace. The envelope Regina gave her crinkles in her pocket, and she wonders briefly what to do with it.

"Happy?" he asks, before directing a mover who has stopped in the doorway to ask where to put a box.

"Definitely," Rose says, realizing it's true. She's never felt so full of possibilities.

They have walked through the house many times at different phases of the construction, but now it is finally complete. Floor to ceiling windows grace every side of the house. Ceiling fans in every room spread the ocean breeze around whenever they choose not to run the air conditioning. Everyone had input into the original plans, and with Violet's blessing, they have created a kind of collective dream house. Life is never perfect, of course. There have been a few bumps in the road, but something about this new adventure and new family feels right to Rose. They will get through the rough spots together.

"Someone's waiting for you on the side porch," Max says.

"Who?" Rose asks.

"Just go," he says as if intent on being mysterious about it.

The inside of the house is organized chaos. Tia and Leisha giggle with two girlfriends by their side and carry boxes to a different wing of the house. Violet, Queenie, and Angela are in the kitchen fixing everyone's lunch. Angie smiles at Rose. Her hair is longer, and her face is minus the piercings. She appears more relaxed and lighter than when Rose first met her.

Spud greets Queenie with a kiss on the cheek. In response, she pats him on the rump and laughs.

Violet has her hair braided with beads like Old Sally used to do when she was a girl. Mother and daughter sing *Michael, Row Your Boat Ashore*, swaying to the melody, their shoulders touching as they cut up peaches. Rose remembers when Queenie sang this in the car and hopes she won't throw in a primal scream to go with it. *Although this crowd could probably handle that, too*, she thinks.

Violet rolls out dough on the countertop for a peach pie and then transfers it onto the pie plate and crimps the edges. In three months, Violet will open a new business called *Violet's Tea Shop* in downtown Savannah. The day before the fire, Violet's shoulder had warned her to move her money from where she kept it in the Temple mansion kitchen.

Rose stops to eat a piece of peach from Violet's bowl. The taste is so completely delicious, she takes another piece and then another.

There's nothing in the world as rich and soulful as Georgia peaches, Rose thinks, as peach juice runs down her chin.

"Welcome home," Queenie says, and her words sound as sweet as the peaches. They exchange a hug full of history.

Rose and Queenie have waited a long time for a moment like this. A time when neither of them is haunted by secrets or shame, and they can completely be themselves. After Violet worked through all the hurt feelings with Queenie, the two women became practically inseparable. Violet spends part of every day learning the Gullah family traditions from Old Sally, as well as creating some special teas and tinctures she plans to sell at her shop.

On her way to the side porch, Rose admires Old Sally's new window seat that has replaced the table and been expanded to her specifications. Colorful cushions have been added for Old Sally to sit on while she nurtures her collection of beautiful and ordinary things, as diverse as the people they represent, including the ones who now live in this house. The sandcastle Rose gave Old Sally nearly thirty years before sits in the center, and next to it, Rose puts the second key.

Later, she plans to talk to Queenie and Violet about what to do with what's in the safe deposit box at the bank, but she has a feeling a big bonfire on the beach may be in their future. She will also tell them that it was Edward who was releasing the secrets and why he felt the need to do it. She likes to think that her brother had good intentions at heart. She only wishes she had known this side of him.

After admiring the view again, Rose walks out the side door to find Old Sally and Katie sitting on the wraparound porch. At almost 102 years of age, Old Sally reminds Rose of the tree in the Temple garden. She has watched over all of them over the years and has also been one of the biggest blessings in Rose's life. When she sees Rose, Old Sally smiles, igniting the love Rose has for this woman.

Rose flashes back to herself as a girl, leaning into Old Sally's wide hip, her strong, brown arms wrapped around Rose. *Those memories make up for everything her mother did or didn't do. As long as you feel love from somewhere, it's enough,* she decides.

Katie holds Old Sally's hand. Seeing the two of them together makes Rose smile. This must be what Max wanted Rose to see. Several times upon waking, she has told him about a recurring dream. In the dream she is living in a house by the sea. A house filled with people who love her.

This is what family is all about, she thinks. Generations all under one roof, honoring and appreciating each other.

"Old Sally's going to teach me some of her spells at the same time she teaches Violet," Katie says.

"That's terrific," Rose says. She wonders what her mother would have to say about Katie learning what she considered "voodoo."

Katie lets go of Old Sally's hand and walks over to Rose to kiss her on the cheek. "I'll leave you two alone and go help Angie," she says.

Rose nods, noticing how pink Katie's cheeks have already become. *This move is going to be good for her, too,* Rose thinks.

As Katie walks away, Old Sally stands to greet Rose. She moves more slowly these days. On the night of the fire, she seemed to pass the mantle to Violet. Yet her eyes remain bright. They embrace. For years whenever she and Old Sally embraced, Rose felt like a little girl in the arms of the Great Mother. This is the woman who not only baptized her with the sprinkler bottle while doing the ironing when Rose was a girl, but also the woman who sprinkled her with love throughout her life. But it's her turn to take care of Old Sally now, with the help of Queenie and Violet, who were also raised in the shade of this grand woman.

Old Sally relaxes in Rose's arms. Confirmation comes from somewhere deep inside that Rose has been moving toward this moment her entire life. A new feeling washes over her like a gentle ocean wave. She is home. She is finally home.

ACKNOWLEDGMENTS

I am grateful for how stories—wherever they come from—enrich our lives, and for books that inspire me to be a better writer. I am grateful for my readers, who have told me what my books have meant to them and encouraged me with such heartfelt reviews and emails.

For information on the Gullah culture, I am indebted to Bill Moyers' story on the PBS show, NOW, as well as an article called Gullah: A Vanishing Culture, by Paige Williams, in the Charlotte Observer, along with lots of other research online.

I am grateful for my first readers: Anne Alexander, Krista Lunsford, Josephine Locklair, Jeanette Reid, Ann Bohan, Liz Gunn, Kendrick Wronski, and Jane Kennedy. Thanks to Nancy Purcell and the Quotation's writers group in Brevard, NC, who gave me feedback on the first chapter of *Temple Secrets*. I also appreciate the feedback given to me by my literary agent, Mary Grey James.

Of momentous importance to my writing life is my business manager, Anne Alexander, who creatively and masterfully does all the marketing and technical things that are so absolutely foreign to me as an author. Holly Adams, my audiobook narrator, is also a treasure.

To my family and friends, thank you for all your support for the last two decades as I acted on this crazy dream of writing novels.

Finally, to my writing assistants Emma and Jack, who are the sweetest mutts in the world, and who spend their mornings in my office at my feet while I write.

P.S.

Insights, Interview & Reading Group Guide

About the Author

Q & A with Susan Gabriel

13 Things I Reveal About Myself in the
   Writing of *Temple Secrets*

Reading Group Guide

ABOUT THE AUTHOR

Susan Gabriel is an acclaimed southern writer who lives in the mountains of Western North Carolina. Her novels, *The Secret Sense of Wildflower* (a Kirkus Reviews Best Book of 2012) and *Temple Secrets* (2015) are Amazon and Nook #1 bestsellers.

She is also the author of *The Wildflower Trilogy* (*The Secret Sense of Wildflower, Lily's Song,* and *Daisy's Fortune*). Other books include *Trueluck Summer,* and *Grace, Grits and Ghosts: Southern Short Stories.* Find out more about Susan and her books at SusanGabriel.com.

Q & A WITH SUSAN GABRIEL

Tell us a little about yourself.

I've been writing novels for twenty-five years. Before that I was a marriage and family therapist with a private practice in Charleston, South Carolina. I grew up in the South (Knoxville, TN), and for years I swore that I would *never* ever write southern fiction. I had enough crazy "characters" in my gene pool to not want to spend any time there. But as they say: *never say never*. It was after living in Colorado for three years that I discovered what a Southerner I actually am.

Now, I live in the mountains of North Carolina, ten minutes from a national forest that has a river that I love to walk along. I have two grown daughters, two rescue dogs, and two cats.

How did you get the idea for *Temple Secrets*?

Right after I returned from Colorado with my newly reclaimed Southern identity, I wanted to write another southern novel. I had already written *The Secret Sense of Wildflower* several years before, which I considered a fluke, as in my "only" southern novel. This was back in my "never" stage. Sometimes our destiny keeps tapping us on the shoulder until it finally throws a brick.

The seed of the idea occurred to me decades ago when I lived in Charleston. A dear friend who lived South of Broad told me about a housekeeper she knew who still worked for the same family who had enslaved her ancestors. This fact intrigued me. Ultimately, I decided to have *Temple Secrets* take place in Savannah. Savannah is a sister city to Charleston and is somewhere I've always enjoyed visiting.

With the setting in place, I began to write. The characters showed up full-fledged as if they'd been waiting for me all those years to tell their story: Queenie, Iris, Violet, and Rose. And of course, Old Sally. I watched and wrote as their lives played out in my imagination.

To me, the ending is symbolic of what I think our culture needs to heal. Acceptance of all kinds of family. Diversity in age, lifestyle, ethnicity, as well as experience.

Who is your favorite character in *Temple Secrets*?

I loved all of the characters, even Iris and Edward, who were quite dastardly at times. But they had reasons for being who they were, as we all do. I loved that Edward got some redemption at the end.

I guess I would say that Queenie was my absolute favorite. I just loved her sense of humor and her resilience. Most of all, I loved writing her dialogue. *Sweet heavens!*

Old Sally was also a favorite. We desperately need wise old women in our lives, so the least I can do is put them in my stories.

I also loved Violet and how she wanted to be an agent of change and open a tea shop. I love tea, by the way, and make a pot of it every morning when I write. (Organic Assam is my favorite at the moment.) Rose was the prodigal daughter returning, and she carries some of my experience of moving from the West back to the Southeast. I adored Spud, too, the vegetarian butcher. We humans are fascinating with all our paradoxes.

So, yes, I loved them all, even with their flaws. When you work on a manuscript for several years, it is crucial to find the story and characters compelling. Otherwise, it's easy to lose interest. I never lost interest in this story, and I am honored whenever anyone chooses to read it.

When are you the most creative?

The mornings are my most creative time. I am usually alone, and I am generally working on whatever my current novel is. A typical morning for me is to write from around 9 am, to around 1 o'clock. Then in the afternoons, I might meet friends for tea or paint in my art studio. For many years I taught writing classes and edited novels to support my writing habit.

Share a favorite quote.

It is hard to only pick one. I love quotes. Here are two by Carl Jung: "Small and hidden is the door that leads inward."

And: "You must go in quest of yourself, and you will find yourself again only in the simple and forgotten things. Why not go into the forest for a time, literally? Sometimes a tree tells you more than can be read in books."

And then one from Maya Angelou: "There is no greater agony than bearing an untold story inside you."

What creative project are you working on now?

Having just completed the Wildflower Trilogy (2019), I am about to start working on a novel that I've already been tinkering with for seven years. It is in a first draft and needs to be revised. No title for that one yet, but it takes place in the lowcountry, near

Charleston. I also have several characters hanging out in my imagination that are waiting for me to get to them.

What were you like as a child?

Very shy and outdoorsy. Some might say a tomboy. I stayed outside riding my bike, playing games with my brother, or playing golf. I rarely read but did well in school. (How is that even possible?) There weren't that many books in our home. It wasn't until I was out of college and having my first child that I began to read children's classics, trying to make up for what I had missed. I am a late-bloomer in many ways. Now I read voraciously. I haven't stopped.

Is there somewhere you've traveled that has influenced your creative life?

As I've mentioned before, I lived out West for a few years, which is about as different from the moist, shady southeastern United States as you can get. I loved exploring this new terrain and the wildlife that resided there. It was in the West that I finally claimed my southern soul. I missed shade. I missed deciduous trees. I even missed kudzu! But I missed moisture most of all. Now I'm back in the southeast living in an area of the North Carolina mountains known for its waterfalls. Life is good.

13 THINGS I REVEAL ABOUT MYSELF

...in the Writing of Temple Secrets

1. Ancestors are important to me. The sense that we aren't alone; that people came before us; that some may even be watching over us.

2. Secrets intrigue me. They make people do strange things. Everybody has them. Sometimes we even keep secrets from ourselves.

3. The spirit world or the invisible world (think ghosts, spirits, the secret sense), fascinate me and are underestimated.

4. Female characters and female voices are underrepresented in our culture. My mission is to get more female characters out into the world who are courageous and have integrity and humor.

5. I think characters over forty are the most interesting.

6. I think happy endings are possible in life, and that it's only to

the level that we've experienced sorrow that we can experience joy. Readers have told me that my books make them laugh and cry.

7. I love to make people laugh, so my books are often humorous. When I was younger, I wanted to be a stand- up comedian. As a girl, I would sneak into the den late at night to watch Joan Rivers on the Johnny Carson show. Since my comedy act never hit the road, I became a writer instead. Well, first, I became a teacher, then a psychotherapist, and then a writer. It was by no means a straight path to writing. I grew into it.

8. Old wise women show up in nearly everything I write because I hope to become one.

9. I am fascinated with death, so there is usually at least one death in my stories. To me, it's just the natural end of living. However, I rarely kill off an animal, especially a dog. (The exception was a dog dying of old age in one of my other books. I'm still sad about that.)

10. I think reading novels opens us to a deeper emotional experience.

11. Sometimes when people are consistently obnoxious to me, I create a character in a novel with some of the same characteristics and then have them be found out for who they really are in the course of the story. I am very good at disguising these real people in the skins of my fictional characters. Novelists do this all the time.

12. I always write about things that interest me. I write the story that I would love to read, trusting that other people will enjoy it, too. Since I spend years writing a book, I have to love the charac-

ters and understand them. After I release a book, I often grieve the loss of not having the story in my life every day.

13. I think we are all trying to find our way "home," in one way or another. Home being a place where we feel the most authentic.

Does anything surprise you? I love hearing from readers. You can email me at susan@susangabriel.com.

READING GROUP GUIDE

1. Who was your favorite character? Why?

2. What do you think motivated Iris? On the one hand, she could be cruel and dismissive to Queenie, yet she had loved Spud Grainger for decades. Do you think she is a sympathetic or unsympathetic character? Why?

3. How much of a person's character would you say is shaped by what has happened to them in the past, or what happened in past generations?

4. Did it bother you that Queenie was willing to overlook so many of Iris's faults to live with Iris? Why?

5. Do you believe that keeping secrets is sometimes justified? Should Queenie have told Violet who she really was from the very beginning? Why?

6. What do you think of Rose coming home to see her mother on

her deathbed? In what situations might estrangement from one's family sometimes be necessary for self-preservation?

7. The author paints Old Sally with a quiet grace and an aura of wisdom about her. How do you think she does this? Have you ever had a wise old woman in your life? If so, what was meaningful about your relationship with her?

8. In what ways do you think racism still shows up in relationships where people of color work for people who are white?

9. How was the Temple Book of Secrets an agent of change for the entire family?

10. How did you feel about Edward's seeming redemption at the end of the novel? Discuss people in your life who have appeared totally one way and then who surprised you with something you never knew about them.

11. What role do you see Violet playing in the novel? What did you think of her ability to perceive ghosts? How might her children end up different from her because of her choices?

12. In the final scene, were you hopeful that all of the characters could live together peacefully? If you were to write a sequel for this novel, what do you imagine happening? (P.S. There is a sequel now called *Gullah Secrets*. It continues where *Temple Secrets* leaves off.)

Gullah Secrets

SUSAN GABRIEL

CHAPTER ONE

Old Sally

Old Sally sits overlooking the Atlantic Ocean, the sunrise stretching toward her like a golden path between this world and the next. At 102 years of age, Old Sally has been teaching her granddaughter Violet the art of Gullah folk magic to ensure their traditions stay alive.

Plenty of troubles in this world are from people forgetting their ancestors' wisdom, she thinks.

Swells of an ocean at high tide slap against the South Carolina shore as pelicans dive in quest of their morning meal. Dolphin Island is on the other side of the Georgia state line, close enough to Savannah that her family always worked there. Old Sally and Violet often meet on the front porch in the early mornings and sit in their favorite rocking chairs while Violet writes what she learns in a hardback notebook. At one time, Old Sally's root doctoring was known all over the Southeast, but nowadays most people take a pill to make their symptoms go away instead of using a root cure.

Even with a household full of people underfoot, Old Sally takes time to ponder things. According to Old Sally's grandmother, Sadie, who taught her everything she knows about Gullah folk magic, silence is where wisdom is found. Over her long life, Old Sally has made a friend of silence. She looks over at Violet, who is mixed race and a lighter shade than Old Sally with her leathered, dark skin. Violet is still as beautiful in her forties as she was when she was young.

"A penny for your thoughts," Violet says.

"Those will cost you a quarter," Old Sally says with a smile.

She laughs when Violet pulls a coin from her pocket and places it on the porch railing in front of them. Their playfulness pleases Old Sally. Often, her memories are from when she was a girl, the end of life circling back around to the beginning.

To the Gullah people, like their African ancestors, time is eternal and continually renews itself like an unbroken circle. Past, present, and future are one. In the Gullah concept of time, the dead still have an impact on the community of the living. While their bodies go into the ground and their souls to God, their presence is still felt as long as they are remembered.

It always touched Old Sally that her Gullah ancestors were buried with their heads turned toward the east. A sacred ritual, her grandmother told her, that signifies the circle of life that rises and sets with the sun. East is also the direction of their beloved homeland. The place her ancestors lived before they were forced onto ships and brought here to the South Carolina and Georgia coasts to be slaves for white landowners.

Remembering their transaction, Old Sally picks up the quarter and puts it in the pocket of her cotton dress.

"I be thinking about my grandmother," Old Sally begins. "She lived with my family the entire time I was growing up. It be my grandmother who always had time for me and who explained things I didn't understand. Before I was born, she had been a slave," Old Sally continues. "The stories she told from those days always made me cry. But she also taught me what it meant to be free, and how to think for myself."

Old Sally pauses, remembering how her grandmother insisted that she learn to read. Before her grandmother's death, Sally taught her how to read and write in return.

"Your great-grandmother was very gifted with folk magic," Old Sally begins again. "She made me look like a beginner. Like I've told you before, you be gifted, too, Violet. You have the family sensitivity."

Violet looks out over the sea as if pondering the responsibility of this gift.

The Gullah women of their family all have different talents. Violet sees spirits and has a shoulder that predicts when something terrible is about to happen. Old Sally's youngest daughter, Queenie, offers laughter as a potion. Her long-gone daughter, Maya, had been an expert at reading tea leaves. Besides root doctoring and spells, Old Sally also helps people transition from this world into the next.

Old Sally pushes the quarter toward Violet, who looks up with a smile. If the light catches her just right, Sally can see Queenie in her, Violet's mother.

"For some reason, I was thinking about Miss Temple and how hard she was on Queenie," Violet says. "Ghosts don't relocate, do they?"

"Not that I know of," Old Sally says, although she must admit to herself she has wondered the same thing.

Old Sally's family and the Temples have a shared history that goes back several generations. Old Sally's grandmother was a slave for the elite Temple family in Savannah before she was finally freed. Then Old Sally worked for Iris Temple in the same mansion for sixty years, even before "Old" was added to her name. When she got too old and tired to work there anymore, her granddaughter Violet took over as housekeeper and cook, and her daughter Queenie became Iris's companion.

Like two trees that have grown together and intermingled roots, the two families sometimes share parentage, which complicates matters even more. Sally's grandmother Sadie gave birth to a baby boy named Adam, who was half Temple and taken from her at the age of ten, sent to a plantation in Charleston. For that evil deed, Sadie was the first of Sally's ancestors to put a Gullah curse on the Temples. Two generations later, Old Sally had Queenie by Edward Temple, Iris's father, making Queenie and Iris half sisters. Then Queenie had Violet by Mister Oscar, Iris's husband. For two hundred years, black servants and lily-white rich folks in Savannah mixed and mingled in all sorts of ways that weren't the least bit socially acceptable.

Of course, Iris's last will and testament changed everything when she left the Temple mansion to Violet, who was not only the housekeeper but also Mister Oscar's daughter. All because of Iris's fear of going against deathbed requests. And not just any deathbed request, but one from her dead husband, who still haunted the Temple mansion.

Old Sally sighs. The spirit world feels so close it's hard to imagine some people never give it a thought.

After the Temple mansion burned to the ground over two years ago—a fire Edward Temple accidentally started in which he also lost his life—no one heard anything else from the ghostly Temples. Old Sally hopes they have finally been laid to rest. But maybe not.

Those Temples are a stubborn bunch, she thinks. *Wouldn't be like them to just fade away.*

Just in case, Old Sally keeps a bowl filled with water in the front room to run the ghosts off like her grandmother taught her, and she continues the protection spells like she always has.

"If we were having the wedding at the mansion today, Miss Temple would try to ruin it for Queenie," Violet says.

Old Sally agrees, thinking that maybe the Temple ghosts are

haunting Violet today, too. "We are lucky to have it here at the beach," Sally says.

Doing battle with Iris Temple, dead or alive, is not something anyone would want to do. Especially not Old Sally. She had her fill of Iris a long time ago.

The sky is a deep blue. The breeze, gentle and warm, with no hints of anything that might ruin the day. But before they get ready for the wedding, Old Sally must think of a Gullah story for Violet to put in her notebook. Lately, she has been sharing the Gullah legends she grew up hearing.

"Perhaps it's time to tell you about the mermaid storm," Old Sally says. "It was my grandmother's favorite story to tell my brothers and me whenever she wanted to mesmerize us, as well as scare us to death."

Violet opens her book, ready to take notes.

"It was October of 1893," Old Sally begins. "Common knowledge to the Gullah people at that time was that whenever a mermaid was captured, a storm brewed." She pauses like her grandmother always did, to pull her listeners in. "Well, a white man on the island did indeed capture a mermaid one day, and he was hiding her in his shed behind his family's beach cottage. He refused to release the mermaid," she continues, "and a few days later a rare hurricane struck the island. It was a horrible storm. The ocean rose and rose until it finally got so high that the captive mermaid was washed back to sea. However, as punishment for the man's misdeeds, his entire family was drowned in the tidal surge."

Violet stops writing. "Well, that story would scare me, too."

"My grandmother always ended the tale with 'Let's just hope no white folks have captured any mermaids lately.'" Old Sally chuckles, remembering her grandmother's laughter.

A bluebird lands on the arm of an empty rocking chair by the front door, surprising them both. A rare shade of indigo blue, the bird's beauty is otherworldly. She watches them as though noting their plainness in comparison to her exquisiteness and chirps a tune before flying away.

"A songbird singing on a doorstep means company's coming," Old Sally says.

"Really?" Violet writes this down.

"And if somebody accidentally drops a dishrag in the kitchen, that means they're coming soon."

Violet jots this in her notebook, too.

The scent of melancholy rides in on the breeze. Sometimes the loneliness of missing all the family and friends who have gone on before her takes Old Sally's breath away. Most notably, her grandmother is on her mind today.

"How did I get to be this old, Violet?"

"Just lucky, I guess," Violet says, still writing. She doesn't realize the significance of Old Sally's comment. "I wish I'd seen all the change you've seen in your lifetime," she adds, looking up from her notebook. "It must be fascinating."

"Overwhelming is the word I'd use," Old Sally says. "To live in the twenty-first century is like holding onto the tail of a comet."

"Well, I'm very grateful that you're here." Violet closes her notebook and looks at her watch. She stands and leans over to kiss Old Sally's cheek.

"I've got to get busy. It's a big day."

Old Sally agrees.

Alone again, she smiles, happy to pass on the Gullah secrets to her granddaughter, just like her grandmother did to her. Not that they are secrets exactly, but they might as well be since so few people know their traditions. Someday soon Old Sally will return to her ancestors, a fact that doesn't scare her in the least. However, she is not ready to go home just yet. She still has unfinished business. Memories of the past must be sorted through, and the last of the Gullah traditions must be passed on to Violet. Not to mention, there is a wedding later today that she doesn't want to miss.

CHAPTER TWO

Queenie

Queenie Temple studies her reflection in her bedroom's full-length mirror, sucking in her ample waistline to no avail. The white plus-size wedding gown she and Rose found in Savannah a few weeks ago is not cooperating. In her sixties, Queenie is not a typical bride, although she is having a traditional June wedding.

"How do women fit into these things?" Queenie says to her daughter, Violet, who inches the zipper upward on the back of her dress.

"It would help if you stood still," Violet says, coaxing the fabric to loosen. "When it comes to squirming, you're worse than when Tia and Leisha were little girls."

Queenie smiles. "I do feel like a youngster these days." The sigh that follows is unexpected. "But the truth is, I'm not a spring chicken anymore, Vi. Hell, I'm not even a *fall* chicken." She cackles. "Is my intended here yet?"

"He got here an hour ago," Violet says. "He's pacing and wearing a path into the kitchen floor."

"Oh heavens, do you think he's having second thoughts?" Queenie's newly tweezed eyebrows float above the glasses she has begun to need.

Violet tugs at Queenie's dress. "I think he's more nervous that *you'll* have second thoughts," she says. "He's wearing a new bow tie, by the way. Wait till you see it."

"That man," Queenie clucks. "Did I tell you about the time he came to bed wearing nothing but a bow tie?"

Violet tugs at the back of Queenie's dress again. "That's what the girls would call TMI," she says. "Too Much Information."

Queenie laughs again. "Maybe you should sew up the back and then cut me out of it later."

"It's bad luck to mend a garment someone is wearing," Violet says. "I imagine that goes for sewing someone into a wedding dress, too."

"Is that another Gullah saying?"

"Yes," Violet admits. "I hope it doesn't bother you, it helps me remember them."

"No problem." Queenie wipes a thin layer of sweat from above her upper lip. "I can't believe how nervous I am. You'd think I'd never been married before."

"You haven't," Violet says, playing deadpan to Queenie's humor.

Queenie cackles again. The more nervous she gets, the more she laughs. She has been this way her entire life. If given a choice between laughter or tears, laughter is the winner every time. Crying is usually reserved for sacred moments, the last time being when Spud proposed. Her eyes mist with the memory. They were eating at their favorite seafood restaurant in Hilton Head—The Spicy Sturgeon. Halfway through the meal, Queenie bit into the best crab cake she had ever tasted and nearly cracked a crown. Wearing a lobster bib, Spud quickly dropped to one knee. Then he spoke the words Queenie had waited forty years to hear, even though she and Spud had only dated for one of those years: *I'd be greatly honored, Queenie Temple, if you would agree to become my wife.*

Leave it to Spud to hide an engagement ring inside a crab cake. In the moments that followed, Queenie cried an ocean of tears. Grateful tears. Relieved tears. Tears she had been holding in for decades. She cried for so long Spud's knee gave out, and two waiters had to help him stand again.

Now, six months later, Queenie and Spud will exchange their vows on the beach in front of the house this very day. Old Sally will be officiating, along with the young priest who buried Iris, Queenie's half sister. Iris was a Savannah matriarch known for being difficult, and Queenie served as her personal assistant for thirty-five years. The priest's signature on the marriage license will make their marriage official in matters of the law, and her mother's blessing—whom Queenie calls Old Sally like everybody else—will make it official everywhere else. Heaven included.

"Did you do the things I suggested?" Violet continues to fiddle with the vexing zipper.

Queenie thinks for a minute. "You mean about wishing on a new moon? Yes, I did that a few days ago. I also said 'rabbit' first thing before getting out of bed on the first day of the month. I'll take all the good luck I can get."

"You didn't happen to dream of gray horses last night, did you?" Violet asks. "That's supposed to be good luck, too."

"Not that I remember," Queenie says. "I think I dreamed I was at the Kentucky Fried Chicken drive-thru in Savannah. The one Iris went to. In the dream, I drove up to that little window and picked up a live chicken instead of a cooked one."

Violet laughs before stepping back to take another look at Queenie's dress. "Not to worry. As far as I know, dreaming of live chickens is not bad luck."

Queenie's cheeks flush hot thinking of how she denied herself and Violet the relationship they could have had for all those years when Queenie was hiding the fact that she was Violet's mother. It is easily the biggest regret of her life. They have always been close. But being mother and daughter feels different from being an aunt and niece. Looking back on it, she realizes now that if she could do it over, she would have told the truth, no matter how angry Oscar might have been or how much she might have feared the outcome. As Iris's husband and Queenie's employer, Oscar had a lot of power over her and took advantage of it.

Thankfully, Queenie no longer has a need for secret-keeping. She wants to shout to the world her love for the one man she's waited her entire life to find: Spud Grainger. A retired butcher from the Piggly Wiggly. Retired thanks to Iris's surprising generosity in her will. Denzel Washington he is not. For one thing, he is about ten shades lighter than Denzel. In other words, he is white to Queenie's black. But life seldom works out as planned.

The zipper finally closed, Queenie and Violet share a mother-daughter sigh of relief. When Queenie turns to the mirror to have a look, her mood shifts like the weather vane on the back porch when a storm is coming in.

"Oh, Violet, who am I kidding by wearing white? It's not like a person can revert back to virgin-hood, even if it was thirty years between dates."

"You look beautiful," Violet reassures her.

They stand at the mirror as if taking in the family resemblance.

"Sometimes I feel like I don't deserve happiness like this." Queenie lowers her head.

"Don't say things like that," Violet says. "You deserve happiness as much as anybody. Maybe more, given you put up with Iris Temple for thirty-five years. For that, you probably deserve life-long happiness *and* a medal."

Queenie walks to the front window, Violet following, and then delivers another sigh as she looks out over the ocean from the second floor. "Maybe Iris was my penance for not being truthful while you were growing up."

"Listen to me." Violet looks into her eyes. "You have waited a long time to be happy, Queenie Temple, and I will not let anyone take this moment away from you. Especially not you. I know you don't think you deserve anything like this, but you do," she continues. "Spud makes you happy. In fact, this last year is the happiest I've ever seen you."

Queenie wipes away a plump tear before giving Violet a hug.

"Thank you for that," Queenie says. "Everybody needs a good talking-to now and again." Queenie stands taller, grateful that Violet feels she can be honest with her.

"I can't believe you went to the Piggly Wiggly with Miss Temple all those years and never even noticed Spud," Violet says.

"Well, he was Iris's old flame, and nobody in their right mind messed with Iris."

They exchange a knowing look.

"Well, I bet wherever Miss Temple is, she's happy for you, too," Violet says.

Queenie turns to look at the overhead light and waits on the ghost of Iris Temple to disagree like she did in the old mansion when her spirit shook the chandeliers. Blissful silence answers her. Queenie has not missed her half sister's haunting presence one bit. Or any of the other ghosts in the Temple mansion, for that matter, who for years gave her the shivers in cold hallways and various rooms of that old house. But it is quite a stretch to imagine Iris happy for her. Iris was notably the most stubborn, controlling matriarch in Savannah, if not the entire Southeast.

"Everything is going too well, Vi. I'm worried something will happen to ruin this day."

"Relax," Violet says. "Nothing is going to go wrong."

"But what if the Temple ghosts find out I'm marrying Spud?"

"Don't be silly," Violet says. "Those ghosts are long gone." But she doesn't look entirely convinced.

If Queenie had to imagine the worst news she could receive on her wedding day, it would be that the one ghost in Savannah she had hoped to sweet Jesus she had rid herself of had returned. A ghost by the name of Iris. A ghost who was once in love with Queenie's intended.

For years Queenie accompanied Iris to the meat section of the Piggly Wiggly, watching her practically marinate all over Spud while at the same time rejecting him. Queenie wasn't sure what game Iris was playing, but it didn't seem fair to Spud. A man Queenie didn't give a second look back then is now a different story.

Queenie begins to pace, imagining every catastrophe that can befall two people getting married.

"Have you and Mama put a protection spell on the wedding?"

"We did spells earlier in the week," Violet says, giving the dress another tug to test its hold.

In the last year, Queenie has found Violet and her mama conjuring up all sorts of awful-smelling things on the kitchen stove. Concoctions that could ward off anything bad within a hundred miles by smell alone. But at this moment Queenie is glad her family tradition includes folk magic and getting rid of any unwanted evil. If that isn't a description of Iris, she isn't sure what is.

After Old Sally passes from this world, Violet will be the keeper of the Gullah secrets. Secrets Queenie has never had any desire to know. The family sensitivity skipped a generation, and Queenie is okay with that. The truth is, she has neither the temperament nor desire to deal with mysterious forces.

Queenie glances at the clock on her bedside table. Guests will arrive in less than an hour. In the meantime, everything has been planned and is in the process of being executed. Old Sally will be the one to give Queenie away and walk with her down the aisle. For months Queenie worried that her mama might not get to attend the wedding. When someone is a centenarian, you figure their days are numbered. But for weeks now Queenie has shoved that thought to the back of her mind with all the other worst-case scenarios.

"In one hour, you will be Mrs. Spud Grainger," Violet says.

"Maybe people should call me Mrs. Potato Head since I'm marrying a Spud." Queenie's laughter tests the strength of her zipper.

Violet laughs, too, something Queenie has seen her do more often these last few months. Ever since she opened her tea shop, Violet has possessed a level of contentment that Queenie has never seen before. It is as if Violet has finally stepped into the role she was meant to play.

Queenie scrutinizes herself in the mirror once again. "There's something off," she says.

"I told you, you look beautiful," Violet says.

Queenie pauses, taking in her reflection until her eyes widen. "I've got it," she says. "There isn't an ounce of color in this whole outfit. Wearing all this white, I look like a milk chocolate Disney princess. That will not do."

Violet insists this isn't true, which only prompts another angst-filled sigh before Queenie begins to pace again, unconvinced.

"Why am I trying to look all traditional? I've never been traditional a day in my life. I don't look one bit like myself," Queenie says, thinking, *Oprah would not approve.* Seeing all this white in the mirror makes her feel like one of Rose's bare-white canvases.

"You're just a little nervous," Violet says.

Queenie pauses. "I need a dash of color," she says.

"A dash of color?" Violet's brows raise as if she thinks that a *dash* of anything would never be enough for Queenie. If Sam's Club sold color in bulk, Queenie would bring it home by the truckload.

Queenie steps into her walk-in closet, her billowing white gown refusing to clear the door. When she breaches the doorway, she nearly falls headfirst into her shoes. When they were designing this addition, she gave up bathroom footage to add more room for storage. The Temple mansion in Savannah, where she used to live, had absurdly tiny closets for such a prominent home.

"Almost there," she says to Violet, who holds Queenie's dress out behind her to keep it from getting wrinkled.

Inside her closet, Queenie ties a bright yellow silk scarf around her neck. Then she trades out her white sequined dressy flats for a pair of purple pumps. Yet, there is still something missing. Queenie sifts through her closet until she finds a large round box containing a hat she has never dared to wear. And for Queenie that is saying a lot. It is bold and big and red. Is now the time to debut it? Or in this case, add it to the veil she already intends to wear? It is a silly notion, she admits, but Queenie is desperate for some color.

For months Queenie planned a traditional wedding like the ones in those wedding magazines. An event meant to finally make her acceptable, in her own eyes and others. Now she is considering wearing a hat that would make even the characters in *Steel Magnolias* balk. The color of fire engines and emergency exits, the wide drooping brim makes her look like a deeply suntanned southern belle.

With Violet's help, Queenie successfully breaches the closet door again, and carefully positions the hat on her head while looking in the mirror.

"Perfect," she says, beaming a smile at Violet.

Violet's initial shock appears to soften. Queenie is now adorned in color.

To calm her nervousness, Queenie takes a deep breath followed by a slow exhale. In less than an hour, she will marry Spud Grainger, the only man in her six decades of life that she has ever truly loved. Nobody and nothing will prevent her destiny.

CHAPTER THREE

Rose

Coming home to Savannah, where she grew up, and now living on Dolphin Island with her chosen family has been good for Rose. She hadn't realized how much she missed shade and moisture until she returned from living in Wyoming. Growing up as a Temple meant Rose grew up facing a lot of expectations. She wasn't anything like her mother—the great and formidable Iris Temple—and every day of her life Rose was aware of how disappointed her mother was in her. But with her mother gone, life seems easier here.

Rose and Violet were up most of the night with preparations for Queenie and Spud's wedding reception. Rose coordinated the event: invitations, flowers, rentals, and helping Queenie find a gown. After Queenie finally decided what kind of ceremony she wanted—a decision process that took months—Rose had only six weeks to get everything arranged. Now Violet is helping Queenie with her dress.

Arranging a wedding is what she had hoped she and her

daughter Katie might do together someday. But it seems that isn't meant to be. Though it has entered a new millennium, the world needs to do a lot of changing for Katie and her girlfriend Angela to get married. Rose doesn't have that level of faith in humanity. Not after the events of last year on September 11.

To stop Spud Grainger's hand-wringing and pacing, Rose gives him a dozen lemons to cut for fresh lemonade. He stands at the granite kitchen counter in front of the cutting board, wearing a purple suit. It never occurred to her that he might need some direction on appropriate wedding attire, but she imagines Queenie will love it.

"Have you talked to Queenie today?" Rose asks Spud.

"She has forbidden it," Spud says, a smile upon his mustached lips.

Rose imagines a romantic relationship with Queenie would require a certain amount of willingness to take orders.

Good for him, she thinks. *Now if only Max could learn that, too.*

The cordless telephone rings in the kitchen. Considering the household living situation, Rose never knows how to answer. Lately, she identifies herself and then hopes the caller knows who to ask for.

"Rose, this is Regina. Edward's wife."

Her missing fingertip throbs in recognition upon hearing her brother's name.

Rose has only talked to Regina once on the telephone since they met last summer at the Temple Garden, a park created by the city where her family's mansion once stood. For decades, Edward kept Regina a secret from their family. A fact that seems poignant to Rose. Has Regina somehow found out about Queenie's wedding and wants to know the whereabouts of her invitation?

They exchange pleasantries, and then Regina's tone grows more serious. "I called to warn you about something," she says.

"Warn me?" Rose sits on a nearby stool, ready for bad news.

The room filled with the puckering smell of cut lemons, Spud has overheard and looks at Rose.

Everything has gone so well with the wedding preparations, Rose has anticipated a giant shoe poised to drop. From the sound of Regina's voice, this call might be it.

"I had an unexpected visitor last night," Regina says. "A young woman." She pauses.

Is her brother's widow the type to dangle a disaster in her face? Perhaps she is more like Edward than Rose initially thought.

"The young woman claims to be Edward's daughter," Regina says.

In her imagination, Rose hears a shoe drop with a thud onto the slate kitchen floor. Somehow, Rose knew her brother would find a way to mess with her life even from the grave.

"Edward has a daughter?" Rose asks.

"It seems so." Regina exhales as though smoking a cigarette. She doesn't seem the type to smoke. Rose has an easier time imagining her at the gym seven days a week. Maybe both things are true.

When Rose asks Regina for details, she obliges. The young woman, whose name is Heather, showed up at Edward's penthouse in Atlanta, where Regina still lives, and announced she was looking for her father.

"It's hard to imagine Edward a father," Rose says.

Regina's laugh is short and unexpected. "I know what you mean. It always surprised me that he could keep an orchid alive."

Orchids? Rose can't envision her brother tending to anything except maybe the stock market. Of course, he didn't seem the type to marry an African-American woman, either. The truth is, she doubts she even knew her brother at all.

Regina pauses and exhales again. Rose can almost smell the burning tobacco.

"It seems Heather's mother was an employee of his for a brief time," Regina begins again. "Twenty-two years ago, Edward gave the mother enough money to get rid of her, as well as abort the baby. But it seems she decided to keep it and raised the child by herself," she continues. "The mother died recently, and the daughter is now looking for her biological father. Namely, guess who?"

"Did you tell her he died in a fire two years ago?" Rose asks.

"She didn't seem surprised by the news," Regina says.

Rose pauses. Why would the young woman go looking for Edward if she knew about the fire? Something doesn't make sense.

"She kept her father's last name?" Rose asks.

"Yes," Regina says. "Her mother was smart enough to list Edward's name on the birth certificate. Heather has a copy with her, but who knows if the thing is real. There are all sorts of cons out there these days, you know." Regina exhales again.

Could Edward have had a secret daughter? He certainly had a secret wife that nobody knew about. The Temple family is steeped in secrets. Not only do they have their own fair share, but they have collected them for over two hundred years to blackmail the citizens of Savannah whenever they needed to boost their influence. There are two ledgers full of secrets, it turns out, though Rose hasn't made time to explore the second.

Phone in hand, Rose walks over to the sunroom and Old Sally's table filled with all the objects that represent the people she watches over, Rose being one of them. The key to the second safe-deposit box is right where she left it.

Perhaps it's time to go see what's in that second book, Rose tells herself.

At the very least, she can see what it contains before destroying it. Somehow the world would seem better off if someone finally laid all those secrets to rest. But first, she needs to get through Queenie's wedding.

Regina is silent like a fisherman slowly moving bait through the water to fool the fish into thinking it doesn't have a hook. But Rose refuses to bite.

"Thank you for warning me," she says, "but I need to get busy here. We're—"

"Wait," Regina says, "there's more."

"More?" Rose doesn't have time for more. She also doesn't have time to figure out Regina's motives.

"Heather visited again this morning," Regina says. "I gave her your address. She left here about fifteen minutes ago, heading in your direction."

"You gave her my address?" Rose returns to the kitchen, where Spud is up to his elbows in lemons. "Why would you do that without asking me first?"

"Is there a problem?" Regina's voice reveals a slight lift. Is she smiling?

"We've got a lot happening here today," Rose says, thinking this is the understatement of the century. A short century so far, since it is only 2002.

"I thought I'd give you a head's up," Regina says, before offering a quick goodbye.

It seems Edward's widow has enjoyed dropping this latest family secret in Rose's lap.

A surprise relative showing up is the last thing she expected, and she doesn't want anything to take away from Queenie's day. The wedding is scheduled to start in less than an hour. Rose pauses, unsure of what to do with this news. A young woman, claiming to be her brother's daughter, is driving from Atlanta to their island today. A trip of just under 300 miles that usually takes about four and a half hours to drive. At this rate, she will miss the wedding, but the party afterward might still be going on.

When she looks up, her daughter Katie—petite, tan, and very pregnant—is staring at her.

"What is it, Mom? Your face has gone all white."

"Nothing," Rose says when what she wants to say is, *Everything*.

Katie drops the dishrag she was using to clean off the counters. When she can't bend over to retrieve it, Rose picks it up. Didn't Violet tell her earlier that dropping a dishrag means company is coming?

Rose will be a grandmother soon. Katie's first attempt at artificial insemination ended in a miscarriage last August. A hard moment for all of them. But the second try worked. Something that Katie attributes to taking Old Sally's root medicines. Rose imagines the rewards of grandmotherhood will quickly outweigh her insecurities of feeling ancient. Katie is two weeks from her due date and looks like she should have given birth a month ago.

But first, a thousand details need to be attended to in the next hour, including keeping the groom from collapsing into a nervous heap. And now a stranger named Heather is driving in from Atlanta?

Katie opens the refrigerator and devours a vanilla yogurt in six bites before excusing herself to go to the bathroom. Both are familiar scenes these days. Katie's small white terrier, Harpo, follows her everywhere, his nails clicking softly on the wooden and slate floors. Only Rose and Spud remain in the kitchen.

"What was that phone call about?" Spud washes the cutting board in the sink.

"We have an unexpected guest arriving later this afternoon," Rose says. His suit reminds her of an eggplant parmesan recipe she hasn't made for a while and needs to find again.

"Well, as my beloved future wife would say, the more the merrier." Spud pets his mustache thoughtfully as if struck with the realization that he will soon have a wife.

But Rose doesn't feel merry. She feels stressed. She wants a smooth send-off to celebrate Spud and Queenie's life together. No complications. How rare is it for two people who have never married before to say vows in their sixties? And these are two people she loves.

In the meantime, Regina's phone call now has Rose angry. Why did Regina give Edward's supposed daughter Rose's address if she felt uncomfortable around her? Was this merely the next logical step, or was her intention more devious?

After glancing at her watch, Rose turns her attention to what she has left to do for the wedding. The rented white tent is already in place on the beach, and Max and Jack are setting up folding chairs. For weeks she questioned the wisdom of a beach wedding, given all the rain they have this time of year, but it is a sunny June day.

Angela, Katie's girlfriend, enters the kitchen carrying flowers she picked from Old Sally's garden in back. Daisies, irises, and lilies. The flowers are to go in large vases throughout the house. While Rose arranges the plates and silver for the reception, Angela cuts the stems and places them in four different jars for Violet to do the final arranging. Angela has proven to be the most surprising addition to their nontraditional family. An author and tattooed feminist, Angela is also quick to help in any situation, with the added bonus of having a way of managing Katie that allows Rose to relax.

When Rose and Angela first met at her mother's funeral, Angela came across as thorny. A northerner with issues. But once Rose got to know her, Angela's brusqueness fell away. Perhaps Angela should answer the door when the young stranger arrives from Atlanta. She could ascertain what the stranger wants and maybe even scare her away. In the meantime, how can she be confident that the young woman really is Edward's child?

When Katie returns, Angela pats Katie's stomach to say hello to the baby. Their relationship was hard for Rose at first, though she pretended it wasn't. If given a choice, Rose would want a more mainstream lifestyle for her daughter, and therefore perhaps a safer lifestyle. But after 9/11 she wonders if anyone is truly safe, no matter what lifestyle they choose. Rose also thought she would have to give up her dream of being a grandmother someday. But it is incredible the medical procedures they can do these days that allow sperm donors—in this case, one of Angela's male friends— and potential mothers to unite.

"I wish you'd tell me what's wrong," Katie says to Rose.

"Everything's fine," Rose says, not wanting to worry her daughter, who worries way too much for someone in her twenties. But as an only child, she has always seemed older and more responsible than most people her age.

In the meantime, something about the stranger coming has Rose on edge. Spud turns up the volume on the small television sitting on the counter in the kitchen. The latest weather forecast reveals clear, sunny skies for today—perfect weather for a wedding—and a tropical storm has formed in the Caribbean. Rose sighs with relief that it won't rain on Queenie's wedding.

Seconds later the weatherman pauses for breaking news, explaining that a tropical storm becomes a hurricane when the wind speed reaches 74 miles per hour. He goes on to explain that every year the National Weather Service starts the naming of storms with the letter *A*, and since it has already been an active storm year, they are already up to the letter *I*.

Upon hearing the name of the hurricane, Rose gasps, and Spud looks like he might faint. Is the universe playing a joke on them? A joke that her dead mother somehow fashioned?

In an ironic—if not uncanny—turn of events, a hurricane named Iris has materialized and is spinning out in the Atlantic, as though she is late for Queenie and Spud's wedding.

CHAPTER FOUR

Violet

Violet returns to the kitchen to find Spud beset with citrus and Rose looking worried. While they spent decades apart, Violet's best friend from her childhood is back. When they were young and Old Sally brought Rose to the beach, she had Rose and Violet do a Gullah charm of washing their hands together in the kitchen sink. This supposedly ensured that they would be best friends forever. For further assurance, Old Sally burned onion peelings on the stove to strengthen the bond. It was a time when little black girls and little white girls—one poor and one rich—weren't allowed to be friends at all, and most certainly not best friends. But that didn't stop them. It seems the Gullah charm is still working.

Over the last few months, Violet has evolved from feeling like an orphan to being part of a large, extended family. To have this many people living together has taken some getting used to. But the house they designed to expand on Old Sally's has two stories and plenty of room, with large porches and floor-to-ceiling windows, as well as a cottage out back for Rose and Max. She has moments when, surprisingly, she misses working for Miss Temple and having time alone, but otherwise, this living arrangement makes her feel more alive. Whole. Useful.

For the first time, Violet notices Spud's purple suit. Perhaps this confirms he and Queenie are meant for each other. At the same time, she wonders briefly if Queenie can be trusted to be left alone. If she adds any more color, she will look like she's leading a gay pride parade. Yet, it appears there are other concerns.

"What's going on?" Violet asks. "Why is everybody looking so strange? We've got a wedding soon."

Rose's pale complexion is even more pale. Come to think of it, Spud looks whiter than usual, too.

"Someone may be crashing the party," Spud says, his eyebrows raised.

"Who?" Violet asks.

"Iris."

Spud loosens his bow tie as though Iris's delicate fingers are choking him from the grave.

"I don't understand." Violet didn't get enough sleep last night and her morning started at dawn with Old Sally. Grouchiness is next if she isn't careful.

Meanwhile, the color returns to Rose's face, and there is a hint of magic in her eyes. "It seems Mother's ghost has finally found us," she says to Violet. "She's hitched a ride on a hurricane!"

Violet smiles, her irritation gone in an instant. However, her confusion is gaining ground. The last time Violet felt this clueless was at the reading of Miss Temple's will two years ago. The day she found out that Queenie wasn't her aunt, but her mother, who had been threatened and sworn to secrecy by her father, Mister Oscar, Miss Temple's husband. Violet isn't in the mood for surprises. At least not until this wedding is over.

For over a week, the spirit of Miss Temple has felt somehow close. After the fire, Violet wasn't sure what happened to the displaced Temple ghosts. Did they disperse to other mansions and find new places to haunt? Or invest in retirement condos in the world's most haunted cities, Savannah being one of them?

Yet, it feels like old times to speak of ghosts. She always knew that funerals attracted them, and now it seems that weddings do, too.

"That hurricane is an interesting coincidence," Rose says.

"I always knew your mother was a force of nature," Violet says, remembering how Miss Temple left critiques in the kitchen in the mornings. Critiques of meals, and initially, critiques of her housekeeping abilities, until Violet figured out exactly what she wanted. To work there, Violet had to grow a thicker skin and not take anything personally, though Miss Temple's critiques were always personal. Telling Violet that she wasn't smart enough to comprehend her needs, or that Violet's cooking skills lacked finesse.

With a white monogrammed handkerchief pulled from the pocket of his purple suit, Spud wipes a smattering of perspiration from his brow. He is right to worry. How will Queenie take this news? She can get stormy herself if she thinks the fates are messing with her.

Katie returns to the kitchen to eat a banana, her latest snack. "What are you guys talking about?"

Violet, Rose, and Spud exchange a look. An entire book is needed to tell this story instead of a sentence or two. It appears Violet has been elected to offer a summation.

"Iris and Spud were an item many years ago," she begins, "and while we initially thought that your Grandmother Temple's ghost was finally resting in peace, now there's a genuine concern that she may be crashing Queenie's wedding."

"At least metaphorically," Rose says.

Angela laughs, as though entertained by hearing about ghosts crashing a wedding.

"That's what you get for moving to the South, sweetheart,"

Katie says with a playful southern accent, all the while holding her belly.

Everyone joins in the laughter before things turn serious again.

"Do we know when the storm is due?" Violet asks.

"The hurricane is a long shot," Rose says. "It may never materialize."

"That's right," Spud says. "Hurricanes never hit Savannah. The big storms head north or south of us, to Charleston or Florida."

Violet is relieved that she hasn't heard a peep out of her left shoulder, her early warning system for bad things.

"There's something else you should know about," Rose says to Violet. "We have yet another unexpected visitor coming."

"Ghost or real person?" Violet asks.

"I'm assuming real," Rose says.

"Good," Violet says. "I prefer real. Who?"

"It seems Edward has a daughter that he didn't tell anybody about."

"You've got to be kidding."

"I kind of wish I were," Rose says. "She's been giving Regina a hard time, so Regina sent her here."

"Here?" Violet can't believe how much has happened while she fought with Queenie's zipper.

"She's driving here from Atlanta this very minute. Evidently, she wants to meet us."

The day is getting more complicated by the minute. While the others scatter to do different tasks, Violet glances at the kitchen clock and speeds up her process. She adds water and sugar to the three large glass pitchers with cut lemons on the bottom, to make lemonade the way Old Sally always makes it.

Violet pauses. Where is Old Sally? By this time of day, she is usually in the sunroom at her window seat, but with the wedding, she is probably taking a short nap. She already dressed hours ago, so now all that's left is showing up.

After finishing the lemonade and arranging the flowers, Violet sprinkles water around the house to keep evil spirits away like Old Sally taught her. A precaution. As far as she knows this ritual doesn't work with hurricanes. But she will welcome any help she can get. Gullah folk magic has proven to be more complicated than she initially imagined. Roots. Spells. Medicines. Rituals. Stories. Spirits. Subtle yet powerful. As with anything, it takes a belief that it will work for it to be effective. And Violet believes.

Many traditions fade away with modern times. However, thanks to Old Sally, the Gullah traditions aren't dying away, they are changing form. To survive, Gullah folk magic is becoming more secretive and protected.

In coming years Violet plans to pass these traditions along to Tia and Leisha, who already spend a lot of time with their great-grandmother now that they all live here on the beach. But first, Violet reheats the gumbo, a meal with an okra base and a host of other vegetables, spices, and meats. The Frogmore stew is on simmer in Rose's kitchen. Violet combined the sausage, shrimp, corn, and potatoes this morning. It will be brought out and served steaming hot at the reception. Both recipes were passed down to her from Old Sally and those who came before her.

"I guess I need to break the news to Queenie," Spud says to Violet. "I wouldn't want her to find out about Iris without me."

Violet wishes him luck. "And tell her that my shoulder isn't concerned," Violet adds.

He says he will.

"Oh, is my bow tie straight?" he asks, before walking away. "It won't be long until I become Mister Queenie Temple." Spud gives a short, nervous laugh.

Violet steps in front of him and tenderly tightens the bow tie of the kindest man she has ever known.

"Where did you find this one?" Violet asks.

"Queenie had it made for me in Charleston," Spud says.

The bow tie is yellow and dotted with purple saxophones. A

couple of years ago, Spud would have never worn custom-made ties, and Violet would have never lived in a big, fancy home on the beach, even if it was an expansion of her grandmother's much smaller house.

Before the reading of Miss Temple's will, Spud was a butcher at Piggly Wiggly, and Violet was Miss Temple's housekeeper and cook. Everything they now possess is thanks to Miss Iris Temple of the Savannah Temples. Naming a hurricane after her seems appropriate. She was an extra-large personality. While Violet hasn't missed dealing with a mansion full of Temple ghosts every day—along with the eccentricities of a *living* Miss Temple—what she did in leaving Violet the estate in her will changed her life, and she is forever grateful. Although the mansion burned to the ground shortly after, the insurance money helped them build this current house, as well as open Violet's long-dreamed-for tea shop in downtown Savannah.

As for Miss Temple, may she finally rest in peace, as well as quietly blow out to sea.

CHAPTER FIVE

Old Sally

While everyone prepares for Queenie's wedding, Old Sally walks down to the breaking tide. Weddings are essential rituals, a moment of light in a family. She pulls her summer shawl tight around her shoulders. Born in the year 1900, Old Sally has stayed on this earth much longer than she thought she would. The only way she can make sense of it is to believe that her Gullah ancestors still have plans for her.

A whirlwind dances up the beach, tossing loose circles of sand, and Old Sally admires the outfit Rose found for her to wear. The cotton dress is the color of sand with red and purple flowers stitched around the collar and hem. If Old Sally had her way, this would be her funeral dress, too. The cemetery at the far end of the island is where her ancestors are buried. All her life Old Sally has known her body would end up there, too, when her spirit rejoins her ancestors. This thought comforts her. No fear involved. Like a story, every life on earth has a beginning, a middle, and an end. Sometimes a life story lasts only hours. Sometimes days, years, or decades. A few last over a century, like Old Sally's, with no rhyme or reason for who goes first or last. It is not about the lucky or the unlucky. The good or the evil. Old Sally knows better than to think she can figure out this mystery. It is not a crime novel, after all. Life and death are in an eternal dance just like that whirlwind. Wind and sand. Sand and wind. A dance across time.

We might as well try to enjoy the dance and the story that goes with it.

Someone calls her from the dunes. It is Jack, Violet's husband, who reminds her of a man from her past she loved with her whole heart. A man nicknamed Fiddle. Someone she has been thinking about more and more, now that the time draws near for her passing.

"Violet asked me to check on you," Jack says as he joins her.

"That sounds like our Violet," she says with a smile.

Jack is a good match for her granddaughter. He is thoughtful and kind and an excellent father to their two daughters. He teaches at the community college and sometimes invites his students to visit with her. With the group of young people gathered around her, she will tell them how things used to be for black people.

Old Sally likes having her great-granddaughters around more now that they are all living here in this great big house. After the Temple mansion was destroyed, Violet presented the idea of adding on to her small home here on the beach, where they could all live together. Old Sally was hesitant at first. Her mind was trapped in a little box of how things had to be. But the Lord's ways are mysterious. Now she has a house full of family again. Family that is related by blood, and the added family that a person chooses. Soul family, she calls them. People found in a moment of grace, while that whirlwind keeps dancing up the beach.

As for family related by blood, there are Queenie and Violet, Violet's teenage daughters, Tia and Leisha, and Jack. Her soul family is Rose, her husband Max, their daughter, Katie, and Katie's special friend, Angela. And after today, Spud will live here, too.

Old Sally even has soul pets. Keeping all their names straight helps her mind stay active. Lucy and Ethel are Rose and Max's border collies. Katie's little white dog is named Harpo. Angela's two cats are Zelda and Gertrude. And Tia and Leisha's pet turtle is named Jake.

Families live so far away from each other these days. Old people go to nursing homes instead of living with their families. Some are perfectly fine. But too many people die lonely. With this arrangement, they all live together yet have their separate spaces. Old Sally might die alone, but loneliness is impossible. Especially with her belief that her ancestors are waiting for her.

As they look out over the sea, Old Sally takes Jack's arm. He is tall and handsome, a lovely black man.

Last fall, to get their minds off the 9/11 tragedy, Old Sally taught Jack and Max how to fish the Gullah way, with weighted casting nets. Now they catch fish, crab, and shrimp from the creeks on the island. Sometimes Old Sally watches them standing knee-deep in water throwing nets and realizes that Dolphin Island is becoming a part of them, too.

Old Sally enjoys having men around again. Her husband, Samuel, died in the Second World War, so she has been a widow for over fifty years. Their wedding was on the south end of the island at the small church, now in ruins.

"Do you want to stay here a while longer?" Jack says. "I need to get back. Guests will be arriving any minute."

"I think I'll walk a little more and gather my thoughts," Old Sally says.

Before leaving, Jack kisses her hand as if they have just finished a dance. She offers him a slight bow.

Old Sally settles into the silence again, memories rising from her bones. Memories of playing on this beach as a girl, living in a house built for her mother by her uncles and grandfather, before Sally was born. Her mother had three children. Two sons and then Sally, the youngest.

Her mother would never recognize this house now. It is beyond grand. Before, it had only two bedrooms, but that seemed like a castle when Sally was a girl. Now it has seven, as well as a cottage in the back. It surprises her sometimes how big her life has become in the last year. Right when most old people's lives are getting smaller.

In June of 1920, it was Old Sally who was preparing to wed. Of course, back then she was called Sally; there was nothing "old" about her. Her mother and her Aunt Polly decorated the small church on the island. Palm fronds lined the aisle, with white hydrangeas tied on the end of each pew. Aunt Sissie Mainer, her mother's older sister, made Sally a beach-shell wedding bouquet with a bleached white starfish lying in the center of purple flowers. She still has the starfish in her collection of unique things.

Her wedding dress was stitched by hand by her grandmother who lived with them—her other grandmother died before Sally was born—who also made sugar cookies shaped like sand dollars, and a wedding cake with two white starfish sitting on the top of sea-blue icing sprinkled with brown sugar to look like sand.

Old Sally still remembers the look of the scars on her grandmother's arms as she made these things. Injuries from a grease fire in the Temple kitchen while she worked there, back in the slave-owning days. She was finally freed in 1865, right after the war ended.

When Old Sally closes her eyes, she feels her mother's gentle touch. Even though her mother always came home exhausted, she would fix Sally's hair before bed to ready it for school the next day. All these years later she still misses her mother. To lose a loving mother is like a heartache that never goes away. However, it was her grandmother she was closest to growing up. Some would call her unlucky to be a servant all her life, but she was lucky to have such loving people around her.

Old Sally looks out over the ocean. Waves were a constant lullaby growing up. A continuous source of comfort. Even now she can recognize the sound of high tide, low tide, and everything in between. Right now, the tide is going out, the beach expanding in time for the wedding.

For seven years—after she married Samuel and before he died in the war—Sally didn't live on the island. They lived in Savannah in a small apartment because Samuel wanted to break free of the old ways. Sally didn't see the point of breaking free of something so central to her, but Samuel was her husband, so she did it anyway.

After his death, Sally moved back in with her mother, young children in tow. Ivy came much later, after Old Sally's other children were already grown and out of the house. She was a change-of-life baby fathered by Iris Temple's father. Making Iris and Ivy half sisters. No consent to it. Old Sally wanted to keep her job. But those days no longer hurt her. She wasn't the one who did anything wrong.

Years later "Ivy" became Queenie, a name given to her by Rose and Violet when they were girls and called themselves the Sea Gypsies. An image rises in front of Old Sally of Rose and Violet running on the beach as girls, the sequined scarves she made for them flowing behind them. In her mind, they will forever be Sea Gypsies.

Old Sally takes a deep breath and walks back to the house. Memory works in strange ways. She can't remember yesterday that well, but she can recall details from eighty years ago. Some memories are painful. Others surprise her with their tenderness. All are a gift.

On the front porch, Violet greets her with a cup of steaming ginger tea—Old Sally's favorite. She places it on the small wooden table beside Old Sally's rocking chair. They each take a rocker, though Violet looks about as harried as Old Sally has ever seen her.

"You okay?" Old Sally says, a shared greeting in their family.

"Just need to catch a breath," Violet says. "Guests are arriving."

"How's Queenie?" Old Sally asks.

"Nervous," Violet says. "She's touching up her makeup."

"And the groom?"

"Nervous, too."

"Marriage be nerve-wracking when you've never done it before," Old Sally says. *Can you hear me?* Old Sally adds, thinking this instead of speaking.

Violet smiles. "I heard you."

"Good," Old Sally says, feeling pleased. "Good," she says again, more to herself than Violet.

Sometimes an opening occurs between two souls where thoughts can get through. It can happen with mothers and daughters, grandmothers and granddaughters, or two people who have been joined together in a common fate. Like Old Sally helping Iris Temple transition to the next world, although that didn't entirely work. Old Sally and Violet are hearing each other's thoughts more often these days. That's because Old Sally's time to leave this world is getting close.

"When you get quiet, what are you thinking about?" Violet asks her.

"I be visiting the past since there's not much future left," she tells Violet. "Lots to explore there."

Old Sally is surprised that Violet is taking the time to be with her with so much going on around them. Cars pulling in the driveway. People walking to the wedding tent on the beach. Max and Jack taking turns telling people where to park or running to get something they need. Yet, it is all getting done, and somehow Violet has accepted that. Anyone who knows Queenie knows that her wedding will not start right on time. It would be out of character.

"You know, if this wedding is too much for you, Queenie will understand," Violet says.

Violet's protection of her means a lot to Old Sally.

"I'm not about to miss this wedding," Old Sally says. "I was honored that Queenie wanted me to take part in the ceremony."

From inside the house, Queenie lets out a frantic call to Violet.

"I'd better go see what's up," Violet says.

Old Sally agrees that may be best.

Violet leaves her on the porch, and Old Sally raises the tea to her lips. Her hand has a slight shake to it these days, like she is getting ready to wave goodbye.

She looks forward to laying her burdens down, as the old spiritual goes. But first, Old Sally must bless Queenie's wedding.

CHAPTER SIX

Queenie

Queenie fans herself with an issue of *O* magazine sporting Oprah's smiling face on the cover. Oprah has Stedman but has never officially married, and for years Queenie was convinced that she was destined to follow in her footsteps. Now she wishes she could call her up and ask her if she knows something Queenie doesn't know. Maybe marriage isn't something enlightened women choose to do in the twenty-first century.

A gentle knock on the door breaks her steady stream of second thoughts.

"You okay, sweet pea?" Spud's voice is muffled through the closed door.

Queenie has forgiven Spud for being in love with Iris for all those years, although she still has trouble understanding it.

"You aren't supposed to see me before the wedding," Queenie calls. "It's bad luck."

"We got all our bad luck out of the way years ago," Spud says.

That little devil sure knows what to say and how to say it, Queenie thinks. "Well, if our marriage only lasts a week, it will be your fault," she says, opening the door.

The look on Spud Grainger's face makes Queenie quit second-guessing herself. Tears spring to his eyes, and hers, too, and she dares them to mess up her mascara.

"You are the most beautiful creature on God's green earth," he says.

Queenie's glee gives her a quick shiver. She is too old to feel like a teenager in love, but there you go. If she has learned anything in the last year, it is not only to seize the day but seize any moments of happiness she can grab.

"Where in the world did you find a purple suit?" Queenie feels the fabric of his lapel to see if it is velvet and then looks on the back to make sure there isn't a picture of Elvis.

"I have my sources," Spud says. "I know your favorite color is purple, and I wanted to make you happy."

Queenie pulls him inside the bedroom and gives him a kiss that steams up his glasses. It still surprises her how her heartbeat quickens every time she sees him. Finding true love with a skinny white vegetarian butcher was not something she saw coming. Ever.

"Why do you smell like lemons?" she asks. "You been cleaning with Lemon Pledge or something?"

"Rose had me cutting lemons to keep me distracted." Spud smiles, sniffing the backs of his hands.

"I guess a wedding wouldn't be a wedding without Mama's lemonade," she says.

He agrees.

"You think we should go ahead and start the honeymoon now?" she asks.

He matches her grin and gives her a loving pat on her ample backside. "I still can't believe I get to do that," he says.

Spud stretches an arm toward the zipper on the back of her wedding gown, and Queenie stops him.

"Come to think of it, honey, I guess we'd better wait. I may never get back in this dress once I take it off."

With a sigh, Spud agrees and takes a handkerchief from his pocket to rub the steam from his glasses.

"How's it going out there?" Queenie asks.

Spud looks away, a sure sign that he isn't telling her something.

"Out with it." Queenie places her hands on her hips. She is not to be underestimated. Something about wearing a wedding gown makes her feel like a superhero. Powerful and gracious at the same time. She may have to wear this more often. Maybe in a slightly bigger size. But then she imagines dragging her train everywhere—through the Piggly Wiggly and the Gladys Knight and the Tints beauty parlor—and thinks better of it.

Queenie regains her focus and waits for Spud to answer.

"It's kind of funny when you think about it," he says, still not looking her in the eye.

Queenie pulls him toward her by the same lapel she admired earlier. They are almost the same height, but she has a good fifty pounds on him.

"Spud Grainger, don't even think about lying to me."

"Two things." His eyes soften as he looks at her. "First, it seems that Edward Temple has a daughter who is coming to visit today."

Queenie laughs. "You are such a joker," she tells him. "This is not April first, and I am nobody's fool."

When he doesn't join in the laughter, she tightens her lips. Queenie has despised Edward Temple with a passion ever since he cornered a teenage Violet in the garden shed at the Temple mansion.

"Since when does Edward have a daughter?" Queenie asks.

"Evidently, it's a recent discovery," Spud says.

"What's the second thing?" she asks, though she isn't so sure she wants to know.

"A hurricane is forming in the Atlantic."

"And why should I care?"

"It's probably nothing," Spud says, "and I hesitate to even mention it, but—"

"But what?"

Spud hesitates.

"All I've wanted for the last six weeks is for this wedding to come off without a hitch. Is that too much to ask?"

"Is that a rhetorical question?" Spud responds.

Queenie lets out a sound that is a cross between a scream and an *oomph*. She drags her train to the window and sees blue skies.

"Seriously, is this a joke?" Queenie asks again. "There's not a cloud in the sky."

"There is a funny part to it," Spud says.

"Funny, ha-ha, or funny strange?" Queenie asks, narrowing her eyes at him.

"Funny strange."

Queenie puts her hands on her hips again, but it isn't the same as before. She doesn't feel powerful or graceful at all. She feels plus-size, awkward, and hot-flashy.

"Tell me before I bust a zipper or something," Queenie says to him, her voice low.

Spud pauses as if being careful of his word choice. "You know how the National Weather Service names storms when they have a certain wind speed and reach hurricane status?"

"Yes, I know that," Queenie says. "Where in the world are you going with this?"

"Well, the letter they've worked their way up to is *I*." He looks at her as though waiting for a lightbulb to go off over her head.

"*I*?"

"Yes, *I*." Spud winks.

"What in heaven's name are you trying to tell me?" Queenie taps her size nine shoe.

Spud's face turns a light shade of red and begins to glisten from the beads of perspiration forming.

"Well . . ." Spud stutters, "they've named the hurricane Iris."

Queenie laughs like she has just heard the funniest joke of all time, but then realizes that she is the only one laughing.

"That witch will not ruin my wedding," Queenie says, thinking the b-word would suit Iris better. When it comes to spoiling a special event, Queenie will not put anything past Iris Temple—dead or alive.

Queenie feels like one of those cartoon characters whose face turns fire-engine red right before the steam shoots out of their ears. Spud tells her not to panic, but it seems that that ocean liner has already sailed. Holding up her dress so she doesn't trip, Queenie pushes past him into the hallway and down the steps that lead to the kitchen.

When they see her coming, Rose and Violet exchange a look that says the hurricane coming starts with a *Q*, not an *I*, and her name is Queenie.

"Try to stay calm," Rose says, meeting Queenie at the entrance to the kitchen. "You look beautiful, by the way," she adds.

"Try to stay calm?" Queenie's voice rises, skipping right over the compliment. She drops the skirt of her gown and enjoys a brief rush of cold air up her legs.

"Don't worry," Rose says. "Edward's daughter isn't due for a couple of hours. It will be the middle of the reception by then."

"Since when does Edward have a daughter?" Queenie asks.

"It was news to us, too," Rose says. "Evidently that was another one of those Temple family secrets."

"God help us," Queenie says. "When in heaven will those secrets finally stop haunting us?"

"Good question," Violet says.

"Do you think she's a fake and just trying to get Edward's money?" Queenie asks.

"She supposedly has a birth certificate that proves his paternity," Rose answers.

"Well, why is she coming here?" Queenie asks.

"I'm not exactly sure," Rose says. "I think Regina wanted to get rid of her. But I could be wrong."

"Well, I'll get rid of her," Queenie says with another tap of her shoe.

Spud places a calming hand on her shoulder. When she looks at him, she is reminded of Barney, that purple dinosaur that all the kids love. Except this Barney is skinny.

"And that's not even the biggest news," Queenie says. "What about this storm?"

"Hurricane Iris is nowhere near here," Violet says, trying to untangle the train of Queenie's wedding dress.

Queenie huffs when she hears the name of the hurricane again.

"Is my wedding a cosmic joke?" Queenie asks Rose. Tears threaten to come next. *Ugly tears,* as Oprah calls them.

Spud, Rose, and Violet look at Queenie as though she is a nuclear reactor threatening a meltdown.

"It's going to be a wonderful wedding," Violet says. "The sun is shining, and we've got plenty of food—"

"Oh my Lord, what time is it?" Queenie shrieks before swooping up the stairs for her last-minute preparations, cussing Iris on every step.

CHAPTER SEVEN

Rose

R ose thinks of Edward's daughter somewhere on the
interstate from Atlanta, curious what this potential niece
might be like. Rose was naïve to believe that the mansion burning
down had brought an end to all the Temple secrets. Another layer
is bubbling to the surface. Maybe her Temple ancestors will never
rest in peace until that Book of Secrets is destroyed. Or should she
say *books*?

Celebrations shouldn't be stressful, she decides.

But she can't quit thinking about those Temple ledgers. Does
Regina have a copy of the secrets that Edward released to the
Savannah newspaper in the weeks leading up to the fire? Maybe
she knows exactly why Edward's daughter is coming. Maybe
Edward kept the juiciest secrets for a future release. Blackmail
goes a long way in business negotiations or in generating cash.
Rose isn't sure why she should even care. However, if the books
exist, they can potentially do harm, and the Temple family is not
free.

Finally dressed, she checks out the tent and seating arrangements on the beach. Queenie will be pleased. She takes a moment to look out over the ocean, comparing it to her former view of the Rocky Mountains. Adjusting to East Coast living again has taken some time.

Rose hasn't been able to paint since she got here, and this concerns her more than she wants to admit. Last week, Rose dreamed her mother hid all her paints and paintbrushes. She couldn't sleep the rest of the night after that and has slept fitfully ever since.

Twenty-five years ago, Rose knew she had to leave Savannah or she would spend her life in her mother's shadow and never recover her self-esteem. Even now, her presence still looms, if only in memory. How ironic that the hurricane out in the Atlantic carries her mother's name. Is the storm reminding Rose that her mother is always watching, always lurking on the edges of her life? Rose takes a deep breath of ocean air to clear the past away. *But will it ever go away completely?*

Painting is the only time Rose feels like she is doing something she is meant to do. Two galleries in Sante Fe, New Mexico, carry her Western landscapes. But she doesn't live in the West anymore, and moving back to the East Coast required more energy than she anticipated. If that wasn't enough, the Temple mansion burned down, which was where they had planned to live. Followed by Plan B, the renovation and move into this house. Followed by 9/11. She hears herself making excuses and stops.

A blank canvas is sometimes a good thing, she tells herself. *I can go in a totally different direction if I want.*

However, new directions take time and patience, and she hopes she is up for the task.

When Rose returns to the house, Old Sally is sitting in the living room by the front window with Katie. Just seeing Old Sally makes Rose feel more settled. Katie rises when she sees Rose and excuses herself to go to the bathroom again.

"Can I get you anything?" Rose asks Old Sally.

"If you could return my teacup to the kitchen, that would be helpful," she says.

It is only lately that Old Sally has been asking for help with little things, like taking a teacup or helping her stand if she's been sitting. The cup rattles gently on the saucer, her hand not as steady as it once was.

Tea leaves deposit a message in the bottom of the cup. Do they spell out danger? Is the stranger coming to town going to change their lives forever? Rose has read enough novels to imagine the worst. If the stranger were anyone other than her brother's offspring, Rose might look forward to meeting a new family member. But Edward was a carbon copy of their mother. Manipulative. Controlling. Always wanting to have the most power in a room. All attributes guaranteed to make Rose cautious about meeting his daughter.

When Rose returns, Old Sally pats her hand and thanks her. They are waiting for Queenie to come downstairs to start the procession as the guests continue to arrive and walk down to the beach.

"Earlier today, I remembered how you and Violet played on this beach as girls," Old Sally says. "You called yourselves the Sea Gypsies. Remember?" Old Sally laughs a short laugh. "You two were the beginning of a promise to me. You gave me hope that someday color wouldn't matter in this world."

"Queenie was always around, too," Rose says. "Now I know why."

"Yes, you do," Old Sally says, patting her hand again.

Rose can't imagine how hard it must have been for Queenie, at nineteen, to have a child that she kept secret. A child that was sired by Rose's father. A fact that still shocks her when she thinks about it.

Do children ever know who their parents really are? Rose wonders.

Family secrets in the South are like kudzu; they grow like

crazy and are nearly impossible to get rid of. For years she thought her father was an honest and kind man. Never would she have imagined that he might take advantage of Queenie in that way, or in any way.

Dear, sweet Queenie, Rose thinks.

Unfortunately, he wasn't the first white man to take advantage of the people who worked for him. Nor can Rose imagine Old Sally's life—living in the South as a black woman for over a hundred years. A servant most of her life. A servant to Rose's family.

A familiar guilt rises and flushes her face. While her mother wore entitlement every day of her life like a set of pearls, privilege has never sat well with Rose. Old Sally has more integrity in her pinkie finger than Rose's mother had in her entire body. Rose looks at her hand, where her fingertip is missing. A small sacrifice to the past, thanks to Edward and a Temple sword.

"You know how much I love you, don't you?" Rose kneels next to Old Sally's chair so they can be eye to eye.

Old Sally covers Rose's pale hand with her dark one. "You be my English Rose. My beautiful girl."

Tears come to Rose's eyes. A moment of peace amidst all the wedding preparations.

Old Sally turns her gaze to the objects on the table, her ritual for as long as Rose has known her. Mementos that stand in for people Old Sally sends healing to and protection from the harshness of the world every single day.

"I have a favor to ask," Old Sally says.

"Anything," Rose says, and she means it.

"There be only a few people left that I watch after these days. Most of them are right here in this house. Would you take over when I'm gone?"

Rose pauses with new tears. It is another day of moisture in the low country. At breakfast, Violet said that she was more emotional than usual today, and Queenie admitted the same. The three of them agreed to not question it and flow with it.

"I would be honored to carry on for you," Rose says to Old Sally.

Old Sally thanks her and takes a deep breath, as if this is one more thing she can let go of before she goes.

Although Rose and Old Sally have never spoken of the key, she is sure Old Sally noticed it there. Rose placed it on the table the day she met Regina, Edward's secret wife. Regina gave Rose an unopened envelope that contained correspondence between her brother and her mother. If Regina had known what was inside, she might never have given it to Rose. Along with the key, there was a letter that told of a second, older safe-deposit box that contained another Book of Secrets. Rose's first instinct was to throw the key away and let that old book rot in the vault until all those secrets could die away, along with her mother and Edward.

Old Sally picks up the key and hands it to Rose. "It be time to lay all the ghosts to rest."

"Lay the ghosts to rest?" Rose repeats, wondering if Old Sally heard her thoughts.

"You're the next in line in the Temple family," Old Sally tells her. "The responsibility falls to you."

Rose has trouble meeting Old Sally's eyes. It's not like a person can choose their lineage. Rose is tired of being a Temple and lugging around all the history that comes with it. Old Sally talks about her ancestors in such a positive way, but Rose wishes hers would leave her alone. She grew up with their lavish portraits staring at her in every room of the mansion. Meanwhile, Old Sally's family seems less encumbered, despite being fated to live in the shadows of wealthy white people.

Rose offers a reluctant nod and places the key in the pocket of her dress. She has no idea what Old Sally means by the Temple history being Rose's responsibility. She has watched Old Sally pass on the Gullah ways and their rich history to Violet—at times, almost enviously. But the Temple traditions are about amassing power and more money than you could possibly spend in a lifetime. Is that a heritage that needs to be passed on?

Despite the warm breeze moving through the house, Rose shivers.

CHAPTER EIGHT

Violet

T he wedding nearly under way, Violet takes a last look at the reception table. She adjusts a serving spoon here and there before deciding it is as good as she can make it. Meanwhile, Tia and Leisha escort guests to the white folding chairs under the rented white tent. The girls wear matching dresses, and their hair is in matching beaded braids that Old Sally fixed for them yesterday, like she fixed Violet's hair when Violet was their age. They were each allowed to invite one friend to the wedding, and wear makeup, which they are usually not allowed to wear. They appear more grown-up than usual. They are beautiful young women.

"Is Queenie ready?" Rose asks Violet in the kitchen.

"She's in her room sitting in front of three oscillating fans to keep from sweating," Violet says. They exchange a smile.

"Should we take her a glass of wine or something?" Rose asks.

"She's fine, just a little nervous."

"It's amazing how much time and energy goes into a twenty-minute ceremony," Rose says.

Violet agrees and pulls a baking sheet of peach turnovers that she had almost forgotten out of the oven.

Rose asks what she can do to help.

"Maybe put these on a serving plate once they're cool?"

Rose nods.

Violet and Rose have agreed that they will be so relieved when Queenie's wedding is over. It has been the topic of conversation between them for weeks—that and the birth of Katie's baby.

Fortunately, the day is sunny, with no hurricanes in sight. The weather people have been wrong plenty of times. Countless storms have been predicted to hit the Georgia/South Carolina coast that never did, and this one is merely a projection, too —so far.

Jack calls Violet from the front door. She doesn't like the tone of his voice. Not upset, but concerned.

Violet meets him on the porch, where he lowers his voice to a whisper. "Have you seen Spud?"

"No," she whispers back. "Where is he?"

"I'm not sure," he says.

"When did you last see him?" Violet lowers her voice another notch.

"I was getting the parking area set up, and he left in his car. Mumbled that he had forgotten something and took off in a flash."

Reflexively, Violet rubs her shoulder, though it doesn't seem to be speaking to her right now.

"He was awfully nervous when I saw him in the kitchen this morning," Jack says. "He isn't the type to leave Queenie at the altar, is he?"

"No," Violet says. "He values his life more than that."

Jack chuckles.

Violet and Spud have been friends for years. It isn't like him to abandon someone, especially at the altar.

"Spud loves Queenie," Violet says. "He would never hurt her like that."

"I didn't think so, either."

"Well, maybe he forgot the rings or something," Violet says.

Jack pulls two silver bands from his suit pocket. "He gave them to me this morning, so he wouldn't lose them."

They exchange concerned looks.

"Is his family here yet?" Violet asks.

"Both his sister and brother are sitting in the first row, groom's side," Jack says. "But Spud left before they even got here."

Violet glances at her watch, thinking how out of character this is. It's time for the ceremony to begin. If Spud doesn't get back soon, the aftermath of Queenie being stood up at the altar may be more devastating than anything they can imagine.

"I'd better tell Rose, just in case," Violet says.

"She's at the tent already, greeting guests," Jack says.

Violet takes off her apron and hangs it over the back of a rocking chair. She finds Rose greeting people at the entrance of the tent. Rose has done a beautiful job creating a simple, elegant beach-themed wedding. White tent, white chairs, white flowers tied to the end of every row. Large potted plants of peace lilies in full bloom on each side of the altar. All very elegant.

Rose talks to a woman wearing a canary-yellow hat who must be Spud's sister. She looks like Spud but with more hair and minus the bow tie. When Rose is free again, Violet steps in and steers them to a section behind the chairs, where they can have more privacy.

"Could you tell that was Spud's sister?" Rose asks with a wink.

"Spud's missing," Violet whispers.

"What?" Rose says, full-voiced.

People turn to look. Rose smiles and waves to convey that all is well.

"Where is he?" Rose asks, her tone matching Violet's whisper.

"Jack saw him leave in his car. He said he forgot something."

"What in heaven's name did he forget?"

Violet shrugs, but not without concern.

"This is not good," Rose says, looking at her watch again.

"It may be nothing," Violet says, looking at her watch, too. They have been checking the time all morning, rushing to get everything handled. Now they may not even have a groom.

"Does Queenie know?" Rose asks.

"It's way too quiet in the house for Queenie to know," Violet says. "There would be screaming and wailing."

"You want to tell her?" Rose asks.

Violet's eyes widen.

"I didn't think so," Rose says.

"Let's give him ten minutes to show up," Violet says. "We have to trust that he'll be back. We have to." She pauses, wondering what the best strategy might be in this situation. "I guess I'll go up and try to prepare Queenie for it, just in case," she says.

"Good luck with that," Rose says.

A minute later, Violet approaches Queenie's bedroom and realizes she has no idea how to tell her mother that her fiancé is missing. When she knocks on the door, Queenie yells for her to come in over the hum of the electric fans. Violet steadies herself and garners her courage before stepping inside.

When Violet enters, Queenie is holding two magazines, one in each hand. She uses them to fan her face, while Oprah's image flutters on the covers, a chaotic photo montage.

"Vi, I've got flop sweat. It's a hundred degrees in here, and I can't stop sweating!"

To Violet, the room is chilly with all the oscillating going on, and the unsynchronized movement makes her feel dizzy. Where did Queenie find all these fans anyway? Maybe Spud is in line at Walmart this very minute buying Queenie a few more, chatting it up with the cashier about the pros and cons of orthopedic socks.

"Please tell Spud I need him," Queenie says. "And tell him to bring clean beach towels. I need to mop up some of this perspiration."

Should she tell Queenie that Spud has vacated the premises? Or that he was called away for a family emergency, even though his only remaining family is sitting in the front row of the wedding tent? She has never been good at lying. But she also has things left to do before she dies.

"What in heaven's name is wrong with you?" Queenie asks. "Don't you see I'm melting here? I'm like the Wicked Witch of the West. Get Spud!"

"I need to tell you something," Violet says finally, her voice reaching for the calmness Queenie lacks.

Queenie stops fanning herself and tosses the magazines on the bed. She approaches Violet in a whoosh of white that feels slightly intimidating. The fans oscillate toward her to observe what will happen next.

"What do you need to tell me?" Queenie asks.

It is the soft volume of Queenie's voice that alarms Violet the most. It can only get louder from here.

"Well—" Violet pauses and holds her right shoulder, even though she has no pain despite the possibility of another Chernobyl. "We can't find Spud." Anticipating an explosion, she cowers. But instead, Queenie rolls her eyes.

"You scared me there for a minute. I thought something horrible had happened. Spud is around here somewhere."

"He left in his car," Violet says.

Queenie hesitates. "Why would he leave in his car?"

"He told Jack he forgot something."

"Well, maybe he did."

"He's not back yet," Violet says.

Queenie looks at the clock and then crosses the room to look out the window. Squinting, she scans the crowd as if looking for a purple beacon of hope.

"He'll be here," Queenie says, but her certainty seems to have taken a hit. "Help me put myself together again, Vi. By the time I get downstairs, I bet Spud will be here. At least he'd better be," she concludes.

While the electric fans toss intermittent waves of coolness in their direction, Violet helps Queenie dry her face and freshen her makeup. Then she straightens Queenie's yellow scarf and red hat. A dash of color, indeed.

They leave Queenie's bedroom for the bride to take her place and begin her procession, no groom in sight.

CHAPTER NINE

Queenie

Q ueenie walks down the stairs and finds Old Sally standing at the front door, waiting to walk her daughter down the aisle. A small bouquet of white roses is tied around Old Sally's slender left wrist.

At the door, Rose hands Queenie the wedding bouquet Violet made for her—white roses mixed in with seashells. Though Spud is nowhere in sight, the three of them act like nothing is wrong.

"That man had better show up at the altar in the next two minutes," Queenie says to Violet, who gives Queenie's stubborn wedding train a final straightening.

Clearly, if Spud doesn't show up, Queenie's heart will be broken. *Perhaps along with his neck,* Queenie thinks.

"He'll be here," Violet says, a dash of hopefulness in her voice.

In the distance, the white tent is filled with seventy-five family members and friends. All of them waiting and shifting in their seats. The young priest looks in Queenie's direction as though wondering what he should do without a groom standing beside him. For sixty years Queenie has imagined being a bride and walking down the aisle. If Spud leaves her stranded at the altar, at least she will have this moment in the spotlight. Or in this case, the sun.

Queenie motions for the priest to start. He pauses, giving her a look that says, *Are you sure?* She repeats her *let's get this show on the road* hand motion. The young priest gives a brief shrug before asking everyone to stand. Family and guests turn in her direction, and Violet kisses Queenie on the cheek. Queenie takes a deep breath and holds Old Sally's arm. Then the two of them walk down the porch steps to where a sheath of white paper leads the way down the walkway through the dunes to the beach.

Queenie decided that there would be no music at the wedding. The sound of the waves would serenade her down the aisle. But that was a mistake. She wants to hear "Here Comes the Bride" or the "Alleluia" chorus. Something to mark such a momentous occasion. In an instant, the wedding she dreamed of is ruined, with no music and no groom.

Old Sally squeezes Queenie's arm as if sensing her growing upset. They begin their slow procession. "It be all right, child," she says. "Enjoy this. It's your day."

Queenie wonders if she is about to be stood up at the altar by the one person in the world she thought incapable of bailing on her. An undertow of grief threatens to pull her beneath the waves.

Suddenly she hears the notes of a familiar melody.

A splash of purple rises from the dunes as Spud emerges, playing his saxophone. It is a jazz rendition of "Here Comes the Bride." The beauty of his playing brings joyful tears to Queenie's eyes. She has cried more today than she has in ages.

Queenie wipes her tears with the yellow scarf tied around her neck, beaming a smile toward the dunes. Spud nods his saxophone in her direction. The melody soars.

As she approaches the tent, all the guests smile at Queenie as if she is the most beautiful bride in the world. Most have tears in their eyes, too. Queenie has never heard Spud play better. After Iris broke off their relationship, he didn't play saxophone for decades and disbanded his jazz quartet. It was only after Iris died that he started playing again.

Iris.

Queenie looks at the sky, expecting angry clouds to greet her, but the day remains clear. A perfect day for a wedding. The hurricane named after her nemesis has stayed away. Her groom has returned. There is music. Queenie's day will not be ruined.

Queenie and Old Sally join the sandaled priest down front, who looks like he might pull out a guitar and sing "Kumbaya" at any moment. Thankfully, Queenie prefers jazz. Spud ends his solo. A rush of purple approaches, and he hands his saxophone to his brother in the front row, who looks like a plump version of Spud with a blond toupée. The young priest who buried Iris invites Old Sally to join him at the front.

Spud and Queenie stand side by side, and Queenie steals a look at her intended. Not only does he play a wicked saxophone, but she loves him with her whole heart.

More tears fill Queenie's eyes, making her grateful for waterproof mascara. Tears that signal a new chapter in her life. A life that a few years ago she could have never imagined would include this much happiness. Or this much purple.

CHAPTER TEN

Old Sally

An image emerges from the past. It is what Old Sally does these days. Remember things. She patches together memories to create a picture of her life. At ten years of age, Queenie wore one of Old Sally's white slips on her head like a wedding veil and walked with great pomp and circumstance down the hallway to the kitchen. Like many little girls, she dreamed of this day. Fifty years later it is finally happening.

Celebrations are as necessary as the air she breathes. Katie stands near the front of the gathering practically busting with another celebration to come.

Death can be a celebration, too, Old Sally thinks. A celebration of a life lived fully.

Old Sally stands at the front facing Queenie, Spud, and the gathering of guests. Goosebumps climb her arms. A signal that a spirit is near. She senses her grandmother in attendance. A woman who passed to the other side many years ago. A strong woman in a long line of strong women stretching into the present day.

A chuckle rises from somewhere deep inside her. Old Sally should have known her grandmother would attend. For years she taught Old Sally the Gullah secrets as Old Sally is now teaching Violet.

To begin the ceremony, Old Sally welcomes everyone and then asks them to stand. Violet joins her at the front and begins to sing an old Gullah spiritual. The song is about how the Gullah people rode the water to this place and how the water will take them home. It is the tempo of a slow walk along the beach. A walk through all the ages that their people have lived here.

Guests sway to Violet's singing, including the young priest from the all-white Catholic church in Savannah. For a time, it resembles a revival meeting instead of a wedding. Old Sally remembers her first love and imagines him playing his fiddle in the dunes, as Spud played his saxophone. For several moments her vision blurs with tears.

In between the verses, Violet leads them on the refrains.

This is how it should be, Old Sally tells herself. *It's Violet's time to lead.*

Old Sally looks beyond the guests to her grandmother watching from the edge of the dunes, nodding and clapping with the passing of the mantle. Old Sally has done her part to not let the traditions die out. So many of their young people have moved away from the island—distracted and enticed by modern times. However, some will return, and some will stay.

Old Sally is reminded of the gathering outside the Temple mansion as the fire raged on. Violet's voice uplifted them in the darkest times. It can bring people closer together in the best of times, too.

In her imagination, Old Sally is transported to another time. A time far away when her ancestors first arrived on this island and named it after the dolphins frequently seen along the coast. She imagines other weddings taking place on this beach, weddings in the past and in the future. When Violet stops singing the guests are silent. Only the waves are heard. Waves from thirty feet away. Waves that sing the ebb and flow of life.

"You must remember the live oaks that grace this coastline," Old Sally begins, her voice clear. "Their roots join under the earth. Now Queenie and Spud be joined, too. The roots of their families now merge. Each of us merges with all Creation. The Creator blesses Queenie and Spud's union because of the genuine love here. This is all you can hope for in this life. To be blessed by love."

Old Sally looks at her grandmother, and for a moment sees a faint reflection of herself standing next to her.

The ceremony continues, and Old Sally steps aside for the priest to say the traditional vows to make Queenie and Spud's marriage official in the eyes of the law.

Queenie and Spud say, "I do," and kiss.

Gullah has mixed with Christianity over the years, adding another layer to the story of Old Sally's people. Most of those who stayed on the island now go to the island church that worships both Jesus and the tides. These are people who believe in the earth's seasons and in the resurrection. Water is central to both faiths.

Finally, the priest takes a step back and leaves Old Sally in front to say the final words.

"Ritual be what unites us all," she begins. "Ritual anchors us to this place and time. With love in place, there be no room for hatred. Love will save us."

Queenie and Spud stand holding hands with their heads bowed, as do all their family and friends, including Old Sally's grandmother in the dunes.

"May we be a lighthouse for each other through every storm," she says, realizing this is not something she had planned to say. Then she looks at Queenie and Spud and adds: "May you spread your joy to all who meet you. May you stay safe from harm and honor your ancestors. May you love each other for the rest of your days."

Violet says, "Amen," and the guests respond with the same. With Violet leading, they call and respond several times, tossing "Amen" across the tent among all those gathered. Laughter and clapping end the ceremony.

CHAPTER ELEVEN

Rose

Never has Rose seen a more colorful bride and groom. Queenie with her white wedding dress, red hat, yellow scarf, and purple pumps. Spud with his purple suit, white shirt, and purple-and-green bow tie. Nor has she ever seen a happier couple.

The wedding reception is at the house and in full swing. Violet is busy refilling different serving dishes.

"Let me do that," Rose says. "You don't work for the Temples anymore."

Rose seldom thinks of herself as a Temple, though she kept the name after she married, as her mother did. Maybe she is more of a Temple than she thinks.

"Don't be silly," Violet says. "I'm good at this."

Violet seems more confident since she started her tea shop a few months ago. Is this what happens when someone finds their true calling? If so, Rose needs to start painting again. Every day that she doesn't, she disappoints herself. But now that Queenie's wedding is over, she plans to get out her easel and paints and set up in the small light-filled studio at the back of their cottage.

The last time Rose mingled was after her mother's funeral, when Savannah's upper crust was paying their last respects and reshuffling the old Savannah power structure.

Rose raises a glass of tonic water with lime, minus the vodka, for an imaginary toast.

Rest in peace, Mother.

Across the room, Old Sally is showing signs of weariness. The priest is unusually talkative, so Rose crosses the room to rescue her. If Old Sally is one of the hundred-year-old live oak trees on the island, the young priest is a sapling.

"Excuse me, Father, can I borrow Old Sally for a moment?" Rose asks.

He offers a brief Kumbaya smile and then pivots to the next listener.

Old Sally holds onto Rose's arm like she is clinging to a life raft. "He kept asking me how all of us could possibly live in this house together without being at each other's throats. You would think a priest would believe in harmony."

Rose agrees. They walk down the hallway toward Old Sally's room, the noise fading as they get farther away from the party. Her bedroom is simple. A bed. A chair. One dresser. Perfectly neat. A knot of "five finger" grass hangs on the bedpost, meant for restful sleep. A large window faces the ocean, with a windowsill filled with seashells Old Sally collects on her walks. One corner holds a piece of driftwood that was the base of an old tree. While Queenie's room is full of color, Old Sally's is the color of the beach. Almost no separation exists between her bedroom and the sand and dunes.

Rose helps Old Sally take off her sandals and lift her legs onto the bed. She lies back onto her pillow and lets out a long sigh.

"I was saving all my energy for the wedding," Old Sally says. "Now I be like a balloon that's lost all its air."

"You rest for a while, and you'll feel much better," Rose says. She gently massages Old Sally's hands as Old Sally did for her when she was getting her ready for bed as a girl. She traces Old Sally's lifeline and the veins on the backs of her hands. Then Rose moves to the end of the bed and massages Old Sally's feet, something she has taken up doing since she has lived here. Old Sally thanks her, her eyes closed. The tops of her feet are the color of leather, the bottoms the color of sand. Cool, wrinkled, and sandpapery dry. Feet that have been walking the earth for over a hundred years. Millions of steps. Walking. Running. Dancing. And at one time, skipping and jumping.

No wonder she's tired, Rose thinks, grateful that she can give back to this woman who gave her so much.

With every second that passes, Rose is more aware that a stranger is coming to the island. A stranger who claims to be Edward's daughter, her brother being the one person in her family she wishes she could forget ever existed.

"Edward's child be almost here," Old Sally says, not opening her eyes.

This is the second time today that Rose has thought Old Sally was reading her thoughts. Is Rose that transparent?

"How did you know that Edward's daughter was coming today?"

"I forget," Old Sally says.

"Should I be concerned about her?" Rose asks.

"Too soon to know for sure."

Rose covers Old Sally with a light blanket from the end of the bed and watches her fall asleep.

When she returns to the living room, Max is greeting a stranger at the door. Upon seeing Heather for the first time, Rose emits a slight gasp. Heather looks like a younger version of Rose's mother. The same upturned nose. The same hair color, though Heather's is long. The same ramrod-straight posture and overture of entitlement. She is dressed like the Junior League version of a

Jehovah's Witness. Heather's blue eyes narrow when Rose approaches the door. No DNA evidence is needed. The resemblance is immediate. Heather is not only her brother's child but her mother's grandchild.

They introduce themselves. Heather's gaze burrows into Rose, before looking around as if to assess the value of the house.

"I didn't mean to interrupt anything," Heather says, though she doesn't seem to mind. "I guess that's what I get for not calling first. I got your address from Regina."

"Yes, Regina called me."

"She did?" Heather's look of surprise appears rehearsed, or maybe Rose imagines it.

"I don't know Regina very well," Rose begins. "I met her once for a short time last year, and we've talked briefly on the phone. She called me this morning to say you were on your way."

Heather nods like someone who has practiced a speech for hours and now must skip several note cards ahead to find a new place to start. A crack in the façade?

"I didn't know you were having a party," Heather says, which feels genuine.

"It's actually a wedding," Rose answers. She starts to say that it is Queenie and Spud's wedding, but she isn't sure she wants to share that much with someone she has only known for half a minute. Someone who also bears an uncanny resemblance to her mother.

Is this a joke? Rose wonders. *Why didn't Regina warn her?* Then she remembers that Regina probably never met her mother.

Rose also questions the timing of Heather's arrival. They are in the middle of a celebration, with a storm barreling toward them, and a long-lost relative has washed up on the beach via Atlanta.

"My father was your brother," Heather says, as if this is a news flash.

"I can see the resemblance," Rose says, thinking it is not only her brother she resembles.

"You can?" Heather's small eyes widen, and Rose notices for the first time her smile. A smile, she imagines, that required several years of orthodontia to achieve. At least the smile is a departure from her mother, who rarely partook in something so frivolous unless she wanted to impress someone.

"You have Edward's bone structure, hairline, even his hair color—at least when he was younger." Rose feels generous saying this much.

Heather's cheeks redden. "Regina didn't seem too convinced."

Regina probably wouldn't admit it, even with DNA proof of paternity, Rose thinks.

She wonders what Heather hopes to gain from their meeting, and then asks herself when she became so cynical. It isn't like her to think the worst of people.

Max gives Rose a look that asks, *Can I go now?* She nods, and he rejoins the party.

For an awkward moment, Rose and Heather stand at the front door, neither speaking. If first impressions are to be trusted, Rose's first inclination is to lock up the silverware. Her second, to return to Wyoming, where she lived for twenty-five years to get away from her mother.

"How can I help you, Heather?" Rose's politeness sounds insincere, even to her. She wants this young woman out of her house.

"I'd like to ask you some questions," she says.

Rose challenges herself to give the young woman a chance. She directs Heather to the rocking chairs on the south end of the porch, where they can have some privacy. Two guests from the wedding are on the other end, but far enough away that they won't be able to hear.

"My mother died six months ago," Heather says. "I didn't know who my father was until I found my birth certificate in her papers."

"I'm so sorry for your loss," Rose says, wondering why

Heather's mother didn't share this information with Heather sooner. Did Edward threaten the woman? Pay her off?

Rose reminds herself to listen, instead of appointing herself judge and jury. She notices how perfectly Heather is dressed. Her sleeveless dress reveals an attractive figure. Tanned legs. Nice sandals. Toenails painted a dusty rose color that matches her purse, as well as her lipstick. Rose half expects her to be wearing pearls.

"Your father and I were never close," Rose says, which is the truth.

"You weren't?" Heather looks almost irritated, like she has come all this way for nothing.

"No, I'm sorry to say we weren't."

Rose's absence of warmth isn't like her. Is this self-protection? They pause again, their awkwardness cresting like the nearby waves.

Until now, Rose has never been an aunt. This will give Katie a cousin, too. A hereditary windfall in some ways. But something isn't sitting quite right. Rose blames it on wedding fatigue and tells herself to be nicer.

"What was my father like as a boy?" Heather appears to renew her excitement, and smiles as if imagining something that involves frolicking.

Rose pauses. How does she tell Heather that her father was a first-class bully? A near-perfect copy of their mother until he betrayed her at the end by releasing the Temple secrets.

"He was older than me," Rose says instead. "He had a totally different set of friends than I did. We rarely played together." Her pinkie finger vibrates where Edward cut it off with one of the Temple Confederate swords when she was five. Is that the kind of story Heather wants? Or does she want to hear how he would shove Rose against walls as he passed or try to trip her on the staircase or trap her in her bedroom?

"Do you know about the fire that took his life?" Rose asks.

"Yes. My mother had a copy of the newspaper article in her things."

Heather straightens her hair, blown by the ocean breeze. Rose can't remember a single time her mother came to the beach, even with it being this close to Savannah. Meanwhile, Heather shows no remorse for Edward's death. No apparent longing for what might have been. Or perhaps she is good at hiding it. Rose was good at hiding her emotion at her mother's deathbed, too. It was the first time she had been back to Savannah since she married Max.

Is Heather here to merely meet her long-lost aunt? Or is she here with a purpose in mind that she isn't talking about? If she is, Rose is intent on finding out what it is.

CHAPTER TWELVE

Violet

The reception is a hit. The crab cakes and shrimp cocktail are well received, and Violet's cocktail sauce—as always—has guests asking for the recipe. When she was in Miss Temple's employ, receptions were frequent. Mounds of seafood, finger foods, and fresh fruits were standard. Depending on Miss Temple's mood, sometimes even a chocolate fountain was prepared, along with strawberries for dipping. At Violet's new tea house, she bakes. Muffins and pastries. Banana and pumpkin bread. Pies and cakes. She must admit she has enjoyed putting together something that doesn't involve quite as much sugar and white flour.

With all the serving bowls and platters full again, Violet turns on the small television in her bedroom for the weather. Tia and Leisha and their friends stand in front of the mirror in her bathroom, putting on additional eye makeup. Tia will be sixteen soon, and Leisha will graduate from high school next week. In a little over two months, Leisha will be leaving for the College of Charleston, a school they never could have afforded a couple of years ago. Edward tried to prove in court that his mother had been out of her mind when she changed the will in Violet's favor, but it was not overturned. Somehow Edward was the loser in the will. Something that surprised Violet considering how loyal he was to Miss Temple. At least she always thought he was loyal, until she found out that Edward was the person who was releasing all those secrets. Evidently, not everything and everyone is as they seem.

On the news, a weather map shows a tight twist of clouds in the Caribbean. The hurricane has made landfall in St. Croix as a Category 3 storm. Violet still can't believe the coincidence of a hurricane named *Iris* forming on the day of Queenie's wedding. It sounds like something Miss Temple might have arranged just for spite. Do spirits have that much power? If any might, it would be Miss Iris Temple.

"What are you watching?" Tia flutters her eyelashes, thick with mascara, in Violet's direction.

"Just the weather," Violet says, seeing no need to excite them any more than they already are. Like Spud noted, Savannah has a history of predicted hurricanes that hit somewhere else. This storm is still far away. She imagines it will fizzle out after making landfall, which they often do.

Honestly, what worries Violet more than a hurricane is the notion of Tia and Leisha leaving home. She's not sure how to deal with an empty nest. Although even without them, their communal nest will be far from empty.

When Violet returns to the kitchen, the party is full of life. Happy to be on the fringes, she loads the dishwasher and then washes a few things by hand. If anyone else knows about the storm, they don't seem that concerned.

Meanwhile, Queenie and Spud dance to Lionel Richie in the living room. Queenie waves for Violet to join them, but Violet

smiles and waves her suggestion away. Even with all the preparations, there is still plenty to do.

Rose enters the kitchen followed by a young woman. Violet
stops washing dishes and her eyes widen. She shivers like the
warm day has suddenly turned cold. Heather could be Miss
Temple's ghost, if she had died when she was twenty instead of
eighty.

Rose lifts an eyebrow as if to say, *You see it, too?*

Her gesture reminds Violet of when she and Queenie used
signals during the long meals with Miss Temple at the Temple
mansion. Meals where silence was required of them.

"Heather found out recently that Edward was her father," Rose
says. "She's come here to meet us."

Heather is taller than Violet and looks slightly down on her. A
position that feels all too familiar. She decides not to bring up the
fact that she is Heather's half aunt. That would require too much
explanation on a day when she is so tired. Besides, she can barely
keep all the family connections straight as it is.

"You have a beautiful home," Heather says to Violet.

She wonders if Heather thinks that she and Rose are a couple.
Their living situation has perplexed many people, especially those
who could never imagine living with a collection of souls who are
in some ways related by blood, and in other ways not related
at all.

"I'd better check the food," Violet says, telling Heather that it
was nice to meet her, though she isn't so sure it was.

Compared to Tia and Leisha, who aren't that much younger,
Heather seems sophisticated, worldly. Violet isn't entirely
convinced it isn't all just an act. She has known families where
genetic traits appear to skip a generation, but this is almost creepy.
Violet recalls dusting early photographs in solid gold frames in
Miss Temple's bedroom that could be of Heather instead of Miss
Temple.

Violet stands at the sink overlooking the wooden walkway that connects the big house to Rose and Max's cottage. The sky is a deep blue with no clouds in sight, but according to the weather reports that could change as the storm progresses.

Katie walks into the kitchen with Angela not far behind. Katie's Lamaze classes usually meet here on Saturday afternoons. Right about now they usually have a living room full of pregnant women and their husbands or partners, pushing and blowing until Violet thinks she might give birth herself from all the encouragement. Because of the wedding, they won't be meeting today, which is probably a good thing. That crowd would have devoured all the food by now.

Angela steps up to dry the dishes Violet recently washed. "Have you heard about the storm?" she asks.

"I doubt there's anything to worry about," Violet says. "We never get hurricanes around here."

She bases her confidence on how her left shoulder would be aching by now if there was a danger. Although, her shoulder has never predicted weather-related incidents before. Probably because there haven't been any.

"We never get hurricanes where I'm from, either," Angela says.

Katie dips a cucumber slice into the avocado dip that Violet will soon return to the reception table. "I guess it's safe to say we're all novices in the hurricane department," she says, offering to help, too.

When all the dishes are dry and put away, Katie and Angela join the party in the living room. Tia and Leisha are now dancing with their friends, eyes brilliant with shadow, mascara, and thick eyeliner, and circles of wine-colored rouge on their dark cheeks.

The music stops and the bride and groom collapse, smiling, onto the sofa. The wedding, as far as Violet can tell, is a complete success. Thanks to Old Sally, the ceremony was lovely and meaningful. Afterward, she heard several people say that they felt part of something extraordinary. They were also complimentary about Violet's singing. Most importantly, Queenie was pleased.

It has only been two years since Violet found out that she is Queenie's daughter. Given how close they always were, it seems obvious now. But sometimes the obvious isn't noticeable at all. Sometimes the truth is hidden right in front of you. She wonders what other secrets have been kept from her, and what secrets are in this room right now. Besides possibly Heather.

Meanwhile, Old Sally is nowhere in sight, and Rose and Heather have moved to the back patio. What could they possibly be talking about that has Rose looking so somber? Somber like she was as a girl whenever she was around Miss Temple, who corrected her almost nonstop. Violet would have asked Heather to leave by now simply because of the creepiness factor, but Rose has always had trouble telling people no. Especially people who look like Rose's mother.

Violet should have known that the Temples weren't the type to rest in peace. Even though Edward's ghost isn't hanging around the rafters, now his daughter has shown up.

Let's hope it's not to make trouble, Violet thinks.

Violet is too tired to deal with trouble. Too tired to deal with anything other than letting her thoughts wander.

If Edward hadn't accidentally started the fire that burned down the mansion, they would be living in that grand old house in Savannah. Yet, despite the tragedy, everything seems to have worked out for the best. Violet is honored to be learning the Gullah secrets and her family's history. Honored to be entrusted with what Old Sally knows. Their Gullah ancestors have been here for almost two centuries. They brought with them a rich ancestry from Africa and built a culture here. A culture based on ancient medicines, rituals, and folk magic. Preserving that history is essential. What they don't know, however, is where their Gullah story will go from here.

CHAPTER THIRTEEN

Queenie

With all the guests finally gone from the reception, Queenie and Spud sit on the couch, their arms entwined. Queenie wants to bottle this happiness and drink from it the rest of her life.

"Hello, Mrs. Grainger," Spud says, his voice soft and affectionate.

"Hello, Mister Grainger," she responds, marveling at how skinny his arm is compared to hers.

What she doesn't tell Spud is that she wants to keep her old name, but she doesn't want to hurt his feelings. It is the twenty-first century, after all. If Oprah ever marries Stedman, Queenie doubts she'll change her name, either. It occurs to her that maybe she could ask Spud to change his name to Spudman, but then thinks better of it.

Marrying Spud has taught her something about change. Mainly that you never know what will be good for you until you try. Before falling in love with Spud, Queenie rolled her eyes at interracial couples. She is sorry about that now.

People can change their minds, thank goodness, otherwise the world wouldn't evolve at all, she thinks, her lightheartedness taking a turn. *Heaven knows we need the world to change.*

Last fall, on September 11, the world changed the instant the first plane hit the towers. Now all these white people think that dark-skinned foreigners are the enemy.

Well, aren't we all foreigners? she asks herself. *Didn't every single one of us come from somewhere else?*

"What are you thinking about, lemon drop? You suddenly went away."

"Those towers," she says with a sigh.

Spud looks puzzled and perhaps surprised she would be thinking of 9/11 on their wedding day, but then he lowers his eyes. After those towers came down, he stayed quiet for days. Queenie likes that he is sensitive. Musicians are often like that, at least the best ones are. But for the life of her, she can't figure out how he was ever a butcher. He will capture a mouse and relocate it instead of killing it.

People are a mystery, Queenie thinks.

Spud squeezes her hand and smiles at her. "Let's not ruin our wedding day worrying about the state of the world," he says.

Queenie agrees, though he's done plenty of worrying as far as she can tell. She shifts her thoughts and looks at him lovingly.

To her unending surprise, Spud Grainger is every bit as sexy to her as her longtime heartthrob, Denzel Washington. Turns out it doesn't matter what a person looks like as long as your two hearts match up.

Queenie gives Spud a full-out kiss right there on the couch. Her shoes drop to the floor and her toes tingle. When Spud played "Here Comes the Bride" on his saxophone she thought she might keel over in the dunes from the surge of love that came through her like a lightning bolt.

A young woman comes in the back door with Rose. A stranger. But someone who looks somehow familiar.

"Who's that?" Queenie asks Spud, motioning toward the kitchen.

"That's Rose's brother's daughter I told you about. Heather."

Queenie's eyes narrow in instant distrust. Mean people should not be allowed to reproduce. Especially someone like Edward Temple.

Queenie pulls her glasses from her cleavage and puts them on. When Heather comes into focus, Queenie covers her mouth and lets out a scream. Mostly it is covered up by the music playing, but a few people turn.

"What is it?" Spud straightens his bow tie with a flash of alarm.

"Edward's daughter is the spitting image of Iris before she got old!" Queenie says.

Spud squints in the direction of the kitchen. If he notices the resemblance, he doesn't let on, which—come to think of it—is a brilliant move. He gives Queenie's love handles a squeeze as if to remind her that they are here to celebrate. But Queenie is not ready to let this go. Violet joins them in the living room and Queenie motions toward the kitchen.

Violet nods, confirming Queenie is not imagining things.

The lights flicker, and Queenie jumps. "You don't think that's Iris, do you?"

Spud laughs and shakes his head like this is the last thing he wants, too.

Even though the spirits of the Temple mansion were silenced in the fire, she wouldn't put it past Iris to figure out a way to haunt her on her wedding day. In fact, it seems the entire Temple clan is conspiring against her. What with Edward's daughter showing up out of the blue, and the news this morning that a hurricane named Iris is hovering somewhere out in the Atlantic. Odd coincidences, at best. Every now and again, Queenie finds herself missing her half sister, which is even more bizarre.

"I've been thinking about the past today," Spud says.

Queenie is so distracted, she forgot Spud was even there. She turns to give him her full attention. Is he going to tell her that his love for Iris goes beyond the grave?

"What is it?" she asks, telling herself not to panic.

"I need to tell you something." Spud looks more solemn than Queenie likes.

"Uh, oh." Queenie holds her breath.

"No, no. It's nothing bad."

She exhales. "You want me to have your love child?" Queenie asks. They laugh, and she thinks about Katie, ready to burst with new life. When Queenie was pregnant with Violet, she did her best to hide it. Mister Oscar told Queenie that if she ever told anyone that Violet was his child, he would have to fire Old Sally and make life difficult for Queenie and Violet. Mister Oscar was weak compared to Iris and could be kind, but he was still surprisingly good at delivering a threat.

"You sure it's nothing bad?" she asks.

"Positive."

"Promise?"

"Promise. Now can I tell you what I wanted to say?"

Queenie pauses while Spud clears his throat.

"I've been thinking about Iris today—"

Queenie puts a hand over her heart to keep it from breaking.

"Let me finish, please," Spud says, his look stern, yet loving.

The lump in her throat tightens with the fear that an annulment is looming.

"When I was with Iris, I was so young I didn't even know what love was," Spud begins again. "It was infatuation if anything, but what you and I have, Queenie, is love. Real grown-up love."

Her eyes mist and she kisses Spud. A passionate kiss meant to curl his bow tie, not caring if anyone sees it.

All those years she was single, she has missed kissing the most, and wants to make up for all that time lost. In an hour, she and Spud are scheduled to leave for their week-long honeymoon in Hilton Head.

A hot flash fans the flames of Queenie's love, followed by a sudden chill that cools her sweat. She breathes in sharply. The last time a chill climbed her spine was before the Temple mansion was destroyed and all those ghosts got displaced. Now she seems to see Iris everywhere she looks. Has her half sister found a new way to haunt her?

CHAPTER FOURTEEN

Old Sally

Waking from her nap, Old Sally remembers why she felt so tired before. A heaviness set in after the wedding. She senses that dark forces are coming together. For the last three nights, she has slept fitfully. Her tea leaves this morning spelled disruption, too.

People wonder how she can read the future from a few leaves left in the bottom of a cup. But the otherworld talks to her whenever she lets it, using anything that is around as a messenger. Sometimes a tree leans in the direction she is to go. Sometimes the mood of the ocean tells the story. Sometimes a whisper hides in the breeze, telling her everything she needs to know.

Old Sally returns to the empty living room. What is left of the party has moved outside. From the front window, she sees Jack and Violet walk arm in arm down the beach, with Tia and Leisha and their friends behind them. Violet stops on the beach and looks back at the house.

Do you need me? she asks, sending her thoughts in Old Sally's direction.

No, Old Sally responds. *But thank you.*

Are you sure? Violet asks.

I'm sure, Old Sally answers.

Old Sally and Violet have begun to converse this way only recently. It is how she knows her time is growing short, and that the opening between this world and the next is growing wider. Old Sally sees this as a blessing. Her spirit is ready to be released.

Rose sits on the front porch with a young white woman. Old Sally narrows her eyes before widening them again. She shouldn't have been napping. A fox has entered the hen house while she wasn't looking.

She goes outside and greets Rose and the stranger on the porch. Some people are like storms and create chaos wherever they go. A trickster, the Gullah people would call her. Someone who turns things upside down and often deceives. Caution is required. Old Sally asks her ancestors for Rose's protection.

"Did you have a nice nap?" Rose asks.

Old Sally nods, not taking her eyes away from Heather.

Rose introduces them.

"I know who you are," Old Sally says. "I be praying for you for a long time."

"You've what?" Heather turns to Rose as if to confirm that the old woman is demented.

"Old Sally is the matriarch of this house," Rose says. "None of us would be here without her."

"Nice to meet you," Heather says, not offering her hand.

In her imagination, Old Sally sees Iris Temple as a little girl hiding under her bed waiting to see how long it would take for her mother or father to find her. Her parents never noticed she was gone. Nobody even came looking except for Old Sally. That little girl became someone who insisted on attention of every kind. This young woman feels the same. Confirmation lies in how much she looks like Iris. The ancestors are offering another attempt for the Temple family to heal and choose something different.

"Can I talk to you?" Old Sally says to Rose. "In private."

Rose follows her into the house and closes the door.

"Something about her makes me tired," Rose says.

"You must be very careful," Old Sally says. "She drains your energy to use for herself. She doesn't do it on purpose, but the Temple wound be so deep you must be careful not to get pulled in."

"The Temple wound?" Rose asks.

"Edward abandoned this girl. Never acknowledged her existence. So, as a Temple, she be looking for you to do that. You're the only one left."

"Can you believe how much she looks like Mother?" Rose asks.

"Traits often skip a generation to remind us there still be stuff to deal with."

"I feel horrible that I don't like her," Rose whispers.

"It be history weighing on you," Old Sally says.

Iris Temple was unrelenting in how she criticized Rose. All to mold her into what she considered to be a true Temple. Edward was treated this way, too. Standards impossible to live up to. Rules that weakened instead of strengthened the Temple family. It surprises Old Sally the burdens parents put on their children when their only job is to love and protect them. And notice them.

"Should I tell her to leave?" Rose asks.

"These old energies never move on unless you take time to acknowledge and understand them," Old Sally says. "You can either do it now or wait until it shows up again."

Rose gives an exasperated sigh. "I thought I'd dealt with this already."

Old Sally removes a small burlap sack the size of a deck of cards from the pocket of her dress. The bag contains a root that looks like a gnarled knuckle, a rough pearl the size of a marble, and a piece of indigo-blue fabric.

"Take this," Old Sally begins. "My grandmother gave this charm to me when I was a girl, and I've carried it every day of my life since. It will protect you from anything harmful."

Rose tries to refuse it, but Old Sally won't let her. "You must take it," Old Sally says, closing Rose's hand around it. "If I need it back, I'll ask for it."

Rose finally agrees, and Old Sally hugs her, telling her everything will be all right. Something still to be seen.

"Do you know where Katie is?" Old Sally asks. "We were supposed to meet after the reception."

"She may be napping," Rose says. "She does that a lot these days."

I do, too, Old Sally thinks.

Births and deaths take place at the same threshold. Old Sally's grandmother said that one is God's inhale and the other is God's exhale. Old Sally likes thinking of it this way. Each of us a part of the breath of our Creator.

Old Sally and Katie spend time together every day to get ready for the birth. If Rose is her *soul* daughter, then Katie is her *soul* granddaughter. Everyone is connected. Blood family and spirit family. Now she needs to make sure that everyone she loves stays safe for whatever is to come.

CHAPTER FIFTEEN

Rose

All afternoon, Rose's unexpected niece has hovered around her like a mosquito looking for a place to bite. With Old Sally off to find Katie and the small charm in her pocket, Rose now feels emboldened enough to tell Heather that their family reunion will have to wait until another time.

Earlier, Rose gave Heather a quick history of the Temple family —it would make Rose's mother proud to know how much Rose has remembered. However, Heather showed only a vague interest in what Rose told her. Had she already researched the Temple family? That would be easy to do these days with the world wide web.

Rose returns to the front porch to find Max and Heather sitting together. Max makes friends easily these days, having traded in his cowboy boots for flip-flops. Sometimes he says more in a day than he said in an entire week at the ranch. Rose doesn't know what brought on this transformation, but it has taken some getting used to.

"We were wondering what happened to you," Max says to Rose, patting an empty rocking chair beside him.

"Old Sally needed my help," Rose says, aware that it was actually Old Sally who helped Rose.

"Heather was asking how we could afford such a beautiful house," Max says. "I told her it was a matter of combining inheritances and—" He stops. The look on Rose's face tells him that he has already said too much.

How is it that the quiet cowboy I've been married to all these years now overshares?

For all Rose knows, Heather is here to collect whatever Temple money she feels entitled to.

"Max invited me to stay the night," Heather says to Rose. Her eyes sparkle like a child receiving precisely what she wanted for Christmas.

When Heather isn't looking, Rose tosses a wary glance at Max. The last thing she wants to do tonight is to have Heather reminding her of her mother and everything wrong with the Temple family.

"I'm sure you have family or pets to return to," Rose says to Heather.

"No, it's only me. No family. No pets."

"But you don't have any of your things with you," Rose says.

Heather smiles as though moving her knight into position to take Rose's queen.

"I packed up some things in the car before I left."

Rose's suspicion may be a direct result of being a Temple. Whenever people in Savannah find out who her family is, they often become intimidated, enamored, or sometimes greedy. Meanwhile, the tip of her little finger throbs and weighs in on her hesitation.

Max excuses himself to go to the kitchen. He knows he's in trouble and food will fortify him to face the fallout.

Heather excuses herself to get her things out of the car. Her profile reveals how much she looks like Rose's mother.

Rose shivers and removes the charm from her pocket.

"You were supposed to protect me," she says aloud with no one to hear.

With the wedding finally over, Rose had planned to put on her pajamas and curl up with a good book. A nice stress-free evening. Now it seems the mystery novel will have to wait, replaced by the mystery of why Heather is here and what old energy, as Old Sally would say, needs to be resolved.

She glances at the sky. It's been hours since she's heard a weather report. Is her mother's storm still out there somewhere? A double dose of trouble, counting Heather's unexpected visit?

Violet walks through the dunes to go to the house, leaving the rest of her family on the beach.

"What's going on?" Violet asks Rose.

"It turns out Heather will be spending the night," Rose says.

"You're kidding."

"I wish I were."

"How did—"

"Max invited her."

Violet mirrors how Rose feels. A stranger in the house means they won't get to fully relax.

"Dinner is fend-for-yourself," Violet says. "I'm too tired to come up with anything else."

Rose agrees. "Have you heard anything about the storm?" Rose refuses to call it Hurricane Iris. The irony is too perfect. Rose's entire childhood was spent avoiding her mother's larger-than-life nature. She thinks again of Heather, whom she hasn't yet figured out how to avoid.

"The hurricane is still in the Caribbean," Violet says, looking unconcerned.

But Rose wonders if her mother is staging a little karmic revenge.

"What did you find out about Heather?" Violet asks.

Rose glances to the left, where Heather's car is parked, to make sure she isn't coming. "I'm not sure why she's here," Rose says. "It appears she wants to know things about her father, but there's something else going on, too. Old Sally thinks she's here to resolve something from the past."

They exchange a look that reminds Rose of how long they've been friends.

"Why do I feel like Mother is messing with us again?" Rose asks.

"It's weird, but I've been feeling the same," Violet says.

"Do you think it's possible for history to bubble up?"

"I do." Violet looks out to sea.

As girls, Rose and Violet were good at putting puzzles together, and it feels like they are putting a puzzle together now. A giant one that includes strangers coming to visit, history bubbling up, and Gullah spells.

"Something about the whole situation feels troubling," Violet says.

Rose's shoulders tense. "Do you ever feel like you're the only one left in your generation to deal with things?"

"I do," Violet says. "I never dreamed I'd be the keeper of the Gullah secrets."

"Just like I'm the keeper of the Temple secrets," Rose says. "Except I don't even know where the Temple secrets are anymore."

"Maybe it's time to go find out what that key opens. And soon," Violet says.

Queenie and Spud emerge from the far deck and the mood shifts. Spud's bow tie is askew, and it appears he has a copper-colored rash on his face from Queenie's lipstick.

"I wondered where you two were." To Rose, mature love seems so much more hopeful than young love.

"I think I'm going to like being married," Spud says to them, causing Rose and Violet to laugh.

The newlyweds go inside. Seconds later, Heather rolls a large suitcase up the front walk, as if she might stay for a month instead of one night. Storm clouds gather in Rose's thoughts. Whatever happens next, she hopes the charm works.

CHAPTER SIXTEEN

Violet

Tiny brass bells jingle to announce another customer coming through the door. First-timers are easy to identify. Violet often catches a moment of delight in their eyes, as if surprised to find her small tea shop tucked away off a side street behind a tiny courtyard full of tea roses. The large front window has fancy purple-and-gold lettering that reads: VIOLET'S TEA SHOP.

Earlier this morning, Violet carried a heavy sandwich board out to the corner of the main street and set it up. A giant arrow below the name points down the alleyway—with the same purple-and-gold lettering—so that people won't miss it. Like most of the structures in downtown Savannah, the building is historic, meaning ivy covers the brick, the water pipes talk to you on occasion, and everything smells like the most ancient of mildew when it rains. But this seems a small price to pay for a sense of history.

When it comes to storms, however, downtown Savannah isn't an ideal location. Even a heavy thunderstorm can flood the street and courtyard. It is hard for Violet to imagine what might happen during a hurricane.

"Don't borrow trouble," Violet tells herself, which is something Old Sally reminds her often.

The next customer through the door makes Violet hesitate, a ghost from the past brushing by her. It is Heather. The Heather who spent the night at the house last night, much to Rose's dismay. Violet was so exhausted after the wedding she went to bed early and was out of the house this morning before anyone was up and about.

Heather glances at the African violets in the large front window. A jungle of purple blooms in clay pots are stacked on bricks at different heights. Bricks that at one time made up the exterior of the Temple mansion and that Violet gathered and carried in the trunk of her car for this purpose. Her only reminder that the estate belonged to her, if only for a short time. Seeing Heather makes Violet wonder if Miss Temple would approve.

Whether at a wedding reception, like yesterday, or a downtown tea shop, Edward's daughter seems somehow out of place. Violet wonders why she isn't at work somewhere or going to college classes. It is eerie how much she looks like Miss Temple.

Violet wonders if Heather will gravitate toward the small tables for two around the edges of the shop, where she'll have more privacy. Or if she will choose the openness of the main tea room, where bigger tables are set up so that people can gather and talk. Heather picks a seat on the fringes and puts her umbrella on a chair.

"Nice to see you again," Violet says when Heather approaches the counter.

"You, too," she says, though neither of them seems to mean it.

Why does Violet feel like she should be wearing her outdated maid's uniform? The one Miss Temple insisted she wear.

"Did you sleep well last night?" Violet asks, pushing the past from her mind.

"I did," Heather says. "Rose told me about your tea shop this morning, so I thought I'd visit."

Is that a dull pain pinging Violet's shoulder again or does she imagine it? She doubts Heather came here only to have a cup of tea. Her entire demeanor is of someone who wants something much more substantial than tea.

"What can I get for you?" Violet asks.

She often tries to guess what people will order. Are they the English breakfast type? Earl Grey? Herbal tea? She has difficulty pinning Heather down.

Heather eyes the pumpkin bread in the glass case.

Too many calories, Violet can almost hear her say.

"Coffee, black," Heather says.

"Of course," Violet says, remembering this is how Miss Temple drank her coffee, too. If she drank tea, she insisted that Violet use two tea bags to keep it from being weak.

If Queenie were here, she would quip something funny in response to Heather's request for black coffee. Something like, *Yes, I am black. Been this way since I was very young.*

But Violet has never had Queenie's sense of humor. If anything, Violet is much too serious. Jack tells her sometimes that she should lighten up. Although Violet has been slow to embrace all the changes of the last couple of years, she has also welcomed them. Violet and Queenie have weathered the storm of Queenie's secret maternity quite well, though she doesn't think she will ever be able to call her anything other than Queenie. As a girl growing up without a mother, Violet would have given anything to have had someone to call *Mama,* but it feels too late for that now. Maybe that will change over time. A lot of other things have.

Violet asked Tia and Leisha to look after Old Sally this morning while Rose went to the bank. Not that Old Sally needs looking after, but at the end of April, they celebrated her one hundred and second birthday. Something about the largeness of that number prompted them to always have someone around if she needs anything. Besides, Violet likes the influence Old Sally has on her girls. After spending time with her, they seem more grounded and thoughtful.

Heather digs into her sizeable purse, as if on a search for buried treasure instead of two dollars and some change.

"It's on the house," Violet says.

Heather stops digging and thanks her. For a moment, Violet wonders if she uses this ploy often.

Violet was good at reading the moods of the ghosts who haunted the Temple mansion and is learning to read the energy of living people, too. But this young woman is not so easy to understand. If Violet had to guess she would say Heather is, underneath all the pretense, desperate for something. A sense of belonging, perhaps. Or a way to fill her emptiness.

"A fresh pot of coffee will be ready in a minute. You can have a seat, I'll bring it to you," Violet says.

Without thanking her, Heather returns to the corner near the window. A table that people often pick their first time in. Violet arranged the tables to accommodate every type of personality. The shy, the outgoing, the college student, the elderly couple, singles, and groups.

As soon as it's ready, Violet brings over the coffee. She refuses to use paper cups except for to-go orders. A person should have a nice cup of tea or coffee in a container that won't begin to disintegrate as soon as hot water hits it. Violet also brings Heather a small slice of pumpkin bread. A slice small enough to not evoke much guilt.

"Oh, I didn't order that," Heather says.

"I know," Violet says. "It's on the house, too."

Heather looks at her as though wondering why Violet is so nice. She doesn't appear to trust easily. Or perhaps at all. Another attribute of Violet's former employer.

"Rose told me that owning this tea shop is like a lifelong dream or something?"

"It is." Violet doesn't mention that before she fulfilled her dream, she was a servant to the Temples, and therefore to Heather's biological father and look-alike grandmother. Violet was someone who wore a uniform to work, lived in a small apartment, and drove an old car. But that has changed.

Violet excuses herself, telling Heather to let her know if she needs anything else.

Most of the morning crowd are older and retired. People who become invisible in the culture after a certain age. Yet, Violet sees them all. At times, Violet thinks she should hang out a shingle. But she isn't so much a psychologist as she is a reader of tea leaves. From Old Sally, Violet has learned to see the invisible clues of who people are. Tea leaves left behind in their cups reveal short journeys. Long journeys. A new romance. A sudden illness. Their lives revealed under their noses and at the bottom of their cups.

The Gullah ways in her family have passed through the maternal line. It isn't always so. There are male root doctors, too. Yet, Violet is becoming well versed in protection spells, healing elixirs, and where to find the different plants and roots needed for both. Not to be forgotten are the teas. Ginger root tea can cure all sorts of female problems. Dogwood root tea mixed with cherry root and oak bark cures muscular swelling. Cockroach tea helps cure coughs. And earthworm tea works on rashes if combined into a salve with lard. However, Violet imagines that most of these teas will never be sold in her tea shop, no matter how beneficial they are.

Violet's favorite customer, Marylou, enters. Her local customers usually come at the same time every day and order the same thing. Orders she begins fixing as soon as they walk through the door. They count on her to remember the teas and pastries they enjoy.

Marylou is twelve years younger than Old Sally and walks with a silver cane. A colorful scarf is wrapped around her neck, her solid white hair in a pixie cut. She used to be a dancer and was quite famous at one time. Every morning, Marylou orders Earl Grey tea with a cheese Danish warmed in the microwave. Violet makes her tea, thinking again how lucky she is to be working at her very own tea shop instead of in Miss Temple's kitchen.

It is still early, just after nine o'clock, but it already seems a lighter crowd than usual. On a typical Sunday, the tea shop is busy. Queenie usually comes in to help with the lunch crowd, but not today. She is away on her honeymoon.

It is probably Queenie's presence that explains why they can barely catch a breath from 11:30 until 2:00 every day. Queenie draws people like bees to flowers with her laughter and folksy manner.

Violet smiles, remembering when they left for Hilton Head last night, Spud's car covered with the JUST MARRIED announcements that Tia and Leisha drew on the sides and back window.

After Violet delivers Marylou's tea and pastry, she stops by Heather's table. The pumpkin bread remains untouched.

"Everything okay here?"

Heather says that everything is fine, but there is something ominous in the way she looks at Violet. Something in her eyes holds a secret.

CHAPTER SEVENTEEN

Queenie

Queenie and Spud walk along the waterway near the lighthouse on Hilton Head Island. A tower built for display, not necessarily function, but that has a lovely panoramic view if you take the time to trek to the top. A feat Queenie only did once, when she started coming here with Spud.

Occasionally Queenie sees tourists looking at them. She imagines a plus-size black woman and an undersized white man wearing a bow tie aren't a typical couple seen here. But diversity is what makes life interesting. At least that's what Queenie tells herself whenever she's being stared at. She would have thought judgment of this nature would be a thing of the past in 2002. Queenie must bite her lip sometimes to keep from saying what she is thinking, which is that people should keep their stares and smirks to themselves.

"What were those men talking about in the restaurant?" Queenie asks her new husband, squeezing his arm to make sure he is real.

"Evidently Hurricane Iris is building up speed and has turned toward the southeastern United States."

"That's us," Queenie says, her eyes widening.

"Well, us, and a whole lot of other places," Spud says.

"Hurricane Iris." Queenie scoffs. "Isn't that just our luck, to be pursued by a storm named after you-know-who?"

"*Pursued* may be too big a word," Spud says. "She may still peter out." But his eyes reveal how seriously he is taking this.

Spud puts an arm around her, telling her not to worry. "No matter what happens, I'll take care of you," he says.

Queenie giggles before she can stop herself. Since when is she someone who titters like a schoolgirl? She hates to admit that she likes the idea of being taken care of, but she can't help thinking it comes at a cost. Doesn't everything have a price, whether it's independence or codependence? For a moment, she sounds like Oprah, and this pleases her. Spud Grainger has become one of Queenie's Favorite Things. A gift wrapped in a bow tie just for her.

More and more people are talking about the storm. When Queenie is paying for a colorful new scarf at one of the harbor shops, Spud tells her he thinks they should talk.

"I don't want to upset you," he begins, "but I think we should head back to the island. The others may need us if this hurricane takes the course they think it might," he continues. "We may need to prepare the house for the high tides and high winds."

Should have known Iris would ruin my honeymoon, Queenie thinks, but what she tells Spud is altogether different.

She says they can leave, sounding more submissive than she feels. But the truth is she doesn't want her mama to go through a storm without her, no matter how many other people are around.

"We can continue our honeymoon after the storm passes," Spud says.

She agrees, hiding her disappointment. "I've waited this long. I can wait a little longer," Queenie says, which is actually true.

He opens the car door for her in the parking lot near the harbor. They will return to his condominium and pack up to go back to Dolphin Island less than twenty-four hours after they arrived. Queenie admires the elegant red-and-white lighthouse again. It couldn't be more different from the one on their island that has been abandoned for years. A structure that may have been helpful at one time, now bolted closed and dark.

A gust of wind shakes the car door as she is getting inside, and Queenie can almost hear her dead half sister laugh. The same half sister who insisted at every opportunity that Queenie wasn't a true Temple but a watered-down version, and who treated Queenie with scorn for thirty-five years.

It's not funny, Iris, Queenie tells the wind, wondering if she will ever escape the woman who haunts her memories at every opportunity. Iris was larger than life while alive and is perhaps even bigger in death in the form of a hurricane.

CHAPTER EIGHTEEN

Old Sally

Y*ou best be waking up now, little girl,* her grandmother says. *Things need to be done to get ready for what's coming.*

Like what, Granny? Sally asks, half-asleep.

You got to build the courage fires to keep everybody safe.

Courage fires? Sally asks. She loves her grandmother more than anyone, but this doesn't make sense.

The water going to get high, over your head. You remember how to swim, don't you, little girl?

Yes, Granny, Sally says.

Don't forget now. Sally's grandmother looks at her with so much love, tears spring to her eyes.

I won't, Sally says.

Promise me, girl.

I promise.

. . .

OLD SALLY STARTLES AWAKE, putting her hand on her chest to calm her racing heart.

"Granny?" she says aloud, wishing the spirit to return. Old Sally's grandmother died ages ago, yet in the dream she was as alive as anything and passing down her wisdom as she was prone to do. Things like the past, present, and future travel together, like three sisters who refuse to be separated. She also told Sally that everything alive grows on top of something that was before. A live oak can grow right on top of another fallen tree and be nourished by it.

But what does any of that have to do with courage fires? she asks herself.

Gullah people have an intimate relationship with nature and spirits. Spirits are benevolent ancestors who are not forgotten. Unlike the Temple ghosts who shocked and scared people, her ancestors try to help. They pass on wisdom to those who will listen.

It isn't always that way. Spirits have different personalities. Some want to do good, and some don't. Whenever her grandmother shows up, Sally knows she wants to help.

Old Sally thinks again of the dream. She's never heard of such a thing as courage fires. And why would her grandmother ask if she remembers how to swim? A tingle travels the length of her spine. Her old bones know something she doesn't.

Old Sally doesn't need a weather forecaster in Savannah to tell her that a storm is coming. She has been studying these things since she was a little girl. She can smell a storm on the wind and feel it in her body. If that isn't enough, the birds act differently. They start preparing long before anybody else. But that doesn't mean it will be a hurricane. They do the same thing before a significant rain.

Old Sally gets out of bed and shuffles toward the kitchen, surprised by how late it is. She usually gets up by sunrise, and here it is almost noon. The house is oddly quiet. Tia enters the hallway, Violet's youngest.

Such a pretty girl, she thinks, *a lot like Violet was when she was this age.*

"Mom is at the tea shop. Can I make your breakfast?"

"That be awful nice," Old Sally says, thinking again of the dream. "You girls know how to swim, don't you?"

"Sure," Tia says. "Daddy taught us when we were young. Why?"

"No reason," she says, although there are plenty of reasons.

In the kitchen, Tia makes Old Sally a bowl of her usual oatmeal, adding a little butter and brown sugar on top. Old Sally could fix it herself, but it seems necessary to let people help her these days. Not only for her benefit, but for theirs, too. After Old Sally is gone, they will know they were helpful to her, and that will comfort them in their loss.

Leisha comes in and gives Old Sally a hug. Violet's two girls are as different as the sun and the moon. One is shy, the other is outgoing. Tia is tall and athletic like her father, Jack. Leisha is more petite like Violet and into making good grades at school. But both are strong in integrity like their parents. Soon they will go off on their own. They are at the beginning of becoming who they are, while Old Sally is at the end.

"Where's your daddy?" Old Sally asks Leisha.

"He and Max are returning the rental chairs," Tia says.

All those wedding preparations now be reversed, Old Sally thinks. Life is a constant building up and breaking down. Ebb and flow. Rise and fall.

Tia and Leisha stand in the kitchen like Old Sally used to stand and wait on the Temple family, meeting their every need. Old Sally eats her oatmeal, thinking how strange it is to be catered to.

"When I was your age, I was living on this island with my mother and grandmother just like you are," Old Sally says.

Tia sits next to Old Sally as if knowing a story is coming.

Leisha pours herself and Old Sally each a small glass of orange juice before sitting, too. Old Sally thanks her.

"Back then, cars hadn't been invented yet, and no one on the island had a telephone," she begins. "My grandmother worked for the Temple family and made seven cents an hour. It felt like a step up to be paid at all. Before that, my family had been Temple slaves."

The girls' attention doesn't waver. Old Sally thinks again of the dream. Courage fires. They will need to call on all their strength soon. The last foretelling dream Old Sally had was before Edward started the fire at the Temple mansion. Old Sally dreamed that Queenie was in danger. Now, this new dream is pointing to something, too.

"Anybody home?" Queenie calls from the front door as Spud carries in the bags. They join them in the kitchen.

"What happened to the honeymoon?" Tia asks.

"We thought we should be here to help out with that hurricane coming," Spud says.

"A hurricane is coming?" Leisha asks, her wide eyes begging it to be so.

"Well, not officially," Spud says.

"You okay, Mama?" Queenie asks Old Sally. "You look like you've seen a ghost."

"A dream has me riled up," Old Sally says, relieved that Queenie and Spud are here. If something big is going to happen, she wants to have all her family around her.

"Where are Max and Jack?" Spud asks. "I thought they'd be boarding up windows by now."

"They're returning the rental chairs in Max's pickup," Leisha answers.

"I thought you said it isn't officially a storm," Queenie says.

"It isn't," Spud says. "There is absolutely no reason to think we may get a hurricane."

According to Queenie, Spud is a person who likes to be helpful. Sometimes too helpful, as far as Queenie is concerned. Last September Queenie had to talk him out of going to ground zero in New York City to help with the recovery effort. Perhaps he would have been more in the way than helpful, but it was an impulse Old Sally admired.

"Mind if I change clothes in your bedroom?" Spud asks Queenie.

"You can change clothes in my bedroom anytime, handsome," Queenie says, and adds a wink.

"Gross," Tia says, which makes everyone laugh.

"Just wait," Queenie says. "Someday, you'll find yourself a handsome hunk of man like this one, and you'll say things you never dreamed of saying, too."

"Doubtful," Leisha says, kidding her sister.

Despite the playful banter among the people she finds dear, Old Sally's concerns deepen. An ill wind is blowing in. She is sure of it. Or near certain. But what do courage fires have to do with anything? She hates a riddle she can't figure out.

While the others talk, Old Sally is deep in thought. Both Queenie and Spud can swim, she's seen them out in the ocean. Rose can, too. In fact, Old Sally taught her one summer when she was five or six. She taught Violet, as well, and she has seen Jack swim with the girls. But Max? She will ask him the next time they have a moment alone. Although she isn't sure why she is so concerned about swimming.

High water. That's what Old Sally's grandmother said in the dream. But maybe that will only happen if Old Sally doesn't heed her warning.

What are you trying to tell me? she says to her grandmother.

Her grandmother doesn't answer, but Old Sally imagines she will find out soon enough.

CHAPTER NINETEEN

Rose

R ose drives over the Talmadge Memorial Bridge into Savannah, the key from Old Sally's table sitting on the passenger seat. A key Regina gave her from the overlooked package Iris sent her son, Edward. At the time it seemed odd that Regina would give it to Rose. Perhaps she hadn't intended to, or maybe she just wanted to get rid of it. Rose had not planned to go to town today, but with Heather showing up and after the strange dream Rose had last night, it felt important.

Living with Old Sally has her paying attention to her dreams. Old Sally is convinced it is how their ancestors communicate. Rose isn't so sure she wants to hear from her ancestors, but at the same time, if it prevents her from doing something unwise, she is all for it.

In her dream, Edward was searching for the second Temple Book of Secrets and wanted to find it before Rose. She has a feeling something inside that second book will change everything.

As if things haven't changed enough, Rose thinks.

Maybe Heather is after the second Book of Secrets, too. She seems to be after something. Rose still can't believe there are two ledgers. Until her return to Savannah, she had forgotten all about the Temple's lifelong obsession with collecting secrets. Secrets that helped leverage the family's power in Savannah. This is not a game Rose has ever played, but she wants to make sure the books don't create further damage. She still has no idea where the first Book of Secrets ended up after Edward shocked Savannah with it around the time her mother died. He released a secret a day in the Savannah newspaper for weeks. An act of revenge to get back at their racist mother. At least that's what Regina said the day she and Rose met for the first time.

When the weather report comes on the radio, Rose turns it up. The storm has taken a turn over the Atlantic and is now heading toward the southeastern coast. After living in Wyoming all those years, severe weather has become routine. Blizzards happened every winter, with tornados in the spring and summer. But she has never experienced a hurricane before. Not even in her first twenty years of life living here in Savannah.

At the bank entrance, Red Mason waits for Rose. His hair has never been red; the nickname is short for Redmond. Red's hair has turned gray, and he wears a pair of gray slacks with a light blue shirt and loafers without socks.

"I didn't know you were back in town," he says to Rose, flashing the same smile he gave her from the varsity basketball court as she sat in the stands back when they went to school together.

"My husband and I moved back to Savannah after Mother died," she says, unsure why she feels the need to tell him she is married, except that the high school crush he had on her was intense.

"I heard you married a cowboy," he says.

"I did, indeed." Her face momentarily warms. She never knows these days if she is embarrassed or having a hormonal surge. She changes the subject. "Do you think that hurricane will amount to anything?"

"Iris?" He smiles again, as if the irony isn't lost on him, either. "Much ado about nothing," he says, from the high school play they were both in.

Rose pauses, wishing she had thought to bring Max along. "Thanks again for meeting me."

"No problem," he says, glancing at his loafers as though they could use a polish.

Rose's mother would like that the Temple name can still get a banker to come into work on a Sunday. It is unusual for Rose to take advantage of that fact. But something about it feels urgent.

"You mentioned finding a key to a safe-deposit box of your mother's?" Red asks.

Rose hands him the old key, and his eyes widen.

"That's from the original bank, the oldest section," he says. "I didn't think there were any of those left anymore."

Red's expression changes to one Rose can't quite interpret. Does he not want her poking around? She chides herself for imagining things, the chiding something her mother did quite often.

After unlocking the front door, Red leads the way up the stairs and then down a hallway. His loafers squeak on the marble floors, sounding almost comical. They enter a section of the building Rose never knew existed. The sign on the door reads ARCHIVES.

"What you're looking for will be back here," he says, opening the door.

They walk into a musty room filled with old wood filing cabinets. Even with windows lining one wall, the place is dark. Red flips on a light switch and fluorescents hum and flicker until they bathe the room with unnatural light.

The farther back they go, the older the furniture gets.

"It's like we're walking through history," Rose says, more to herself than to him.

"Yeah, I guess we are."

At the end of the room is a large walk-in safe that takes up an entire wall. Red takes a small index card from his shirt pocket and turns the silver dial to the correct numbers like in every old movie she's ever watched with a bank vault scene. She looks around to make sure they aren't in the middle of a film set.

"You have the number with you?" Rose asks.

Red pauses, like he didn't think she'd notice.

"I had it just in case." He beams his charm at her again, but this time it isn't the least bit charming.

"You acted surprised when I showed you the key," Rose says, thinking something doesn't add up.

Red swings the door open and ignores her comment. A whiff of old papers and history rush toward them, suddenly disturbed. Rose steps into the vault and feels instantly claustrophobic. She steadies herself against the cold metal of the safe, taking deep breaths of the musty air, the smell something akin to old attics.

Red asks her for the key that Rose had forgotten she was holding. He goes over to an iron box that looks like it could be pre–Civil War. A safe within a safe, the size of a small coffee table. He opens it with the key.

"A couple of years ago, I let Edward in here," he says, as if feeling a need to confess.

"Edward was here?" Her throat tightens. "What was he looking for?" she asks.

"No idea," Red says. "But he was acting strange that day."

"What do you mean by strange?" Rose asks.

"Like secretive, but full of himself at the same time," he says. "Come to think of it, he was almost gleeful, and shortly afterward those secrets started showing up in the paper."

Rose imagines Edward's delight was from knowing he was finally getting back at their mother. But Rose admits she didn't see this need for revenge coming. She always thought Edward adored their mother.

"Edward came in again a week before the fire," Red begins

again. "He stood right where you're standing now. That was horrible about the fire," Red adds, sounding genuine.

Rose's little finger tingles, remembering its sacrifice in the war with her brother. When he died, her grief was more about what could have been instead of what was.

"Do you know what Edward was looking for?" Rose asks.

"The same thing you are, I imagine." He lifts an eyebrow.

"But I don't know what I'm looking for," Rose says.

"You don't?" Red's voice registers mild surprise.

Rose wonders what Red knows that she doesn't. Do bankers have access to every vault and safe-deposit box and what's inside? Or maybe her mother was right about Rose imagining things.

"This is where I disappear," Red announces. "You can stay up here as long as you like. I'll be in my office on the first floor." He hands her back the key that she had already forgotten about.

Red exits the long room, his squeaky footsteps growing softer in the distance as Rose's sneaking suspicions grow. She reminds herself she is not a reliable witness as far as sneakiness is concerned. In the past, Rose imagined complicated plots and ulterior motives where nothing was confirmed.

Alone now, Rose pulls a wooden office chair into the vault and sits in front of the open safe-deposit box, at eye level. Timid, she reaches inside the box, almost expecting to fall headfirst into the past.

Inside the box is a metal drawer at the top, deep enough to hold an old fountain pen and a bottle of petrified ink. A blotter like the one that sat on her father's desk when Rose was a girl sits next to it. Below is a stack of papers and different ledgers. She is surprised cobwebs aren't strung between the pages. Except that Edward was here before her.

One after another, Rose carefully lifts out the papers crisp with age. Ledgers. Deeds of different properties dated before the Civil War, along with stacks of receipts for various goods: furniture, weapons, the chandelier that used to hang in the Temple mansion.

Then an entire folder holding receipts for large deposits to different people—the faded ink a light gray—for services unknown. Payoffs?

Rose regrets she hadn't stopped at Violet's shop to order a large coffee to go. She needs caffeine if she's going to sift through the Temple past. An abundant and dark past, if she imagines correctly.

Minutes later she comes across an old ledger that looks familiar. Wasn't this in her father's office when she was a girl? The Book of Secrets was leather like this one. Could the second book be the same? And how did Edward even know there was a safe here full of Temple papers? Did their mother tell him about it? Or perhaps their father? Rose can't remember a time when so many unanswered questions rushed at her.

When she opens the ledger, she realizes it is actually the Book of Secrets that Edward used when he leaked the confidences to the Savannah newspaper before their mother died. This information was never shared with Rose, but maybe as the male heir, her brother had access. It seems the quest for secrets and leverage was generational and never-ending until now.

Rose is relieved that Regina doesn't have the book. At least in this old safe, it can't do any more harm to reputations. Power is a fascinating thing, and if you combine power with secrets, it can be both dangerous and advantageous for whoever has access to the secrets.

Rose puts the ledger back where it was for safekeeping. She will give some thought to what she wants to do with it now. A bonfire at the beach is still a possibility.

Rose goes through more papers, digging through the Temple past. Mostly records of everything acquired and ample evidence of status. It is hot in the safe, the air conditioning unable to reach inside. She tires quickly, not even knowing what she is looking for. Then she stops, deciding on a different tactic. She pauses and closes her eyes, asking her ancestors what they want her to find. This is something Old Sally or Violet might do.

Rose waits, feeling silly at first and then recommitting to the question. When she opens her eyes, she is drawn to something about halfway down in the right corner of the large safe-deposit box. It is another thick ledger, similar to the Book of Secrets, except the pages are more yellowed, and the cover is faded. She opens it to find that the pages are indeed more brittle, the ink even more faded. The dates are from the early 1800s. Pages have fallen out and been stuck back in. If this is the precursor to the Book of Secrets Rose saw as a girl, she feels she should be wearing gloves. It is like a museum piece. It seems to be a diary containing dates and meetings. Some of the things are written in her great-great-grandfather Temple's hard-to-read scrawl. Page after page gives a list of names and dates of transgressions. It's not the second Book of Secrets. It is the original one. Confirming that the secrets Edward leaked to the press were much newer.

After thumbing through several more pages, Rose comes across a list of names, knowing immediately what it is. A shudder passes through her that feels as old as the names. Does she want to see the evil deeds of her ancestors? She thinks of Old Sally and Queenie and Violet—people who are dearer to her than any family member other than Katie and Max—who are the descendants of the people listed in this ledger. Page after page.

Most of the names are written in the same hand, but with varying dates and shades of ink. A first name only. Age. Children. Where they were assigned to work. Near the middle of the third page, Rose recognizes the name Sadie, Old Sally's grandmother, whom Rose has heard stories about her entire life. A child is listed. A boy named Adam. Sent to the Temple plantation near Charleston at ten years of age.

Rose pauses and closes her eyes. "Forgive us," she whispers.

Even if the people are no longer living, an apology is inadequate. She closes the book to erase the truth written in the ledger.

A boy was taken away from his mother at age ten? Old Sally's grandmother must have been heartbroken. And what must it have been like for the boy?

Rose covers her mouth, feeling queasy, and leaves the vault to find a restroom. Her footsteps echo on the marble floors.

How does someone several generations later make up for the sins of her family's past? she wonders.

In the restroom, Rose splashes cold water on her face and dries it with paper towels. The bank is as quiet as the Temple crypt in Bonaventure Cemetery. She could probably spend weeks in the bank vault exploring the past. But for now, she needs to figure out what Edward was searching for. She guesses that it is somehow linked to Heather being here.

After returning to the vault, she takes another deep breath of history and allows herself ten more minutes to look through the ledger to see what she can find. It isn't fair to keep Red here much longer.

Rose wonders what else her ancestors want her to see.

Near the middle of the book, she finds more secrets. She recognizes the name Rivers. Bo Rivers was her mother's attorney. But this is a Harrison Rivers who was living in 1834 and had an unlawful child named CeCe, who was sent to Vicksburg to live with a maiden aunt. She imagines how scandalous it would have been and thinks of Edward's daughter. A present-day scandal hardly worth noting.

Another name comes to her attention: Mason. She imagines this is one of Red's ancestors. She leans forward to read the faded ink. Several dates follow the name along with a series of numbers, all to do with embezzling from the bank. This bank. The oldest bank in Savannah.

"You about done?" Red says, suddenly behind her.

Rose jumps. "You scared me!"

His apology sounds sincere, but she wonders why she didn't

hear him walk up. Perhaps he knows what secrets concerning his family may be in there. Or perhaps it is simply a coincidence.

"I promised my wife I'd spend time with her and the kids today," Red says.

"Of course," Rose says, momentarily flustered. "Sorry, Red. I lost track of time. Can I take this?" She holds up the faded ledger with the yellowed pages stuck in here and there.

"Everything in there is yours," he says, his eyes on the papers, not her. "You can take anything you want."

She closes the fragile ledger and then carefully puts it in her purse, grateful that she is carrying one of her bigger bags today.

"Find anything interesting?" Something about the way he asks makes her question his intention.

"Just a bunch of old papers."

Rose realizes how inconsistent this is to her calling him on a Sunday morning with a special request to get into the bank.

"Your family is one of the reasons this bank has survived," he says, as if no apology is needed.

For years Rose didn't question how her mother could get anything she wanted from just about anybody. She wouldn't have thought twice about keeping a banker from his family for an entire Sunday for weeks or months on end. Her mother's needs trumped anyone else's.

They walk down the marble stairs, Red holding her arm. Manners are essential in Savannah. Important all over the South. Southern men have impeccable manners, even while embezzling, siring illicit children, or laundering money.

Instead of going home, Rose drives to Violet's Tea Shop. After she parks, she pulls the faded ledger from her purse. Rose has no idea why she is bringing it home. Or why she is sitting here in the car wanting to hold it. But something about this record of the past feels significant, and she is determined to find out why.

CHAPTER TWENTY

Violet

When the bells jingle to announce the next customer, Violet looks up to see Rose enter the tea shop.

"What are you doing here?" she says when Rose reaches the counter.

"I need coffee," says Rose, who seldom looks this weary in the afternoon.

Violet reaches for the pot, but Rose insists on fixing it herself and is even more adamant than usual. Rose has helped Violet out enough to know where everything is and comes behind the counter for a coffee cup.

"How did it go at the bank?" Violet asks.

"You don't want to know." Rose doctors her coffee with cream and two sugars, cleaning the counter after she finishes.

"You seem upset," Violet says. She was surprised that morning to hear Rose's plan to visit the bank on a Sunday and when a storm was coming, but she trusts her friend had a good reason.

"I'll fill you in later when we have some privacy," Rose says.

Violet agrees and then nods in Heather's direction. Rose looks and then quickly turns away. They stand behind a display of pastries and cookies, keeping their voices low.

"What is she doing here?" Rose whispers. "And who is that guy with her?"

"He came in a few minutes ago. I guess he's a friend." Violet looks out into the tearoom at the two people, who are deep in conversation.

"Isn't he one of those Goth people?" Rose asks.

"Complete with trench coat," Violet says.

"Doesn't he know it's ninety degrees outside?"

"I don't think he cares," Violet says. "They're a very odd-looking couple, aren't they?"

Rose agrees. "But in a weird way, they look kind of related."

"I think that, too," Violet says. "It's like they wear the same mascara and eyeliner."

Rose laughs. "I'm serious."

Violet apologizes. "Maybe they're in on something together," she says.

"You sound like me," Rose says. "I hate thinking the worst of people."

"You're not thinking the worst, you're cautious," Violet says. "It's okay to be cautious." Violet narrows her eyes while looking in their direction, a model of cautiousness.

The bells on the door jingle again, and Violet leaves Rose still blowing on her coffee. While Violet fixes an order, Rose watches the corner table near the window.

"I think I'll confront them," Rose says after Violet finishes the order. A sentence Violet doesn't think she has ever heard Rose say.

Before Violet has time to stop her, Rose is already approaching the table. From a distance, Violet tries to decipher what they are saying. Regarding their body language, it is the young man with the black lipstick who appears to be the most ill at ease. Rose seems to be holding her own. Every now and again her childhood friend surprises her. She didn't expect Rose to be this bold.

The door jingles again and Tia and Leisha enter, pulling Violet's attention away from Rose. Jack is behind them. When Violet worked for Miss Temple, her family never stopped by. Not once. But now, since Violet owns the tea shop, they visit often.

"Mom, the storm is coming straight for us!" Tia's excitement is tangible.

Jack gives Violet a quick kiss.

"Is it true?" she asks, her shoulder offering a twinge for the first time in months.

Jack nods. "We're under a hurricane watch."

From Violet's understanding, a hurricane watch means that the storm is still only a possibility. It is a hurricane warning they fear, saying the wind is imminent.

Leisha eyes the pastry counter. This adventure might require a lemon poppy seed muffin.

"When is the storm supposed to be here?" Violet refuses to call it Iris. It is too strange.

"Sometime in the early morning," Jack says.

Mondays are her slowest days, so at least the storm may not affect her business too much.

"Have you been busy?" Jack asks.

"Not really," she says. "I guess the possible hurricane is keeping people away. Even the threat of a tropical storm has people standing in line at the Piggly Wiggly, their carts full of canned food, bread, and milk."

"You're right, it's a zoo. We picked up bottled water just in case," Jack says. "Max has plywood in the truck to board up your windows. He's right outside."

Violet glances at the large window, the most beautiful and fragile part of the shop. The door jingles again and Max comes in, waving to her and Jack.

"Isn't it a little early to board up windows?" Violet asks. "It's only a hurricane watch. Still a long shot."

"Better safe than sorry," Jack says. "Max is dropping off the plywood. We'll be back right before closing, and if it looks like it's not going to happen, we won't do anything."

"I still think you're overreacting," Violet says.

Everyone gathers at the counter—the girls and Max and Jack—and then Rose returns, looking flushed. "What did they say?" Violet asks.

Rose greets the others before pulling Violet into the back room, keeping her voice lowered like they did when they shared secrets as girls.

"Evidently he's a friend that goes to Savannah Art and Design," Rose says. "Heather said they grew up together."

"Okay, so nothing to worry about, right?" Violet asks.

"Something still feels fishy to me," Rose says.

"What are you two doing back here?" Jack asks.

"Just talking," Violet says. She will fill him in later about the Heather saga.

"We need to catch the latest weather report," Jack says.

"Did I miss something?" Rose asks.

"Looks like we may get that hurricane after all," Violet says.

"Worse-case scenario, downtown Savannah could get six to eight feet of water," Jack says. "Dolphin Island even more."

A sharp pain shoots through Violet's shoulder, putting to rest the concern she had about losing her sensitivity. Her thoughts immediately turn to preparations for the storm.

CHAPTER TWENTY-ONE

Queenie

Queenie stacks several wedding gifts in the top of her closet to deal with later, along with the thank-you notes.

"You've got nerve messing with my honeymoon," Queenie says to her deceased half sister. She looks up at the closet light to see if it flickers with Iris's answer.

When still alive, Iris Temple was known for her revenge tactics, and for all Queenie knows she has ordered this hurricane from the grave. According to Spud, they are under a hurricane watch. It is still far away, a Category 3 storm and growing. Knowing Iris, she will settle for nothing less than top tier, a Category 5.

When Queenie lived in the Temple mansion there were daily hauntings by various dead Temples, Iris being the last of the Temple spirit legacy. Cold air rushed down hallways or rattled dishes and glasses when no one was in the kitchen. Plants tipped over for no reason. Ancient perfumes and scents lingered in bedrooms. As far as she knows, however, all the Temple spirits were destroyed along with the mansion, along with Edward, who died in the fire.

Of course, Queenie knows that a hurricane named Iris and the woman who made her life miserable for over three decades are not the same. Or are they? Unexplained mysteries happen all the time. Like the fact that she loathed Iris, yet still misses her. Queenie is a perfect example of what occurs when you combine Gullah folk magic and an old Savannah family. All her life she has struggled to find her place in the world—she, herself, is a mystery. Since Iris died and Queenie is no longer her personal assistant, she hasn't known what to do with herself. Until recently, her entire life revolved around Iris's needs, not her own.

Spud told her they must take this storm seriously, and Queenie is doing just that. She checks on Old Sally, who is busy making a smelly concoction on the stove. It is not unusual to smell strange substances brewing. Things that don't, in Queenie's opinion, belong in a cooking pot. Gnarled roots, parts of frogs and chicken bones, human hair and sometimes fingernails. Along with the ever-present graveyard dirt kept in an old metal canister at the top of the kitchen cabinet over the sink. A canister Queenie remembers from when she was a girl, the FLOUR label already faded with age.

Long ago Queenie stopped asking what these ingredients were for. Lately, Violet has been brewing things with Old Sally, writing complicated recipes down in her notebook while standing alongside the stove, though not today.

Queenie has never been interested in spells. It never made sense to her how the bark of one tree and the mud from a certain Georgia swamp could heal or prevent something bad from happening. It also never made sense to her that putting a favorite cereal bowl at someone's gravesite will keep the spirit happy forever. Do people eat Cocoa Puffs in the Afterlife? She hopes not. She hopes there are better options. Like croissants from a heavenly bakery, covered with real butter and homemade raspberry jam. Her mouth waters.

"What are you cooking up?" Queenie asks Old Sally, not really wanting to know, but she is suddenly hungry.

"A protection spell." Old Sally seems more thoughtful than usual. She gets this way when something is going on *between worlds*, as she calls it. Evidently, there are two worlds instead of one. The visible one that Queenie is standing in here in the kitchen and the invisible one her ancestors live in, and where everyone who dies crosses over to.

Queenie has never understood the Gullah ways. The only time in her life she took an interest in folk magic was when she asked her mama to make her a love potion for a boy she had a crush on in the fourth grade. Her request did not go over well. Gullah magic was not to be used to manipulate matters of the heart, she was told, so Queenie never asked her to do it again.

She knows that if she had somehow managed to marry before now, it would not have been the *right* man for her. Her eyes tear up, and it's not from what is cooking on the stove. She cannot believe how much she loves Spud Grainger.

Well, not his bow ties, she tells herself. *I could spend the rest of my life without those.* But he doesn't wear them much anymore since he has retired.

Queenie never dreamed someone would treat her so well. Bringing her socks to put on in bed if her feet are cold. Putting a Hershey's Kiss on her pillow every night, even though she has recently brushed her teeth. Giving her a neck rub if she has the least bit of a pain. Iris was an idiot to end her affair with Spud Grainger all those many years ago.

With Old Sally stirring smelly stuff on the stove, Queenie wonders if her mama has ever loved someone as much as she loves Spud. Queenie's father was Edward Temple, and Old Sally's only husband had already died before Queenie was born. Old Sally had Queenie when she was in her early forties, having long before planned to not have any more children. But life, it seems, rarely goes as planned.

"Mama, who was the love of your life?" Queenie asks. She doesn't usually speak of intimate things with her mama like some daughters do, but she is genuinely curious. She takes a seat to wait for the answer.

"A man named Everett Moses," Old Sally says, without hesitation. "But everybody called him Fiddle. He was said to be the best fiddle player east of the Mississippi."

"Everett Moses?" Queenie pauses. She has never heard that name before. "Why haven't you ever told me about him?"

"It was a long, long time ago." Old Sally gives the pot another stir.

"Well, how did you meet him? What was he like?"

Old Sally stops stirring and looks up, surprised by Queenie's interest. But then she returns to it, this time like she is stirring her memories.

"Everett was from Charleston," Old Sally begins. "We met at a revival my family took me to over at Edisto."

"I've never heard this story," Queenie says.

"I never told anybody before." Old Sally chuckles when she sees Queenie's face. "Nice to know I can still surprise you," she says.

"I'll stir. You talk." Queenie takes the spoon and motions for her mama to sit in one of the chairs. "I need to hear what happened between you and Fiddle."

The smell coming from the pot makes Queenie want to gag. But it is the price she is willing to pay to hear her mama's story. This concoction smells strong enough to ward off anything. Iris the hurricane *and* Iris the ghost.

"Fiddle be eighteen, with me two years younger," Old Sally begins. "He was playing at a three-night revival. A gorgeous man if ever you saw one. Black as a moonless night, with beautiful eyes and straight white teeth. He could smile at you and weaken your knees."

Queenie stops stirring. Her mama looks suddenly younger. Her eyes sparkling with the memory.

"The first night, he watched me," Old Sally continues. "On the second night, we talked before and after the service. By the third night, Fiddle and I snuck away from the tent and talked the night away under a live oak with a full moon watching over us. My family thought I was spending the night with a girlfriend," she continues, "but I was spending the night with Fiddle under the stars. Then the next week he drove over from Charleston and tried to talk me into eloping with him. But I didn't want to hurt my mama by moving so far away."

"Charleston was too far away?" Queenie asks, thinking it is a two-hour drive if that.

"It seemed far away back then," she says.

Old Sally looks out the window, as though looking into her past. The sparkle in her eyes begins to fade.

"That night, I snuck out and met him at the lighthouse. Most wonderful night of my life." Old Sally lowers her head, as well as her voice. "On the way back to Charleston the next morning, he died in a car accident. A bus hit his car straight on."

Queenie gasps mid-stir. "Oh, Mama, I'm so sorry." She walks over and hugs her, being careful not to embrace her too tightly. She seems so fragile these days. "I can't imagine losing Spud so soon after we found each other. I'm not sure I would ever get over it."

"I'm not sure I ever did."

Old Sally pauses for what feels like a long time.

"A baby girl came out of that night at the lighthouse," she begins again, her voice even softer. "A baby girl who died at six days old. Broke my heart into tiny pieces."

Queenie's eyes fill with tears. She can't imagine losing Violet, either, even if she didn't officially claim her for over four decades.

"Is that why you walk to that lighthouse all the time?"

Old Sally nods. "Life be full of heartache, daughter," she continues, emotion choking the words. "That's why when love comes you got to celebrate it as big and loud as you can."

Queenie gets them both tissues.

"I wish you had told me sooner," Queenie says.

"Sometimes we lock hurtful things away, just so we can carry on," Old Sally says.

Queenie thinks of the secret she kept for so many years. Maybe she locked that away so she could carry on, too.

"What was the little girl's name who died at six days old?" Queenie asks.

"Annabelle," Old Sally says. "She looked like Fiddle, too. Dark and sweet as sunlight."

"Annabelle," Queenie repeats. She realizes now that she's had two half sisters: one black and one white.

"He came to me in a dream the other night," Old Sally says.

"Fiddle did?"

Old Sally nods. "At first I only heard him play. But then I saw him, and he had so much love in his eyes I woke up crying."

"You missed him so much," Queenie says.

"No. I be crying because I get to see Fiddle soon."

Queenie puts a hand to her heart. For years now, her mama has been ready to go. But it doesn't mean a daughter wants it to happen. Violet will be the one to help Old Sally transition to the next world since Queenie knows so little about the Gullah tradition. But she does see the importance of death rituals on the Gullah side of her family.

"I need to lay down for a minute," Old Sally says.

Queenie asks her if she's okay, knowing that nothing can make losing a child okay, no matter how long ago it was.

"I be fine," she says, though she doesn't look fine. Queenie turns off the stove and follows her into the bedroom. She helps her take off her sandals and lie on the bed.

"It's been a big weekend," Old Sally says. "More excitement than I've had in a long time. I just need a quick nap, and I'll be fine."

Queenie closes Old Sally's door and returns to the living room. She goes over to the collection of objects near her mama's chair and finds a small black-and-white photograph, worn with age, of a dark man playing a fiddle. Next to it sits a small square of pink fabric with an *A* embroidered on it. Almost threadbare, it is as if someone held this piece of cloth every day for over eighty years. How many times has Queenie passed this table and never taken in how each object is a story in her mama's life? Not a shallow connection. Not a collection of ghosts. But an assortment of living memories of the people she continues to love.

CHAPTER TWENTY-TWO

Old Sally

S *ally, honey, wake up.*
      Her grandmother Sadie bustles around the room, a stooped-over Gullah woman.

What is it, Granny? What are you doing? Sally asks.

It be time to light the courage fires, girl. The driftwood be already piled high on the beach. Your grandpa piled it up this morning.

But I don't have anything to light it with, Sally says.

Yes, you do. You be the only one who has the light. If you don't light it now, everyone will be lost.

As a girl, her grandmother expected Sally to know things that she had no way of knowing.

What time the tide be, girl? she would ask. *If you don't know, we all be sunk.*

Sally's mother was tired before her time. Her grandmother was a different story. She had the energy of three people and expected Sally did, too.

Old Sally floats in and out of the dream like she is time traveling. One minute she is young Sally searching for matches, the next she is Old Sally watching everything unfold.

Her grandmother looks under the bed and all around the room, repeating that she must find the light, or everyone will be lost. She repeats it until Sally covers her ears and can't hear it anymore. She wants to go back to sleep. The island school doesn't start for another three hours. The sun isn't even up yet.

Then her grandmother grabs her by the shoulders and lifts her from the bed.

This be serious, girl. Go to the lighthouse. The water's coming. Get up those stairs!

Old Sally wakes with a start, gasping for air as if coming up from a giant wave. Fully awake, she sits up, her heartbeat echoing in her ears.

CHAPTER TWENTY-THREE

Rose

Rose decides to stay and help Violet at the tea shop, her time at the bank still on her mind and in her nose. The smell of musty old ledgers has seeped into her clothes. Her purse hangs on a hook in the back room of the tea shop. When she has a chance, she wants to look through it. If this is the original Book of Secrets, she can't imagine anything it contains is pertinent today. But the question remains of why Edward would have gone to the bank to try to find it. And why is Heather in Savannah hanging out in the wings like that crazy storm?

"You seem distracted," Violet says to Rose between customers.

"I'm still thinking about that trip to the bank," Rose says. "I barely scratched the surface. There were receipts, deeds, and accounts from the last two hundred years. Most of it useless, I imagine."

"Might as well check it out just in case," Violet says.

"Might as well," Rose repeats.

"I wonder what my Gullah ancestors would have kept in a

bank vault," Violet says. "Recipes, maybe. Spells or different folk magic remedies. Maybe a few special roots." She smiles.

Rose doesn't tell Violet about the lists of dozens of her Gullah ancestors who were slaves owned by Rose's family. If the situation were reversed, she imagines Violet would feel a similar shame. But the situation isn't reversed. A long line of Temples owned people. Lots of people, it seems like. People forced to run not only the mansion but a Charleston plantation as well.

To keep an eye on the storm, Rose suggested last night that Violet bring in a small television from home to sit on top of a filing cabinet in the back. Violet, Jack, Rose, and Max gather in front of the local weather report. It reminds Rose of when they watched the towers go down on 9/11. Like the dust of the buildings that fell that day, a profound sense of helplessness fell over Rose. But this isn't a terrorist attack. It's a hurricane. A hurricane spinning wildly out in the Atlantic Ocean, due to turn further inland any minute, where it will collide with a low-pressure system and determine their fate.

Minutes later Rose's fear is confirmed when the weatherman reports that the hurricane watch has just been upgraded to a hurricane warning. Their fate sealed, they exchange looks revealing their surprise. The hurricane is heading this way.

The news report now includes information on how to prepare for the storm. Stocking up on bottled water is recommended, as well as canned goods and batteries. Jack tells them about driving up to Charleston to help some cousins clean up after Hurricane Hugo hit in 1989.

"I've never witnessed anything so destructive," he says, shaking his head.

The word "evacuation" flashes across the television screen. Rose feels a knot in her stomach. She doesn't want to evacuate her new home. Her life has seen enough upheaval lately. Half of the people she talks to are skeptical the storm will even hit. People keep saying how many storm paths predicted for Savannah don't materialize.

Meanwhile, possible evacuation routes are shown on the screen.

"I think you should close early," Jack says to Violet.

"I do, too," Rose says.

Heather walks into the back of the shop and startles Rose, who is standing closest to the door.

"I didn't hear you walk up," Rose says.

"I'm wondering if I should go back to Atlanta," she says to Rose.

"That's up to you," Rose says. Her distrust of Heather nags at her again. When Regina first talked about Heather on the tele-phone, she practically called her a con artist, and she implied birth certificates could be forged.

"Do you mind if I come back after this storm has blown over?" Heather asks her. She looks back at her friend standing at the door.

Rose says she doesn't mind, which isn't the truth. The truth is she wishes Heather had never shown up in the first place. She would prefer to not deal with this hurricane, either. Or the mystery of whatever is in that old bank vault. Rose wants a peaceful life. One without drama. But at this moment, that seems an impossible request.

CHAPTER TWENTY-FOUR

Violet

While Violet makes out Sunday's bank deposit, Max and Jack nail plywood over the large tea shop front windows to protect them from breaking during heavy winds. They also get everything off the floor, since the street Violet's shop is on floods during a hard rain. Before they leave they stack sandbags in front of the door to keep high water from coming in.

When Violet locks the door from the outside for the day, she offers a silent prayer that her tea shop is here when she returns. She wishes now she had brought some of Old Sally's graveyard dirt from home to spread around the shop to protect it. Violet is not someone who enjoys starting over. Who does? But she will if she must.

On the drive home, Jack and the girls are in their other car somewhere in front of her. Weatherwise, it has been a perfect day in Savannah, though hot, and the thought of a hurricane bearing down on them is hard to imagine. The sunset in her rearview mirror is a masterpiece of yellow and orange. Despite the hurricane warning, forecasters say there are still other paths the storm could take. Hitting their island is only one of them. She finds comfort in the possibility that the hurricane may veer north at the last minute and amount to nothing.

Home again, Violet sees that the house is lit up as if they are hosting another wedding party. A peculiar odor greets her on the front porch. A root mixture has been rubbed along the door and window frames of the house. Old Sally's doing, no doubt, for further protection against the storm.

Violet finds everyone in the kitchen except for Old Sally. An animated discussion is going on about the storm. Jack puts an arm around Violet when she steps close. Tia and Leisha have made iced tea for everyone, placing lemon slices on the rims of the glasses like Violet did for Miss Temple's fancy dinners. She hasn't missed serving the silver-headed patriarchs and their wives who keep old Savannah alive. Although they are welcome to visit her tea shop at any time, not one of them has passed through its doors. She offers a wry smile.

Angela fixes Katie a snack. Green grapes and green olives have been her latest craving. When Violet was pregnant with Tia, she ate her weight in apple slices dipped in Peter Pan peanut butter. She looks forward to having a baby around. Good practice for when Tia and Leisha have babies, if they choose to. But before any new life is welcomed, they need to get through this hurricane.

Queenie and Spud enter the kitchen. "We're going back to Hilton Head as soon as this storm passes," Queenie says to Violet, after noting her surprise at seeing them back.

Spud gives Violet a wave, sporting one of the many Hawaiian shirts he has collected since he retired, his idea of leisure wear.

For years Violet thought of herself as an orphan, her mother deceased and a father who had no name. But now she has Queenie and a stepfather in Spud. Violet smiles at this thought despite her tiredness and sits on a stool at the kitchen island. She will check on Old Sally after she rests for a moment.

Weather reports now play on the hour. Violet sighs. She is already tired of this storm, and it hasn't even happened yet. Katie turns up the volume on the television on the kitchen counter, and they watch yet another update. The forecaster has taken off his suit coat and rolled up his sleeves. The storm is skirting past Cuba with 150 mile-per-hour winds, still heading in their direction.

The inevitability of the hurricane reminds Violet of childbirth —that moment during her labor with Leisha when she realized there was no turning back. Nature rules over everything and everyone. Like a newborn, the storm will arrive whether they are ready for it or not.

Violet is curious why her shoulder isn't hurting anymore. She had one sharp but brief pain at the tea shop, and now nothing. At times she has prayed that this sensitivity would go away, but she didn't realize how much she relies on it.

"I need to check on Old Sally," Violet tells Jack.

"Good idea," he says, not taking his eyes from the weather report.

When Violet gets to Old Sally's room, she finds it empty. She checks the bathroom before finding the side door slightly ajar. She goes outside and calls Old Sally's name and then follows the deck around to the front of the house. It is almost dusk, and Old Sally is standing on the beach looking out over the ocean. Violet walks through the dunes to join her, the crests of the waves tipped in the last moments of sunlight. Violet often finds Old Sally like this these days. Deep in thought. Visiting a silence that takes her full attention.

"Are you okay?" Violet asks her.

Old Sally nods as she studies the waves.

"An ill wind be blowing in," Old Sally tells her.

"I thought so," Violet answers. "How should we prepare for it?"

Old Sally doesn't answer and keeps staring at the waves. "Do you know what courage fires are?" she asks after a long pause.

"No. What are courage fires?"

"I'm not so sure myself," Old Sally says. "But they sound important."

It is not often that Violet sees Old Sally at a loss or confused. But something has her off balance.

Together, they look out over the waves as if the sea holds the answers they seek. The tide is coming in.

"Are you worried about the storm?" Violet asks.

"This one be different somehow."

Old Sally's words make Violet uneasy. She shudders and wraps her arms around herself.

"I may need you later," Old Sally says.

"Of course," Violet answers. "Just tell me what you need."

"My grandmother came to me in a dream yesterday. She told me to build courage fires, but I don't know what that means."

"Well, whatever they are, we'll figure it out." Weary, Violet glances back at the ocean, wishing the waves could carry her tiredness out to sea so she could be more available to Old Sally.

"Thanks for your faith in me," Old Sally says, touching Violet's arm.

It strikes Violet as an odd thing to say. She has never lost faith in Old Sally. She has counted on her to be there every moment of her life, and Violet has never been disappointed. It never occurred to her that faith might be involved.

"Has everyone made it home?" Old Sally asks.

Violet says they have. "I need to go in. You coming?"

"Soon," Old Sally says.

Violet turns and heads back to the house. Two crows pick at a dead crab on the beach. They stagger away when Violet walks by. Life and death hold hands here on the island, where land and ocean meet. To see crows this late in the day is odd. Depending on who you talk to, they can either be a sign of good luck or death coming.

The crows take flight, their wings flapping loudly as they pass on both sides of Violet. Close enough that she can feel the wind from their wings on her face. She walks through the dunes, remembering a story Old Sally told her about a Dr. Crow who lived on one of the barrier islands near here. He was a root doctor like Old Sally. Rumor was that he could take the form of a crow whenever he set a notion to. But these are not human crows as far as she knows. She hopes they are bringing a sign that good luck is coming. Sounds like they could use it with this storm.

An ambitious gust of wind causes the dune grasses to twirl—a whisper, perhaps, of the shouting to come.

CHAPTER TWENTY-FIVE

Queenie

Several of Queenie's housemates gather in the kitchen to view the latest weather report. The weather map on the television shows a giant swirl of tight clouds heading toward the southeastern coast of the United States.

"Heaven help us," Queen says, a frequent phrase of late.

"Looks like that hurricane is building steam," Spud says. He puts an arm around Queenie, resting it on her hip. "Don't worry, we'll be fine, Sugar," he adds.

Queenie gives him a sideways glance. "Mister Grainger, since when do you call me *Sugar*?"

His smile is followed by a quick kiss. "Husbands and wives are supposed to have pet names for each other, aren't they?"

Queenie resists slapping him. This storm has her agitated. Not only has it cut her honeymoon short, but now Iris is sucking up all the wedding excitement. A bride is meant to bask in the glory of her wedding day for weeks. But that once-in-a-lifetime memory is now replaced by weather maps and preparation lists.

"Max and I call each other 'honey,'" Rose says. "We haven't called each other by our real names in years."

"We do 'honey,' too." Katie smiles at Angela.

"What would you like to be called?" Queenie asks Spud. Not *Sugar*, she hopes.

For a moment, he looks perplexed, but then another smile crosses his face. "How about, *You sexy devil, you?*"

She gives Spud a playful nudge in the ribs. "You wish, old man."

Everyone laughs, except for Tia and Leisha, who roll their eyes. Queenie imagines this is more than they want to know about their grandmother and new step-grandfather.

For decades, Queenie's love life was only a periodic fantasy that involved movie actors. But now, in her sixties, all has changed. The first time she and Spud made love she was literally weak in the knees. She had heard the phrase before but never experienced it. Now she doesn't feel weak but emboldened. At times, she even feels forty years younger. However, this storm is aging her fast.

"Lord have mercy," Queenie says after the weather report ends. "Are those weather people deliberately trying to scare us? Every time we watch, the news gets worse."

Amidst the chatter, Queenie reminds herself to ask Rose what happened to Heather, as well as what happened at the bank today. It seems a lot more is going on besides this storm, and Queenie hasn't had a spare minute to catch up.

"We need to get busy," Max says to everyone gathered in the kitchen. "You know what they say: prepare for the worst and hope for the best."

Queenie moans. This is not what she had in mind for entertainment this evening. Max and Jack hand them rolls of masking tape and instruct them to put a large *X* on each window that doesn't have storm shutters. Canned goods and other foods are to be gathered. Water jugs filled and labeled. Batteries and flashlights collected. Matches and candles put in dry, waterproof containers.

Queenie gets tired just hearing them talk about all that needs to be done. She hasn't recovered from the last big event, and now they are getting ready for another one.

Nor has my honeymoon adequately commenced, she thinks.

With that thought, Queenie gives Spud a wink that appears to confuse him. Who, after all, gets amorous during hurricane preparations? It seems her sexual prime has coincided with her AARP membership and senior discounts.

But it's good to surprise yourself, she decides, *especially as you age.*

The kinds of surprises she doesn't like are unexpected weather events. But truth be told, this hurricane could ruin a lot more than Queenie's honeymoon. Just a little while ago Jack showed her some photographs of the aftermath of Hurricane Hugo. Oprah even did a show there at the time, but Iris refused to let Queenie attend. Hugo left houses on Sullivan's Island and Isle of Palms in shambles or swept them off their foundations. Some of the homes were washed a block or two away. It didn't help that the drawbridge to the islands was blown off its hinges, too, and people couldn't get home for weeks. A bridge very similar to the one on Dolphin Island.

Hurricanes, like Iris Temple in her day, are never to be underestimated, in Queenie's opinion. Iris was a blowhard for sure, and she was also destructive, especially if you got on her wrong side.

Not that Iris had a right side, she thinks.

Queenie had thought those evil days were over. But it seems her stormy stepsister is making an encore appearance with the clear intent to destroy Queenie's happiness.

CHAPTER TWENTY-SIX

Old Sally

For all the years Old Sally has looked out over this same sea, she has never seen it with this many deep purple hues. Something is churning up from its farthest depths. A similar churning is happening in her gut. Her grandmother was the one whose intuition was the most refined in her family. She predicted the loss of her boy, Adam, who was sent away to the Charleston plantation, and ultimately put a curse on the Temple family for sending him away. She predicted the First World War and the Second. In fact, she predicted her own death right down to the hour.

Old Sally isn't as good at predicting world events, but her gut tells her when something dangerous is close to home. The ill-tempered wind she sensed earlier is growing in anger and heading in their direction. Old Sally's dreams were different last night, too, churned up by the sea. Every night it seems that some-thing new washes up on the beach of the dream world that she is to look at.

This isn't the first time this has happened. The night the Temple mansion burned to the ground a dream warned her. The morning Fiddle died in a car crash her dreams foretold that, too, as well as the death of their child together, and Maya's death—from a tragic car crash, too, more than forty years ago. Now her latest dreams have her grandmother telling her to prepare for something dangerous. Something that requires courage.

Old Sally pulls her shawl tighter and thinks again of Violet. The Gullah ways have been perfected over several centuries stretching back to Western Africa. It would be impossible for anyone to learn everything in only a few months, and harder still for modern people to embrace the old ways. What more does she need to pass on to her? Every human thinks they will have more time, but the truth is, nobody has any guarantees of living any longer than the next second.

Only recently did Old Sally and Violet begin to experiment with tonics Violet might sell in her tea shop. Root teas. Teas that keep sickness at bay, as well as dark forces. But Old Sally wonders if Savannah is ready for such cures.

She walks in the direction Violet went moments before and falters. For the last twenty-four hours, dizziness has visited her. At first, she thought it was the excitement of Queenie's wedding. Now she realizes it may be the storm.

Once inside the house, she stands in the entryway to steady herself. Then Queenie comes to greet her in the hallway like a sudden gust of wind, if the wind were happy to see someone.

Because of her advanced age, Old Sally is often the center of attention, as if everyone is anticipating her keeling over in front of them. The older she gets, the more her final day crosses her mind. But it doesn't frighten her like it seems to scare them. To Old Sally, it is her reward for living. Her last breath here will be followed by her first breath there—the land of her ancestors.

However, it seems that since she is still breathing, her work in this world is not yet finished. Thank the heavens she is good at waiting. Otherwise, it would be harder than it is. Longevity has burdens, too, as well as lessons—as does everything in life. In the meantime, Old Sally directs an unspoken message to Violet to further test their ability to communicate with their thoughts.

Violet emerges from the kitchen.

Was that you? she asks, without speaking.

Old Sally gives a single nod, and she and Violet exchange a smile. Their connection is getting stronger.

Is there something more we should be doing about this storm right now? Violet asks.

Even our best conjuring spells can't keep this storm away, Old Sally tells her. Although she did create something earlier to try.

The truth is this hurricane is as inevitable as Old Sally's passing. The wind and sea are riled. Once nature sets things in motion, there is nothing humans can do.

Old Sally joins Violet in the kitchen, feeling a sense of urgency.

"With this storm, things be speeding up," Old Sally says aloud. "There are a few things left for me to tell you and now seems the time. Can we talk later?"

Violet agrees. As far as Old Sally knows, Violet's notebook contains the first written record of the Gullah beliefs and potions, as well as the stories going back to when her people first arrived on this island.

Until she began teaching Violet, the stories Old Sally heard when she was young were part of an oral tradition. But Violet's book of Gullah secrets gives her hope that their traditions will live on in written form, too. Tia and Leisha also give her hope. They have Gullah blood in them, and an interest in the old ways.

Old Sally yawns. She naps a lot these days to conserve her energy for what is coming. She tells Violet she needs to lie down, and on the way to her bedroom, she glances at the front door. Someone is about to arrive. The doorbell rings and Rose answers it. Old Sally lingers long enough in the living room to hear that it is Edward's daughter again. She is certain Heather is part of the ill wind blowing in.

Tiredness threatens to overcome her as she continues to her bedroom. She must sleep and gather her strength.

CHAPTER TWENTY-SEVEN

Rose

Seeing Heather at the door reminds Rose of that saying about how bad pennies always turn up. After they last spoke at the tea shop, she imagined she wouldn't hear from Heather again. At least not anytime soon.

"Did you forget something?" Rose asks.

"Let me explain." Heather pushes past her, reminding her of how her mother always insisted on being center stage.

Rose would never walk into someone's home uninvited. Southern manners were bred into her as habitually as brushing her teeth. She rubs her temples with the beginning of a headache.

"This isn't a good time," Rose says. "We're getting ready for a storm here."

Heather doesn't move and readjusts her purse on her arm.

Rose wants her out of the house and steps onto the front porch. Thankfully Heather follows. A bitter smell around the door reminds Rose of the roots Old Sally cooks on the stove for her different spells. Rose crosses her arms, body language for *Go away*. Words Heather doesn't appear to understand.

"First of all, I appreciate you talking to me," Heather begins. "Second of all, I don't think you realize how important it was for me to find you. I never had a family growing up except for my mom and now that she's gone—"

Rose's arms loosen their grip. For the first time that day, Heather appears to have broken character.

"How did my brother meet your mother?" Rose asks, taking advantage of the opportunity.

"She worked for him in Atlanta."

It doesn't surprise Rose that Edward would take advantage of someone under him.

"Did you tell Regina that?" Rose asks.

"I was afraid to," Heather says, which sounds honest enough. "I wasn't sure if they were already together by then."

"That was probably smart," Rose says.

"Well, it didn't work, anyway."

"Why?" Rose asks.

Rose is surprised by her own directness. Directness is not a southern thing.

Heather pauses. Is she revisiting her strategy? Or maybe choosing her words carefully?

"I read the article in the newspaper when the Temple Garden was dedicated," Heather says. "It said you had returned to Savannah after being away for a long time. You sounded like an outsider," she continues. "Someone who might understand my situation."

"Regina didn't understand your situation?"

Heather rolls her eyes. "She threw me out of her apartment."

"Threw you out?" Rose doesn't reveal her wariness. This is more drama than she wants to deal with today or any day.

"She didn't actually touch me," Heather says, "but she strongly suggested that I leave, or she would call the police."

Heather sounds convincing. Not that Rose knows Regina that well, either. But why should she believe anything either woman says? Heather is Edward's daughter. A brother she never trusted. And Regina married her untrustworthy brother. It also makes no sense that Regina would threaten to call the police. From what Rose remembers, Regina has some muscle to her. If anyone were in physical danger, it would be Heather. And why did Regina give Heather her address without even asking her?

"I'm confused," Rose says, uncrossing her arms.

"She thinks I want my father's money," Heather admits.

If Heather is covering up her motives, she sure is sloppy about it. At least in this current version of herself. Besides, isn't Edward's money now Regina's money?

There must be more to this, Rose thinks, feeling even more cautious.

"I didn't know who my father was until six months ago," Heather continues. "When I was a kid and asked my mother, she said he was an anonymous sperm donor who was college educated and athletic."

"Well, he was those things, too," Rose says.

"He was?" Heather smiles and then twists a silver bracelet on her wrist. Is she imagining father-daughter dances and doubles tennis matches?

"I'm athletic, too," she adds. "I haven't gone to college yet, but I plan to."

Rose can't discern if Heather is innocent or cunning or both.

"Edward was a lot like our mother," Rose offers, wondering if Heather has any idea how much she looks like her.

"What was your mother like?" Heather's attention doesn't waver.

A simple search at the library would reveal a wealth of information about Rose's mother *and* her mother's wealth. Newspaper clippings from the society section don't tell the real story of who a person is, but they do offer clues. Given Heather's way of presenting herself, Rose would have thought she had studied Iris Temple for years.

"Look," Rose says. "I can't do this with you right now." She sounds like her mother, a fact that makes her recoil.

While Rose withers, Heather stands taller. It seems the Temple ghosts are back after all, in the form of inherited behaviors. For as long as Rose can remember, her quest was to be nothing like the infamous Iris Temple. Or Edward, either, for that matter. Her mother's prized son. Yet, as much as Rose has tried to get away from them both, it seems they have been personified in Heather.

After going to the bank this morning, she now knows the Temple ruthlessness goes back many, many generations. Documented proof is in the faded ledger in her purse.

Rose softens her voice. "We'll have to do this another time, Heather. A hurricane is coming, and we need to prepare."

A hurricane with the same name as my mother, she thinks.

A flash of anger crosses Heather's face that comes and goes so quickly Rose wonders if she imagined it.

"I need to go back inside," Rose says. She takes a step toward the door and stops, aware that Heather is about to follow her again. "You mentioned coming back after this storm has blown over," Rose says. "Let's do that. We can meet at Violet's Tea Shop and have a talk about your father and grandmother and any other Temple you want to know about."

Instead of retreating, Heather steps forward, blocking her way. It reminds Rose of when Edward cornered her as a girl. Or when her mother lectured her on how she should act. Both made her feel trapped.

Rose extends her arm and takes a step forward, refusing to play the game. "Give me a call after the storm, and we can set up a date." A generous offer on her part. She could be like Regina and threaten to call the police.

Heather takes a step back, and Rose goes inside. She considers locking the door but doesn't want Heather to hear the latch.

Meanwhile, she can feel her presence on the other side. When Heather finally walks away, Rose takes a breath and finds herself hoping that her long-lost niece never returns. Something about this whole mess doesn't add up.

To Rose, the world became more complicated after 9/11. The entire country now lives with a heightened sense of danger. Reminders of how safe or unsafe they are on any given day come in yellow, orange, and red alerts. Here on Dolphin Island, they are probably safe from terrorist attacks. But Rose's trust in humans has lessened.

Violet enters the living room wearing casual shorts and a sleeveless top, as though ready to get to work on storm preparations. "You look upset," she says to Rose.

"Heather was here."

"I thought she went back to Atlanta."

"That's what she said at the tea shop, but then she ended up back here again."

Violet rubs her left shoulder.

"Are you getting a hint of something dangerous?" Rose asks.

"No, I'm not getting anything. That's what's odd. Do you suppose intuition can go on the blink? I got a hit at the tea shop, and then nothing again."

Rose cannot relate to Violet's sensitivity, though she did sometimes see the spirits in the Temple mansion when she was growing up.

"Can you believe all those ghosts we put up with over at the other house?" Rose asks. "It seems the memories still haunt me. I think of them quite often."

"I can't say I've missed that crew," Violet says.

"Me, either," Rose says, thinking again of the ledger in her purse. In a way, that book is full of ghosts, too.

Marrying Max and moving to Wyoming was a way to escape everything the Temple family represented. Rose wanted a new

life, and Max gave her that. Now Rose has given him a *new* life
back.

"You look a thousand miles away," Violet says.

"Two thousand, actually. Can I tell you something unrelated?"
Rose asks.

Violet says she can.

"I feel a little shaky with this storm coming."

"Do you?" Violet says, touching her arm. "I do, too."

"You do?"

Violet nods. "It's important to remember that it may not
amount to anything, though."

"I hope you're right," Rose says.

Queenie joins them near the door. Without thought or plan, the
three of them lock arms like they did when they were Sea Gypsies.
A celebration of lightheartedness.

"Are we having a secret meeting?" Queenie smiles.

Queenie was an honorary member of the Sea Gypsies, the
secret club created by Rose and Violet when they were young.
Rose wonders if Katie's child will grow up to be a Sea Gypsy, too.
The thought pleases her, even if he is a boy.

"Sea Gypsies aren't afraid of storms," Violet says, as though
speaking it will make it so.

"They are absolutely not afraid of storms," Rose says, her tone
perfectly serious.

"Tell that storm to stay the hell away," Queenie says, snapping
her fingers.

"Stay the hell away!" Rose repeats with a smile, her voice raised.

Violet snaps her fingers, too, and says the same, matching
Rose's volume.

They laugh, the three of them snapping their fingers at the
ocean to keep the danger away. As girls, they would have liked
nothing better than a hurricane coming ashore to give their lives
some adventure during the long, dull days of summer. Rose some-

times wonders what happened to that little girl in her. It's like she was never seen again after she left home. Hidden away in the scrapbook pages of her memories.

While Rose could never get close to her mother, Queenie and Old Sally were the people she depended on to love her no matter what. They have never let her down in that regard. Rose feels better thinking these old friends will be with her during the storm. And a small part of her now thinks of it as an adventure.

Max comes in the back door, and they unlock arms as if their playfulness is as secret as the Sea Gypsy handshake. He hands them each a roll of masking tape.

"What's this for?" Rose asks, although she knows perfectly well.

"Taping the windows that don't have storm shutters," he says.

They weathered plenty of storms on their ranch in Wyoming, and none required masking tape.

"I thought we did that already," Rose says.

"There are still a few left upstairs," he tells them. "Iris's ETA is about nine hours from now," he continues. "She'll come ashore somewhere, we don't know where. But we might as well be prepared."

Queenie and Violet leave, and Rose leans into Max's broad shoulder. "Tell me what your gut says. Do you think we're in danger?"

After thirty years of marriage, Rose trusts Max's hunches.

"Honestly?" he asks her.

"Yes, honestly."

Max pauses, his brow furrowed. "Truth is, nobody has any idea what this storm is going to do, but my guess is we're in for a humdinger."

"Then let's get ready for it." Rose thinks of Heather again. She has no idea what Heather is going to do, either. But there's no time to worry about that now. With masking tape in hand, Rose sets off to prepare for their unexpected summer adventure.

CHAPTER TWENTY-EIGHT

Violet

Violet makes sandwiches enough for everyone in case the power goes out. She puts them in a cooler and then packs chips and fruit to go with them. Whatever happens, they will have food.

With a few more minutes of light left, Violet decides to go on a short walk down the beach. She breathes in the salt air, letting it take her tiredness away. After all those years of dreaming about having a different life, it seems she is finally living her dream. Not only of owning her tea shop but having a purpose to her days. A life in which she is learning about her Gullah ancestors from Old Sally and creating a written record.

Though she is half-white, like Queenie, she can relate more to the Gullah side of her family. A side more mysterious than she ever realized. Increasingly, Violet can hear Old Sally's thoughts when the intention is set. A gift she is counting on to continue after Old Sally returns to the ancestors, as her grandmother calls it. And a gift she hopes will make what feels unbearable more bearable.

Darkness falls quickly now. Violet stops before getting to the lighthouse, uncertain of why she even headed in this direction. She usually walks down the beach instead of up. Violet makes an X in the sand before turning around and going back. A ritual that is written in her notebook of Gullah secrets. She isn't sure why the X is essential, except that many of their rituals are related to avoiding lousy luck or attracting good fortune.

Violet glances at the lighthouse before turning around. For years, it faded into the background of her life, as though hidden behind an invisibility cloak, like in the *Harry Potter* books her daughters have read. Then one day she started seeing it again. Violet has done this with people, too. For many years she took her Aunt Queenie for granted until she found out that Queenie was her birth mother. Then memories of her always being there for Violet rushed forward.

The water birds on the beach move frantically along the shore, using the last seconds of daylight to eat their fill. All the while, several pelican formations head north, zigzagging up the coast like an airplane pulling a banner behind to advertise tours of the island. Other than these clues, it would be impossible to imagine a storm on the way. What was it like for her Gullah ancestors who didn't have Doppler radar and advanced warning systems?

Violet remembers the mermaid story Old Sally told her yesterday and hopes that if someone has captured a mermaid they soon return her to the sea.

Home again, Violet is grateful the foundation of the house was raised eight feet during the renovations. A suggestion made by their contractor. With this hurricane, this could be a crucial eight feet. Even a thunderstorm can be dangerous when you live on a barrier island and are exposed to the elements.

Leaving her sandy sneakers on the top step, Violet shakes out the small, colorful rag rug outside the front door and wonders if

Old Sally is up from her nap. Every evening Violet sweeps sand from the wooden floors, something she remembers Old Sally doing when Violet was a girl. Tradition gives her comfort these days. The knowledge that some things carry on, despite death and natural disasters.

The only voices in the kitchen come from the television someone left on in the corner. A different weather reporter talks about a best-case-scenario, which has Iris skirting the coast with winds of 80–100 miles per hour. A storm surge of 4–6 feet. That would have waves breaking against their front steps before returning to the sea.

This is the best case scenario? she asks herself.

Violet goes to check on Old Sally. She knocks gently and then opens her door. Eyes closed, Old Sally lies on the bed. Violet watches for her gentle breathing, the movement of her chest up and down—signs of life. When someone is Old Sally's age, the end is expected. Like the hurricane, it cannot be ignored and falls somewhere on the prediction spectrum between a Watch and a Warning.

"I be awake," Old Sally says, her eyes still closed.

"Did you have another dream?" Violet asks.

Old Sally pats the bed beside her, and Violet comes to sit. When Old Sally opens her eyes, there is a weariness there that Violet hasn't seen before.

"These days, the ancestors come every time I close my eyes," she says.

"Does it scare you?" Violet asks.

"Oh my, no," Old Sally says with a chuckle. "I welcome them."

Violet wonders if she will be like Old Sally when her time comes. Not fearing death but looking forward to it as a family reunion. Old age is a privilege, not a birthright, Violet heard some-where. Not everyone gets to grow old.

"My grandmother came again in the latest dream," Old Sally begins. "She was braiding my hair on the old front porch, and I sat cross-legged a step below her with my favorite rag doll in my lap. It was a brown doll she made me that wore an outfit that was made from the same fabric of her favorite dress," Old Sally continues. "That doll had black buttons for eyes and black yarn stitched on for her hair." Old Sally pauses as though seeing the doll anew. "In the dream, I could feel Granny's breath at my back. Her soft touch working to tame my hair into a braid after rubbing the oil into it that makes it relax."

Violet's scalp tingles.

"You feel her presence, too?" Old Sally asks.

"I do," Violet says, "at least I think I do."

"That be your great-great-grandmother," she says.

Violet soaks in the feeling of another presence in the room. The vibration is like a fan on its lowest setting, except it makes no breeze. The tingling spreads from her scalp into her torso and then down into her arms and legs.

"Why do you think you have so many memories from back then?" Violet asks.

"Because it be close to my time."

Violet lowers her head.

"No, sweet girl," Old Sally says, with a gentleness Violet has come to expect. "Don't be sad for me. I have been here long enough. I am ready for the Great Beyond. More than ready. I overdue."

Violet never thinks of people being overdue, as in late to depart this life. A jar in the kitchen is full of change for when it takes Tia and Leisha longer to finish a library book than the due date allows. Ten cents a day for an overdue book. She wonders what the cost is for an overdue person.

"I'm worried more about me than you," Violet says. "I hate thinking of you not being here anymore."

"But I will be here." Old Sally smooths out the wrinkles on Violet's forehead with her warm, soft touch." *And we can still talk to each other.*

Violet hears the last statement in her thoughts, transmitted on a secret Gullah airwave. A few months ago, she would have never thought it was possible to talk to her grandmother this way. Violet still questions sometimes if she imagines it.

When Violet looks up, Old Sally is watching her.

"What's troubling you?" she asks.

"I hate it when you talk about going," Violet says. "I know you're ready to go and all that, but I've learned so much from you, and I don't know what I'll do without you here to teach me."

"I felt the same way about my grandmother," Old Sally says. "It was much harder on me when she died than anyone else in my family. But after a bunch of years, I finally figured out that this is exactly how nature works," she continues. "We're like flowers that bloom for a while and then fade away to make room for the next blooms."

Violet thinks of the blooms on her African violets at the tea shop. They love the window they sit in front of and bloom for months on end. She likes to think of people flourishing that way if they find the right spot to thrive.

Except for the mother she thought she had lost when she was a little girl, Violet hasn't lost anyone close to her. Jack's mother died a few years ago, but Violet and her mother-in-law didn't have a close connection like she does with Old Sally. Old Sally raised her. Violet lived with her for the first twenty years of her life until she married Jack. Besides Queenie, Old Sally is the most constant presence in her life.

But Violet doesn't want to bloom at Old Sally's expense. "I'm not sure what to say." Words feel inadequate to express the weightiness of the moment.

Old Sally touches her hand. "You don't have to say anything."

"Will you tell me what you need me to do? I mean when the time comes?"

Old Sally says she will. *Though I imagine even if I couldn't, you would know.*

Violet pauses, hearing her thoughts and wondering if this is true.

Moments later, Old Sally sits up. "What's the weather doing?" she asks.

"I guess you could call it the calm before the storm," Violet says. "It's absolutely beautiful out there. A clear and glorious night."

"That will all change soon," Old Sally says.

Violet's left shoulder twitches for the first time in hours, as if waking from a long nap. It has given her mixed signals or no signals all day. Either way, Violet must prepare for what is coming.

CHAPTER TWENTY-NINE

Queenie

Queenie's bedroom is in total disarray from the ceremony the day before. Her wedding gown is thrown over a chair near the far window, along with her red hat, yellow scarf, and purple pumps. Several fans sit in silence. Queenie has been known to thrive on excitement, but this weekend has been too much even for her.

A hurricane is churning out in the Atlantic and according to the weather forecasters has just turned inland. Spud's place up the beach was to have summer renters living there starting this week since he would be living with Queenie after their wedding. But an hour ago, they called to cancel their stay because of the hurricane.

Last week, Queenie cleared half of her walk-in closet for Spud and gave him two drawers in her large dresser. One for his socks and underwear and another for his bow ties. Spud has a bow tie for almost every day of the year and in every color. Queenie has yet to see the fascination, but Spud doesn't understand her loyalty to Oprah, either. She supposes living with each other's weirdness is what marriage is all about.

"Honeypot?" Spud steps out of the bathroom, naked, every gray hair on his head sticking straight up.

"Who are you calling *Honeypot*?" If he weren't so cute Queenie might throw something at him. "Why are you so obsessed with finding me a nickname?"

"I don't know," he says. "Maybe I should just call you Queenie."

"Now there's a novel idea," she quips. "It is my name after all." But in truth, she is not the least bit irritated. She likes how hard he tries to please her. So far in this marriage, she has no complaints. Well, except for the fact that a hurricane named after his ex is threatening to spoil everything.

A knock on the door has Spud ducking back into the bathroom.

Violet enters.

"I need to talk to you," she says.

"You mind if I stay here in my chair?" Queenie asks. "This weekend has tuckered me out."

Violet says she doesn't mind at all and sits on the end of her bed.

"What is it?" Queenie asks. "You look worried."

"It's Old Sally," Violet says. "She's talking about things she doesn't usually talk about."

"Like what?" Queenie sits straighter.

"Like dying."

Queenie bolts from the chair. "Does she think she's dying now? I just saw her a couple of hours ago, and she seemed as good as ever."

"She's fine," Violet insists, "but she's having a lot of dreams about when she was a girl, and her grandmother keeps visiting her in her dreams, too. She seems to think it's a sign."

Queenie calls to Spud in the bathroom. "Can you get out here, please?"

When Spud comes out his hair is combed, and he has a bathrobe tied tightly around his skinny waist. It smells like he got a little overzealous with the aftershave.

Is all that primping in the bathroom for my benefit? She smiles at the thought.

Spud's legs are white and thin and remind her of a chicken's legs, which then reminds Queenie of Kentucky Fried Chicken, and Iris, and the stupid storm heading in their direction.

"What is it, sweet cakes?" Spud says. "You look upset."

"Oh, good heavens," Queenie answers with a reluctant smile. "I am nobody's sweet cake."

Spud greets Violet like they are old friends, which they are. Queenie sometimes forgets how close they were before Spud and Queenie started dating.

"Violet says Mama is talking about dying."

Queenie tells Spud about how hard it will be when her mama passes. She has been her only parent, after all, for her entire life. Her father for sure never claimed her. He only barely claimed Iris, who was his legitimate daughter.

When Spud hears all this, he gives her such a loving and compassionate look that tears spring to her eyes.

"What should we do?" Queenie asks him, dabbing her eyes with a tissue.

He pauses for what feels like a solid minute. "I don't think you'll like what I have to say."

"Tell me." Queenie trusts him to tell her the truth, even if she won't like it.

"I think we should let her go," Spud says.

"Let her go?" Queenie glances at Violet, who to her surprise doesn't appear as shocked as Queenie is. This is the last thing she expected to come out of the mouth of Spud Grainger, who has a hard time letting go of anything. He still has bow ties he wears from back in the sixties.

"What else can we do?" Spud asks.

Queenie puts her hands on her hips. It is all she can do not to scream or cry. She is a big woman after all, with big thoughts and big feelings. Spud knows how much Queenie hates feeling helpless. It is her least favorite feeling in her feeling collection. And with this storm coming she was already heading in that direction. She is tired. And when she gets tired, she is not good at handling anything.

She had hoped to hide all her oversized emotions from Spud for at least the first year of their marriage, but here it is on the second day.

"I just thought you should know," Violet says to them.

"You did the right thing by telling me," Queenie says. "Did she say anything else to you?"

"Only that she is ready to go," Violet says.

Tears rush to Queenie's eyes again. Spud arrives at her side, a look of genuine concern on his freshly shaven face.

"I can't believe I'm crying like this," she says to him, hoping it isn't the "ugly cry."

To her surprise, it feels good to release the stress and worry she has stored up for way too long. The last time she blubbered like this was when those twin towers came down. It was such a sad day, being aware of all those people who would never get to go home again. Life is more difficult than Queenie likes to admit. The truth is, sometimes crying is the sanest thing a person can do when the world gets crazy. Crying or laughing. But Queenie isn't feeling that funny right now.

While Queenie's tears are rare, Spud will openly weep during Hallmark and dog food commercials. Not to mention the Olympics—a Championship Cry Fest that happens without fail every two years. Queenie witnessed tears in his eyes more than once at their wedding, and she had some of her own.

Queenie blows her nose on the handkerchief Spud provides. It has been an emotional two days, and she can't believe she is falling apart now. It doesn't help that a hurricane is bearing down on them. A hurricane bearing the name of her dead nemesis.

In the next moment, a gust of wind rattles Queenie's windows, and the three of them jump as if Hurricane Iris has just offered to give Queenie something new to cry about.

CHAPTER THIRTY

Old Sally

O*nce the dreams start, it won't be long,* Old Sally says to herself.

Dreams change when people get to the end of their life. Or so her grandmother told her. During Sadie's final days, Sally sat by her bedside and listened to her grandmother tell her dreams to her in great detail. Long-gone friends and relatives walked through every scene, as well as many people she had unfinished business with. Sometimes the dreams finished things up for her.

Old Sally's latest dreams have Fiddle playing at a wedding on the beach, his music as beautiful as ever. In the dream, the wedding is the one that she and Fiddle didn't get to have. Her daughter Annabelle is alive and well, in her arms and part of the ceremony. Their silver wedding bands were made from a silver spoon taken from the Temple kitchen by her grandmother. Stolen from the Temples because they stole her son Adam and sent him away so long ago.

Sometimes dreams deliver the only justice to be found during this transition from life to death, and the dreams come regardless of whether they are welcome or not. Those who believe in a spirit world have an easier time with these visitations, her grandmother told her. And Old Sally believes in the spirit world. A world where mysteries live. Not just the ancestors, either, but the Creator who set everything in motion and watches over all of them. The Gullah way is to see everything in creation as sacred. The plants, the trees, the animals. Everything on land and sea.

Love is the most sacred thing of all, she tells herself, thinking of the people she loves.

Up from her nap, she looks at herself in the round mirror over the sink in the bathroom. Sometimes she can't believe how many wrinkles she has. Like the rings of a tree revealing her age. But it is her eyes that say the most. The soul's windows, they've been called. If that's true, her soul looks hopeful and sincere, though tired.

The wind is finally picking up outside. Not much. But enough to hint at what's to come. Though the weathermen haven't committed to the exact path the storm will take, Old Sally already knows the outcome. It will come here to the island, and perhaps then Iris will help Old Sally with her transition, just like Old Sally helped her two years before. Except this time, Iris will be in the form of a hurricane.

CHAPTER THIRTY-ONE

Rose

I s it Rose's imagination or has the wind started blowing harder? Max and Jack have stored all the outdoor furniture in the garage and closed the storm shutters on the main house and cottage. Now they stack sandbags on the porch to put in front of the door. Water can do more damage than hundred-mile-an-hour winds, reports say, so whether they stay or leave they need to prepare for a possible storm surge.

Weather fascinates Rose. When they lived out West, she learned to pay attention to it or suffer the consequences. The Rocky Mountains served as a magnet for extreme weather. Tornados. Blizzards. Thundersnow. Twisters that took aim at entire neighborhoods, scattering houses like dice on a board game. And thunderstorms so fierce lightning shot sideways with nothing to ground it.

However, a hurricane appears to be a different beast. Hurricanes don't miss one house and then grab the next in a flash of fate. Hurricanes churn for days out over warm ocean waters to gather strength. High winds team together with a tidal surge to destroy whatever is in its path. Thankfully, they are also slow enough to allow the time for people to get away.

After filling several water jugs in case they lose power and water, Rose goes back to the cottage to rest for a moment. She lifts the faded ledger from her purse and sits on her bed. It smells like the bank vault and paper molecules breaking down and deteriorating. She turns more pages, being careful with the bindings, which look like they could easily break apart. Near the back, she finds notations written in a kind of code. Is it a manifest? She wonders how anything so old could be of any importance today. Yet, something about the book feels valuable.

Max comes into the bedroom and turns on the television. "Look," he says.

The mayor of Savannah is standing in front of town hall suggesting people evacuate Savannah and the surrounding islands.

Max's face has a look that Rose wishes she hadn't seen. Is that fear?

"Are we going to evacuate?" Rose asks.

Max shrugs. The old Max. The one who wears cowboy boots and doesn't share what he thinks unless she pries it out of him.

"But where will we go?" Rose asks. "If we get on 95 going north, we'll probably get stuck in a standstill. Queenie said it was already backed up yesterday when she and Spud were coming back from Hilton Head."

The news of the evacuation spreads fast given the sounds of the voices in the kitchen.

"I guess we'd better go see what the others are thinking," Max says finally.

Rose agrees.

In the kitchen of the main house, everyone talks at once, offering different solutions. It is the first time they've had to make any group decisions other than chore lists. Do they go separately or together? Which cars do they take? How much do they have room for? And—mainly—where do they go?

"Maybe we should vote," Rose says, raising her voice above the others.

"Well, we don't all have to do the same thing, either," Violet reminds them.

"I think we should stick together," Queenie says, looking at Violet.

"No matter what, we've got to keep Katie and the baby safe," Angela says.

Max agrees.

"I was in Charleston in 1989 after Hurricane Hugo hit," Jack begins. "The bridge going to Sullivan's Island and Isle of Palms was destroyed, and people couldn't return to their homes for weeks," he continues. "I don't want to get stuck on the mainland and not be able to get back."

"I agree with Jack," Max says. "We need to be here to fix any damage right away, as well as keep everybody safe. We've collected supplies for two days," he continues, "including a stack of tarps in the garage in case the roof is damaged."

"I appreciate how prepared we are," Rose says to Max. "But we don't want to do anything unwise." Sometimes the cowboy in Max does things regular people consider risky.

At that moment Rose realizes how easy it is to let the men make all the crucial decisions. The thought goes contrary to her Smith College days. Yet, it fits right in with the culture she was raised in.

"What do you think we should do?" Rose asks Old Sally.

Everyone turns. Old Sally is the only person who appears calm in the middle of the chaos. They wait in silence for her to speak, and when she does, her voice is softer than Rose expects, though it is still strong.

"This old house has withstood plenty of storms over the

hundred years I've been here," she says. "But we can't afford to put anyone in danger."

Violet's girls interrupt with the latest news.

"They're saying the evacuation is now mandatory," Leisha says. "All barrier islands on the Georgia and South Carolina coastline."

"And anyone who refuses has to leave the name of their next of kin with authorities." Tia's eyes widen, and Violet crosses the kitchen to calm her.

It is agreed. The next hour will be spent getting ready to evacuate. Before the group disperses, Max tells everyone to limit their things to a single suitcase. A suggestion that has everyone talking again.

Back at the cottage, Rose fills one suitcase with a few clothes, an extra pair of shoes, and loose photos she pulled from the family scrapbook, along with a couple of pieces of jewelry her mother gave her when she graduated college. Rose lovingly called these pieces her nest egg. It is a troubling exercise to discern, after a life-time of collecting things, what to put into a single suitcase.

In a separate, smaller bag she packs dog food for Lucy and Ethel, as well as bowls and two leashes. She returns the Temple ledger to her purse—she doesn't want to risk losing it until she figures out its importance. If indeed it is important at all.

An hour later, they stand at the door ready to leave. Twelve people with twelve suitcases. Three dogs, two cats in a carrier, and a pet turtle in a small dry aquarium. They get outside, and as soon as they lock the front door, Max and Jack pull sandbags in front of it. As they stand in the dunes, Rose looks at the house that has become her home over the last few months. She takes a mental photograph in case it isn't here when they get back.

The night is dark with thick cloud cover. No stars or moon to light the way. The ocean tide can be heard in the distance as they take the walkway through the dunes to the cars. Something about the storm coming at night has Rose unnerved. It is one thing to see a storm coming and wind whipping at trees. It is quite another to only hear it.

In his truck, Max leads the caravan of four cars. They plan to drive inland for an hour and stay at a motel they have booked for the evening. Rose is in the pickup, their two dogs in the back seat already drooling their excitement. In the back are water jugs and the food, along with a chainsaw, a canister of gasoline, and different tools Max might need. She trusts his instincts. He helped them survive many blizzards in Wyoming and a flash flood threatening their home.

The first few blocks the traffic isn't bad, but then everything comes to a stop at the two-lane road that will take them off the island. The road runs along the waterway, with steep shoulders down to the marsh. A steady line of red brake lights leads the way for them to exit the island. At most, six hundred people live on this barrier island. But when they are all in their cars, it seems like more.

Spud and Queenie and Old Sally are in Spud's ten-year-old Toyota directly behind them. Old Sally can be seen holding onto the Jesus bar despite their snail-like speed. Even though Spud could afford something much more expensive, he has not invested in a new car. Queenie is in the middle of the back seat, already talking. It is hard to imagine Queenie taking a back seat to anyone, except for Old Sally.

In the caravan behind Spud are Angela and Katie, followed by Jack and Violet and the girls, with Jake the turtle in the back window.

"Why are we stopped?" Rose asks Max.

"Not sure."

Rose remembers her last trip home to Wyoming after her mother's funeral. Max picked her up at the airport. She would never have guessed when she presented the option of moving back to Savannah that he would have taken her up on it so readily.

As many cars are behind them as ahead of them.

"Should we be worried?" Rose asks Max.

Max shrugs, his eyes staring straight ahead. He doesn't show his fear often, but the look that passed between him and Rose in the bedroom earlier still haunts her.

"What if we can't get off the island?" Rose asks, wishing she had an alcoholic beverage of some kind. Or at least a cup of coffee.

"If we can't get off the island, we'll go home." He sounds slightly irritated. Or maybe that's his worried tone.

"But what about the storm?" Rose asks.

He pauses. "We'll manage."

Rose's worry intensifies. High winds. Storm surge. Katie.

"The last thing we need is for Katie to go into labor," Rose says to Max.

He drums the steering wheel with his thumbs as if this thought hasn't occurred to him. Meanwhile, the line of traffic moves like inchworms out for a leisurely stroll. The truck finally comes to a stop.

The truck idles. Ten minutes pass. People start to turn off their cars. Max puts on the parking brake, although the terrain is perfectly flat, and turns off the engine.

"I'm going to walk up there and see if I can see anything."

"I'll come, too," Rose says.

Windows down, they get out of the car, telling Lucy and Ethel to stay. They drool their disappointment. Then Rose walks back to tell Spud and Queenie what they are about to do.

"Catching another ride?" Queenie asks when Rose shows up at the window. Despite her joke, she looks concerned.

"We're going to walk up ahead and see what we can find out," Rose says.

"It be too late for that," Old Sally says, looking toward the horizon as if seeing the future. She appears both diminutive and formidable.

"You know something you aren't telling us, Mama?" Queenie asks from the back.

"Just that we be staying here on this island, storm or no storm."

Rose and Queenie trade looks. Neither are willing to question her.

"Well, we might as well stretch our legs anyway since we're stuck in this line," Rose says.

Everyone mills around among the long line of parked cars. The only person in their makeshift caravan who is still in the vehicle is Old Sally. Violet joins Rose to go check out what is up ahead. They have barely talked since the evacuation began. As they walk, the warm breeze coming off the ocean has a sudden chill to it. Rose zips up her light jacket as though her mother—in the form of Hurricane Iris—has suddenly brushed against her.

CHAPTER THIRTY-TWO

Violet

During the evacuation, the lane coming onto the island is closed, and they walk down that side of the road. Violet holds her left shoulder, questioning its silence. This has never happened before when she has wished her shoulder would give her a sign.

The air is filled with the smell of salt marsh. A pungent mixture of land and sea that makes Violet's nose itch. The marsh creates an ecosystem unique to this area. The salt marshes are regularly flooded with seawater during high tide, servicing the clams, mussels, and snails, as well as various fish that come and go with the waves. Fiddler crabs, ghost crabs, and blue crabs feed on the bacteria in the muds, creating a feast for the seagulls, snowy egrets, and great blue herons. A banquet put on every day by nature.

Along the edges of the marsh are salt-stunted oaks, a few loblolly pines, and scrubby saw palmettos. At low tide, the water gives way to pluff mud and seven-foot-tall spartina grass. But water is coming in with the tide, and all that mud will soon disappear. Later the sea will shift again and call her salty presence home.

Rose points and Violet turns to look. A giant egret flies by on ghostly white wings, its coarse call spreading the word of something coming.

Meanwhile, Violet nods a greeting to people standing by their cars as they wait for the limbo to lift.

"I never noticed what an interesting mixture of people live on this island," Rose says.

Violet agrees. "The diversity is one of the things I love about living here," she begins. "As many blacks as whites. As many rich people as poor and everything in between," she continues. "All ages, too, ranging from newborns to Old Sally, the only centenarian on Dolphin Island."

"It has a totally different feeling to it than Savannah," Rose says. "I love living here."

"I love that you love it," Violet says, as they lock arms.

Violet's Gullah ancestors settled this island and named it after the dolphins living in the waters off the coast. White masters didn't want to put up with the mosquitos, the heat, or being so far away from the luxuries of civilization, so they let the Gullah people live here mostly undisturbed. Her ancestors made their own fishing nets, wove sweetgrass baskets, made their own clothes. Grew indigo, sugarcane, and rice, as well as all sorts of vegetables.

Many of the stories that Old Sally has shared with Violet include Gullah superstitions and the use of folk magic—potions and spells—to protect and heal. She wonders how much Gullah history Rose knows. Someday she will tell her, and maybe the island will come even more alive for her, too.

Without the occasional streetlight, they would have trouble seeing along this stretch. The island didn't have electricity until Old Sally was a grown woman. She told Violet stories about how strange it was to have a light bulb that lit a room instead of a lantern. Her mother and grandmother sometimes stared at the bare bulb in the evenings like they were witnessing someone walk on water. Miss Temple took pride in the fact that the Temples were the first family in Savannah to get electricity. It came to the island years after that.

An orange traffic cone is placed in the middle of the road where Max has stopped, giving Violet and Rose time to catch up. They unlock arms. On the edge of the marsh, a tree has fallen across the road, bringing down a power line with it. A sheriff's deputy is on his radio. When he finishes, Max asks him how long it will be before the road is passable again.

"Two hours," the deputy says. He is a young black man who Violet doesn't recognize. His uniform is perfectly pressed. He is someone who takes pride in his appearance.

Max thanks him. "We might as well go home and try again later," Max says to Violet and Rose.

"We can't evacuate?" Violet asks, aware that Old Sally already predicted this.

"Not for at least two hours," Max says.

Violet looks at Rose. Are they thinking the same thing? There is no other way off Dolphin Island. For years, islanders petitioned for a second bridge so what happened up the coast on Sullivan's Island and Isle of Palms during Hugo didn't happen here, too. But government funds are slow to come to this part of the country.

Walking back to the car, people ask them what they found out. "Two hours," Violet says.

Various moans come from the cars, and engines start. Exhaust fumes mingle with the smell of the salt marsh, making Violet feel a tad nauseous.

"Let's go home," Violet tells Queenie and Spud. "A tree and a downed power line are blocking the road. They hope to have it cleared in a couple of hours."

"Sweet Jesus," Queenie says, her eyes wide. "Does that mean we can't leave the island?"

Violet reassures her that everything will be fine, though at this moment, she has doubts.

"What does your shoulder say?" Queenie asks Violet, as though consulting an oracle.

Violet gives Queenie a quick shrug. "Nothing to report."

Queenie exhales as though this is good news.

Cars begin making three-point turns, which Violet practiced here on the island before getting her driver's license and has never used. She is relieved that it is Jack who turns the car around, not her, as they head back toward home. Now the traffic jam faces the other direction. She doesn't often view their island at such a slow pace. It is interesting to note how things haven't changed much since she was a girl and rode the school bus to the mainland and observed her world.

The main intersection on the island contains a convenience store that also houses a tiny post office in one corner, as well as a back wall that carries beach balls, flip-flops, and T-shirts with DOLPHIN ISLAND written on the front and either a dolphin or a lighthouse on the back. A seafood restaurant called Dolphin Shrimp is next door and is only open from Memorial Day to Labor Day. Alongside the restaurant is a gas station with two pumps that are currently out of gas. Violet goes to Savannah for groceries, gas, and the post office, as most islanders do.

Back at the house, they gather again to talk about Plan B. It feels anticlimactic to be here.

"Do we try again?" she asks Jack.

"Two hours was probably a best-case scenario," Jack says. "I'd be surprised if they get that mess untangled by morning."

Max agrees.

"But isn't the storm supposed to make landfall before then?" Queenie asks, holding onto Spud's arm.

No one answers.

Violet turns to Old Sally. Every time Violet looks at her, she seems smaller somehow, and older.

"That storm be the least of our worries," Old Sally says.

A moment later Katie lets out a loud moan, doubling over from the pain.

A flash of panic crosses Angela's face, and Rose steps to Katie's side. Meanwhile, Katie looks down at her belly as though an alien is about to burst out of her skin.

"Maybe it's false labor pains," Violet says, purposely sounding calm. "I had those a lot with Tia."

Katie looks instantly relieved, as does Rose, and the relief passes to Angela.

"That's what it is," Angela says, giving a convincing look to Katie. Nobody mentions the fact that they couldn't get off the island if they wanted to. Not to a hospital or a birthing unit. It is a time to stay calm and endure.

"Heaven help us if that sweet baby comes during a hurricane," Queenie says.

"We'll be fine," Violet says, turning toward Queenie, her expression relaying the message to not alarm Katie and Angela. It is Violet's opinion that babies need to come into this world with love surrounding them, not fear, and the concern in the room is growing.

How people enter and leave this life fascinates Violet. Old Sally calls it a threshold. She regrets she missed Miss Temple's passing. She would have liked to be a part of Old Sally helping Miss Temple transition. Old Sally describes herself as a midwife for the dying. Perhaps she can be one for the living, too, and deliver this baby if it decides to come.

Violet remembers the bluebird on the rocker. A sign that company was coming. At first, Violet thought the bird was announcing Heather. But could it have been announcing the baby, too?

Katie rubs her belly, Harpo at her feet looking up. At least if they are real labor pains, they aren't close together yet. Hopefully, the road to the mainland will be open soon.

Violet catches Old Sally watching her, perhaps reading the tea leaves of her mind.

What? Violet asks her. Their unspoken conversations are a kind of underground railroad. Thoughts safely transported to their destination.

We must keep everyone calm, Old Sally answers.

How do we do that? Violet says.

We be examples, Old Sally says.

Whether a baby is coming or a hurricane—or both—they are in for a long night.

"Anybody hungry?" Violet asks.

The response is animated.

Violet unpacks the sandwiches she made before they left to eat when they reached the motel. They forego formality and eat standing at the island in the kitchen.

After eating, Old Sally suggests that everyone get some rest, even though it is only eight o'clock. Tia and Leisha look at their mom, questioning if this could possibly pertain to them, too. The thought of going to bed now doesn't appeal to Violet, either, but she knows Old Sally is right. If the storm is coming at three or four, it would be nice to have slept some before the night gets interesting. Violet yawns with the knowledge that her body could actually use the rest. It has been an unusually busy weekend.

Meanwhile, Old Sally is already in her bedroom. Whatever is coming, she appears to know she needs her full energy. Violet trusts she is right. Others leave, thanking Violet for the sandwiches. Finally, it is only Violet, Queenie, and Spud in the kitchen.

"There's no way I could sleep now," Queenie says. "Anybody up for a game of Twister in honor of the hurricane?"

Spud laughs. "How about a game of Hearts in the bedroom?" he suggests with a wink.

With this storm on the way, Violet has forgotten that there are newlyweds in the house. She kisses each of them on the cheek as they say their goodnights and go upstairs.

Left alone in the quiet kitchen, Violet washes and dries the last of the dishes and puts them away. This is her favorite time of day, the hour before bedtime when she can look back and see what she accomplished that day. But this hasn't been an ordinary day.

Being turned away at the bridge was distressing, knowing that they are trapped on the island. At least temporarily. Then Katie's false or possibly real labor pains. Violet can't imagine what is to come. A sudden gust of wind rattles the shutters as if to confirm that the night has only just begun.

CHAPTER THIRTY-THREE

Queenie

Queenie watches in disbelief as Spud puts on his pajamas and gets in bed like it is any other night.

"How in the world can you think of sleeping with Iris rattling our windows?" Queenie asks.

"Old Sally is right to tell us to get some rest," he says. "It's going to be a long night."

"This is not how I thought I'd be spending my honeymoon," Queenie says, a pout threatening to form.

"Come lay down next to me, Buttercup." Spud opens the covers and pats the bed.

"Where in heaven are you getting these names?" Queenie asks. "Is there a book somewhere called *Lame Nicknames to Call the Woman You Love?*"

As soon as she hears the words, Queenie regrets saying them. Queenie doesn't know much about relationships, but it seems that apologies are a big part of them. She tells Spud she's sorry. Sarcasm has never looked good on her. In fact, she has never known anyone it looked good on. Iris Temple perfected it to the point that she could cut you wide open with a few choice words, leaving you to bleed out on one of the Oriental carpets, the blood not even clashing with the design.

During the thirty-five years Queenie lived with Iris, there were a million things done to Queenie that would have warranted an apology. The correcting. The criticizing. The condescending looks. Sometimes downright meanness. Scheduling events on Queenie's birthday so Queenie couldn't take a day off. Making Queenie take multiple trips to the bank or post office on any given day, instead of letting her combine trips. The fact of the matter was that Iris Temple loved ordering people around.

But she would never have apologized even if her life depended on it, Queenie thinks.

It takes a certain amount of humility to know that you can be wrong about things or to admit that you can hurt people, even if you don't mean to. Iris, however, seemed to enjoy gutting people on occasion. Nothing accidental about it.

Spud accepts Queenie's apology, and they kiss. Love at sixty is the best kind of love. No time to waste or take things for granted. And who cares if they don't have the bodies of twenty-year-olds. The biggest surprise is how much passion Queenie stored up for so long. Thankfully, Spud doesn't seem to mind making up for all those years they weren't together.

Queenie remembers the weekly trips she took with Iris to the Piggly Wiggly where Spud worked. She not only judged that book by its cover, but she put him in the wrong section of the library, too. A section called *Not Interested.*

Boy was I wrong, Queenie thinks.

They kiss again. When Spud unhooks her plus-size bra to view what he calls her "chocolate truffles," she gets a hot flash unlike any before. The heat forces her to rush to the balcony and step outside, but not before grabbing the light robe on the back of her chair to cover her nakedness. The warm breeze greets her, and Queenie fans the flames prickling up her arms and neck.

Spud steps out onto the balcony with her, his pajama top blowing in the wind and revealing his pale chest, her kimono revealing a glimpse of her untethered breasts. A photo opportunity for the cover of a geriatric, interracial romance novel if ever there was one. Queenie silently scolds herself for comparing him to Denzel in a moment like this. Who cares if the man of her dreams is a different color? It is what's in his heart that matters.

"You okay, honey bun?" Spud asks.

"I can't believe how riled up I am over this storm," Queenie says, fanning herself with both hands. "Can you believe the day after our wedding we are dealing with a hurricane? A hurricane with the same name as your ex-girlfriend and my deceased half sister?"

Queenie knows she is bringing up Iris and this storm a lot, but she can't seem to get over the coincidence of it. If Iris somehow found a way to transform from a ghost into a natural disaster to destroy Queenie's life she would do it.

"Don't panic," Spud says.

"I'm not panicking," Queenie answers. Heat climbs up her face and neck, and she bites her lip.

A gust of wind grabs at her robe and the porch light illuminates the dune grasses swaying in the breeze. A figure in white stands on the walkway below.

Is that Iris's ghost visiting to rub it in? Queenie wonders.

She has no patience for apparitions at this moment. Real or imagined. She retrieves her glasses from the pocket of her robe and puts them on, letting her vision focus. Thankfully, it isn't a ghost after all. It is Old Sally standing on the walkway, looking out at the dark sea. Her long white nightgown blows in the wind, as well as the shawl that is wrapped around her shoulders, giving her an ethereal look. No wonder Queenie thought she was a ghost.

"Mama?" Queenie calls from the balcony, but Old Sally doesn't hear her.

"What's she doing?" Spud asks Queenie.

"Standing on the walkway looking out at the ocean," Queenie says. "I doubt she can see a thing."

"Maybe she's listening," Spud says. "Should I go check on her?"

"Wait. It looks like she's talking to somebody," Queenie says, squinting her eyes behind her glasses.

"Who would she be talking to?" Spud asks.

Queenie leans over the small balcony. "Nobody I can see."

Old Sally is always doing peculiar things. Peculiar, at least, to someone who isn't familiar with the Gullah ways.

A chill climbs Queenie's arms that feels wonderful after so much heat. She can't shake the feeling that something big is about to happen. Big, as in life-changing. A plus-size adventure.

"Let's go back inside and go to bed," Spud tells her.

"Spud, honey, do you think we'll be okay?" She turns to face him.

"Yes, my dearest."

Dearest, she can handle. It's all the food nicknames she has a hard time stomaching. Plus, they make her hungry.

"Are you sure?" Queenie asks.

He puts an arm around her. "In all probability, we'll be fine," he says.

"In all probability?" Queenie doesn't like the sound of that. "What do you mean by fine?"

Spud looks confused.

Voices rise from the kitchen. Their housemates must be gathering again, and it sounds like the television is on. Soon, Queenie will talk to her mama and get her inside, but first, she and Spud will join the others. Animated voices mean something is going on.

Downstairs they watch the latest coordinates of Hurricane Iris, which are being given on the television screen. Iris has been upgraded to a Category 4 storm with the potential to be a Category 5, which could have catastrophic results. Hugo was a Category 4, and it took years for people to recover from the destruction. If they ever did.

Graphics show the latest predictions of where Iris will come ashore. Bright red arrows point to her destination like a bull's-eye on the map of the southeastern United States. Dolphin Island is ground zero.

CHAPTER THIRTY-FOUR

Old Sally

The storm makes Old Sally agitated. It has been impossible to sleep. She stands outside, her nightgown flapping in the wind. The waves crash against the shore in the darkness. The chaos from the sea churns inside her. She holds a hand over her heart and can feel it beating faster than usual. Forces are aligning that she has never experienced. This may be the type of storm that comes once a century. Or maybe once every two hundred years. Perhaps Old Sally's ancestors never saw a storm like this in their lifetimes. But it is Old Sally who is called to witness it now.

If the road leading off the island is clear, perhaps they should drive inland as quickly as they can, ignoring speed limits as they try to outrun Iris. Yet, at the same time, she realizes that everyone will be trying to do that. Best to be in a stronger structure. Old Sally has never felt safe in a car given how Fiddle died, as well as her daughter Maya who was killed here on the island.

In the time Old Sally has been standing here, the wind has ratcheted up its power another notch. These aren't the calm ocean breezes that air out a soul. These are winds that come to destroy. Not because it is angry, but because it is what nature does. It destroys and renews. Even the strongest Gullah folk magic must bow to nature.

An owl hoots in the live oak next to the porch and Old Sally turns toward it with alarm.

To the Gullah people, a hooting owl is a bad omen. A bad omen is the last thing they need on a night like this. Old Sally pulls from her memory what her grandmother taught her. If she is outside and barefoot, she can counteract the evil by pointing a finger at the owl to cancel out its power. Old Sally tosses off her sandals, doing as her grandmother taught her. With silent wings, the owl flies away. She relaxes her shoulders.

Meanwhile, the sea smells different somehow. Saltier. A more pungent version of itself. Tiny particles of sand cling to Old Sally's lips. The dune grasses begin to dance, while the clouds periodically reveal the stars and moon behind. Celestial witnesses to a tempest that from their perspective is a grain of sand. The wind lets out a low growl like a lion cub finding its voice. A voice with plenty of room to grow.

When faced with a storm of this magnitude, her ancestors would have sought refuge on the other side of the island. The highest point is a rise near the cemetery where the old abandoned church sits, falling in on itself, among the live oaks. It is where their old village was before people left for the mainland. Not because of storms, but to find work and raise families because the island could no longer support them. The second highest point is the lighthouse.

Ancestors clamor for Old Sally's attention. Spirits, not ghosts. Never ghosts. Or hags. Hags possess you and don't let you go. They are like the past that you can't get rid of. Guilt and shame ride a body until it is tormented thoroughly. All used up.

Spirits are good. Benevolent. Helpful. Old Sally could use help now. The others look to her for wisdom, though she doesn't feel that wise.

An ancient weariness comes over her. Exhaustion that comes from living a long time and being ready to go. Life is precious. Yes. But life isn't all there is. The time spent with the ancestors is sacred, too. With death also comes renewal. A different part of the same journey.

The past comes in like the tide. Old Sally remembers when she was a girl and sat by the deathbed of her Grandpa Joe, Granny Sadie's husband. A roomful of relatives and friends waited by his side, singing softly, sending prayers to get heaven ready for him. It was high summer. With candles burning, it was stifling hot in Grandpa Joe's room. This was in the house her grandmother used to live in before she moved in with Sally's family.

The night he died, everyone held paper fans that moved the air around to little good. Paper fans that to Sally looked like butterflies filling the room. Every now and again Sally would feel the wind from their wings. Her grandmother held a young Sally in her lap. Sweat mixed with tears rolled down her grandmother's face. Sally traced their path and tasted their salty essence. Tears were nothing to be afraid of, her grandmother told her. Nor was grief. Grief meant you had loved well. Grief meant you were alive. Mourning was a regular part of living. A necessary part of being alive.

A hand on her shoulder pulls Old Sally away from the past and back into the here and now. She turns to see Queenie's new husband.

"Queenie sent me to check on you," Spud says, standing close enough to be heard. "Anything I can do for you?"

Old Sally shakes her head no. "Tell my daughter not to worry."

"She's worried about everything right now," he says. "But mainly this storm."

His gray hair lifts with the wind like wings that might lift him into the night.

"Tell her I'll be right in," she says, patting his arm.

Spud nods and then leaves.

People treat her like a child these days. Always checking in on her to make sure she's okay. Checking to make sure she hasn't fallen out of bed, or some such nonsense. Old Sally has been getting up and out of bed for over a hundred years. They need to trust that she has gotten the hang of it by now. Old age doesn't make a person automatically senile. Though it does make a person frail when bones get this old. She understands their concern. But people get caught up in the number of years she's been on this earth instead of their experience with her. They mean well, she knows. And with this storm coming she must admit she feels vulnerable, too. A strong wind could blow her over, that's true. But if she is to leave this world by way of a hurricane, then so be it. She will move on any way she can.

When her grandmother died, many years after Grandpa Joe, people said it was the most peaceful crossing they had ever witnessed. Like Old Sally, her grandmother was ancient and ready to go. In the last year of her life, she passed on everything she could to Old Sally.

A tear rolls down her face, the wind catching it and tossing it away. Human tears are powerful in potions. But now isn't the time for making spells. It is time to let life do as life does.

Can you hear me, Grandmother? Old Sally asks.

Goosebumps come. A sign that a spirit is near. A vision comes, too. Her grandmother stands in the dunes, untouched by the wind.

Remember what I taught you, she says.

Old Sally pauses. Is this real? Or maybe she hears what she wants to hear. Needs to hear. Her grandmother's scars from the out-of-control fire in the Temple kitchen so long ago are illuminated by the moonlight. They look somehow beautiful.

You taught me so much, Old Sally says. *What part do you want me to remember?*

You be solid. It's the ground that be shaky, her grandmother says.

Old Sally narrows her eyes, reaching for understanding. Leave it to her grandmother to pose a riddle from the Afterlife.

What do you mean? That makes no sense, Old Sally says.

Her grandmother doesn't answer, and in the seconds that follow, her image fades away. What is she to remember? Looking out over the dark landscape, Old Sally feels utterly alone.

CHAPTER THIRTY-FIVE

Rose

Though Rose hasn't had a drink for over a decade, she wants one now. Perhaps a glass of red wine, or a vodka tonic with a slice of lime. It is hard to say what beverage is better suited for a hurricane. Perhaps both. One after the other. Instead, she goes into the kitchen to make a pot of coffee. The digital clock says it is after midnight, 12:34 to be exact. Spud waves from the stairway as he returns to Queenie's room. She imagines Queenie has sent him to check on Old Sally. Something they all do these days.

They are opting to stay in the big house tonight instead of their cottage to keep everyone together. They are on the pull-out sofa, the dogs on the floor nearby. The house is quiet except for the sounds accompanying the storm. The wind is steady and slowly growing in power. Palm fronds beat against the side of the house like a drumroll announcing the main event. Every now and again Rose hears something hit the house. Things left unsecured on the island. A plastic bucket clatters through the back patio. When she looks out back, an aluminum lawn chair flies through the air, looking like something from the tornado scene in *The Wizard of Oz*. Will she see her mother riding a bicycle next, a basket on the back for when she steals Toto?

In the past, Max has slept through blizzards and crackling thunderstorms that had Rose on her knees praying to the saints of her childhood. However, something is different with this hurricane. He is wide awake and wanting coffee, too.

Rose pours two cups and retrieves the faded ledger from her purse, handing coffee to Max and then curling up in a side chair. With all the excitement of the storm and Katie's false labor pains— at least they hope they are false—Rose hasn't had time to further explore the old journal. The musty smell causes her to rub her nose and Ethel the dog sneezes. Rose opens the book somewhere in the middle and tries to read the ornate cursive writings from the 1820s, written by Rose's great-great-grandfather, give or take a "great." A portrait of him was at the end of the hallway near her room in the Temple mansion. A stern-looking patriarch if there ever was one, who had the Temple nose. In the portrait, he wore one of the swords Edward played Cowboys and Indians with when they were young. Not that cowboys carried swords usually, but to Edward, anything that let him have power over her was fair play.

Rose thinks of Heather, who also possesses the Temple nose. The more Rose reflects, the more Heather showing up this weekend doesn't seem like an accident. Like the storm, it feels like a convergence. Or in the case of the ledger, a kind of reckoning. A time to take stock of the Temple wreckage.

Rose turns another page, reading a mystery set in the past. A more readable script follows. Lists of numbers. Notations about property deeds, including a rice plantation in Charleston and a property in Richmond, Virginia. Another page lists investments into tea farms in India. More numbers. More names of people who were property.

Rose's face turns warm, but already she is less shocked. Did no one think that slavery wasn't a good thing? Or that in a hundred years or so it might be considered evil? These were her ancestors. Elite southerners. Owners of slaves. Who for whatever reason crossed a vast ocean to forge their way in a new world. *And make money,* she thinks. The Temples have always been good at making money and keeping money. Old money.

When Rose left Savannah after marrying Max at twenty-one years of age, she didn't want any part of the Temple money, and her mother was happy to oblige. At various times, Rose and Max struggled to keep their ranch in Wyoming going, and Rose had a certain amount of pride about their struggle. But in the end, it was her mother's last will and testament that enabled them to come back to Savannah. Would she have ever returned otherwise?

Rose closes the ledger. What exactly is she searching for? If the book contains more secrets, she hasn't found them. To what good are the secrets of dead people, anyway? At some point, the scandals don't matter anymore. Rose wonders now why she went to that old bank vault anyway. Then she remembers what Red told her. Edward was looking through these same papers a few days before he died. Why? What was he looking for? And what is the significance of Edward's daughter showing up literally on their doorstep?

Queenie enters the kitchen, looking wide awake. "I thought you were going to try to get some sleep like the others," she says to Rose.

"It didn't work. You, either?"

"Not a wink," Queenie says. "And Spud is sawing logs like he works at a lumberyard."

"Coffee?" Rose asks.

"No, thanks." Queenie points to the journal. "What's that?"

"I thought it was another Book of Secrets," Rose says. "But it appears to be a list of assets and property."

"Sounds like something that could help you sleep," Queenie says.

"You'd think," Rose says, "but this storm has me wired."

"Me, too." Queenie sits on a kitchen stool.

"So, how's married life?" Rose asks, giving her coffee another stir.

"Too soon to tell," Queenie says. "At least I haven't killed him yet."

"Nothing like a hurricane to put stress on a new relationship," Rose says.

"No kidding," Queenie says, her face serious.

"What's up?" Rose asks.

Their dog Lucy has a fondness for Queenie and ambles over to greet her in the kitchen. At first, Queenie didn't welcome her attention, but now she seems much more at ease. She bends down to pet her.

"Have you ever noticed that I've never owned a dog or cat?"

Rose pauses. Considering everything else going on, this seems an odd question. "You know, to be honest, it never occurred to me."

"Of course, your mother would have never allowed a pet, anyway," Queenie says.

Rose agrees. Her mother wasn't fond of animals. It seemed she wasn't fond of anything living. People tested her patience. Animals served no purpose except to be eaten. It wasn't until Rose moved out of the house that she had her first cattle dog at the ranch. Lucy looks up at Rose, as if hearing her thoughts.

"But even if I had wanted a pet," Queenie begins again. "I could never get past knowing that I would probably lose them at some point. I didn't think I could bear losing something that I loved."

"Is that what this is about? Are you afraid of losing Spud?"

Queenie's eyes fill with tears.

Rose doesn't expect such a robust show of emotion from Queenie and immediately stands and hugs her broad shoulders.

"Oh, Queenie. It's okay," she says, thinking how interesting it is to know someone your entire life and never know them at all. Not the most vulnerable parts, anyway. "It's better to love someone," Rose says, "even with the risk of losing them. Honestly, it is."

Queenie pulls a clean tissue from her robe pocket. Her crying sounds a little like her laughter. Big, bold, and full-bodied. Rose keeps talking, despite not knowing what to say. "Sometimes I think simply living our lives fully is one of the bravest things we can do."

"You sound like Mama," Queenie says. "And in case you haven't noticed, I'm not a very brave person, Rose." She lowers her eyes.

Rose isn't feeling that brave herself with a hurricane building outside. And she, too, has noticed how they are all beginning to sound a little like Old Sally.

"I wish I could be like you," Queenie says. "You're the most courageous person I know."

"Don't be silly." Rose has never been called brave in her life. In fact, her mother reminded her on a consistent basis what a coward she was when she was growing up.

"I'm serious," Queenie says. "You moved out West when you got married after college, and then you moved back here. You stopped drinking when you realized it was becoming a problem. My God, that takes the heart of a lion. All that and you've been married to the same man all these years and raised a child." Queenie pauses to think of more things, and Rose stops her.

"I guess it's a matter of perspective," Rose says. "According to Mother, I was too lazy to ever reach anything close to my potential."

"Well, your mother was an ass," Queenie says, "and I speak from personal experience. I knew her. Iris wasn't even one-fourth the person you are, Rose Temple."

Now it is Rose's turn to tear up. She thanks Queenie for saying that, even if she has trouble believing the last part.

The lights flicker and then flicker again.

"You think we made Mother mad?" Rose asks.

Queenie cackles. "Well if we did, then Lord help us. Especially if she has anything to do with this storm."

In the next second, the lights go out with a clap, leaving Rose and Queenie in total darkness.

CHAPTER THIRTY-SIX

Violet

Violet wakes suddenly when someone shakes her shoulder. Her first thought is of the old Temple ghosts who used to startle her on occasion when she worked at the Temple mansion. Her second thought is Old Sally. However, it is Tia standing next to the bed with a lit candle.

"Mom, the lights went out."

Jack wakes up as Leisha shows up behind Tia with another candle lit, her eyes wide.

"Do you hear that wind?" Leisha says.

Storms scare her, even relatively tame ones. As a little girl, she would hide under the dining room table after a thunderclap, covering her ears.

"Nothing to worry about." Jack sits up in bed and rubs his eyes. "We're safe here."

Violet wonders if he truly believes they are safe this close to the sea, the house so exposed to the wind.

"We should have evacuated," Tia says.

"We tried," Leisha says. "Remember?"

"Maybe we should try again," Tia says.

They are close to bickering. Everyone is stressed.

"Well, the road is probably still closed," Violet says. "But we'll be fine. You'll see."

The girls sit on the end of the bed, looking toward the windows.

"I wish we could see what's happening," Leisha says. "It's like having a blindfold on."

"The wind gives me the creeps." Tia's hand trembles, making the candlelight dance.

"What should we do, Mom?" Leisha asks, resorting to biting a nail.

"Storms are temporary, honey. They move in, and they move out. That's their job."

"I'd better get up and see if there's anything I need to do," Jack says to Violet.

As soon as he gets up, Tia and Leisha put their candles on the nightstand and climb in with Violet. She has missed snuggling with her girls. Even though they are practically grown, they still act like children sometimes. The hurricane looming out over the Atlantic is making Violet feel shaky, too.

"You coming?" Dressed now, Jack grabs a flashlight from their dresser.

"In a minute," she says, stroking Leisha's hair.

Violet hates to admit how much she has missed the closeness she had with her daughters before adolescence hit. They are still close, but she doubts it will ever be the same as before.

"Mom, what if the hurricane blows our house away?" Leisha says.

"You mean with us in it?" Tia scoots closer.

"We'll be fine," Violet says again, her throat tightening. Nature is never to be underestimated. Two scared teenagers are not to be underestimated, either.

After some coaxing, the girls go back to their rooms to get dressed. Violet dresses in candlelight and makes her way down the dark hallway and into the kitchen where Max hands her a flashlight. Rose sits in the living room with Katie and Angela, who are also up. Tia and Leisha are now with Jack in the kitchen. Queenie, Spud, and Old Sally are the only ones not here. However, Rose tells Violet that Queenie was just here and went upstairs after the power went out to try to get some rest.

Violet asks if anyone has seen Old Sally and no one has. She retraces her steps down the hallway and knocks on Old Sally's bedroom door. When Violet opens the door, the bed is empty. The wind rattles the side door that leads out to the deck. Jack and Max had put sandbags against the door, but they have been pushed aside.

Where are you? Violet asks, using their underground network.

Old Sally doesn't answer.

Violet steps out onto the dark deck and instantly regrets it. Though the storm is still young, the wind is already strong. Sand burns her eyes. She steps back inside to find something to cover her face and grabs Old Sally's summer robe on the back of the door and puts it on. It smells of her and reminds Violet of their early-morning talks, before Violet leaves to go to her tea shop.

With the robe pulled up over her nose and mouth, Violet goes back outside. Her flashlight highlights the grasses on the dunes frantically waving like they are warning her away. If this is only the beginning of the storm, what will it be like later?

"Old Sally?" Violet calls, her words quickly tossed aside by the wind. She holds onto the railing and follows it around to the front of the house. A bigger pile of sandbags blocks the front door, a flimsy fortress against the storm surge predicted to come. Though it does no good, Violet calls out Old Sally's name again and then walks down the front steps toward the ocean. The wind in her ears reminds her of flapping sails.

How would Old Sally ever be able to stand up against this

wind? Violet is more than fifty years younger, and she can barely navigate it. The wind steals Violet's breath away. Her shoulder begins to throb. But is it phantom pains like Katie's false labor?

Where are you? she asks Old Sally again. She imagines the channel opening between them but hears nothing in response.

Violet shines her flashlight up the beach toward the abandoned lighthouse, the destination of many of Old Sally's walks. She has never understood her grandmother's fascination with the place. It's like an altar she visits every day to worship some unseen god.

Surely, you wouldn't have gone there, Violet thinks, looking up the beach. *Not with a storm coming.*

Turning her flashlight back toward the house, Violet sees Jack waving at the top of the stairs for Violet to come inside.

When she joins him, he hugs her close, and they walk together around the side of the deck to Old Sally's room. Once they are inside, he pulls the sandbags as close as he can and closes the door.

"What were you thinking?" he asks, though she can tell his question is more out of concern than anger.

"I can't find Old Sally," Violet says.

He looks at the empty bed, as though not noticing it before.

"Let's go back to the kitchen and see if anyone else has seen her," Jack says. He leads the way back to where everyone is now gathered.

In candlelight, they listen to the wind. It is 1:30 on a Monday morning and the full force of the storm isn't even due to hit until 3:30 or 4 A.M. Violet asks if anyone has seen Old Sally. They go from silence to everyone talking at once, but the consensus is that no one has seen her.

"Let's search the house just in case," Jack says, giving instructions on who is to go where.

They each take a candle or flashlight and head off in different directions. Rose and Max go back to search their cottage. Katie and Angela search the garage. Queenie and Spud, who until recently were napping, join them and look in every bedroom and bathroom upstairs. When they all meet back in the kitchen, their concern has reached a new level.

"Lord in heaven," Queenie says, "I just saw her a while ago from the balcony. Spud checked on her. Where in the world would she go? Doesn't she know a hurricane is coming?"

Spud puts an arm around Queenie and tells her to stay calm. It doesn't work.

"Maybe it's nearing her time," Violet says, and then questions the wisdom of saying that now.

"Her time?" Queenie asks, picking up on Violet's fear.

Tia and Leisha look at Violet. "What are you saying, Mama?" Tia asks.

"Never mind," Violet says, refusing to alarm them any more than they already are.

A lightning bolt of pain shoots through Violet's shoulder. Definitely real this time. In the next second, Katie grabs her stomach and leans over with a half grunt, half scream. Holding the edge of the countertop, her knuckles are white from the strain.

Tension crackles through the kitchen as looks are exchanged. Who will deliver this baby if they can't get to a hospital? Only Old Sally has done this before. In fact, she delivered Violet. Now they have even more reason to find her.

"That sure didn't feel like false labor pains," Katie says, no longer leaning over.

"You are not allowed to have this baby during a hurricane. Do you hear me?" Angela's panic feels almost contagious.

"It could still be Braxton-Hicks, right?" Rose turns to look for Violet to agree with her. But Violet isn't so sure.

With Old Sally missing, Katie possibly in labor, and a hurricane approaching, nobody speaks. Violet feels almost paralyzed, not knowing which action to take.

"It's a first baby," she says finally to reassure everyone. "First babies take their time coming. I was in labor with Leisha for almost twelve hours."

Angela sends a grateful look in Violet's direction, and Katie appears visibly relieved.

"Just in case, we need to find Mama," Queenie says. "She is the only one who has ever delivered a baby before."

"Should we look on the beach?" Spud asks.

"Have you heard those waves?" Rose says. "Why would she risk life and limb to go to the beach?"

"I think she may have gone to the lighthouse," Violet says.

"But why would she go there?" Rose asks.

They all talk at once with different theories until Katie lets out another long moan. All the while, Angela reminds her to breathe.

"Better start timing those," Violet says, and Angela nods.

"Do you know something about this lighthouse that we don't?" Queenie asks.

"It's like a touchstone for her," Violet answers. "She walked there every day until a few months ago."

"Actually, that makes sense," Queenie says. "It holds special memories for her."

"I'll go see if she's there," Jack says.

"I'll go, too," Spud offers.

"Not without me, you won't," says Queenie.

"Have you forgotten a hurricane is coming?" Violet says to Queenie, concern in her voice. She is not about to lose her mother again, having only recently found her.

"She may need us," Queenie says, which is hard to argue with. "And we sure need her," she adds, looking at Katie.

Meanwhile, Violet's shoulder appears to be waking up with a clear and steady warning of what is to come.

CHAPTER THIRTY-SEVEN

Queenie

"Sweet Jesus," Queenie says to herself. "The last thing I expected was for Mama to go missing during a hurricane."

She doesn't know whether walking to the lighthouse during a storm is the smartest thing to do, but she trusts Jack and Spud to keep them all safe.

Before they go in that direction, however, Queenie and Spud circle the house with flashlights to make sure her mama isn't somewhere outside and has fallen and can't get up like those television commercials that advertise medical alert systems.

The wind increases in power, making Queenie glad she has some substance to her. Otherwise, Iris might knock her over. It helps that Queenie and Spud are in an armlock, each carrying a flashlight so they can see ahead of them.

For better or worse, her marriage vows said. But she didn't expect the *worse* to come a day after the ceremony.

The first thing they notice from circling the house is all the debris. Plastic bags cling to the trees like SOS flags. Palm fronds are everywhere. Drifts of sand have blown against the house. The patio has disappeared, covered with sand, with no possibility of finding footprints to confirm where Old Sally might have gone.

Within seconds of being outside, an airborne milk jug causes them to duck. An excellent test of aging reflexes. Then an empty soda can nearly hits Queenie in the head. She jerks sideways just in time. She feels like she is fielding foul balls at a World Series between the Hurricanes and the Newlyweds.

There's no way Mama is out in this, Queenie thinks. *If the wind doesn't blow her away, a soda can might take her out for good.*

Heaviness sits in the center of Queenie's chest. Why would her mama risk her life to go out in this storm? How could she even find the lighthouse in this darkness? It would help if the beacon still worked, but that hasn't been turned on in decades.

When they turn the corner of the house, the wind is so strong they struggle to move forward. Spud turns them around to go back the way they came, the wind at their backs. At least they can breathe again. The wind pushes them back to the house. Once inside, they shake the sand from their shoes, clothes, and hair. Now that they've gone around the house, they have a sense of what it will be like to get to the lighthouse.

Rose sits next to Katie, waiting for the next real or fake contraction. Meanwhile, Angela looks like she could use a strong sedative. Katie—distracted as she is by potential motherhood—asks if there are any signs of Old Sally. The two have become close over the last few months.

"Nothing?" Violet asks Queenie when they return.

"Nothing," Queenie repeats.

She remembers Old Sally's story of the love of her life. Would that be enough to get her to walk through a hurricane?

"I think we need to check the lighthouse," Queenie says. "If she's not in the house, it's the one place she might go."

"The other day she told me that her father helped build that old lighthouse in the 1920s," Spud says.

"She told me that, too," Leisha says, and helps Queenie brush the sand out of her hair.

"She hated that it was abandoned," Tia says, as she helps her sister.

"It's supposed to be locked," Spud says, "but when I checked it last fall, the lock had rusted off the door."

"So, she could go inside?" Queenie asks.

"I think so."

"Max and I will check it out," Jack says, asking Spud to stay at the house and watch out for everybody.

Queenie could kiss Jack for giving Spud a reason to stay behind. She doesn't want to lose her new husband in this storm along with her old mother. Was her wedding only yesterday?

Iris is due to come ashore in two hours. Her mama is missing. Katie is in labor. Or not. Her one and only honeymoon has been rescheduled like it is only a dental appointment. Could it get any worse?

A pounding on the back door is her answer.

CHAPTER THIRTY-EIGHT

Old Sally

Old Sally stands on the beach below the lighthouse. The wind rips at her raincoat, wanting to tear it from her body. Hurricane Iris is already a formidable presence, just like Old Sally's former employer, who asserted her stubborn power up until the last moment of her life. She knows this because she helped Iris transition. Or tried to. Old Sally doesn't begin to understand the forces that call together a storm of this magnitude. For all she knows, the spirit of Iris Temple is riling this hurricane up. If anyone could, it would be her.

The power Old Sally possesses isn't the harsh power of lording over, but the soft power of her Gullah ancestors. It is the power of knowing the land, as well as medicines and charms. Some might say her beliefs are based on superstition. However, it is much deeper. She also believes in the white man's religion, and the idea that help is everywhere. Not just in the spirit world but here on earth.

It isn't like her to leave the house in the middle of the night.

But the dream that woke her was so vivid, more real than real, she felt like she didn't have a choice. The visions of her ancestors that have been coming for weeks now mostly have to do with going on a long journey or getting things ready. Preparations. The destination being a hard-earned peace.

In her most recent dream, her grandmother told Old Sally to meet her at the lighthouse to build the courage fires. Her grandmother looked like she did when Old Sally was a girl, with her dark skin and solid white hair. She was a strong woman. A strong woman who taught Old Sally everything she knows.

The wind wails that it doesn't care about dreams and ancestors, and especially not strong women.

But Old Sally does, and she will honor them as long as she has breath in her body.

You coming, girl? Her grandmother's spirit stands a hundred feet away, at the top of the lighthouse steps, unaffected by the wind. The concrete lighthouse looms behind her.

Old Sally hasn't been called *girl* for close to a century. It makes her smile, despite a hurricane bullying her.

I'm coming, Old Sally tells her. She steps from the solid sand of high tide into the deep, soft sand of the dunes, struggling until she reaches the concrete steps that lead up to the lighthouse. She questions the wisdom of leaving the house as a storm approaches, but Old Sally has spent most of her lifetime visiting this lighthouse.

In a way, she feels like she is still dreaming. She has no idea how she got here through the growing winds, the waves crashing ever higher on the beach, and the salt spray reaching for her with every wave. The moon gave her very little help in finding her way. If not for the large flashlight Jack left on her nightstand earlier that evening, she might never have made it. But at the same time, she could find her way to this lighthouse with her eyes closed, her body over the years having memorized every step.

At the bottom of the steps, a sun-bleached sign warns people that the lighthouse is closed. No trespassing allowed. The wind howls around her. Old Sally closes her eyes to rest them. The wind has dried them out, and the sand makes them burn.

What do you want with me here? she asks, looking up at her grandmother. But when she opens her eyes, the image is gone.

The lighthouse continues to loom up ahead. She has a history here. A past that haunts her, as well as sustains her. After she got too old to work for the Temples, her visits to the lighthouse increased. She needed rituals to fill her days that didn't involve dusting and running a vacuum cleaner. For many years a walk to the lighthouse was what she did first thing in the morning when the sun came up. She rarely missed her daily walk unless the weather refused to cooperate, but sometimes she even walked in the rain. All this training must have helped her get here.

The beacon was turned off sometime in the 1980s. Decommissioned, the officials said. Another NO TRESPASSING sign went up by the only door. A lock added. For twenty years it has made her sad to think of a lighthouse not shining its light. Not fulfilling its purpose for being. Too many people don't know what their light is, either. They convince themselves they don't have one. Or other people convince them. Or they say their light isn't good enough, bright enough, or is too bright when all that's required is to stand in their Truth. Thankfully, Old Sally can see her light.

However, the lighthouse is also a monument to her biggest regret. A memorial to youth and a life she could have had if things had gone differently. After Fiddle died, she felt unmoored, like a boat on a vast sea in danger of crashing ashore. Grief does that to a person. The ground gives way, and people are set adrift. The lighthouse saved her. It gave her a way to honor the past and finally make peace with it.

Old Sally rests. She must garner her strength to climb the concrete steps. A long life carries so much grief. Not only from her own life but also the losses passed on to her from her ancestors. Sorrow from those days of not being free and not getting to choose what to do with their lives. Old Sally carried this history with her to the Temple mansion every day she worked there. She scrubbed grief into the floorboards as she cleaned the Temple mansion. Old Sally cooked grief into every meal. She polished grief into the silver until it shone like a full moon. That is why that old house burned down. It was a necessary sacrifice. All the grief needed to burn away and turn to ash, so her people could finally be free. And so the Temple grief could be set free, too. Sadness from knowing what they did, even if they never acknowledged it.

Not much longer now, her grandmother says, reappearing at the top of the steps near the entrance of the lighthouse.

Why did you bring me here? Old Sally says, now concerned that it was too much to ask. *To get my old heart to finally stop beating? To push it beyond what it can do?*

Fear hits, nearly staggering her. When she doesn't resist it, it moves on with the wind.

After working in the Temple mansion for so many years and going up and down the spiral staircase thousands of times, Old Sally kept up her exercise by climbing these concrete steps stretching between the beach and the lighthouse. Forty-two of them, to be exact. She started counting them after reading an article in *Reader's Digest* about how to keep her mind active by counting things and working on crossword puzzles. The old iron railing still stands, except for one section about halfway up. There, she must rely on balance to keep herself upright.

One at a time, she takes the steps now. Every five steps she rests. Where the railing disappears, her grandmother takes her hand. Real or imagined, it is a great help.

When the lighthouse was being built in the early 1900s, the government hired Gullah men to be the laborers and paid them less than white men. Her father was one of those men and was proud that he had a part in the lighthouse being here. When she was a girl, he walked with her up the beach to show her his handi-work. He told her stories of mixing concrete to make the floors and walls inside, as well as the steps outside that hold her now.

Back then, you could see the beacon from their house, which was the closest thing to having God looking over her in the darkness that she could imagine.

You did good, Daddy, she says to his memory.

It feels strange saying "Daddy" as a hundred-year-old woman. It has been decades since she uttered the word. Just like it has been decades since she has been called a *girl*. But the girl still lives inside her even now, and Old Sally remembers her often these days. Her endless curiosity. Her delight in simple things. Sunshine. A beautiful seashell. A sweet breeze. The sound of laughter and the playful chatter between family and friends. Like school photographs causing her to recall specific memories, every year of her life is documented inside her. She is the girl she once was, even as an old woman. Remembering that makes her life evergreen, even during the bleakest winter.

The Gullah menfolk tended to die off early, leaving the women —her mother, grandmothers, and aunts—to keep things going. Even in her dreams, it is the old women who visit her, rarely the men. Maybe it is true what she has thought for years, that women are the stronger ones. Raising children and tending homes. Midwives for births and deaths. Storytellers. Magic keepers.

Her father died when she was nine. She remembers his massive arms and how he would lift her up as a young child and carry her on his shoulder like she was as light as a seagull's feather. He smelled of tobacco and taught her how to have a poker face and not reveal—with wide eyes or a sudden gasp—what cards he held in his hand when he played blackjack with his friends. These memories live in the past and feel further away than the recent dreams of her ancestors. One is a remembrance, the other a visitation. Whenever her grandmother shows herself, it is like she is standing in the room with her. Flesh and blood. Sometimes she can even feel the weight of her sitting on the end of Old Sally's bed.

At the top of the outside concrete steps, Old Sally stops. Her

knees quake with the task. Finally, she touches the familiar coolness of the metal door, corroded from age and salty air. Her hands
shake as she pushes against the door. A door that will not open.

Her grandmother now stands next to her, a calm presence in
the growing chaos.

I need help, Old Sally tells her.

Her thoughts create the opening between the worlds. The
threshold Old Sally and Violet have begun to explore.

Be gentle, and it will come, her grandmother says, regarding the
door.

This makes no sense to Old Sally. This door does not need a
soft touch, but a man-sized shove. Or two. Or three.

But Old Sally heeds her advice. A harsh wind at her shoulder,
she turns the handle and gives it a gentle push. The door swings
wide open with the help of the wind, nearly pulling her inside.

Steady, her grandmother tells her. *You must save your strength to
build the courage fires for the others.*

If only someone would tell her what that means. It is June in
the South. Humid and hot. No need for a fire of any kind. Not a
literal fire at least.

As Old Sally steps through the threshold, the past greets her
with a metallic, musty smell. She blinks, shining her flashlight into
the dark room, her eyes adjusting to the new darkness. The
absence of the wind is a blessing. Yet, the sudden silence disori-
ents her. She falters as past and present collide, steadying herself
to keep from dropping to the concrete floor. To reorient, she aims
the flashlight at the old metal cot still in the corner, and the metal
desk chair nearby, companion to the metal desk across the room.
An old gray army blanket covers the bed with its edges tucked in
over the narrow mattress.

No one has ever lived here full time. For decades, old Mr.
Harrison stayed on stormy nights to make sure the light stayed lit
for passing vessels. A set of metal stairs winds up the center of the
structure into a small observation deck, where the great beacon

holds center stage. For something so old and so close to the sea, the moisture has done little damage. Everything inside is remarkably well preserved.

This is where she met Fiddle on their one night together. The closest she has ever come to loving someone with her whole heart. From the pocket of her raincoat, Old Sally takes out the only thing she brought with her when she left. A piece of worn pink fabric with an *A* embroidered on it. *A* for Annabelle. Her sweet baby girl who died after only six days of living on this earth.

Dark and sweet as night, Old Sally says to herself as she fingers the cloth, remembering the warmth that at one time lived beneath the fabric.

The wind wails outside and reminds Old Sally of her howling grief when Annabelle died. If only she could have traded some of her time here on earth so that Annabelle could have lived longer. No need for Old Sally to have so many days, years, and decades when a tiny creature so pure and beautiful gets only six days. It doesn't make sense to her how life-and-death things are decided. So many things just don't make sense. Automobile accidents. Slavery. Random blessings and curses everywhere.

Meanwhile, she can't remember a time when she was more tired. She lies down on the old cot and closes her eyes, feeling she could sleep for another lifetime. Every bone in her body confirms her journey through the hurricane.

Seconds later, the spell of the past is broken, and she realizes for the first time why her grandmother has brought her here: to get the others to follow.

CHAPTER THIRTY-NINE

Rose

The pounding on the back door brings everyone to see who it might be. When Queenie opens the door, she shakes her head and says, "What are you doing here?" as though the storm has decided to introduce itself.

When Queenie steps aside, Rose hides a grimace. In the back doorway stands Heather, windblown and breathless from the storm.

"I thought the road onto the island was closed," Rose says, a flashlight the only light between them. "A power line had fallen."

"They moved it," Heather says. "The road had just opened again when I drove up. I was the only person not heading off the island. But those people won't get far," she continues. "The interstate is at a total standstill. People are stranded and running out of gas."

While Rose takes this in, Heather steps past her into the dark kitchen. She takes off a hooded windbreaker and throws it on the kitchen counter. Rose's jaw tightens with the familiarity Heather assumes.

"What did you find out at the bank?" she asks Rose.

Rose pauses. "That's an odd question given what's going on outside."

"Is it?" Heather shrugs in the shadows of the kitchen.

"Wait, how did you know I went to the bank?" Rose asks.

"You told me you were going to the bank," Heather says. "Remember?"

"No, I don't remember that." Rose is confident she didn't share this bit of information with Heather. A person she doesn't know or trust.

"Yes, you did." Heather smiles and cocks her head, looking almost pleased with Rose's agitation.

However, Rose refuses to bite the wormy hook Heather dangles in front of her. She has more important things to deal with.

"What's going on?" Max approaches, his flashlight spreading more light into the foyer.

"You remember Heather," Rose says to Max.

Max nods at Heather and looks back at Rose like a bouncer in a bar waiting for instructions to bounce. But Rose's lifelong goal has been to avoid conflict, not engage in it. As a girl, if she had ever questioned her mother's criticisms, she believed the earth might open and swallow her. Back then, Rose stayed in the kitchen with Old Sally or played with Violet in the courtyard. Even today it challenges her to confront anyone, even if they deserve it.

"Is the road open again?" Max asks Heather.

She says it is and repeats what she reported to Rose. "Have you decided to stay on the island?" she asks Max.

"Sounds like we don't have a choice," Max says.

Like all previous encounters with Heather, something about it doesn't make sense. When they tried to evacuate before, both lanes of the road leading off the island were being used for evacuation. How would Heather get back on the island? And why would someone drive directly into a storm when the island is being evacuated? Was she hoping to find the house empty? Also, how did she know Rose went to the bank?

Violet returns to the kitchen and looks at Rose as if to ask, *What the hell is she doing here?*

Rose answers with an *I have no idea* shrug of her shoulders.

Violet holds a piece of paper. "It's a note from Old Sally," she says to Rose. "I found it next to her bed. I'm not sure why I didn't notice it before."

"The old lady is missing?" Heather asks.

No one answers.

The windows rattle with stronger gusts, and the thought of Old Sally out in this storm somewhere makes Rose tremble.

"What does the note say?" Rose asks Violet.

They gather around the kitchen island, which looks somewhat romantic with all the candles burning. "The only thing it says," Violet begins, "is how important it is for us to meet her at the lighthouse."

"The lighthouse?" Rose looks at Max, worry etched in her eyes.

Violet nods, mirroring Rose's concern.

It was only last week that Rose and Max walked up the beach and explored the old lighthouse. The outside steps were crumbling. Part of the railing was gone. Not the safest place for an old woman to go.

"Was the note to all of us, or only you?" Rose asks.

"I have no idea," Violet says. "It isn't addressed to anybody."

"Sounds like she means all of you," Heather says.

Rose and Violet turn toward Heather. Does she want them out of the house? Does she think they keep the Temple jewels in their closet or something? Although her closet was precisely where Rose kept her nest egg for years.

"Why the lighthouse?" Max asks.

"I'm not sure," Violet says.

"How did she even get there in this wind?" Rose asks.

"Maybe the old lady is losing it and just wandered off," Heather says.

"She left a note." Rose shoots Heather a look that says, *How dare you.*

"Old Sally is a lot sharper than most of us," Violet says.

And definitely a lot sharper than you, Heather, Rose wants to add, her anger rising.

In the next moment, hairs raise on the back of Rose's neck, and it's not from her anger at Heather. A loud creaking noise quickly crescendos like a giant rusty nail being pulled out of an equally giant piece of lumber.

A crashing sound follows, and the entire house shakes. Violet's girls scream like extras in a horror film and the dogs bark. For a moment nobody moves.

Rose grabs Max's arm and tells him to check on Katie and Angela, whose bedroom is upstairs. He points his flashlight into the darkness and dashes away. Rose follows Queenie and Spud up to Queenie's bedroom, where the sound appears to have originated.

When Queenie opens her door, she screams something that evokes the entire Holy family: Jesus, Mary, and Joseph. The live oak that had been growing for two centuries next to the garage has fallen into Queenie's room. Most of the roof went down with the tree, as well as a considerable chunk of the porch and wall. Queenie's bed is crushed underneath massive limbs, where only a short time ago Queenie and Spud were lying. The strong wind rattles the leaves and whistles through where a wall once stood. Spanish moss clings to the limbs like ghosts hanging on for dear life.

The tree was one of the oldest on the island and has withstood storms for hundreds of years. The oaks on the island are second in age only to the Angel Oak up the coast near Charleston, is estimated to be over four hundred years old.

When Rose questions how the situation could get any worse, it begins to rain.

CHAPTER FORTY

Violet

T he rain forces everyone into action. Violet grabs anything in
Queenie's room that she can lift that is not destroyed and
takes it to a dry part of the house. Jack and Max disappear to get
tarps to nail over the gaping hole in Queenie's wall and ceiling.
Within seconds, everyone is soaked, as the rain comes down
harder.

When the men return, Jack reports to Violet that most of their
cars are crushed under the giant limbs of the tree. Max's truck is
the only one that appears to be drivable. His look confirms that
there is no way they can evacuate now.

Panicking is not helpful, Violet reminds herself.

She has attempted to reach Old Sally via the underground-
between-worlds-radio, and Old Sally is not answering. To make
matters worse, Violet's left shoulder has finally woken up with a
hurricane warning of its own.

"What will we do?" Violet asks Jack.

He pauses. "I have no idea," he says.

The thought of Jack not knowing what they should do unnerves her even more.

Violet helps Queenie spread a smaller tarp over her dresser, and Queenie wipes tears and rain from her eyes. Violet hugs her, telling her everything will be all right. But she doesn't know if that's true. This could be only the beginning.

"They're just things," Violet hears herself say. She said something similar when Queenie lost everything in the Temple fire. However, Queenie helped her understand that losing things can be devastating, too. In a way, it's like losing your identity and a feeling of safety in the world.

We need you, Violet tells Old Sally, trying again to reach her.

She wishes this mysterious communication system of theirs also had an answering machine. Violet would leave a frantic message asking her to come home immediately.

"My wedding dress is ruined," Queenie says, pointing to the chair where it was draped, now crushed by the tree.

"Maybe it's still salvageable," Violet says.

Was it only yesterday that her mother and Spud spoke their vows to one another? It seems like weeks ago.

"I thought Iris might *crash* the wedding, but it seems she waited until the honeymoon," Queenie says.

From the floor, she picks up the red hat she wore at her wedding and puts it on to keep the rain from her eyes. Leave it to Queenie to be colorful even during a hurricane.

"After this storm blows over we'll see what we can do about your dress," Violet says, making her voice sound hopeful.

"It's not like I'll ever wear it again," Queenie says. "I'm just hoping it's not a sign."

"Since when do you look for signs?"

"Since Iris crashed a tree into my bedroom," she says, water dripping from her brim. "Is Mama still missing?"

"She's at the lighthouse," Violet says. "I found a note. She wants us all to meet her there."

"How did I not know this?" Queenie asks, pulling Spanish moss from her lampshade, delivered by the tree.

"I have no idea," Violet says.

"Why is she at the lighthouse?"

"I have no idea about that, either."

Pain pings Violet's arm. She can't believe just a few hours ago she was convinced her sixth-sense shoulder had somehow given up the ghost, so to speak.

While the others work to salvage more of Queenie's things, Violet returns to her bedroom. She can't just do nothing. The lighthouse is only a ten-minute walk if she runs some of the way. She can get there and back with Old Sally in half an hour. That is, if she can convince her that she should come home. Violet puts on her raincoat. She has taken this walk a thousand times or more, although not in the dark, and not with a hurricane offshore.

Violet leaves a note on the dresser telling Jack what she's going to do. He will try to talk her out of it if she speaks to him directly. Either way, he will be upset with her for wanting to do this. The first rule if someone gets lost is to not go looking for them, or you might get lost yourself. But what if Old Sally needs her? What if this is her time to transition and Violet isn't there?

Violet leaves the house with one of the bigger flashlights. She keeps her raincoat and hood pulled close and wraps a scarf around her nose and mouth. Seeing the downed tree is like seeing an old friend struck down. It takes her breath away as much as the wind. Their cars are indeed crushed underneath. The wind pushes her through the dunes and down the beach, a giant hand on her back urging her to get to the lighthouse. The waves are like an advancing army inching their way up the beach. But it is the wind, by far, that is a different beast than anything Violet has ever experienced. It has teeth and a bite to it. Yet, it is only an infant compared to what it will grow up to be.

How did Old Sally walk in this? It was earlier in the evening, but it would still be difficult. And why would she go to the light-house, anyway?

The ancestors, Violet thinks. It is the only explanation that makes sense. Old Sally must have had another dream.

Increasingly, Old Sally has lived in both worlds. The everyday world marked by days, months and years, and the timeless world of her ancestors. Ancestors, Old Sally told her only a day or two ago, who seem as real to her as Violet.

When Violet visited the lighthouse as a girl with Old Sally, its presence felt unlike when she went up into the attic at the Temple mansion. At the mansion, Violet dealt with a whole house full of dead Temples that rattled her with their creepiness. At least at first. However, her Gullah ancestors are more benevolent spirits. Preferring to be helpful, instead of obnoxious.

Violet stops walking. Her thoughts have been racing, and she hasn't kept track of where she is in relation to the old lighthouse. Thick clouds cover the moon, which doesn't help.

Thanks to Old Sally, the island's history is alive to her now. It isn't just the place she grew up, but a place with a past. A past with hidden treasures. With the distraction of modern life, Gullah traditions are more threatened than ever before. The winds of change want to clear the coastline of all evidence that the Gullah culture ever existed. Old Sally's primary concern is that every-thing will be forgotten.

At times, it feels to Violet like an overwhelming mission to be the person who remembers. The person working to preserve an entire culture. Yet, without Old Sally, Violet would never have recognized the imprint her people have made on this island, as well as the mark they have made on her own life.

Using her flashlight, she searches for familiar landmarks. She finally sees the shape of the lighthouse up ahead. Between the beach and the structure are the dunes. Beyond the dunes is a forested part of the island with a cluster of live oaks and underbrush.

The only remnants left of the Gullah culture are a one-room schoolhouse on the far end of the island, stone ruins around their cemetery, and the small praise church Old Sally went to when she was a girl, now covered from floor to rafters with wisteria. These structures blend in so well with their surroundings they are almost hidden.

This area is always where the wild indigo grows, another reminder of the past. A crop that was cultivated and used to dye clothes for hundreds of years. The roots of the plant are used for medicines. Last week Violet and Old Sally collected and dried some of the roots for indigo root tea, known to be good for digestion and kidney ailments.

Violet's mind remains active as the wind continues to push her up the beach. It is slow-going; she can only see two or three feet ahead of her with the flashlight. It is her intuition that reminds her to turn where the island juts left.

When she goes in this new direction, the wind pushes her sideways. She steadies herself to keep from falling. What propels her forward is the thought that Old Sally might need her. In a way, her grandmother is like the lighthouse. A beacon to future generations, yet also somehow abandoned and not appreciated for the history she holds.

Aiming the flashlight upward, Violet sees the lighthouse looming above her. She heads into the dunes that lead to the steps. Climbing the steps from the beach, her left hand clutches her raincoat and flashlight while her right uses the railing to pull herself forward. The wind tugs at her clothes while burning her eyes and stretching her skin wherever it is exposed.

Violet can't imagine what the full thrust of this storm will be like in two hours, when it is supposed to finally make landfall. Surely, no one will be able to stand, much less walk in this wind and driving rain. It is a challenging climb in a storm. She pulls herself up each step until she reaches for the railing and nothing is there. Her body lurches forward, and she screams as she tries to not fall headfirst into the dunes. Her heart takes a quick elevator to her throat until she steadies herself. For the next few steps, she places each foot solidly before moving it to the next level. Finally, the railing returns. She stands for the longest time, not moving, appreciating the railing's support. Her heartbeat calms as she stands on the landing in front of the lighthouse. She made it.

When Violet tries to open the large metal door, it doesn't budge. With one fist, she beats on it. If Old Sally is inside, she doubts she will hear her.

If, she hears herself say.

What if Violet has come all this way for nothing?

Shining the light on the handle, she pushes against it with her right shoulder. Someone pulls from the other side, and Violet stumbles into the lighthouse. An instant later, the wind grabs the door and slams it behind her.

CHAPTER FORTY-ONE

Queenie

Queenie's bedroom is soaked with water and filled with the pungent destruction of live oak and unearthed soil. For a moment, she feels much sadder about the tree than her bedroom. A bedroom can be rebuilt.

"It's a good thing we weren't celebrating our honeymoon when it happened," Spud says, with a wink she assumes is meant to reassure her.

Queenie leans into him as they survey the damage, a large puddle forming on her oval rug. "This is serious, Mister Grainger. Please don't make light of it. Where are we going to live now?"

"My place, Mrs. Grainger, until we get everything fixed good as new."

The *Mrs.* catches Queenie by surprise. She prefers *Ms.* to *Mrs.* Besides that, she hasn't told him yet that she plans to keep her old name—Queenie Temple—given that's how everyone in Savannah and on the island has known her for the last forty years. She claimed the Temple name after working for Iris for only a year. If

she was going to be treated like someone lower than the graveyard dirt her mama keeps in the flour bin, she decided to legally
change her name. Since she resided in South Carolina, nobody in
Savannah even knew about it until it was official. It was an act of
pure defiance, and something she has not for one instant regret-
ted. The Temple name gives her a little prestige, like driving a new
Mercedes instead of taking the city bus.

When Iris married, she refused to change her last name, too, to
keep the power that came with the Temple title. It doesn't matter
to Queenie that she is a Temple by way of the back door, as the
illegitimate child of Iris's father, the second or third Edward
Temple in a long line of Edwards that Queenie can never keep
straight.

Meanwhile, all this chaos and debris has stirred up Queenie's
past. Besides Spud, the only other man Queenie ever slept with
was Iris's husband, Oscar—Violet's father. Not that it was Queenie's idea for one second. Although she did develop feelings for
him. Complicated and confusing feelings. None of which she has
for Spud.

*Come to think of it, natural disasters don't offer a whole lot of choice,
either,* she reasons. Maybe that's why she is all of a sudden
thinking of these things again.

Oscar had his demons, too. The only time Iris showed him any
respect, as far as Queenie observed, was to change her will at the
last minute and honor his wishes that Violet inherit the mansion.
Oscar knew that Iris's only weakness was deathbed requests and
the fear of what might happen if she didn't fulfill them. Queenie
still can't believe Iris did it. If not for her falling into a coma soon
afterward, she probably would have changed the will back lick-
ety-split.

"What are you thinking about, sweet-tart?" Spud kisses
Queenie on the cheek.

Queenie doesn't comment on his latest confectionary nickname, except to note that it could be taken in the wrong way. She

is not a tart or a loose woman by any imaginative stretch. However, she is certain Spud didn't intend it as anything bad. She also doesn't answer his question. He might not understand her flirtation with prestige. She will wait for the ideal moment to broach the subject of keeping the Temple name.

"Maybe the good Lord wanted to teach me a lesson that it's not good to get attached to things," Queenie says.

"Possibility," Spud says, "although it could also be about an old tree doing battle with a strong wind and losing."

"True." Queenie appreciates Spud's practical nature. "Let's hope we don't lose the battle, too."

"Indeed," Spud says, reaching to straighten a bow tie that isn't there. He asks if she is okay and she says she's been better. She assumes he knows how much this house means to her. Not only was it her childhood home in its previous rendition, but it has also been her first real home since Edward burned down the Temple mansion. At least everybody thinks it was Edward who burned it down, given he was walking around in the mansion that night and didn't get out alive.

To this day, it perplexes Queenie why Edward would do such a thing. She knew he could be a pompous jerk, but she never thought he would try to murder her in her sleep by committing arson. Something about all that didn't make sense. Anybody in Savannah who had a secret would have a motive. But instead of scrutinizing the whole city of Savannah, investigators determined Edward did it, and it's not like he could object.

Queenie was the only person living in the mansion at the time, though Rose and Max had just arrived from Wyoming and were spending the night, too. However, it was Queenie's bedroom and all her possessions that were destroyed in that fire. As far as personal items, she had to replace everything from underwear to books. What she couldn't replace were her journals from the last twenty years, and Rose's letters she had kept for decades. The loss still makes her tear up if she thinks about it long enough. In their new house here on the beach, she finally had everything to her liking. And now this.

Queenie sighs. It never occurred to her that a tree could crash into her bedroom and do this much damage. That old oak was thought to be the oldest on the island. As a girl, Old Sally told her trees are our elders and should be respected as much as people. This old tree provided shade during the boiling summers when Queenie was a girl. She sat under it while Old Sally braided her hair. She played with her dolls under it. In a way, it is like an old friend. An old friend pushed over by a playground bully named Iris.

When Queenie and Spud ventured outside a little while ago to see the damage from the other side, the entire root system of that sweet old tree had been unearthed and was dangling above the ground. All its secret parts exposed for the world to see.

Queenie thinks again of her wedding dress. It was in the garment bag it came in, the bag lying across the big armchair in her room where she did her journaling. The new chair was never quite as comfortable as her old one that burned in the Temple fire, but it didn't deserve to be destroyed.

Tears cling to her eyelashes as she takes stock of her current losses. Yet, like Spud said, it could have been a lot worse. What if they had been in bed celebrating their nuptials, or Queenie had been reading or journaling in her chair?

She imagines the headlines in the Savannah newspaper the next day:

ELDERLY NEWLYWEDS MEET TRAGIC FATE DURING HURRICANE IRIS

Well, I'm not dead yet, Queenie thinks, *and I'm not willing to meet a tragic fate.*

In typical fashion, Queenie asks herself, *What Would Oprah Do?* The answer is easy. Oprah would err on the side of gratitude. There would be no room for feeling sorry for herself. No spending time with the thought that she might be somehow cursed with bad luck. Nothing is required but gratefulness.

Queenie will have to start over again, at least regarding a few items, but the one thing she knows for sure is that she is resilient.

Queenie and Spud return to the candlelit kitchen. Only Jack is there.

"Who died?" Queenie asks, seeing his face.

"Vi is out in this storm somewhere looking for Old Sally."

Queenie gasps. She can't believe she has been worrying about a stupid wedding gown when Violet may be in trouble. "What should we do?"

"I'm not sure," Jack says. "They may be on their way back already. That's what I'm hoping, anyway."

Queenie has never seen Jack look this worried. "Where is everybody?" Queenie asks.

"Tia and Leisha are in their room," Jack begins. "Rose is somewhere with that Heather woman. Max is taking a quick nap, and Katie and Angela are in their bedroom resting up for the big event."

"Which big event?" Queenie asks. "Baby or hurricane?"

"Hurricane, I guess. The latest word is that the earlier contractions were a false alarm."

"Thank goodness," Queenie says with a relieved sigh.

Queenie remembers very little about giving birth to Violet. She was incredibly young, for one thing. But she does remember that having a baby feels as life-changing as a hurricane coming. No one can stop a force of nature. Just like no one can predict where exactly Iris might come ashore. Queenie wishes now that they had made it off the island. She and Spud could be sleeping soundly at a Days Inn without a single worry except what they might come home to. Instead, they are right in the middle of a disaster waiting to happen.

"Are you sure we shouldn't go after Violet and Old Sally?" Queenie asks Jack.

"No, I'm not sure," he says. "But for now, it makes sense to stay put. They both know how to take care of themselves."

Queenie is not so sure non-action is the course to take. Spud sends her another reassuring look. But how could she not worry? Two of the most important people in her life are somewhere out in a hurricane. Or at least the beginnings of one.

Do Max and Jack believe that a few storm shutters and sand-bags are going to keep an ocean out of their house? Nothing prevented the poor unfortunate tree from falling into her bedroom and taking half the porch and several cars with it.

Queenie can usually laugh her way through anything, but she finds nothing at all funny about their current danger. As if to prove her point, one of the tarps rips away from the roof, and the wind whips through the house. If she could get on her knees with any ease, she would be on the floor praying by now.

A shiver climbs Queenie's spine as she thinks of Violet and Old Sally out in the storm. A storm that seems determined to challenge them in every way possible.

CHAPTER FORTY-TWO

Old Sally

O ld Sally wakes to find Violet sleeping in the chair next to her. Then she remembers Violet's arrival and her disappointment that Violet didn't bring the others. The steady drone of the storm outside sounds like a wild lullaby. She recalls the dream where her grandmother told her to build the courage fires for what is coming. Old Sally thinks now that the dream was telling her to get everyone to the lighthouse and light the beacon. It will be the safest sanctuary for them.

Violet's head tips forward, and she startles awake. "I must have fallen asleep," she says. "Are you okay?" Violet moves to the cot and Old Sally's side.

"I be fine," Old Sally tells her, but even to herself she doesn't sound fine. Her voice has a quiver to it that is new since her walk to the lighthouse.

"We didn't talk about it after I arrived. Why did you come here?" Violet says this gently, as if speaking to a cherished child who was lost and who is suddenly home.

Old Sally has noticed how the young and the old change places at some point. Old Sally took care of Violet. Now it is the other way around. A mantle passes there, too.

"My grandmother told me to come here and light the courage fires," Old Sally says. "Our ancestors were sending me a message through the dream."

If anyone can comprehend the urgency, it is Violet. Yet, she doesn't wear the expression of someone who understands.

"Well, we've got to get back to the house," Violet tells her. "Everyone is so worried about you."

"I left you a note, so you could bring everyone here," Old Sally says.

"We can't stay here during a hurricane." Violet looks around the inside of the lighthouse as if gathering reasons why this won't work.

"It not be safe at the house," Old Sally says. "The storm is angry, and the ocean, too. This is the safest place we can be if we stay on the island."

Violet pauses and takes another look around. "That live oak next to the house came down after you left," Violet says. "Everybody is fine, but it fell into Queenie's bedroom and smashed several cars."

A wave of loss crashes over Old Sally. That tree kept her small house shaded during the hottest summers and protected it from the wind all year long. Not to mention its beauty and the number of creatures it supported. Birds. Chipmunks. Squirrels. Insects. Even that old owl she scared away earlier. The live oaks on the island have long outnumbered the people here. The roots of the live oaks grow shallow and cling to the sandy soil, weaving an immense tapestry just beneath the surface. Being rooted is vital for humans, too. No matter how long they live in a place. This particular tree has grown alongside Old Sally for a century. It is an ancestor, as well.

"So sorry to hear that," Old Sally says, a wobble of emotion in her throat, along with the quiver.

"I loved that old tree, too," Violet says. "Remember how I sat under it to eat my breakfast?"

"You fed it oatmeal," Old Sally says. "I had to teach you that a tree's food was the sun, rain, and nutrients in the ground."

"You were teaching me even then," Violet says.

"Yes, I was." Old Sally thinks again of how the tree was already ancient when Sally was a girl. A storm this size will topple many trees. The pines may stay rooted—most of the damage will be to the branches and upper parts of the trees. But the wind will do different injury to the oaks. The live oaks are top heavy, with roots that don't go that deep in the sandy soil. The most vulnerable ones will be pushed right over, roots and all.

Violet looks at her watch. "We don't have much time left before the full brunt of the storm is here. What are you suggesting?"

"You need to get the others here as quickly as possible," Old Sally says. "We must keep everyone safe. My grandmother has never been wrong about anything like this."

Violet takes a deep breath, as though her belief in Old Sally is faltering.

"I wouldn't want to walk back in this storm, either," Old Sally says, "and I wouldn't even suggest it if lives weren't at risk."

Violet nods.

A few days ago, Old Sally's tea leaves predicted a great disorder would occur before order returns. She didn't realize the full extent of the danger until now. Sometimes in the dark of night, things become clear as day. Her people have survived many storms on this island, but the coming storm is more extensive than any of her ancestors have ever seen before. One that will be documented in history books. One that will change everything.

CHAPTER FORTY-THREE

Rose

Rose excuses herself to go out to the cottage to check on things, but the real reason is to get away from her newfound niece. Unfortunately, Heather doesn't take the hint and follows Rose to the cottage. Now Rose must look busy and like she has a reason for being here.

A hurricane is hard enough without a stranger hanging around. A stranger with hidden motives. Rose has never figured out Edward's hidden motives for burning down the Temple mansion with Rose in it, and she can't help but wonder if that same family trait has passed to Heather. A character trait that destroys instead of preserves. A trait that could be true regarding Rose's mother, as well.

"Do you mind if I ask you something?" Heather has cornered Rose again, something she seems quite good at.

"I guess not," Rose says, a thin veil hiding her irritation.

"What kind of man was my father?" Heather asks.

Oh, good God, Rose thinks. *Now?*

The storm is due to hit in two hours. Now is not the time to give Heather a character analysis of her brother, and yet the question causes her to pause. Hasn't she asked this before? Should she offer a feel-good version of Edward, so Heather can walk away thinking he has contributed something endearing to her gene pool? However, there is also something to be said for knowing the truth.

"If he hadn't been my brother, I probably wouldn't have spent any time around him at all," Rose says.

This admission bolsters her. Yet, the candle in their small cottage kitchen illuminates Heather's disappointment.

"He was older than me by a few years," Rose continues, feeling a bit stormy herself. "I irritated him simply by being alive, and sometimes he tormented me, too."

There, Rose thinks, *let her chew on that for a while.* Maybe it will stop any further questions.

"When my mom was dying, she told me he was a real jerk," Heather says. "She said she didn't like him that much."

And the truth shall set you free, Rose thinks.

For years she tried to understand why her brother was the way he was, attributing all sorts of childhood wounds and Temple family karma. But the truth is whether you were family, friend, or stranger, Edward was an alpha dog who played dominance games. You never knew when he might try to pee on you, hump your leg, or toss you to the ground.

"But I thought she told you that your father was a sperm donor," Rose says.

"Yes, she did," Heather says. "Initially. Then when she was dying she told me the truth."

Rose pauses. Didn't Heather tell her that she found out while looking at her mother's documents?

"We were very close," Heather adds. "Like friends instead of mother and daughter."

Rose can't imagine being her mother's friend. As far as she

knows, her mother didn't have friends. She had connections to assert her influence. People who witnessed her wealth and status. Not close friends like Rose is with Violet.

Violet. How could she forget her best friend is out in this storm? She left a while ago to look for Old Sally. Has she even come back? Heather has distracted Rose from what is essential. Two of Rose's chosen family members are in danger: Violet and Old Sally. Two people who helped Rose survive her mother's dominance and are directly responsible for the person she is today.

Rose leads the way back from the cottage to the big house, her light jacket doing little to protect her from the wind and blowing sand. Heather is even less prepared for the elements and uses Rose's back as a buffer. Once inside, the ongoing weather report now has the forecasters calling the storm a potential hundred-year-event. A destructive storm, like her mother could be, who if crossed had no problem destroying lives and making you wish you had never met her.

Seconds later, Violet bursts through the back door, her hair sculpted in the direction of the blowing wind. She leans over to catch her breath. The others come from all corners of the house to greet her.

"We need to go to the lighthouse," Violet says, still leaning over. "Old Sally says we're in danger here. The lighthouse is where we'll be safe."

"We should go, right?" Rose says, looking at Max.

"I'm not going to some dirty lighthouse," Heather says, standing straighter.

Everyone turns to look at her, as though suddenly noticing the stranger in the room.

"Well, I'm not," she says. "That old lady probably has dementia."

"I trust Old Sally with my life," Rose says to her. If Rose were one of their dogs, her hackles might raise. "If she says we should go to the lighthouse, then we should go."

Violet agrees.

Max and Jack debate logistics. One truck. Twelve people and various animals. Can it be done? They challenge each other to think creatively.

Meanwhile, Rose goes to check on Katie and Angela, who have no idea what is happening. Their room is upstairs, the other side of the house from Queenie's. Rose knocks on the door and finds Katie lying on her left side, a recommendation from her doctor a month ago when her blood pressure was creeping up. Angela coaches her to breathe deeply; the smell of unearthed live oak fills the hallway like meditation incense.

"Sorry to interrupt," Rose says, "but we need to go to the lighthouse, the house isn't safe."

Katie sits up and holds her stomach. Where Rose expected panic, there is calm.

"The lighthouse?" Angela asks.

"Old Sally says to. We need to keep you and the baby safe."

"Then we should go," Katie says.

Angela looks at Katie, then at Rose, as if the calmness is a surprise to her, too. Rose and Angela help Katie stand and cover her shoulders with the light blanket on the bed. One thought reassures Rose. If this baby comes during a once-in-a-century hurricane, then they are better off with Old Sally than without her. As always.

CHAPTER FORTY-FOUR

Violet

T he wind fights against Violet as she puts the food and water in the back of Max's truck, the only vehicle spared by the capsizing of the giant live oak. In the car are Katie and Angela, along with Lucy, Ethel, and Harpo. A cat carrier with Angela's two cats inside—Zelda and Gertrude—sits at Katie's feet, and Angela holds a terrarium containing Tia and Leisha's turtle, Jake. Lives are seldom set up with an evacuation in mind. They have animals. Too many possessions. But at least they have a destination that should keep them safe.

Queenie starts the truck, revving the engine, and then waves goodbye to Violet like she is off for part two of her honeymoon, instead of evacuating from a hurricane for the second time. Provided it is still passable, she will take the old gravel road to the back entrance of the lighthouse. The rest of them will walk through the dunes and up the beach to the same destination.

Standing on the back patio, where the wind is less intense, Jack and Max secure a rope around everyone's waists and attach them, allowing six feet between each person. Violet wonders if this is necessary, but when they step away from the shelter of the house and into the dunes, everyone immediately stumbles backward. For several seconds they struggle as a group to stand upright again.

Violet is willing to be tethered if it will get them all there safely. Max leads. By way of the beach, it is a simple ten-minute walk. At least any other day it is. By road, it is half that, but the storm is fast approaching, and they don't have time to make multiple trips. It is still over an hour or so before the storm is due to hit, but someone needs to tell the wind that. It is already intense.

Like passenger cars attached to a train, they follow the person in front of them. Rose follows Max, followed by Heather and then Jack. Violet is next. Behind her is Tia, then Leisha, and then Spud as the caboose. Despite Heather's insistence, Rose wouldn't let her stay at the house alone, which Violet thinks is a good idea, and not only for safety reasons.

They shuffle toward the lighthouse, their human locomotion severely limited in comparison to the storm. Hurricane Iris pushes and pulls against them. Violet's cheeks stretch like they've become elastic. She lowers her head to get the short, shallow breaths the wind will allow.

Meanwhile, sheets of rain begin to fall, hitting them from every direction like thousands of tiny bee stings hitting their exposed skin. The steady roar of the wind makes Violet's ears ache. Periodically she looks back at Tia and Leisha, beaming courage in their direction. The storm of 2002 will be something they tell their children and grandchildren about.

Provided we survive, Violet thinks, and then tells herself to not even hold that result as a possibility. Her doubts create an opening to question the wisdom of their decision to walk up the beach. The lighthouse now feels like an impossible distance to cover with the intense rain and wind. But they are all tied together. If anyone falters, the rest of the group will pull them forward. Whatever happens, they will have to do it together.

Perhaps that occurs with whoever we attach ourselves to in life, she thinks. *Family and friends.*

The waves crash closer. How many times has she walked up this beach and seen only its beauty? Now she witnesses the sea's dark side. Its ominous presence feels as dangerous as the wind. Old Sally is right about the lighthouse. It is built for storms like this. Solid concrete. Their house is only wood. Wood may be too vulnerable to withstand the storm surge promised to come.

They follow the curve of the land and Violet spots light up ahead. Someone must have figured out how to turn on the beacon. How is that possible? It hasn't been turned on in twenty years. A surge of hope fills her. Violet jerks on the rope to get everyone's attention and points ahead to the light. Their rope line stops. Then they rock the line in celebration like a spectator wave in a football stadium. Every few seconds the beacon rotates in their direction. A rush of adrenaline pushes away Violet's tiredness. Her great-grandfather helped to build this lighthouse. In a way, it is like her ancestor helped construct this shelter for them years ahead of time, all the while knowing that they might need it someday.

The rain comes again, pinging against her raincoat. They turn inland toward the light. As before, walking is difficult in the soft sand of the dunes until they reach the concrete steps that lead up to the lighthouse. They're going to make it. She's sure of it now. Only a few more yards to get to the lighthouse. With each step, the wind vibrates the ropes ahead of and behind her.

In the next instant, Violet remembers the missing railing where an hour or so before she almost fell into the dunes. If one person goes down, the others will, too, including her. She stops and yells to warn the others. The wind silences her. Violet pulls hard on the rope and Heather stumbles toward her. Violet helps her up, and everyone finally stops and looks around to see what has stopped their forward motion.

"Danger up ahead!" Violet yells to Heather, pointing to the handrail.

The look in Heather's eyes reminds Violet of how young she is. Only a little older than Tia and Leisha. The message gets passed up the line. They move more slowly now, and each person points out the danger as they pass the missing railing. She just hopes everyone can keep their balance. Now is not the time for clumsiness. Meanwhile, the beacon radiates light 360 degrees above their heads. A literal beacon of hope.

Finally, at the top of the cement stairs, the human chain stops again. Bodies huddle together at the entrance while Max pounds on the door. Slowly, the heavy metal door opens. They shuffle their way inside and turn as one body to push the door closed and latch it. Queenie, Old Sally, Katie, Angela, and all the animals await them.

Wild hair, bloodshot eyes, and red chapped skin tell the story of their escape. They are not only windblown but beaten up. Violet's ears ring, and she can barely hear. Tia begins to cry, and Violet comforts her, while Jack goes to Leisha. Everyone talks louder than usual. Perhaps their ears are ringing, too. Lucy and Ethel greet them, licking faces, while Angela's cats let out cautious meows.

It takes several minutes for Violet's hearing to return to normal. "Most definitely a bad hair day, Mom," Leisha says.

Both daughters laugh, and Leisha helps Violet unzip her rain jacket. The look they exchange has a new dimension. Is that appreciation she sees in her daughter's eyes? A new level of maturity?

The storm continues to rage outside, but it is now a muffled rage. Muffled through layers of concrete that make up the lighthouse. The constant fight with the wind to stay upright has made Violet numb. When the numbness begins to wear off her skin tingles to the point of pain.

The metal door rattles from the wind but holds secure. The lighthouse has the faint smell of wet dogs and an old musty attic.

Yet, it is relatively dry considering how close it sits to the sea. The lighthouse, wide at the bottom and narrow at the top, has a set of metal stairs in the middle that spiral upward to a small section with just enough space to walk around the beacon. Small windows dot the walls all the way up to the top, where that smallness expands to a panoramic view of land and sea. The beacon bathes them in a dull, golden glow. Below the beacon, an old generator emits a continuous, almost comforting hum.

Violet thinks about what a shame it is that the lighthouse has been abandoned, as many have been over time. Given advances in sonar instruments on ships and on land, people are kept safe by other means. Now lighthouses have become symbols more than anything. Reminders of how things used to be, and a belief that something manmade might have the power to dispel darkness and bring hope and safety.

Jack and Max untie the ropes between them, and they begin to settle. Once free, Violet walks over to Old Sally, who embraces her.

"You did it," Old Sally says. "Thank you for bringing everyone here."

"You're welcome," Violet says. "Who turned on the beacon?"

"Angela," Katie says, sitting nearby on the cot, Harpo in her arms.

Violet turns and smiles at Angela, as word passes through the small space. The others thank her, too, and Angela takes a quick bow before returning to Katie's side.

Violet sits and rests her back against a cool wall. Suitcases are piled under the spiral metal stairs to give them room to walk around a little. If everyone in the lighthouse stood shoulder to shoulder they would reach the entire way across, with maybe a little room to spare.

Violet turns to see Rose watching her.

You okay? Rose's expression asks.

Violet nods, asking her the same.

Rose nods, too.

Violet thinks of the unspoken conversations she used to have with Queenie at the dinner table when Miss Temple ate. Now Violet has unspoken mysterious discussions with Old Sally, too. So much communication happens when she doesn't even realize it. Body language. Facial expressions. She looks at Rose again. She sometimes forgets that they are not only best friends but also half sisters, given what Miss Temple's will revealed about Violet being Mister Oscar's child.

They exchange a secret Sea Gypsy look. When they were girls, they played in this abandoned lighthouse. A secret hideaway. A prominent NO TRESPASSING sign was posted next to the door, so they were not supposed to be here. By accident, they discovered where the old lighthouse keeper had hidden a spare key in a dried-out old paint bucket under a rusted-out wheelbarrow on the north side.

As girls, when they let themselves inside, Violet and Rose would climb the steep metal stairs to the beacon. Looking out over the ocean, they made up stories and pretended ships at sea relied on them to find their way. Using a conch shell as a radio, they sent messages warning the ships of gales and storms, offering anyone in trouble safe harbor. Never imagining, of course, that someday the lighthouse might be a safe harbor for them, too.

They exchange a smile, as though remembering the same things, before Rose turns back to check on Katie.

"How are you holding up?" Jack asks Violet, taking her hand while the girls doze.

She shrugs. Truth is, she won't be entirely okay until this storm is over.

Jack leaves to help Max investigate their current haven.

While she rests, Violet begins to tremble from their harrowing walk to the lighthouse. It reminds her of the tiny birds that sometimes hit the front picture window. Stunned at first, they then begin to shake and let the trauma pass. It always takes longer than Violet thinks it will before they fly away again.

It is the middle of the night, and she hasn't slept. The only light, besides the diffused light coming from the beacon, comes from two battery-operated camp lanterns.

The beacon sends its rhythmic, sweeping light out into the darkness. If there are any ships at sea, they are in for a rough ride. Violet's thoughts drone on like the wind. She remembers a story Old Sally told her about an entire crew on a Civil War ship that sunk in a storm off the coast and ended up somewhere at the bottom of the ocean. It was near the end of the war and they carried much-needed supplies. Some say the ship's sinking helped seal the fate of the war for the South. She imagines a ghost ship somewhere at the bottom of the Atlantic, complete with skeletons and fish swimming amongst them. A vessel never found. All those men and supplies buried at sea.

In the distance, the surf pounds the land. Is it her imagination or is it even louder than minutes before? The life raft of safety Violet clings to disappears when she remembers what the weather forecasters said in the last report before the power went out. The storm surge is easily the most destructive part of the storm, its severity based on where the hurricane comes ashore.

Jack comes to check on her and the girls again, who are still dozing, as are several of the others. Violet lowers her voice and asks him about the storm surge.

"There's no way of knowing," he whispers back.

"But haven't we been getting the full force of the hurricane?"

"I wouldn't doubt it," he says.

"Then we'll also get the full force of the storm surge, right?"

"I don't know, sweetheart, but let's not panic."

Violet nods, repeating his words to herself, *Let's not panic.*

Getting everyone afraid will do no good, especially while they are so exhausted. However, shouldn't everyone be warned about the possibility? Just in case there is some way they can prepare for it?

According to Violet's watch, it is now 2:30. Everyone is either sleeping or sitting in silence listening to the storm. The small window to the left of the door reveals a dark and colorless world. A predator lurks outside in the form of a hurricane.

Trees snap and crash in the distance. Violet half expects them to moan with pain. If this part of the shoreline is supposed to be more protected, what is happening in the *un*protected areas? She imagines the dunes being beaten down with every wave of the unrelenting surf. Without the dunes, there will be nothing to stop the ocean from crashing into the lighthouse, as well as their home down the beach.

Ropes, raincoats, backpacks, and various supplies are piled on the floor nearby. Rose's two dogs lie together, their backs touching. They pant and salivate like they do whenever they go to the vet, their ears following the sounds of the storm. Hurricane Iris rages outside. The only thing left to do is wait.

CHAPTER FORTY-FIVE

Queenie

W hen Spud entered the lighthouse after his harrowing walk up the beach with the others, Queenie rushed to his side. Every strand of his thin, gray hair stood straight up like a geriatric rapper, unable to withstand the teasing of Iris. If she had known the walk would be so perilous, she would have tied Spud to the top of the truck.

Even now, Queenie attempts to tame his hair. "You sure you're all right?" she whispers to him while the others sleep.

"I'm fine, pumpkin spice."

She tires of his continuous search for a sweet nickname, but he could say anything right now and she would feel nothing but gratitude.

Earlier, while waiting for the others, Queenie and Angela clanked their way up the metal steps to the top of the lighthouse— Queenie holding onto the railing with a death grip, as she has never liked heights—to see if they could get that fool light on. Thanks to Angela's handiness, their multiple efforts, and giant-sized luck, they were able to get the generator going with the help of the spare canister of gasoline Max always keeps in the truck. Seconds later, with the flip of a switch, the old beacon groaned to life.

Nice to know that even an abandoned old lighthouse can still have some life to it, Queenie thinks.

Now they don't have to wait on this fool storm to be over in total darkness. It's even kind of romantic as the soft, throbbing light cascades down the stairs. Queenie thinks again of her aborted honeymoon and smiles with the thought that everyone she cares about is in this massive concrete phallic symbol.

In the meantime, a hurricane named Iris is huffing and puffing and threatening to blow the door down.

The human Iris was a blowhard, too. Not giving a hoot what anybody else had to say about anything. A big, bad wolf in pearls.

Queenie isn't sure how anyone can sleep with a hurricane right outside the door. Instead of whispering, she wants to yell: *What's wrong with you people?*

But instead, she is quiet and holds Spud close. To her surprise she finds herself dozing off, too. Something about the constant wind outside is like a white noise machine. Her shoulders relax. A dream peeks around the corner of her awareness. Then Katie lets out a moan that grows into a scream. Everyone, including Queenie, startles awake. It seems Katie's baby isn't that fond of hurricanes, either, and wants to vacate the premises, pronto. Although, in Queenie's opinion, it would be much smarter to stay put where it is for a while.

Rose rushes over to Katie and takes the free hand that Angela isn't holding. She says the things that mothers say to kids who are about to panic. Things like *Everything is going to be okay,* and *I'm here,* and *breathe, sweetheart.* Angela rubs Katie's back like she is helping the words sink in.

"Sweet Jesus," Queenie whispers to Spud. "What if this baby comes right here in this lighthouse in the middle of a hurricane?"

"Then he or she will have a great story to tell every year on their birthday," Spud says. "Don't worry, sugarplum."

Queenie gives him a look that now is not the time to bring up the *Nutcracker Suite* and sugarplum fairies. Not unless he wants his own nuts cracked. He offers a quick apology as if aware of the risk.

Though the sounds are muffled in the metal building, Iris's ferocity is growing. If this were the human Iris, Queenie would call this a great big hissy fit. Iris's hissy fits were infamous all over Savannah. They happened whenever a downtown chef didn't get her order just right. Or when someone at the Junior League or the Daughters of the American Revolution meetings didn't pay Iris what she deemed was adequate respect.

Katie lies on the cot with Harpo by her side, and Old Sally sits next to Katie on the only chair in the room. Angela is nearby. Both focus on what Old Sally is saying. The part Queenie overhears has to do with trusting the process. Old Sally reassures Katie that this baby knows exactly what to do even if she doesn't. Katie nods her agreement.

If Queenie were the one giving birth during a hurricane, she would probably already be cussing a blue streak, whatever a blue streak is. Her pain tolerance is practically nonexistent. She hates any type of pain, from small discomforts—like the pain in her knees after she stands too long at Violet's Tea Shop—to the pinched nerve she gets in her back sometimes. Her foremost intolerance is for stupid people. But thankfully, she manages to avoid them for the most part.

Old Sally tells Katie to be patient and breathe. Queenie must admit she barely has the patience to wait for toast to pop out of the toaster, much less breathe deeply.

In the meantime, Rose is focused on Katie. Becoming a grandmother appears to be nothing short of a holy experience. Queenie became a grandmother twice, though she didn't get to claim it at the time. Keeping that secret robbed her and Violet of the closeness Rose and Katie have now. The worst kind of disappointment is when she disappoints herself, and Queenie never wants to feel that again.

Tia and Leisha are awake now and take turns braiding each other's hair. They periodically look over to see what is happening on the cot. Violet looks tired. Queenie makes a point to catch her eye and smile at her. Violet returns the smile. No more secrets.

Queenie looks around at those waiting out the storm. Heather sits alone near the door, looking like a young Iris who doesn't want to get her hands dirty, first in line to leave once the storm is over.

"What are you thinking about?" Spud whispers to Queenie.

"About how Heather is a great big nothing burger," Queenie whispers back.

"A nothing burger?" Spud shakes his head, as though never knowing what his new wife will come up with next.

"It's like she's not even here," Queenie whispers again.

"Maybe she's afraid," Spud says.

Queenie nods with the knowledge that she is afraid, too. Perhaps Queenie would be more compassionate if Heather didn't look like someone who tried to make every day of her life miserable.

Meanwhile, Max and Jack speak in hushed tones near a large footlocker underneath the spiraling metal stairs. Whatever is in the footlocker is guarded by a rather large lock. Queenie wonders what they are talking about. Whatever it is, they look concerned. Except for Heather, it seems everyone else has been drawn closer together by this experience.

Iris rattles the windows, reminding Queenie who is in charge.

You are such an attention hound, Queenie tells her. *I'm onto you, even if nobody else is.*

Iris was at her brightest and most content whenever the newspaper photographer from the society section showed up at one of her philanthropic forays. For years, one of Queenie's jobs as Iris's companion was to clip these photographs and any write-ups that appeared in the newspaper and put them in a monogrammed album with the gold Temple name on the cover. A collection Iris kept in the sunroom to remind her of her importance. Something she could flip through after reading the newspaper and having her morning tea. Queenie, of course, was not in any of the photographs in the scrapbook, except for an occasional brown arm in the corner next to a sea of white people—the rest of her cropped out because Queenie wasn't a *true* Temple, only an imitation.

Queenie shakes her head. She can't wait until this damn storm is over and Iris is out of her life for good.

Before the power went out at the house, the weather reports predicted where the storm might make landfall. The highest storm surge totals would happen north of wherever the storm comes ashore. That would also be the area with the most significant destruction. Queenie remembers the arrows pointing to Dolphin Island. In a way, it is like those adventures where a damsel is tied to the railroad tracks with a locomotive coming straight for her. The storm increasingly sounds like a train engine, too.

Katie lets out another moan. A wave of tension vibrates through the lighthouse. Iris is right on top of them. The lighthouse is one of the highest spots on the island, the other being the ceme- tery. A ten-foot storm surge has been predicted. Are they ten feet up from the sea? Is a lighthouse waterproof? Queenie wishes now she had worn her pink flip-flops instead of her sneakers, which are already squishy wet. But her complaints are hiding a more pressing issue.

"Why are you so quiet?" Spud takes her hand, waiting for an answer.

"Well, the truth is . . ."

Queenie whisks a tear away.

"Tell me," Spud says, looking into her eyes with so much tenderness she looks away.

"I'm scared," Queenie confesses. "I've never been in a hurricane before."

Standing, Spud pulls her into his arms, which isn't as effortless as she would like. Queenie is taller by at least an inch, though Spud insists they are the same height. But she is happy to give him an inch if he needs it.

"We're all frightened," he says, his words soft. "I truly believe we are in the safest place on this island we could possibly be."

Every inch of Queenie's full-figured body wants to believe this. Yet, her knees are quivering and remind her that there were times in her life when she has been a weakling. She is not proud of those times. They were mainly in the past and had to do with keeping secrets for way too long. Storms are a different matter. With storms, she has absolutely no control.

Katie lets out another moan.

For a moment Queenie flashes back to the night she gave birth to Violet. It was also summertime, and every window of the house was open. Old Sally had been by Queenie's side, just like she is with Katie now. That night, Old Sally was equally calm and reassuring. Old Sally knows what she is doing. She has done this before. Queenie breathes deeply for the first time since the storm began and wants to cue a Bette Midler song. Not to sound too hokey about it, but Old Sally is the wind beneath Queenie's wings. Her light through every storm. A beacon lighting the path her entire life.

CHAPTER FORTY-SIX

Old Sally

Old Sally closes her eyes. She hears the faint music of a violin playing in her memories. The man with the violin would have been her husband if fate had been kinder. It was here in this lighthouse that she experienced the most profound love she has ever known—an attraction to last a lifetime, even an unusually long one.

Because of how well he played the violin, he was nicknamed Fiddle. He played for her here in this lighthouse, the rich sound echoing against the concrete walls. Old Sally hears the haunting melody that captured her imagination so many years ago.

Memory, like so many things in life, can be both a blessing and a curse. Memories like this one haunt Old Sally, while at the same time uplift her. To remember him is to know who she is. To remember her ancestors is to understand why she is here.

Old Sally opens her eyes to see Max trying to unlock the rusty metal footlocker underneath the stairway with a small pocketknife. Old Sally remembers when that old footlocker first arrived. Until the 1980s, when it was abandoned, this lighthouse was never locked.

Old Sally gives Katie's hand a reassuring pat and tells her she will be right back. Her back and legs are stiff with pain when she walks over to Max and Jack.

"Please pull the footlocker away from the wall," Old Sally tells him.

He pauses and then does as she asks.

Old Sally leans behind the box and pulls out the key from where it was left decades before. She hands it to Max, who grins.

Opening the footlocker is like opening a forgotten time capsule. First-aid supplies are there from back in the days of World War II. Including three army surplus wool blankets. They pass two out to the others, and Old Sally keeps one for Katie.

Jack pulls out two small hurricane lamps—aptly named—and gets them going with some old but dry matches in a metal box. He wasn't sure if the oil would still be usable, but it is. The smell of lamp oil and sulfur mixes with the musty, salty air. Everyone comes over to investigate the metal trunk, even Lucy and Ethel, who both sneeze when exploring the contents. The lighthouse fills with chatter and light and feels almost homey.

Old Sally sits in the chair again and leans back, listening to the storm. Its dull roar has become familiar now. When she closes her eyes, she hears her grandmother singing in a long-ago kitchen. A song from a faraway home before she came to this new world. A new world where their lives were not their own. At least not at first. She hums along with the melody, wishing her grandmother were here.

In the next moment, the sounds outside change. The raging wind stops. Old Sally opens her eyes. No one moves. It is as if the world is holding its breath to see what will happen next.

Following the steady chaotic roar of the wind, the silence is almost painful. With caution, Max opens the door of the lighthouse as if Iris might lurch out at him if given a chance.

It is the eye of the storm.

To OLD SALLY, it feels like they have landed by spaceship onto a new planet. In a matter of seconds, their nightmare has become a paradise of stillness. Yet, evidence of the ordeal is everywhere. Trees down. Battered shoreline. Dead things spit up by the sea. The rain has stopped. Total calm surrounds them. Overhead, the clouds open and reveal a deep blue sky. The moon and stars, visible hours before, appear again. It is a glimpse of heaven. Iris has revealed a side of herself Old Sally didn't expect. After showing no mercy, the hurricane has presented a moment of grace.

Old Sally stands a few feet from the door, mesmerized by this strange, dark world. Her eyes continue to adapt to the darkness, and goose flesh crawls up her arms from the fresh, damp air. In the distance is the steady sound of the surf. A promise that never stops. No matter how still the earth becomes. The strong smell of salt and sea mixes in with broken trees—the odor of Christmas trees dipped in the ocean, decorated with seaweed.

An unexpected gift is found in the center of the storm. Old Sally puts a hand over her heart. Pledging allegiance to all that is good, real, and true. In some ways, it feels like she has been waiting her entire life for this scene to be revealed to her. A perfect chaos. Light inside darkness. Good inside evil.

Tears pool in her eyes. If this were her last moment on earth, all would be well. It is almost time. She can feel it in her bones. She clings to this promise. But there is at least one more thing she must do.

One more thing, Old Sally repeats.

She turns to look at Katie sleeping on the cot, lovingly holding her belly. She knows what it is like to rest up for a big transition.

The beacon rotates, offering periodic glimpses of the shoreline. A vast sea stretches where the dunes and beach used to be. A graveyard of debris litters the adjacent land. A door here. A bathtub there. Pink building insulation is spun into the limbs of trees like cotton candy.

All are silent as they step into the moonlight to witness this new world. Part of the walkway is missing. Pieces of porches and docks are everywhere, making it difficult to walk even a few inches. A large chunk of twisted metal, a boat before Iris got to it, blocks the stairway.

One by one, they venture farther out into the dark eye of the storm. Max cautions them not to wander too far. The eye won't last for long.

Tia and Leisha stay close to their dad, and Rose and Violet are arm in arm. Max goes out back to check on the truck, while Queenie and Spud stay close to Old Sally. Heather stands just inside the lighthouse, all alone. A trickster without a trick, and still someone not to be trusted.

"You okay, Mama?" Queenie asks.

"Yes, baby," Old Sally says. A mama can still call her children "baby" even if her children are in their sixties. No harm in that.

They stand inside the eye of the hurricane, and for the first time in her long life, Old Sally understands what it means for time to stand still.

THE WIND BEGINS to blow again. Slowly at first. Softly. And then the clouds gather again to cover the moon. With the same quickness that the eye came, the second half of the storm begins. The eye is only the halfway point. From the weather reports they heard, it is the second half of the storm that is the most destructive because the wind reverses itself. Yet, how can anything be more destructive than what Iris has delivered so far?

They quickly gather inside the lighthouse again. At that moment Old Sally remembers that humans are both a resilient and a fragile species. A young species. Governed by the laws of nature.

A species that needs guidance. The others look at Old Sally as though needing something only she can deliver.

At first, she thought that building the courage fires meant getting the beacon going. But it seems that more is required of her. She hesitates, wondering what might be helpful. When nothing comes, she calls on her grandmother. Old Sally waits, but she doesn't appear.

Not the best time for you to disappear, she says to her grandmother.

Again, no answer.

But Old Sally knows what she must do.

She closes her eyes, drawing her words from somewhere deep inside herself, where all her people reside.

"We must be strong for one another," Old Sally says, opening her eyes again. "We each hold a spark of courage. It may not feel like enough when you are alone, but together it will be enough," she continues. "Together all those sparks build a fire. A fire of courage."

Outside, the wind and rain quickly surpass where the storm left off before the eye. Nobody talks about the storm surge that is destined to come. At the top of the lighthouse stairs, Old Sally's vision returns, and her grandmother nods her approval. The courage fires have been prepared for whatever is to come.

CHAPTER FORTY-SEVEN

Rose

Katie's contractions have sped up along with the storm. What they had hoped were fake have proven themselves real. Rose doesn't let her daughter see how frightened she is that this grandbaby is almost ready to come with no hospital, telephone, or any way to communicate with the outside world.

Rose pulls the charm from her pocket that Old Sally gave her and holds it in her left hand. She feels the roundness of the pearl, along with the gnarled root. Along with her prayers to God for protection, Rose calls on the charm to keep them from harm. She will take whatever help she can get. She opens her hand to show Old Sally what she is holding, who nods her encouragement.

Angela rubs Katie's back to help her relax before the next labor pain. Rose regrets now her harsh judgments of Angela when they first met. It turns out that she is everything Rose would want Katie to have in a mate. Kind, respectful, and unwavering in her care for Katie.

Old Sally told them they each have a spark of courage and

together they make a fire. Rose returns the small sack to her pocket, and Katie squeezes Rose's hand, the sign that the next labor pain is coming. Like Katie's grip, the storm outside isn't letting up. Angela and Rose exchange a look that contains the spark. They take turns comforting and reassuring Katie. They must stay calm. Together, Rose and Angela have enough courage for the three of them.

Between pains, Katie becomes talkative, something she did as a girl whenever she was afraid and needed a distraction. Katie motions her head toward Heather, asking Rose what she intends to do.

"Not sure," Rose says, which is the truth. Heather is the least of her worries now.

Needing her own distraction, Rose glances over at her purse across from the cot. Inside is the first faded ledger. Every hour or so she checks to make sure it is still there. She can't imagine what is in that old book that Edward would have been looking for before the fire, and she can't help but wonder if that is why Heather is hanging around, too. Rose doesn't believe that she only wants to get to know who her father is. They could do that over the phone. She is apparently searching for something else. Like Edward was searching for something else other than the secrets.

Rose remembers what Heather told her earlier in the day about her mother's job when she worked for Edward. She had been hired to research and compile the history of the Temple family for a possible book. Was Heather's mother given access to either of the ledgers in the bank vault? Doubtful. But she might have found something out through other means. And would she have shared that *something* on her deathbed with her daughter?

Rose looks around at the menagerie of people and animals gathered. Talking is sporadic. It is like a makeshift Noah's Ark. Katie and Angela are on the cot, Harpo at Katie's feet. Max and Jack speak near the stairway. Max's two dogs stand nearby. Queenie and Spud lean into each other while sitting on the metal stairs. Tia and Leisha and Violet rest against the wall. Old Sally and Rose are near the cot. Heather is at the door like someone whose adventure took an unexpected turn, and she no longer knows who she is in this new setting. For the first time since they met, Rose feels compassion for her. Like her mother, Heather is all alone and doesn't know how to connect.

Rose leans back, looking at the building towering over them. She hasn't been inside this lighthouse since she was a girl. When she takes walks on the beach, it always looks lonely sitting back from the ocean, overlooking everything. Solitary. Unapproachable. But she doubts it is lonely now.

Old Sally rocks her body while sitting in the gray desk chair. She hums something that is barely audible.

"How did you know we should all come here?" Rose asks Old Sally.

Old Sally pauses. "Do you remember the night of the fire at the mansion?" she asks.

"Yes, of course," Rose says. "Max and I had just driven across the country."

"That night I had a dream that Queenie was in danger, and the dream told me to get Queenie and you and Max out of that house, so I telephoned until Queenie finally answered."

"I never knew that," Rose says. "Or if I did, I'd forgotten."

Many times, Rose has thought about what might have happened if Queenie hadn't rushed into their room and told them to get out. She saved their lives. What Rose didn't know was that Old Sally had saved all of them.

"Earlier today, I had another dream," Old Sally begins again. "This one told me to get everyone to the lighthouse."

"Oh my," Rose says, wondering if she has had dreams she ignored and shouldn't have. She guesses everybody does.

"I guess I've lived long enough to know that when a dream gives me explicit directions, I follow them," Old Sally says.

"Thank goodness," Rose says. "I might not even be here if you hadn't listened."

Rose remembers the dream she had recently of her mother hiding her paints. Storm or no storm, Rose is tired of being distracted from what feels necessary to her. When the storm is over, she will start to paint again. She promises herself this.

In the meantime, Rose trusts Old Sally with her life and the life of her family. She helped Rose survive her childhood. If getting them to this old lighthouse is what Old Sally's dream told her to do, this is precisely where they should be.

CHAPTER FORTY-EIGHT

Violet

The hurricane's peaceful eye had almost lulled Violet into believing the worst was over. But what's true is that they hold front-row seats to a drama that has only reached intermission.

Violet's throat tightens as she sits against the wall with Tia and Leisha. She tells them not to worry. However, there appears to be plenty to worry about.

The storm crescendos. Hurricane Iris is outdoing herself. The more Violet tells herself that they are safe, the more the hurricane begs to differ. The question remains: Will this lighthouse protect them from a wall of water? An alarm pounds its warning into her left shoulder with such intensity it brings tears to her eyes. A fear she can't verbalize, or it might scare the people she loves.

In the meantime, Old Sally sits calmly next to the cot as though awaiting a special guest. Violet can hear her humming and tries to discern the melody. She finally recognizes "Amazing Grace." She begins to hum along, the tune vibrating in her throat. On the second round, Rose starts to hum, too, as do the girls. Queenie and Spud join in, as well as Jack and Max, who add a bass line to the hum. Only Heather is quiet.

In the distance, Hurricane Iris pounds the shore like a boxer poised to win the heavyweight championship of the world. Waves crest closer to the lighthouse, and the winds grow in volume yet again. Violet has heard eyewitness accounts of tornados and hurricanes where it's said that the wind sounds like a locomotive barreling down the tracks. She can hear the train coming now.

They continue to hum as the lighthouse vibrates with each crashing wave. The storm has its own song. Nothing stands between them and the ocean, except this lighthouse. If not for this structure they would already be lost, perhaps never to be found again.

A low rumble grows in the distance, and everyone stops humming to listen. At first, it sounds like a stomach growling. A huge stomach. Violet can feel the vibration deep inside her.

Jack yells that the storm surge is coming. Everyone is to get up the stairs as fast as they can. At the bottom of the spiral steps, Max and Jack remind everyone to move quickly and stay calm, an impossible feat. One by one they climb the winding metal staircase toward the beacon of light, their shoes echoing against the metal stairs. Violet's legs feel like she is attempting to run in pluff mud.

Jack yells for them to stay away from the glass around the beacon of the lighthouse. Queenie and Spud are first up and they stop at the top of the stairs. Tia and Leisha and Violet pack in closely behind her, followed by Old Sally, Rose, Katie, and Angela, who holds Harpo. All of them help Katie climb the stairs. Max tells them to move closer together, while Jack grabs dogs, a cat carrier, and a turtle in a terrarium and passes them up the steps. He holds out his hand to Heather, who is still sitting on the floor. The look on her face is terror, her body frozen, unable to move.

Violet cannot remember a time her heart has beat this wildly.

She yells at Jack to not do anything heroic and get himself hurt. She and the girls need him. But he isn't listening. When he takes Heather's arm, she slaps him away with her backpack, causing the faded ledger to fall out onto the floor, several of the pages falling loose. Like a game when someone yells "Unfreeze," Heather scrambles for the pages. Violet looks at Rose, who is searching in her purse for what is now on the floor of the lighthouse.

"Get up the stairs!" Jack yells at Heather.

The hairs prickle on Violet's arms. The storm surge is growing. Electricity is in the air, the energy building and moving toward release.

Heather is on her hands and knees gathering up the pages.

Violet screams at Jack to come on. To leave Heather if he must. The low rumble grows louder, and Violet's entire body involuntarily shakes. Beyond the small windows, the sea swells. Finally, Jack picks up Heather while she is leaning over to get the remaining ledger pages and carries her up the metal steps.

Through a small window near the top of the lighthouse, all Violet can see is water. The wave crests. She feels like one of the minnows she and Rose collected in her plastic beach bucket when they were Sea Gypsies. Like the minnows, they are about to be sacrificed to the sea.

"Hold onto the railing as tight as you can!" Violet yells to Tia and Leisha. The roar of the wave swallows her voice. She secures both girls between her and the metal bars and turns to see Queenie and Spud doing the same with Old Sally.

The big wave hits its apex and prepares to fall. Violet tells Tia and Leisha that she loves them with all her heart. She feels her lips move, unable to hear the words.

The giant wave crashes against the lighthouse. Windows around the beacon shatter above them. The door crashes open, swept off its hinges. For a few seconds the lighthouse seems to rock backward but then holds firm. Freezing water pours down the stairway and takes Violet's breath away. She coughs and gasps to get it back. Old Sally said the ocean was warm for this time of year, but to her, it feels freezing cold. It pours from overhead, forming a steadily rising pool of water in the bottom of the lighthouse. The generator flickers on and off several times and mercifully stays on. Without the beacon, they would be in total darkness.

Violet holds onto her girls so tightly she can barely feel her hands. She refuses to let them be washed away into the dark, freezing water. Her teeth chatter, her body longing for sunlight and warmth. For an instant, she imagines sitting with Old Sally on the porch when Violet was a girl. A sunny, warm day stretching out in front of them.

Like someone filling a glass of water from a giant faucet, the frigid water fills the lighthouse frighteningly fast. It rises a third of the way, and then halfway up the wall. In seconds it is below Jack and Heather's feet, who cling to the railings like everybody else. They are all stacked like sardines in a metal tin on the top half of the steps.

In the next instant, Violet loses her grip on the railing, and the force of the water pulls Tia away from her. Tia screams and is washed down to the step below. Spud grabs her and pulls her between him and Queenie. One by one they inch themselves higher up the steps to get away from the rising water. Finally, Violet and Leisha are at the top of the lighthouse stairs looking down. If they go as far as the landing they will have nothing to hold onto. The cat carrier, along with the turtle terrarium, are passed up the steps to keep them safe from the rising water. Lucy and Ethel and Harpo stay with their owners.

The papers Heather had in her purse float on the top of the water, a swirl of off-white pages. Rose grabs as many as she can and stuffs them in the pocket of her raincoat before the rest of the faded ledger floats away. Along with the pages are their suitcases, rising from under the staircase. They swirl like part of an oceanic baggage claim area. Violet gasps, seeing her suitcase begin to swirl on a conveyor belt she cannot get close enough to claim. She thinks of all the photographs she crammed into her one suitcase, the special ones she would be the most bereft at losing. But she has no time to grieve her losses now. The sea threatens to swallow them whole.

Time slows, perhaps the last seconds of her life ticking away. Thankfulness fills her like the water filling the lighthouse. She thinks of how much she loves Jack and the girls. How much she loves her makeshift family and the home they built together. How much she appreciates finally getting to open her dream tea shop. Her shop may be underwater, too. But she can't think about that now. If she is lucky enough to survive, she will deal with whatever the aftermath brings. Grateful for the chance.

The storm surge finally slows and stops rising.

Seconds later Queenie begins to giggle. Adrenaline releasing, no doubt. Before long they all are laughing, tears in their eyes. Giddy with relief that they have survived the most dangerous part of the storm, couples kiss. Family members hug. Friends embrace and pat each other on the back. All except Heather. But then Violet notices that Old Sally isn't laughing, either. In the next second, she realizes what Old Sally already knows. All waves—big or small—must return to the sea. The storm surge is only half over. This awareness passes to the others. The wall of water is on its way back out. If there is worse news, Violet can't imagine it.

A new surge of water rushes in, coming from the other direction. The water swirls its wildness and starts to rise again. It makes Violet dizzy to watch it.

Along with the tons of ocean water comes tons of debris into the lighthouse. Fish, some floating dead and others frantically trying to stay alive, swirl in the water with pieces of trees and houses. Things living and dead churn together in the crucible of the lighthouse. Drowning is no longer their primary concern. They must also avoid being crushed by debris.

The water edges its way up the walls again, surpassing the

high-water mark from moments before. It leaves Jack and Heather halfway underwater.

Violet prays to the lighthouse to keep them safe. The beacon light flickers again as if wanting to offer them hope on such a dark night. It groans and clanks. The water forces them even higher, edging them toward the beacon. Broken glass litters the way and crunches underneath Violet's shoes. No longer is there a danger of water coming in from the top, it is now on its way out. The new threat comes from below, the threat of being pulled out of the lighthouse with the receding floodwater.

From Violet's new vantage point, the intermittent beacon illuminates a horrifying sight. The land has disappeared entirely. The ocean is everywhere. As a girl, the sea had been her playmate, but now that playmate has turned dark and has come to claim her.

From now on, Violet and her family and friends may be part of a tragic story on the island, like the family that lost their lives because they captured a mermaid. They will be the unfortunate people who fled to a lighthouse during a hurricane and didn't survive. But Violet doesn't want her story to end this way. She refuses to end up as fish food.

The sea lunges forward one last time. Violet isn't sure how much time passes before the water starts to recede like water draining from a bathtub. Eventually, the wind also ceases to rage. Then, slowly, Iris begins to leave.

CHAPTER FORTY-NINE

Queenie

The orange-and-yellow sunrise filters in through the top of the lighthouse. They have remained crouched on the steps for what feels like hours and Queenie's sciatica is giving her fits. Wet, shaken, but alive, they wait for the water to recede. Spud holds Queenie in his arms and tells her the worst is over.

"That had better be true, Mister Grainger." Queenie is weary from having not slept and is so hungry if she had a way to fry these fish thrashing around she would have some breakfast.

Katie shrieks with the labor pains that are coming with growing frequency. Everyone wearing a wristwatch checks the time. The pains are only a minute apart now. It is all Queenie can do to not shriek with her. One of those primal screams like she used to do when driving over the Talmadge Bridge from Savannah on the way to Dolphin Island.

Old Sally, Violet, Rose, and Angela are now with Katie at the top of the lighthouse, by far the driest place they could be. Queenie likes that it also gives Katie a little privacy. Anticipating the storm surge, Max and Jack created a spot near the beacon for Katie to give birth, the floor padded with army blankets. They also brought the first-aid kit from the old footlocker. It is not ideal, since everything is wet, but it is better than nothing.

At least a foot of water still stands in the lighthouse and keeps them from venturing down the metal stairs. A baby shark thrashes around in the low water, trapped inside as the wave went out. Max and Jack grab two boards and stand on each side of the baby shark to help guide it through the doorway. But the shark is frightened and swims into the darkened corners of the lighthouse.

A metal trash can lid floats in. Queenie fishes it out and bangs it against the metal stairs to discourage the shark from swimming near them. It works. Their unwelcome guest finally finds its way outside and into the small river of water returning to the sea. Given the shark's example, one by one they carefully wade through the debris.

In stark contrast to the dark eye of Iris, the sunrise is so bright that Queenie has to cover her eyes. A new day greets them. A perfect summer day, from the looks of it. However, this day isn't at all typical. Even though the wind and rain have stopped, the morning light reveals a chaotic scene that reminds her of 9/11.

Queenie remembers that awful day last fall. They had only been living on the island for a few months when they sat around the television in the living room watching those towers go down, all of them disbelieving that this horrific event could happen here in the United States. Old Sally went silent for days, as did Spud. No one knew what to do. Life seemed suddenly dangerous and unpredictable, just like now. All distractions fell away. A few weeks later, Spud proposed to Queenie. And Katie got pregnant again after miscarrying a few months before. The most essential elements of life seemed clear. Humans aren't meant to be isolated and alone. We are destined to be together and create community. No matter what that might look like. And together they became survivors in a way, just like now.

"I have something I need to say to you," Queenie says to Spud. "But I don't want to hurt your feelings."

"Go on," Spud says, a look of concern in his eyes.

Queenie pauses. She isn't someone who usually needs the courage to speak her mind.

"I want to keep my old name," she says.

"Yes?" Spud says, waiting for her to say more.

"That's it," she says. "Just that one thing."

"Of course, gingersnap." Spud gives her a relieved smile, as though much more concerned that he was about to be asked to find new homes for his bow ties.

"You don't mind?" Queenie asks.

"Not one bit," he says. "You'll still be my wife, and that's all I really want."

Now it is Queenie's turn to look relieved.

Spud helps Queenie leave the lighthouse.

"Careful, sweetheart," he says, wading through the water in front of her. "Watch your step."

Queenie watches every step and then some. She has no intention of falling into what smells like the inside of a dumpster at Red Lobster.

Outside, water continues to make its way back to the sea, cutting jagged ruts deep into the soft earth. Large puddles create a natural obstacle course. Queenie hangs onto Spud's arm. It seems years have passed since they made their way to the lighthouse last evening.

Live oak trees, once majestic and beautiful along the shoreline, lie wounded on their sides, their roots exposed like the one that now rests in Queenie's bedroom. The ones that have not entirely fallen over lean in unison in the direction Iris came, like witnesses pointing out a murderer in a courtroom.

In addition to the fallen oaks, pine trees are snapped halfway up, as if Iris took a giant ax and knocked all the trees down with one blow. Queenie feels oddly satisfied. Iris has thrown a massive temper tantrum for everyone to see, not just Queenie. A hissy fit of hurricane proportions.

A butterfly crosses in front of them, following a jagged flight pattern, drunk from the storm or perhaps disoriented by its surroundings. A visible mark graces the outside of the lighthouse about fourteen feet up. Is it possible that the storm surge was this high?

Max reports that his truck is nowhere to be seen. Washed away by the storm surge.

Spud squeezes Queenie's hand. "I hope we still have a home."

Queenie hasn't thought that far ahead. When the Temple mansion burned down, she felt displaced for months. But once they moved to the beach, she felt like she was finally home.

Sweet God in heaven, Queenie thinks, *please don't ask me to start over again.*

But from the looks of things that seems entirely possible. She reminds herself that houses don't make homes, but the love and the people in them do. It seems trite to even think that way, but she will settle for any comfort she can find.

With Spud nearby, Queenie takes in the scene of the chaos on their island. When they were outside during the eye of the storm, Queenie would have never thought the destruction could get any worse. Unfortunately, it did. The dunes are gone. Debris is everywhere, dotting the beach. Vast rivers of water return to the sea. The one-lane road to the lighthouse has been washed away, water still standing everywhere. They have no way of letting anyone know where they are.

Unexpected things have traveled on the wind or washed up with the swollen tide. Next to the lighthouse are a variety of displaced objects: a rake, an unopened bag of diapers, the gate of a white picket fence, a yellow rain boot, a container of mint-flavored dental floss, and a pink toilet seat that Queenie hopes no one was sitting on.

The concrete steps leading from the beach to the lighthouse

have disappeared, along with the railing. There is some question of how they will get home. Heather sits on an overturned tree a few yards away. The storm seems to have taken away all her rough edges. She still looks like a younger version of Iris in this light, but also like someone who is lost (like in "Amazing Grace") and not yet found.

During their time at the lighthouse, Heather made no effort to connect with any of them. Hard times usually bring people together. But not Heather. If anything, it seems to have reminded her of how separate she is.

The sunny, humid day feels more like late August instead of June. However, the sky is the bluest Queenie has ever seen it. If not for the astounding physical evidence around them, no one would believe a hurricane had hit a few hours before.

Isolated at the lighthouse, she has no idea how far the damage extends. For all she knows, Iris may have devastated not only Dolphin Island but Savannah, as well. It is the not knowing that is the worst.

In the distance, Queenie hears what sounds like Iris returning. But then they realize it is a rescue helicopter flying along the coast. Excited, everyone gathers near the lighthouse and waves as it hovers nearby.

A man on the helicopter uses a bullhorn to ask how many of them there are, promising to return with help soon. They look at each other, counting, yelling different numbers until Queenie finally gets it right: "Almost thirteen!"

In the aftermath of Hurricane Iris, the most devastating event Queenie has ever witnessed, it seems that the most significant development is happening now, as Katie pushes a new life into their world. Lucky number thirteen.

CHAPTER FIFTY

Old Sally

Old Sally hasn't delivered a baby in years, but Violet is a great help, and of course, Katie and the baby know through pure instinct what to do. Overhead, helicopter sounds drown out Katie's efforts for a time, before it moves away. With the final push, Old Sally catches a perfect baby girl in her arms.

After the cord is cut and the mother and baby are resting, Old Sally takes out a thimble she put in her pocket right before she came to the lighthouse.

"What are you doing?" Violet asks.

"The first water taken by a new mother must be sipped from a thimble," Old Sally says. "This will ease the baby's first tooth."

Violet helps Old Sally pour a tiny bit of bottled water into the thimble before giving it to Katie. Then Rose and Violet help Old Sally finally stand. She has been on the floor for over an hour, with only a soggy folded army blanket underneath her knees. She is wobbly, at best, yet also exhilarated to have helped a new life come into this world.

"What's this?" Rose asks, picking up a small glass container filled with what looks like dirty sand.

"Oh, that be mine, too," Old Sally says, returning the small bottle to her pocket along with the thimble. "Childbirth be a dangerous time," she continues. "Mother and baby are vulnerable to spirits who may wish them harm. But I brought along some graveyard dirt to protect them."

Violet and Rose exchange a look of surprise.

A warm, salty breeze drifts through the broken windows at the top of the lighthouse. Old Sally looks out over the island. Her island. The island of her Gullah ancestors. The last time she stood in this spot was the night she and Fiddle stayed here. On that night, so long ago, it was romantic to look out over the island because she was so much in love. Her knees were wobbly then, too.

The baby cries and Rose helps Katie place her new daughter at Katie's breast to feed.

"Birth be such a hopeful process," Old Sally says. *As is death,* she wants to say, looking out over the eternal sea.

"Do you have a name yet?" Violet asks.

Angela and Katie exchange a look, and Katie nods, giving Angela permission to say it.

"Sally Rose."

Old Sally lets out a short laugh, and tears rush to her eyes. Rose takes Old Sally's hand.

"What an honor," Old Sally says to them.

"Truly," adds Rose, who is a mixture of tears and smiles.

This lighthouse holds a vibrant part of her history. From now on, Sally Rose will have a history here, too, just like Old Sally, and everyone who survived the storm. Someday, Sally Rose may even run down the beach and play here. A descendant of the light.

DOLPHIN ISLAND EXPERIENCED the full force of the storm. Not only were the winds devastating, but most of the island was underwater. It turns out that the lighthouse was the safest place they could have been.

While most people experienced the storm sitting in long lines on the interstate, those who stayed on the island sought refuge on the second floors of their houses or in their attics. After the storm, there were stories of resilience everywhere. Stories of people climbing into live oaks in their backyards to try to outrun the sea —rescue workers found them the next day, clinging to limbs, battered and bruised. Stories of people coming from all over the United States to help the residents of Dolphin Island with the aftermath of the storm. Helpers who brought bottled water, food, supplies, and generators because they were told it would be months before the power would be restored. Miraculously, only one person died on the island, an elderly gentleman who had a heart attack while hammering up plywood before the storm.

The winter after Hurricane Iris, bulldozers droned up the beach, rebuilding the fragile dunes that were destroyed by the storm surge. Like the helicopter that found them, the sound of the bulldozers reminded Old Sally and the others of Iris's roar. Iris changed everything on Dolphin Island. Even now the ocean spits out reminders of the storm. Pieces of houses. Pieces of people's lives.

When they returned to their home after the storm, two feet of water was still in the house, but it had been much higher. The high-water mark stopped right below Queenie and Spud's wedding presents in the top of Queenie's closet. A fact that made Queenie cackle, as well as cry. While most of their things were destroyed, the structure and foundation of the house stayed strong. Old Sally attributes this to the graveyard dirt she used to surround the house. Dirt she gathered at midnight, the night before the storm hit, from her grandmother's grave. Midnight being when the graveyard dirt is the most potent.

Like everybody else on the island after the storm, they started a massive cleanup that took months to complete, and then they began rebuilding. Like the pains of childbirth that most mothers forget, Old Sally has mostly forgotten the pains of starting over. What matters most is that Katie and her baby are healthy, and they all survived.

ON THE ONE-YEAR anniversary of the hurricane, Old Sally sits facing the sea in her favorite rocking chair. Life has a habit of keeping on. She has lived on this same piece of land her entire life. A rare occurrence these days. In extreme contrast to Iris's storm surge, waves break gently along the shoreline. Now that things are starting to return to normal, there are some days she can fool herself into thinking that the storm didn't happen at all.

There will always be storms. Storms of the heart and mind, and storms on land. Storms that have a beginning, a middle, and an end, and storms that seemingly last forever.

Where the old live oak once stood, a new oak is rising. An upstart, as we all are upstarts in one way or another, with the clear purpose of sinking roots where its ancestor once stood.

Without speaking, Old Sally sends Violet a message to join her. She has a final ritual to share with her, and then the passing on of the Gullah secrets will be complete.

Violet has seemed different since the storm, somehow lighter, but also more purposeful. Her tea shop suffered no damage. But it is more than that. She is growing into her wisdom.

We're getting good at this, Violet says to Old Sally when she steps outside.

Old Sally agrees.

"Have you seen the painting Rose is working on?" Violet asks, speaking aloud this time. "I just saw it." Her eyes dance with pleasure.

"She showed it to me last night," Old Sally says. "She told me it be the first portrait she's ever done. It's for sure the first portrait of me to ever exist."

"She did a wonderful job," Violet says. "It's a great likeness of you. And we've already decided where we want to put it in the living room."

"Oh my." Old Sally's face warms.

"The one she wants to work on next has all of us standing in front of the lighthouse," Violet says.

Old Sally remembers the storm and thanks her ancestors for helping them stay safe. A sudden awareness reminds her that her work is finished. She has done enough.

"I be so glad Rose is painting again," Old Sally says. "How are things at the tea shop?"

"Queenie and Spud are covering the breakfast crowd this morning," she says. "How are you feeling? Still a bit dizzy?"

"I have moments. But nothing to worry about."

Old Sally sleeps more than she is awake these days, her world full of dreams. When she isn't sleeping, she is here in her rocking chair overlooking the sea. Or telling Gullah stories to Katie and Sally Rose. Her walks on the beach with Rose are now short ones. She can no longer make it to the lighthouse. Yet, its purpose in her life has been fulfilled.

"Just a reminder that Rose is in Savannah today to handle the court issue," Violet says.

"Did you tell me about this before? I can't remember what it was about," Old Sally says. She has very little interest in worldly things these days. Not the news or the weather or anything that doesn't have to do with this island and her place on it.

Violet sits in the rocker next to Old Sally and reminds her about the ledger pages that Rose rescued from the rising water in the lighthouse. It seems they contained a manifest for that old Civil War ship that sank off the coast. It turns out that the boat didn't have soldiers on it, but gold to subsidize the war.

"It was a Temple ship," Violet concludes.

Old Sally chuckles. "Too bad Iris didn't live to see that. She would have been tickled pink. But why does Rose have to go to court?"

"Heather says the ledger was in her possession and belonged to her father. She's suing Rose for the contents of that old ship," Violet says.

"Oh my," Old Sally says again.

"Rose and I have been trying to put all the pieces together," Violet begins again, "and it looks like Heather and her half brother planned the whole thing based on information their mother gave them before she died last year. Heather's brother goes to college in Savannah, and Rose and I saw them in my tea shop one day."

"Fascinating," Old Sally says, always amazed by the drive of humans to amass money when true riches are never—ever —tangible.

"Years ago, their mother was researching the Temples and found an old newspaper article that told about the ship," Violet continues. "Then she must have heard about those secrets being released in the Savannah newspaper and put two and two together."

"You know, I saw Heather take that old book from Rose's purse when we were outside during the eye of the hurricane." Old Sally rocks gently in her rocking chair.

"You did?"

Old Sally nods. "It's a good thing that the storm surge took most of it. All those secrets needed to finally be buried at sea. And all those Temple ghosts finally put to rest."

"Rose said something very similar," Violet says. "The attorney seems to think it's an open-and-shut case. Heather doesn't really have any rights in this situation. But we'll see. In the meantime, there are no plans on locating the ship yet," Violet continues. "I guess they have to figure out who has rights to it first."

"And just as that old Temple ledger be buried at sea, the Gullah Book of Secrets be born."

Violet holds up her notebook, held together with a sturdy rubber band, and filled with everything Old Sally has told her over the last two years.

"I be relieved it wasn't lost in the storm," Old Sally says.

Violet agrees. "I had it stuck in my shirt, as close to my heart as I could get it," she says.

"That be very smart," Old Sally says. "You want to finish up our lesson out here?"

Violet pulls a pen from her pocket and opens her book to take notes. Old Sally notices that it is near the end of the book, and Old Sally is at the end of what she needs to share.

"Ready?" she asks Violet.

Violet nods, her book open, pen in hand.

Old Sally pauses again, gathering her thoughts. She tells Violet how very few people remember the funeral rituals used when Old Sally was a girl in the early 1900s. In those days it was believed that if a dead person didn't have a proper funeral, their spirit would be unable to join the ancestors and be doomed to wander around and cause trouble as ghosts. In the Temple mansion, this unfortunate dilemma played out all the time.

"I remember that dilemma quite well," Violet says. The two of them exchange a smile.

"When I be four years old," Old Sally begins again, "I be passed over the open grave of my Grandpa Joe at the cemetery. Several times, in fact."

Violet's expression is one of disbelief, but Old Sally crosses her heart that it is true.

Violet shivers. "What if they had dropped you?"

"That happened to one of my cousins once, but thankfully not to me."

"But why would they pass you over an open grave?"

Old Sally pauses again, remembering how her grandmother explained it to her.

"I be his favorite grandchild," Old Sally begins. "There was a worry that our attachment was so strong that he might pull me into the spirit world and that I would die, too. Passing me over the coffin was the Gullah way of cutting our connection to each other so that he could go to the ancestors, and I could stay here and finish out my time on earth."

Violet writes swiftly to capture every word.

"Children can hear the voices of the dead, you know," Old Sally begins again. "Even more if they are close to the person who died. I remember my Grandpa Joe talking to me long after he was buried."

Violet gasps but doesn't let it deter her from writing. The sound of Violet's pen flowing across the paper, documenting her words, gives Old Sally a sense of deep satisfaction. A written record will exist now, instead of only a spoken one. As a girl, she was proud of herself for learning to read and has read books her entire life. She was the first in her family to learn to read, and after her everybody did.

"Rituals were part of everything, especially deaths," Old Sally continues. "The night before he died, my Grandpa Joe had a 'sit up.' A vigil that goes on all night. Relatives and friends sang and shouted over him."

"They shouted?" Violet's eyes widen.

"You bet they did," Old Sally says. "My grandmother told me the reasoning behind it all later, but with Grandpa Joe I was old enough to see it with my own eyes."

Old Sally remembers how hot it was that night. It was high summer.

"First they said prayers to strengthen him as he passed by death's door," she continues. "Then the instant he died everyone in the room shrieked and shouted to scare off the spirits of hell that always roam the earth and search for a soul to claim."

"Oh my," Violet says, still writing. "What happened next?"

"After the shouting, there was all this sobbing and grieving from everybody there," Old Sally says. "I remember sitting in my grandmother's lap, who cried so much my little dress was soaked straight through."

Old Sally waits for Violet's ballpoint pen to slow and then finally stop.

"This is fascinating." Violet smiles and looks at Old Sally as if receiving an unexpected gift.

"That's not all," Old Sally begins again. "After that, several women came to our house to wash and dress Grandpa Joe and prepare his body. Coffee was placed under his arms, legs, and open spaces, then his body was dressed and kept for three days." Old Sally pictures it as she describes it, remembering more of the ritual. "They used water in an earthen pot to clean him, and they made a big deal about how the water inside must never touch the ground. The water was sacred. Later, the pot and remaining water would be placed on the top of the grave."

Like her dreams these days, the scene she describes is so real Old Sally can almost smell the coffee grounds. She waits again for Violet's pen to stop and gives her a moment to rest. Violet nods when she is ready to begin again.

"Some of his favorite things were placed on his grave," Old Sally continues. "The knife he used his entire life. His favorite coffee cup. His plate and silverware. A deck of cards in a wooden box—the box he had carved himself. A layer of white seashells was created on top of the grave to look like the ocean. The ocean that brought him here and the ocean that would return him to the ancestors."

This morning, Old Sally visited the graveyard. Jack drove her over there first thing. Several markers had washed away when Iris came ashore, but last winter Violet hired someone to return it to how it looked when Sally was a girl.

Space is saved for Old Sally, overlooking the ocean, under the live oak in the back that survived Hurricane Iris. She will be next to her husband, who died in the war, and both her parents and her beloved grandmother on the other side of the tree. Close enough to hold hands if they wanted to. This morning when Old Sally walked among the simple graves, she was aware that she wouldn't exist if not for the people who came before her. To those people she owes everything.

"I don't expect you to do all that for me, Violet, but when the times comes, hopefully very soon, Sally Rose must be passed over my grave. And you must put this on my grave." Old Sally hands her the piece of cloth with her baby's embroidered A.

Tears spring to Violet's eyes, and Old Sally reaches over and takes her hand.

"Please don't be sad, sweet girl. It be a celebration."

"But, I'm going to miss you so much."

"I know you will," Old Sally says, squeezing Violet's hand. "But we can still talk to each other. And when it's your time, I'll be right there to help prepare the way."

Old Sally thinks how lucky they are to get to say goodbye. Not everyone does.

Violet leaves the rocking chair and gets down on her knees in front of Old Sally. She puts her head on her lap, her tears making Old Sally's dress wet. Salty tears by the salty sea. Old Sally caresses Violet's face and wipes her tears like she used to do when Violet was a little girl.

"I know a lot about grief," Old Sally tells her, her voice soft. "When someone you love dies, grief comes like a hurricane and threatens to destroy you. But grief isn't bad," she continues. "Grief means you've loved someone with your whole heart. Love and grief go hand in hand. There's no other way."

Old Sally was right to pass the mantle of Gullah secrets to Violet, and perhaps Tia or Leisha will be the next to carry the secrets. Or maybe even Sally Rose. Everyone else has died off. Families have left the island. But it is important to remember the history. We stand on the shoulders of our ancestors. Those known to us and those unknown. Some we can be proud of and others we would like to forget. But all are important. And our job is to always try to do better.

"Last night, I dreamed of my grandmother again," Old Sally says to Violet.

"You've been doing that a lot." Violet takes a tissue from her pocket and blows her nose before returning to her own rocking chair.

"Would you like to hear the dream?" Old Sally asks.

Violet nods.

"My grandmother was walking down the beach toward this house," Old Sally begins. "She was as real as anything, and she was wearing the indigo-colored dress she wore whenever she had reason to celebrate. She was buried in that dress."

Before the hurricane, Old Sally still had indigo plants out behind the cottage that her grandmother had cultivated to make dye. But since the storm, those plants are gone.

"In the dream, I realized how much I had missed her," Old Sally says.

"I wish I could have known her," Violet says.

"You'll know her someday," Old Sally says. "When it's your turn to celebrate."

Violet retakes her hand. "I need to tell you something."

"Yes?" Old Sally says, looking into Violet's eyes.

"It has been a great honor to learn the Gullah secrets from you."

Now it is Old Sally's turn to use a tissue. "It has been my great pleasure to teach them to you."

For several seconds they sit together in silence. A moment of grace by the sea. Then Violet glances at her watch and apologizes for having to get to the tea shop.

"I can send Katie and Sally Rose to sit with you if you'd like," she says to Old Sally.

"No, no, I'm fine. I like sitting out here alone sometimes. Did you know that I was born almost exactly in this same spot? It was back when babies were born at home."

"I never knew that," Violet says. "But come to think of it, I was born in this spot, too."

"You were indeed," Old Sally says.

A Gullah person wants to die in their place of birth. Even if they move away, many want to come back home to die and be buried there if they can. Old Sally is lucky that she never had to leave.

I love you, Violet, Old Sally says in their unspoken way of conversing.

I love you, too, Violet answers. She leans over and kisses Old Sally on the cheek before walking away. *Can we talk more when I get home?* she asks.

Of course, Old Sally says, knowing how important this will be.

ALONE AGAIN, Old Sally overlooks the vast ocean. Waves rise and fall and break gently on the shore. After months of staying away after the storm, dolphins have finally returned to the inlet. One swims now in the distance, its fin gracing the surface of the water, and then it is joined by another. The sky is a vibrant blue. It reminds her of the bluebird singing on the porch before the storm. A sign of company coming.

The June day feels somehow new. It reminds Old Sally of the eye of the storm and the feeling of absolute calm that came over her on that dark night. All the chaos ceased. Millions of stars embraced her, along with a full moon, and she felt part of the entire universe.

Violin music begins to play. A lilting, floating melody. Fiddle, her love from long ago, stands in the dunes. It reminds her of Queenie's wedding. Sweet Queenie. Old Sally is so glad she finally found love. Her daughter will be fine now. As will the others. They will continue on as we all do, risking love and risking grief.

Meanwhile, Fiddle looks the same age as the night she last saw him. His smile makes her feel young again.

A sense of deep joy washes over her like a gentle tide. Seconds later, her grandmother approaches, wearing her indigo dress. The one reserved for celebrations. Old Sally takes her grandmother's hand as she leaves her old body behind. She always knew it would be her grandmother who came for her.

THANK YOU FOR READING!

Dear Reader,

Even before I began writing this sequel to *Temple Secrets*, I knew that *Gullah Secrets* would end with Old Sally's death and that the character wouldn't fear it, but welcome it. Perhaps I wanted to believe that it is possible to leave this life—as we all must—with gratitude and a sense of completion.

I began writing *Gullah Secrets* in 2016. Since then several monstrous hurricanes have impacted the United States, most recently Hurricane Florence which devastated the eastern part of my state of North Carolina. My heart goes out to everyone who has suffered in those storms. In 1989 I was living with my two young daughters in Charleston, SC when Hurricane Hugo hit the area. My experiences in that storm greatly informed *Gullah Secrets*.

I am grateful to you, dear reader, for taking the time to read this book and others that I have written. It is an honor to create stories for you. I love hearing from readers, and I welcome your emails. Feel free to let me know what you think of *Gullah Secrets*.

Thank you again for spending time with me and these characters I create. I hope this story somehow helps you keep your courage fires burning.

With every good wish,
Susan Gabriel

P.S. If you want to be notified when I publish new books, sign up on my website at SusanGabriel.com/new-books/. Also consider joining me on my facebook author page: SusanGabriel, Author.

P.P.S. Next, I just finished the final book in the Wildflower trilogy, called *Daisy's Fortune*. Turn the page to learn more.

The Wildflower Trilogy

The Secret Sense of Wildflower

Named a Best Book of 2012 by Kirkus Reviews. Small southern towns have few secrets in Appalachia, 1941. When thirteen-year-old Louisa May "Wildflower" McAllister is targeted by the town's teenage bully, she may need more than her "secret sense" to survive.

Lily's Song

A mother's secrets, a daughter's dream, and a family's loyalty are masterfully interwoven in this sequel to *The Secret Sense of Wildflower*. A compelling tale set in 1956 Appalachia that captures the resilience and strength of both mother and daughter, as secrets revealed test their strong bond and ultimately change their lives forever.

Daisy's Fortune

Tennessee, 1982. Wildflower McAllister returns to the small mountain town that stole her innocence and cast her out. Can she stop a harrowing legacy from spreading to another generation? If you like strong women, generational tales, and the power of family and the land to heal, then you'll adore this compelling finale to the Wildflower trilogy.

Available in ebook and paperback.

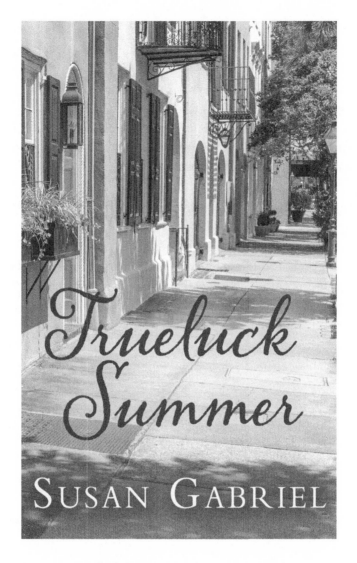

Trueluck Summer: A Lowcountry Novel

A hopeful grandmother. A sassy young girl. Their audacious summer stunt could change their southern town forever.

Charleston, 1964. Ida Trueluck is still adjusting to life on her own. Moving into her son's house creates a few family conflicts, but the widow's saving grace is her whip-smart granddaughter Trudy. Ida makes it her top priority to give the girl a summer she'll never forget.

When a runaway truck nearly takes her life, Trudy makes fast friends with the boy who saves her. But since Paris is black, the racism they encounter inspires Trudy's surprising summer mission: to take down the Confederate flag from the South Carolina Statehouse. And she knows she can't do it without the help of her beloved grandmother.

With all of Southern society conspiring against them, can Trudy, Ida, and their friends pull off the impossible?

Trueluck Summer is a Southern historical women's fiction novel set in a time of significant cultural change. If you like courageous characters, heartwarming humor, and inspirational acts, then you'll love Susan Gabriel's captivating tale.

Available in ebook, paperback and audiobook.

ABOUT THE AUTHOR

Susan Gabriel is an Amazon & Nook #1 bestselling author who lives in the mountains of North Carolina. Her novel, *The Secret Sense of Wildflower*, earned a starred review ("for books of remarkable merit") from Kirkus Reviews and was selected as one of their Best Books of 2012.

She is also the author of *Trueluck Summer, Lily's Song, Daisy's Fortune, Grace, Grits and Ghosts: Southern Short Stories* and other books. Discover more at SusanGabriel.com and facebook.com/SusanGabrielAuthor/.

BOOKS BY SUSAN GABRIEL

FICTION

The Wildflower Trilogy:
The Secret Sense of Wildflower
(a Best Book of 2012 – Kirkus Reviews)
Lily's Song
Daisy's Fortune

Trueluck Summer

Temple Secrets Series:
Temple Secrets
Gullah Secrets

Grace, Grits and Ghosts: Southern Short Stories
Seeking Sara Summers
Circle of the Ancestors
Quentin & the Cave Boy

NONFICTION

Fearless Writing for Women:
Extreme Encouragement & Writing Inspiration

Available at all booksellers
in print, ebook and audiobook.